Tuesday May

By Cassandra Doon

Written 2009 First Published 2024

First Edition 2024

Cover Art by Elyon from TheBookCoverDesigner

Don’t Give up, Sometimes things take years, and sometimes they take seconds.

6

Chapter 1

1985
Father David

The air in Willow's End was like chilled glass, fragile and biting as it swept through the narrow streets of the small country town. Nestled in a valley, ringed by weeping willows that stooped low to kiss the surface of a silent lake, it was a place that time had caressed with a tender hand but ultimately decided to pass by. Each morning, fog clung to the cobblestones like a shroud, and twilight found the town bathed in hues of amber and rose, shadows lengthening across porches where rocking chairs whispered secrets to the wind.

It was on such an evening that I, Father David, stood before the ageing church, its steeple piercing the violet sky like a solemn prayer. The stillness was a living thing, a companion I had grown to cherish and fear in equal measure. In the solitude of my parish, I often felt the weight of unseen eyes upon me, the heaviness of stories untold pressing against the walls of my heart.

"Lord," I murmured, my breath clouding before me, "grant me the strength to bear what I cannot change."

A soft whimper shattered the stillness, drawing my gaze downward. There, swaddled in a blazer of deep navy and wrapped in a shawl that seemed too delicate for this world, lay a tiny infant abandoned on the cold doorstep. My hands trembled as I reached out, brushing the fabric back to reveal a face so innocent, it seemed an affront to the cruelty of its circumstance.

"Forgive them, for they know not what they do," I whispered, cradling the child close. The bitterness of the air did little to mask the warmth that blossomed within me, a protective instinct flaring to life. She was so small, yet her presence filled the chasm of loneliness that had long since settled within the walls of the church and my own weary soul.

I hesitated only a moment before striding inside, the heavy door closing behind us with a sound that resonated like finality. My fingers fumbled with the rotary phone, the numbers a litany under my breath as I dialled the authorities.

"Police? Yes, it's Father David from St. Clement's. There's been...a child left here. Please, send someone quickly." My voice was steady, but the ruby ring on my finger—a symbol of my commitment to God and this community—felt heavier than ever.

"Is she alright?" A voice crackled over the line, concern lacing the question.
"Alive," I answered, peering down at the baby now resting in the crook of my arm. "But alone. So terribly alone."
"Help is on the way, Father."
"Thank you," I said, hanging up. As the silence reclaimed the church, I rocked the infant gently, her cries softening to whimpers. The sanctity of the space around us felt hollow, echoing with the absence of the love she deserved.
"Tuesday," I found myself saying, the word slipping out unbidden, a name for the day of her discovery, though I knew it wasn't mine to give. In her eyes, I saw reflections of all the love lost and found in this quaint, isolated town. The red ruby glinted once more, my promise to keep her safe until help arrived—an ember of hope in the encroaching darkness.
"Your story begins here, little one," I told her, "but it will not end on this cold step. I swear it."

Nurse Amanda

I stood at the back entrance of the emergency room, my hands trembling as I held onto the tiny, fragile life that had been thrust upon me by the paramedics. The baby's cries pierced the sterile silence, her little body shivering against my

chest. I knew I had to act fast but couldn't shake off the overwhelming feeling of responsibility.
"We need a cot," I pleaded with the doctor who rushed towards us. He took one glance at the infant and immediately recognised the urgency of the situation.
"Get her hooked up to an IV, stat," he ordered, his voice firm but compassionate. His eyes met mine, offering a brief moment of reassurance as he whisked the baby away from me.
As they examined her, I could see the shock on their faces when they noticed she still had the umbilical cord attached. It was clear this newborn couldn't be more than a few hours old. My heart ached for this innocent child, abandoned so early in her life. The thought of someone deliberately leaving her to fend for herself ignited a slow-burning fury deep within me.
"Will she be okay?" I asked, my voice barely above a whisper.
“We'll do what we can," the doctor replied, his face softening. "We'll do everything we can."
For three months, I watched over her like a guardian angel, ensuring she received the love and care she deserved. Each day, I marvelled at her resilience, her tiny fingers grasping onto life with a fierce determination. Her cries turned into coos, her wide-eyed gaze taking in the world around her as if she understood the magnitude of her survival.

In time, Mr. and Mrs. Smith, a kind and loving couple, were chosen as her foster parents. They came to the hospital, filled with excitement and trepidation. As I handed the precious bundle over to them, I couldn't help but feel a pang of loss.
"Take good care of her," I whispered, my voice cracking with emotion. "She's been through so much already."
"Thank you for everything you've done," Mrs. Smith said, her eyes glistening with tears. "We promise to love her as our own."
With one last look at the baby girl who had fought her way into this world, I turned and walked away. Despite the sorrow that weighed heavy on my heart, I knew that she would be surrounded by love and warmth in her new home. And as I returned to my duties, I couldn't help but wonder about the dark secrets that had led to her abandonment.

Tuesday May

At three months old, I was given to Mr. and Mrs. Smith, my first foster family. They nurtured me with love and tenderness, raising me as their own. But life, with its cruel twists, had other plans. When I turned five, Mrs Smith was diagnosed with cancer, and I was thrust into the arms of another family - the Hamiltons.

"Welcome home, Tuesday," Henry Hamilton said gruffly, his rough exterior matching the hardness in his heart.
Night after night, I lay in bed, paralysed with fear as he came to me under the cover of darkness. The others slept, oblivious to my silent suffering. I yearned for the safety and warmth of the Smiths' embrace, but the memories became increasingly distant like wisps of smoke slipping through my fingers.
"Please, make it stop," I whispered to myself, my voice barely audible beneath the creaking floorboards and stifled sobs.
But it didn't stop. Not until I was eight years old that fate intervened once more and placed me with the Munro's. Mr. and Mrs. Munro enveloped me in their love, providing a sanctuary where I could start to heal.
"Tuesday, you're safe now," Mrs. Munro said softly, her eyes brimming with compassion. "We'll take care of you."
"Promise?" I asked, my voice trembling with vulnerability.
"Promise," she replied, holding me close.
Only she broke that promise.
The rain slapped against the window, like a metronome ticking away the time I had left in this house. The Munro's were getting a divorce, and with their separation came my own dislocation. I was turning 10, but there were no candles to blow out, only the cold realisation that I was being passed on to yet another foster family.

"Mrs. Kent is going to love you, dear," Mrs. Munro said, her voice wavering as she tried to smile. "They're a lovely couple."

"Are they really?" I asked, my eyes locked onto the raindrops racing down the glass. Inside, I already knew better than to believe that any family would truly love me.

"Of course, sweetheart. It's going to be perfect," she lied. I sighed, knowing that she needed to cling to that illusion as much as I did.

As we pulled into the driveway of my new home, the Kents stood on the porch, their arms folded and faces stern. Mr Kent, a tall man with a long beard, wore an expression that suggested he had bitten into something sour. Beside him, Mrs. Kent sneered, her pinched features scrutinising me as though I were an unwelcome insect.

"Welcome to your new home, dear," Mrs. Kent said, the words dripping with insincerity. "I hope you'll learn to behave here."

"Behave?" I frowned. Apparently, my reputation had preceded me.

"Your room is upstairs, second door on the left," Mr. Kent grunted. "Get settled in and don't cause any trouble."

Within days, Mrs. Kent's taunts burrowed under my skin like splinters. She delighted in berating me for every perceived slight or mistake, ensuring that I knew my place in her twisted hierarchy. But it was Mr. Kent's nightly visits that truly broke me. How could Mrs. Kent not know? Did she turn a blind eye, or was she simply too absorbed in her own torment to notice mine?

"Please," I whispered each night as I huddled under the covers, praying for it to end. "Please."

But my prayers fell on deaf ears.

When I turned 12, I was given to Mr. Jennings, who ran a foster home for teenagers. It was a house full of lost souls, and in their company, I found no solace. The abuse continued, now at the hands of Mr. Jennings and two other foster children. I was trapped in a never-ending cycle of pain and betrayal.

"Stop it! Leave me alone!" I screamed one night, lashing out with trembling fists.

"Shut up!" one of the boys snarled, his grip tightening around my arm.

As the months rolled by, something inside me snapped. I had endured enough – too much. My rage boiled over, and one fateful day, I tried to stab everyone in the house. My vision blurred red, and all I could see was my own fury reflected back at me.

"Get away from me!" I shrieked, brandishing a knife like a shield.

"Tuesday, put the knife down!" Mr. Jennings barked, but his words were swallowed by my own internal cacophony.

Ultimately, they had me committed. They labelled me psychotic, but what did they expect? I was just a child, broken and battered by the cruelty of those who should have protected me. As the padded walls closed in around me, I wondered if I would ever find a way out of this darkness, or if I was doomed to be forever shackled by the demons of my past.

Chapter 2

1997
Tuesday May

The moment I set foot inside the mental health facility, a suffocating wave of despair washed over me. The air was heavy, tainted with the echoes of anguished cries and desperate whispers that seemed to seep through the sterile white walls. As the massive iron doors shut behind me, the inescapable sound of their metallic clang reverberated through the hallway, sealing my fate.

"Please sign here, Ms. May," a disinterested nurse instructed as she handed me a clipboard filled with forms. Her eyes didn't meet mine; instead, they focused on some distant point beyond my shoulder, as if I were nothing more than a ghost passing through her world.

"Tuesday," I mumbled, scrawling my name in shaky letters. My hand trembled as I gripped the pen, my fear manifesting in every clumsy stroke. "My name is Tuesday."

"Very well, Tuesday. Take a seat, someone will be with you shortly."

I sank into one of the uncomfortable plastic chairs that lined the room, feeling the weight of isolation pressing down on my chest. A thousand questions swirled in my mind like a dark storm threatening to drown me. How did I end up here? What would become of me within these cold, lifeless walls?

"Hey," a timid voice said beside me, pulling me from my tumultuous thoughts.

I glanced at the girl sitting next to me, her eyes wide with an innocence I longed for. She looked as lost as I felt, a fragile bird caught in an unforgiving storm.

"Are you scared too?" she asked, her words barely audible. I wanted to tell her that I was terrified, that I felt the same crushing uncertainty she did. But my throat clenched, unwilling to let my own vulnerability escape.

"Sometimes it's okay to be afraid," I managed to choke out, hoping that my words would offer her some comfort, even if they couldn't ease my own fears.

"Thank you," she whispered, a small but grateful smile tugging at the corners of her lips. As we sat there in shared silence, I wondered if this place could ever truly save us, or if we were all simply lost souls trapped within its walls.

I watched the other patients move about, their faces etched with the same sombre expressions that mirrored my own. I couldn't shake the feeling of being a caged bird, longing for

freedom but knowing that the world outside was far too dangerous to bear.
"Tuesday May?" A gentle voice called out my name, and I instinctively tensed. I lifted my gaze to see a woman standing in front of me, her warm smile and genuine demeanour a stark contrast to the sterile environment that surrounded us.
"Hi there, I'm Nurse Kylie," she introduced herself, extending a hand toward me. Her short, curly blonde hair framed her face perfectly, drawing attention to her bright green eyes which seemed to radiate kindness. It was disarming, almost too good to be true.
"Hello," I murmured, hesitating before taking her hand in mine. The warmth of her touch provided a momentary relief from the coldness that had taken residence within me.
"Please follow me, Tuesday. We're going to get you settled into your room," she said softly, her voice soothing like a balm on my frayed nerves. I nodded and rose from my chair, my legs trembling beneath me as I followed her down the hallway.
"Is this your first time at a place like this?" Nurse Kylie asked, her tone gentle and nonjudgmental.
"Y-yes," I stammered, my voice barely above a whisper. "It's all new to me."
"Change can be scary," she acknowledged, giving me an empathetic glance. "But it can also bring healing and growth when we open ourselves up to it."

My heart clenched at her words, the truth behind them cutting through my defences. A part of me wanted to believe her, to hope that maybe this time, things would be different. But my past traumas still haunted me, leaving me wary and guarded.
"Thank you," I managed to say, my voice thick with emotion.
As we continued down the hallway, Nurse Kylie's presence brought a sense of comfort that I hadn't felt in a long time. Maybe, just maybe, she could be a beacon of light within this dark place.
"Here we are," Nurse Kylie announced as we stopped in front of a door. "This will be your room, Tuesday."
"Thank you, Nurse Kylie," I said softly, stepping inside and taking in the small space that would become my sanctuary for the foreseeable future. It was sparse, but it was mine.
"Remember," she told me before leaving, her eyes brimming with compassion, "you're not alone here. We're all here to help you heal, Tuesday."
The door closed behind Nurse Kylie, leaving me alone in my new room. I glanced around the sterile space, feeling a chill run down my spine. Despite her warmth and kindness, I couldn't help but remain sceptical of everyone here, including Nurse Kylie. The scars of my past had taught me to be cautious and to trust no one.
I sank onto the narrow bed, my heart heavy with conflicting emotions. On one hand, I wanted to believe that Nurse Kylie was different, that she truly cared. But on the other, I couldn't

shake the memories of those who had hurt me, who had betrayed my trust when I was at my most vulnerable.

"Hey Tuesday, how are you settling in?" Nurse Kylie appeared again later that day, her eyes filled with genuine concern.
"Fine," I muttered, looking away.
"Is there anything you'd like to do? Maybe take a walk or join one of our group activities?"
"Maybe later." I shrugged, not committing to anything.
"Alright, just remember that we're here for you whenever you're ready," she said sincerely.
"Thanks." My voice was barely a whisper, as the walls I had built around myself began to show small cracks.
Nurse Kylie's persistence slowly chipped away at my defences, and though I remained guarded, there was a flicker of hope deep within me. Maybe, just maybe, I could learn to trust again. But it would take time, and I knew that healing wouldn't come easily.

The sun had long since set when I heard a soft knock on my door. It cracked open, revealing Nurse Kylie bathed in the dim glow of the hallway lights, her short curls casting playful shadows on the walls.
"Tuesday, would you like some hot chocolate?" she offered, holding up a steaming mug.

"Uh, sure," I hesitated, carefully taking the mug from her hands and feeling its warmth spread through my fingers.

"Mind if I join you for a bit?" Her tone was gentle, and inviting but not imposing.

"Okay," I whispered, making space for her to sit at the edge of my bed.

"Tell me about yourself, Tuesday. What do you enjoy doing when you're not here?" She blew on her own mug before taking a sip.

I pondered her question, allowing myself to drift back to a time before my life had been consumed by darkness. "I used to love drawing," I admitted quietly, my gaze fixed on the swirling patterns in my hot chocolate.

"Really? That's wonderful. Art can be such a healing form of expression." Nurse Kylie's eyes sparkled with enthusiasm. "Would you like some supplies so you can draw while you're here?"

"Maybe," I allowed, the faintest hint of a smile tugging at my lips. The thought of losing myself in art again felt foreign, yet comforting.

"Great, I'll see what I can find for you tomorrow." She paused, sipping her drink again before speaking. "I want you to know that you're not alone here, Tuesday."

Her words stirred something within me, a longing for connection that had lain dormant for far too long. And though

I still hesitated to fully trust her, the sincerity in her voice chipped away at the fortress I'd built around my heart.
"Thank you, Nurse Kylie," I murmured, finally meeting her gaze. "I appreciate that."
"Of course," she replied warmly, placing a reassuring hand on my shoulder. "And remember, I'm always here if you need someone to talk to."
As the days turned into weeks, Nurse Kylie's unwavering support began to break through the barriers I'd erected. Her constant presence in my life provided a sense of safety I hadn't felt in years, and slowly, ever so slowly, I let my guard down. I allowed myself to trust her, to lean on her as I faced the demons that haunted me. And it all began with the kindness of one nurse, who refused to let me drown in my own darkness.

Chapter 3

Tuesday May

The sterile white walls of the mental health facility always felt suffocating, but today they seemed to close in tighter than ever. I sat on the edge of my bed, fingers fidgeting with the frayed fabric of my hospital-issued sweats. Nurse Kylie stood nearby, her warmth and compassion filling the room like a soft blanket.

"Dr. Harper will be here any minute," she said, trying to sound upbeat. Her bright green eyes were full of concern, but she did her best to hide it. "She's really looking forward to meeting you."

"Is she?" I muttered, not bothering to look up. It didn't matter who came or went; none of them could truly understand the darkness that had rooted itself inside me.

The door creaked open, and Dr. Elizabeth Harper entered the room. Her calm demeanour was a stark contrast to Nurse

Kylie's bubbly nature. She closed the door behind her and took slow, measured steps towards me.
"Hello, Tuesday," she said softly, extending her hand. "I'm Dr. Harper."
I hesitated for a moment before reluctantly shaking her hand. As I pulled away, I took in her appearance. Dr. Harper had shoulder-length brown hair that framed her face, and glasses perched on her nose. The most striking thing about her, though, was her eyes – they bore into me with an intensity that was impossible to ignore. It was as if she could see straight through me, into the depths of my soul.
"Nice to meet you," I murmured, averting my gaze. I didn't need another person prying into my life, picking apart my thoughts and memories.
"Likewise," she replied, pulling up a chair beside my bed. "I've been reading your file and I think we can work together to help you heal." She spoke with a quiet confidence, as though she held the key to unlock the chains that bound me.
"Everyone keeps saying that," I said, my voice barely above a whisper. "But nothing going to change."
Dr. Harper leaned in slightly, her eyes never leaving mine. "I know you've been through a lot, Tuesday. But I believe that with time and the right support, you can find your way out of this darkness."

I wasn't so sure, but the sessions commenced with or without my consent, cause that was what this place was, a place with no consent just rules.

The sun streamed through the window, casting a warm glow over the sterile room as I sat across from Dr. Harper in our first therapy session. She arranged her papers on a clipboard, her glasses perched on the bridge of her nose, reflecting the sunlight. I fidgeted with my hands, my heart pounding in my chest.

"Let's start by discussing your medication," Dr. Harper began, her voice calm and patient. "I understand you've been experiencing some side effects."

I hesitated, my eyes fixed on the floor. "Yeah," I mumbled, feeling the familiar weight of shame settling in my chest. "I feel like a zombie when I take them. I wish I didn't have to."

"Side effects can be frustrating, but sometimes they're necessary for progress," she said gently. "However, we can always consider adjusting the dosage or trying something else if it becomes too unbearable."

Her empathy was unexpected, and it softened my defences slightly. "I just want to feel normal," I admitted, my voice barely audible.

Dr. Harper nodded, understanding etched into her features. "We'll work together to find a balance that helps you heal without making you feel disconnected from yourself."

She paused, studying me for a moment. "Now, let's talk a bit about your past. I know it's difficult for you to discuss, but opening up is an important part of the healing process."

I swallowed hard, my pulse quickening. The memories were like a dark cloud, threatening to consume me if I allowed them to surface. "I don't know where to start," I whispered, my voice shaking.

"Start with whatever feels most significant to you," she suggested, her gaze steady and supportive.

Taking a deep breath, I closed my eyes, allowing fragments of my past to drift into my consciousness – the sound of shattering glass, the harsh grip of hands on my skin, the echoes of cruel laughter. A tear slipped down my cheek, but I didn't wipe it away.

"Everything was just... so chaotic," I murmured, my voice strained with emotion. "I never felt safe."

Dr. Harper leaned forward in her chair, her eyes filled with concern. "You don't have to relive those moments now, Tuesday. Just know that I'm here to help you process and understand them when you're ready."

Relief flooded through me, mingling with the lingering tendrils of fear and pain. She was offering me a lifeline, an anchor amidst the storm of my emotions.

"Thank you," I whispered, feeling a small measure of hope beginning to blossom beneath the weight of my past. As the sunlight continued to filter through the window, casting a warm glow over Dr. Harper's face, I dared to believe that I might one day find my way back to the light.

As the days passed, I couldn't shake the feeling of being trapped in an endless loop. The medication they prescribed made me feel numb and detached, like a ghost drifting through my own life. Dr Harper had said it would help stabilise my moods – an anchor to keep me from losing myself to the whirlwind of emotions that threatened to tear me apart. But every time I swallowed one of those tiny pills, I couldn't help but wonder if I was trading one prison for another.

One night, as I lay in bed staring at the shadowy patterns on the ceiling, my thoughts spiralled into darkness. What good was it to be alive if I couldn't truly feel anything? If all that awaited me was the cold grip of emptiness, why not just... end it?

"Tuesday?" Nurse Kylie's gentle voice pulled me from the abyss of despair. "Are you alright?"

I blinked away tears, realising the door to my room was ajar and she was standing there with a look of concern etched on her face. "Yeah," I lied, wiping my cheeks with the back of my hand. "Just didn't sleep well."

"Would you like to talk about it?" she offered, her eyes filled with genuine care. As much as I wanted to push her away, something deep inside me whispered that maybe, just maybe, she could help.

"Please," I choked out, the weight of my pain finally breaking through the walls I'd built around myself.

She sat down beside me, offering her hand to hold. Tentatively, I took it and began to unravel the tangled threads of my past. I told her about the psychotic episode that landed me in here – the whispers that turned into screams, the shadows that morphed into monsters, and the crushing weight of despair that threatened to swallow me whole. I recounted the times I'd tried to escape the agony by attempting to take my own life, only to find myself unsuccessful.

"Tuesday, I'm so sorry," Kylie whispered, her voice thick with emotion. "But I promise that we're here to help you. Both Dr. Harper and I are dedicated to supporting you through every step of your journey towards healing."

As she spoke, something inside me began to shift. For the first time in as long as I could remember, I didn't feel completely alone in my battle against the darkness. Her words were like a balm to my aching soul, and a flicker of hope sparked within me.

"Thank you, Kylie," I murmured, clinging to the fragile thread of trust that connected us. "I don't know if I can ever truly heal, but... maybe with your help, I can at least learn to live with the pain."

She squeezed my hand gently, her eyes shining with determination. "Dr. Harper wanted me to remind you that she'll be here for your therapy session in the morning," Kylie

continued, her tone warm and reassuring. "She has some new strategies she'd like to discuss with you."
"Alright," I murmured, nodding slightly. The thought of facing Dr. Harper again filled me with a mix of dread and hope – dread at the prospect of delving deeper into my troubled past, and hope that perhaps she might hold the key to unlocking the door that stood between me and freedom from my pain.

"Tuesday, remember to breathe," Dr. Harper's calm voice instructed me as I sat across from her during our session. She had a way of grounding me, bringing me back to the present moment when my thoughts threatened to spiral out of control.
"I'm trying," I whispered, my hands trembling in my lap. "It's just... sometimes it feels like I'm drowning, and there's no one around to save me."
"Believe me when I say that we're here to help you navigate these stormy waters," she replied, her gaze steady and resolute. "But first, you must find the strength within yourself to take that first step towards healing."
As I left the therapy room that day, something inside me felt different – lighter, somehow. Perhaps it was the knowledge that I wasn't alone in my struggle anymore, or maybe it was the realisation that the power to change my life lay within my own hands. Whatever it was, it filled me with a sense of determination I hadn't felt in a long time.

"Thank you," I whispered to Kylie as she walked me back to my room, my heart swelling with gratitude for her unwavering support.

"Of course, Tuesday," she smiled, squeezing my hand gently. "Remember, this is just the beginning. There's still a long road ahead, but I have faith that you'll find your way to the light at the end of the tunnel."

As the door to my room closed behind me, I knew she was right. The path to recovery wouldn't be easy, and there would undoubtedly be setbacks along the way. But with Dr. Harper and Nurse Kylie by my side, I was finally ready to face whatever challenges lay ahead – and to begin the slow, arduous journey towards healing.

Chapter 4

2008
Tuesday May

My heart raced with anticipation – today was my twenty-third birthday, and I couldn't help but feel an unfamiliar excitement bubbling within me. For the past ten years, I had been confined to the walls of this mental health facility, each day another step closer to freedom.

"Happy Birthday, Tuesday," I whispered to myself, staring at the familiar cracks in the ceiling. A sense of hope surged through me, daring me to dream of a life beyond these suffocating walls.

As I sat up, the door to my room creaked open, and Nurse Kylie peeked in. "Someone's here to see you, dear," she said softly, her eyes holding a mixture of curiosity and concern.

"Who?" I asked, puzzled. Visitors were rare, and I couldn't think of anyone who'd want to see me.

"Mr George Wellington," she replied, motioning for me to follow her.

I stepped into the sterile hallway, following Nurse Kylie towards the visitor's room. My mind raced – why would someone with a name like that want to visit me?

Upon entering the room, I saw a tall, imposing man sitting in one of the chairs. His salt-and-pepper hair was meticulously groomed, and his cold, calculating eyes scanned the room before landing on me. He stood up, extending a hand to me.

"Tuesday May, I presume?" he asked, his voice deep and authoritative.

"Y-yes, that's me," I stammered, hesitantly shaking his hand.

"Let me cut to the chase," he began, taking a seat and gesturing for me to do the same. "I believe I am your biological father."

I stared at him, incredulous. This man, with his expensive suit and air of superiority, didn't look anything like me. My dark hair and piercing blue eyes were nowhere to be found in his visage, yet he claimed a connection.

"See, you look like your mother, Lillian" he explained, noticing my scepticism. "But we can confirm this with a DNA test if you're willing."

I hesitated, my mind racing with questions and doubts. Could this man truly be my father? What did he want from me? But the thought of finally knowing my family – of having a connection to someone – was too tempting.

"Alright," I agreed, trying to steady my voice. "We'll do the DNA test."
He nodded, a small, satisfied smile playing on his lips. As we made arrangements for the test, I couldn't help but feel both excited and apprehensive about what the future held.

The hours I spent waiting for the DNA test felt interminable. Mr. George Wellington had left me with a whirlwind of emotions, and I couldn't shake the mixture of hope and fear that gripped my heart. The memories of my abusive foster parents haunted me, making it difficult to trust anyone who claimed to care about me. I reminded myself not to get too attached to the idea of having a family, as I'd been disappointed before.
"Tuesday, are you ready?" Nurse Kylie's gentle voice brought me back to the present moment. I nodded, trying to keep my face impassive. Inside, though, doubts swirled like thick fog.
"Let's go," I said, my voice barely above a whisper. She led me down the white hallway to the small room where the DNA test would be conducted. As we entered, I noticed a lab technician waiting for us, her eyes kind but professional.
"Hi Tuesday, I'm Lisa. I'll be administering the DNA test today" she said, extending her gloved hand towards me. I shook it cautiously, feeling as if I were entrusting this stranger with the key to my past and future.
"Alright," I agreed, swallowing hard. "Let's do this."

"Please open your mouth wide," Lisa instructed, holding a long cotton swab. I complied, trying to ignore the dryness in my throat. She gently swabbed the inside of my cheek before placing the sample into a sterile container.

"Thank you," she said softly. "We'll have the results for you in a few days."

"Days?" I croaked, mortified by how desperate my voice sounded. "Can't it be sooner?"

"Unfortunately, these tests take time" Lisa explained apologetically. "But I promise, we'll contact you as soon as we have the results."

“Okay," I whispered, trying to hold back tears of frustration. As we exited the room, Nurse Kylie wrapped an arm around my shoulders, offering silent support.

"Tuesday," she said, her voice full of warmth and understanding, "no matter what happens with this test, remember that you're strong and resilient. You've survived so much, and I know you'll continue to do so."

"Thanks" I replied, touched by her words but still fearing what the future might hold. As I returned to my room, I couldn't help but replay every interaction with George Wellington in my mind, looking for any signs of deceit or ulterior motives.

The days dragged on, each one slower than the last. My thoughts were consumed by the upcoming results, making sleep nearly impossible. I kept asking myself: Could he really be my father? Or was this just another cruel trick fate had in store for me?

When the day finally arrived, my heart pounded so fiercely in my chest that I feared it would burst. The truth was within reach, but what if it wasn't the answer I wanted? What if all my hopes were shattered once again?

"Tuesday" Nurse Kylie called softly from the doorway. "It's time."

With a deep breath, I rose to my feet and stepped forward, ready - or as ready as I could be.

I stood next to Nurse Kylie, my knees weak and my palms slick with sweat. The small office felt suffocating as the doctor's words hung in the air, heavy with significance.

"Mr George Wellington is, without a doubt, your biological father."

His words echoed in my ears, and I felt as though I were drowning in a sea of emotions, each wave threatening to pull me further under. Relief washed over me, followed closely by disbelief, and then a faint glimmer of hope flickered in the darkness.

"Thank you, doctor," George said, his voice steady and confident, betraying none of the turmoil that surely must be churning within him. He turned to me, his eyes searching mine. "Tuesday, I know this is a lot to take in, but I want you to know that I'm here for you. You're not alone anymore, you can live with me now."

"Thank you," I whispered, my throat tight with unshed tears. "I... I just... need some time to process all this."

"Of course," he replied, his voice gentle and understanding. "Take all the time you need."

As we left the doctor's office, I pulled Nurse Kylie aside, my heart aching at the thought of leaving her behind.

"Kylie, I don't know how to thank you for everything you've done for me," I choked out, my vision blurring with tears. "You've been like a sister to me, and I'll never forget you."

"Tuesday, I'm so happy for you," she said, her own eyes glistening with tears. "You deserve a chance at a better life, and I truly believe that your father will give you that. Just promise me one thing: Don't ever forget who you are and how strong you've become. No matter what happens, you always have a friend in me."

"I promise," I whispered, hugging her tightly.

"Tuesday" George called from the doorway, his voice gentle and patient. "Are you ready? I can sign you out of this facility today?"

I hesitated for a moment, my heart pounding with both fear and excitement. The prospect of leaving the mental health facility and starting a new life was thrilling but also terrifying. Could I really trust this man who claimed to be my father? What if he turned out to be just like all the others?

"Okay," I said finally, taking a deep breath. "Yes, I'm ready."
"Good" he replied, a small smile playing at the corners of his lips. "Let's go home."
As we walked toward the exit, I glanced back one last time at Nurse Kylie, who stood watching us with a bittersweet smile. Taking a deep breath, I stepped into the unknown, a fragile flame of hope burning within me.

The car pulled up to the wrought-iron gates, and I could feel my heart pounding in my chest. As we passed through and made our way up the long, winding driveway, the mansion loomed before us like a fortress from another world. The grandeur of the place was overwhelming, with its ornate architecture and vast gardens. I felt as if I had been transported into the pages of a fairy tale.
"Welcome home," Mr. Wellington said softly, placing a hand on my shoulder as we stepped out of the car. His touch sent an involuntary shiver down my spine, but I tried to ignore it. This was my new life.
"Thank you," I murmured, my voice barely audible.
As we entered the mansion, I couldn't help but gaze in awe at the opulence that surrounded me. Crystal chandeliers hung from high ceilings, casting a golden glow over the polished marble floors. Oil paintings adorned the walls, depicting scenes of enchanting landscapes and regal figures that seemed to be watching me as I walked by.

"Would you like a tour of the house?" George asked, his eyes scanning my face for any sign of discomfort.

"I'd love that," I replied, trying to sound enthusiastic despite the knot of anxiety twisting in my stomach.

"Very well," he said, leading me through the sprawling estate.

We wandered through room after room, each one more breathtaking than the last. There was a library filled with leather-bound books, a grand dining room, and a conservatory where exotic plants reached for the sun.

"Your mother loved this place," George said wistfully, pausing to run his fingers over the petals of a rare orchid. "I hope you will come to love it too."

"Me too," I whispered, though I couldn't shake the feeling that I didn't belong here.

"Tuesday," George called one evening, rousing me from my thoughts as I sat curled up on a velvet chaise lounge. "I have someone I'd like you to meet."

"Who is it?" I asked, my heart pounding with trepidation.

"My friend, Dr. Raymond," he replied, gesturing to a tall man with salt-and-pepper hair and kind eyes. "He's a psychiatrist, and I think he could help you with your...transition."

"Nice to meet you, Tuesday," Dr. Raymond said gently, extending his hand.

"Hi," I managed, taking his hand hesitantly.

"Your father has told me a lot about you," Dr. Raymond continued, his tone warm and reassuring. "I understand you've been through a great deal, and I want to help you find peace."

"Thank you," I whispered, feeling a strange mix of gratitude and fear.

"Let's start by talking about what medication you are on," he suggested, guiding me into a plush armchair.

Chapter 5

Tuesday May

The next day the housekeeper, Mrs. Collins, greeted me with a warm smile and a slight curtsy. She was an older woman, grey hair pulled back into a neat bun, her eyes kind but tired. "Welcome to Wellington Manor, Miss May," she said, her voice soft and comforting. I nodded, managing a weak smile in return.

"Thank you, Mrs. Collins." My voice sounded so small in this vast, imposing space.

"Allow me to introduce Mr. Thompson, our butler." She gestured to a tall, slender man standing nearby. His posture was impeccable, his silver hair immaculately combed, and he regarded me with a polite nod. "Miss May."

"Hello," I replied, feeling the weight of my new life beginning to settle on my shoulders.

"Your father is expecting you in his study," Mrs. Collins informed me, leading me through the opulent halls of the mansion. Paintings of people long dead adorned the walls, their eyes seeming to follow me as I passed.

As we approached the study, I hesitated for a moment, my heart pounding in my chest. With a deep breath, I pushed open the heavy oak door and stepped inside.

The study was dimly lit by the glow of a dying fireplace, casting flickering shadows across the room. Towering bookshelves lined the walls, filled with leather-bound volumes that seemed to whisper tales of secrets and power. And there, behind a large mahogany desk, sat the man I'd only known for a week.

"Tuesday," he said, his voice deep and commanding, sending a ripple of unease through me. He was an imposing figure, his salt-and-pepper hair framing a face etched with experience and authority. Those cold, calculating eyes bore into me as if he could see every hidden thought lurking in the depths of my mind.

"Father," I replied, feeling the word taste strange on my tongue. I'd never called anyone that. My hands clenched at my sides, betraying my nerves despite my best efforts to remain composed.

"Please, have a seat," he gestured to a plush chair across from him. As I sat down, I couldn't help but notice the way his gaze lingered on me, as though he was trying to piece together the puzzle that was his long-lost daughter.

"Thank you for having me," I said, trying to sound grateful while keeping my guard up. This man was still a stranger to me, and I had no idea what to expect.
"Of course, my dear." He paused, steepling his fingers together as he studied me intently. "You've grown into quite the young woman, Tuesday May."
I shifted uncomfortably in my seat, feeling exposed under his scrutiny. "Thank you, Father." I didn't know what else to say. The silence stretched between us, heavy with unspoken questions and uneasy truths. What did he want from me? And, more importantly, what would it cost me to find out?
"Your new life begins now, Tuesday," he finally said, his voice a low rumble that reverberated through the room. "And I expect great things from you."
"Of course," I murmured, forcing myself to meet his icy gaze. "I won't disappoint you."
"See that you don't," he warned, his eyes never leaving mine. And in that moment, I knew that secrets lurked in the shadows of this mansion.
I hesitated, picking at the frayed edges of my sweats as I mustered the courage to ask him. "Father...why didn't you ever come for me? Why did you leave me on that doorstep all those years ago?"
Mr. Wellington's eyes narrowed slightly, and I could see him weighing his words. "Your mother, Lillian," he began, his voice measured and deliberate, "was a beautiful but troubled

woman. She left me when she was pregnant with you and disappeared without a trace. I had no idea where she'd gone or if she'd even given birth." He paused, looking away for a moment. "Then I eventually gave up hope of finding her."

A heavy silence settled over us, punctuated only by the ticking of an ornate clock on the wall. The room felt colder, and more oppressive than before.

"So, how did you find out about me?" I probed gently, my curiosity getting the better of me.

“I came across a letter hidden in one of the rooms," Mr. Wellington replied, his face unreadable. “It was hidden amongst her belongings. It mentioned her desire to leave you somewhere, so someone else could raise you." He sighed deeply, a rare display of vulnerability that I hadn't expected. "By then it had been 21 years since she ran. I did some digging and found you."

I couldn't shake the feeling that something was missing, some crucial piece of information that he wasn't sharing. I chewed on my lip, hesitating before asking one more question. "What happened between you and Mother? What drove her away?"

"Ah," he breathed, a guarded expression crossing his features. "That, my dear, is a tale best saved for another time. Your mother and I...we had our differences, but that is of little importance now."

"Little importance" – somehow I doubted that. But I knew better than to push further. Instead, I nodded, feigning acceptance as I filed away my unanswered questions for a later date.

"Thank you for telling me," I murmured, looking down at my hands as I fought to keep my emotions in check. My past was a jumbled mess, full of shadows and whispers that never seemed to add up. But finding the truth would have to wait, at least for now.

"Go and explore," Mr. Wellington said, his voice softening ever so slightly. "This place is huge and filled with stories, go discover them." As he stood, signalling the end of our conversation, I couldn't help but feel a chill run down my spine. This man, my father, held the key to understanding my past, and something told me that unlocking those secrets would be far from easy.

"Ok thank you, Father," I whispered, rising to leave the room. His eyes followed me to the door, a silent reminder that I was stepping into an unfamiliar world where nothing could be taken for granted.

The morning sun bathed my room in a warm glow, casting shadows that danced across the aged wallpaper. I stood by the window, taking in the vast expanse of land before me. This was mine now – a fresh start, a place where I could belong. I hesitated for a moment, thoughts of my father's vague explanation from before momentarily clouding my mind, but I pushed those feelings aside. Today was a new day.

"Would you like to take a walk around the grounds?" Mrs Collins asked, her eyes sparkling with enthusiasm as she popped her head through my door. "It's a fine day, and I'm sure you'll find the gardens quite lovely."

"Thank you, that sounds wonderful."

As we stepped outside together, the air was crisp and cool, carrying the scent of dew-kissed grass and blooming flowers. The mansion's grounds were meticulously maintained, with perfectly trimmed hedges and vibrant flower beds arranged with an artistic eye. Everything seemed so perfect; it was as if I had walked into a painting.

"Your father takes great pride in these gardens," Mrs Collins explained, leading me down a winding path lined with rosebushes. "He spends hours out here, tending to each plant and flower as if they were his own children."

"Really?" I couldn't help but feel a pang of jealousy at the thought of my father nurturing these plants with such care, while I had been left to fend for myself all these years. But I brushed those thoughts aside, focusing instead on the beauty that surrounded me. This was a new beginning, and I wasn't going to let my past cloud the possibilities that lay ahead.

"Indeed," Mrs Collins continued. "He's always been a man of few words, but his love for this place is evident in everything he does."

We walked in companionable silence for a while, taking in the serene atmosphere. I found myself drawn to a small pond

nestled amidst a grove of weeping willows. Their long, slender branches swayed gently in the breeze, casting dappled patterns on the water below.
"Is it true what they say about Willow trees?" I asked Mrs Collins, my voice barely above a whisper. "That they're the keepers of lost dreams and forgotten memories?"
"Perhaps," she replied, her eyes softening with a hint of nostalgia. "But sometimes, it's better to leave the past where it belongs and focus on the future."
I couldn't help but wonder if she was speaking from experience, but I decided not to pry. Instead, I gazed at the delicate beauty of the willows and allowed myself to get lost in the tranquil scene before me. For now, I would let myself believe that everything was perfect in my new life – that in this place, I could finally find the sense of belonging I had always yearned for.
As the sun dipped lower in the sky, painting the horizon with hues of gold and crimson. We strolled back towards the mansion, the shadows lengthened, stretching their dark tendrils across the lush landscape like a veil slowly being drawn over the day. I couldn't help but feel a sense of melancholic beauty in the scene before me – it was as if the world itself were sighing with bittersweet longing at the end of another day.
"Miss May, dinner will be served shortly," the gravelly voice of the butler, Mr. Thompson, called out to me from the open

doors of the mansion. His stern features softened into a small smile as he added, "I trust you found your walk enjoyable?"
"Very much so, thank you," I replied, returning his smile with one of my own. My heart swelled with gratitude for the kindness shown to me by the staff, yet there was still a lingering uncertainty that gnawed at the corners of my mind. What secrets did this place hold?
"Shall I escort you to your room, Miss May?" Mr. Thompson offered, his gaze steady and unyielding.
"Please," I murmured, suddenly feeling the weight of the day settling upon my shoulders. The warmth of the dying sun still caressed my skin, but it was tinged with a hint of chill that whispered of the impending night.
Mrs Collin patted my arm and walked off towards the kitchen.
As we ascended the grand staircase, I couldn't help but notice the portraits lining the walls, their eyes seeming to follow me with every step I took. Were they watching me, judging me? Or were they simply echoes of a past long gone, trapped within the confines of their frames?
We reached my bedroom door, and Mr. Thompson opened it for me with a quiet grace. "I will return to escort you to dinner when you are ready, Miss May," he said, inclining his head before departing down the hallway.
As I stepped into the sanctuary of my room, I allowed myself a moment to drink in its soothing ambience – the soft glow of

the setting sun filtering through the lace curtains, the scent of lavender wafting from a delicate porcelain vase on the vanity, the plush embrace of the bedspread beneath my fingertips as I ran my hand over it.

But as I prepared for dinner, the melancholic beauty of the evening outside my window served as a constant reminder that even the brightest of days must come to an end. And as the sun finally disappeared beneath the horizon, I couldn't help but wonder what darkness lay waiting just beyond the edge of sight.

Chapter 6

Dimitri Costa

The sound of keys jingling echoed through the empty apartment as I unlocked the door and stepped inside, my weary limbs aching from another long day at work. I closed the door behind me, flicking on the lights to chase away the shadows that pooled in the corners of the room. My stomach grumbled loudly, reminding me that I hadn't eaten since breakfast, and I was suddenly grateful for the takeaway Thai I'd picked up on the way home.

"Pad Thai again, huh?" I muttered to myself, chuckling softly as I set the plastic container down on the kitchen counter. The rich aroma of spices and noodles wafted up, making my mouth water. As I grabbed a fork from a nearby drawer, I couldn't help but think that it would be nice to share this meal with someone other than my own reflection in the microwave door.

"Enough of that," I scolded myself, shaking off the thought and digging into the steaming food. With each bite, I felt some of the tension and exhaustion from the day seep out of my body, replaced by the satisfying warmth of a good meal.

I had just closed a particularly gruesome murder case – a man found shot in his own home. The victim's brother ended up being the culprit, driven by jealousy over his sibling's newfound wealth. He had thought he would inherit all the money once his brother was out of the picture. But instead, he was now in custody, and justice had been served.

As I ate, I found myself reflecting on the case and how I'd pieced everything together. There was something about unravelling the truth that filled me with a sense of accomplishment and pride. I loved being a detective, despite the long hours and the emotional toll it sometimes took.

"Another case solved," I murmured, staring at the crime scene photos I'd left scattered across the living room coffee table. It was hard not to get lost in the images of despair and destruction, but it was a part of the job I'd come to accept. In the end, it was about bringing closure to the families and making sure that those responsible paid for their crimes.

With a sigh, I finished off the last of my Pad Thai and tossed the container into the trash. The apartment felt cold and empty as I stood there, surrounded by the remnants of the day's work. Grabbing my laptop I sat down and scrolled through old case files, a glass of bourbon in my hand. I couldn't help but feel a pang of loneliness as I sat there, surrounded by walls that seemed to close in on me with each passing day. But the job was my life – and, in many ways, my one true love.

"Guess it's just you and me again tonight," I muttered to the screen, taking another sip of the amber liquid. The burn was comforting, a reminder that I was alive and still capable of feeling something other than the emptiness that had become all too familiar.

I let my mind wander back to the few relationships I'd attempted over the years, brief flares of warmth snuffed out by the relentless demands of my career. There was Jenna, a sweet girl who tried so hard to understand why I spent countless nights hunched over evidence and reports instead of cuddled up beside her. But the disappointment in her eyes when I inevitably cancelled yet another date haunted me long after we'd said our goodbyes.

"Sorry, Jenna," I whispered into the dark, my voice thick with regret.

And then there was Sarah, a fiery redhead who shared my passion for justice but couldn't quite grasp the toll it took on my soul. Our arguments were fierce, echoing through the apartment like rolling thunder. In the end, though, even she couldn't compete with the ghosts that clung to me, demanding to be avenged.

"Looks like it's just you and the job, Dimitri," I thought bitterly, remembering the pain in her eyes as she walked away, knowing that I couldn't - wouldn't - follow.

"Can I ever find someone who understands?" I asked the empty room, not really expecting an answer. The silence was deafening.

"Maybe it's time to try again," I murmured, the idea taking root in my heart like a fragile seedling. "Or maybe I'm just too far gone."

The amber liquid in my glass swirled as I pondered the question, the soft glow of the computer screen casting shadows on the walls. My heart yearned for connection, for love that went beyond the all-consuming passion I had for my work. But deep down, I knew that it would take someone truly special to break through the barriers I'd built around myself.

"Maybe," I whispered into the darkness, daring to let hope flicker within me. "Maybe someday.”

Chapter 7

Tuesday May

Three months had passed since I moved in with my father, and the mansion's once-grand facade now felt like a prison. The days dragged on, blending together as my supposed father's abusive behaviour became increasingly apparent. His eyes, cold and calculating, followed me through the corridors, and with each passing day, I felt more like prey than his daughter.

"Tuesday, where have you been?" he demanded one evening, grabbing my arm tightly as I tried to slip past him into the safety of my room.

"Out for a walk," I muttered, wincing at the pain of his grip. "Just needed some fresh air."

"Next time, inform me or Mr. Thompson," he said, his voice low and threatening. "You're not to leave this house without my permission."

As I lay in bed that night, the moonlight cast eerie shadows across my bedroom walls, and I couldn't shake the feeling of unease. It was during these dark hours that my father would sneak into my room, calling me Lillian as if I were his long-lost wife. My heart raced, and I buried my face in my pillow, why did the medication leave my body so pliant, but my mind so awake?

"Please," I whispered silently, my voice trembling as I clutched my bedsheets. "Don't let him come tonight."

But my prayers went unanswered. The creaking floorboards announced his arrival, and I could feel his presence looming over me, my body paralysed with fear.

"Lillian," he murmured, his breath hot against my ear. "My beautiful Lillian..."

I wanted to scream, to fight back, but my night-time medication left me trapped in a fog of drowsiness, leaving me vulnerable to his abuse. My thoughts turned inward, desperate to find some semblance of strength in my darkest moments. I knew I couldn't continue like this. Something had to change.

"Stop," I managed to choke out, the word barely audible as tears streamed down my cheeks.

"Stop what, dear?" he asked, feigning innocence. "I'm just checking on you."

"Leave me alone," I whispered, my voice a mere shadow of the strength and resilience that once defined me. "Please..."

He paused for a moment, then chuckled darkly. "Very well, Lillian," he said, his fingers brushing against my cheek before he retreated from the room.

As the door closed behind him, I wiped away my tears, my fear and anxiety intensifying with each passing night. I couldn't go on like this, living under the constant threat of my father's twisted desires. My medication, which was meant to provide some semblance of stability, now felt like a prison of its own, holding me captive in a nightmare I couldn't escape.

"Enough," I whispered to myself, determination steeled within me. "You are strong, Tuesday. You will survive this." I thought as I finally drifted to sleep.

I woke to the sound of rain tapping gently against the windowpane, my thoughts still clouded by the lingering haze of sleep. I curled up beneath the blankets, seeking solace in their soft embrace as I tried to piece together the fragments of my shattered psyche.

"Focus, Tuesday," I whispered to myself, my voice barely audible above the pattering rain. "You need to figure this out."

Gathering what little strength I had left, I climbed out of bed and made my way over to the desk nestled in the corner of my room. My fingers trembled as I opened my laptop, the screen flickering to life with a soft hum.

"Okay, let's see..." I muttered under my breath, typing in a search for my diagnoses, and others that looked the same. As

the results loaded, I couldn't help but feel a sense of dread coiling within me, tightening its grip around my heart.
"Flashbacks... nightmares... anxiety... avoidance of reminders..." I read aloud, feeling my chest tighten with each word. It all seemed to fit—like pieces of a puzzle finally falling into place. Could it be that the awful memories that haunted me weren't just remnants of a troubled past, but symptoms of something far more insidious?
"Tuesday?" The voice startled me, and I quickly closed the laptop, my heart racing.
"Are you okay?" It was Mrs Collins, the House Keeper, her eyes filled with concern as she stood in the doorway.
"Y-yes," I stammered, trying to mask the fear that threatened to choke me. "I'm fine."
"Your father asked me to bring you your medication," she said softly, handing me a small paper cup with two pills nestled at the bottom.
"Thank you," I murmured, taking the cup from her trembling hands.
As soon as the door closed behind her, I stared down at the pills, deep in thought. The medication was supposed to help me, and yet it left me feeling more trapped than ever before. Frustration bubbled within me, and at that moment, I made a decision.
"Enough," I whispered defiantly, my determination renewed. "I don't need these."

With a flick of my wrist, I sent the pills tumbling into the trash can beneath my desk, their hollow clatter echoing through the room like a promise of freedom. It was time to take control of my life—to face my demons head-on and fight back against the darkness that sought to consume me.

"Tuesday May, you will not be a victim any longer," I vowed, my voice steady and resolute. "You are strong, and you will survive this."

As the sun broke through the clouds outside, casting a warm glow across the rain-slicked streets below, I felt a newfound sense of hope blossom within me. And with each step I took towards reclaiming my life, I knew that one day, the shadows of my past would finally be vanquished, leaving only light in their wake.

In the days that followed my decision to stop taking the medication, a new clarity slowly took root within me. I began to see the fine lines of my reality, the twisted threads of deception that had woven themselves around my life. My resolve hardened with each passing moment like the cold steel of a blade being tempered in the fire.

I was no longer going to let others hurt me; I had reached my breaking point. At 23 years old, I was an adult with rights. Determined to take back control of my life, I began hiding knives and other sharp objects around my room in case my father tried to harm me again at night.

"Tuesday," I whispered to myself one night as I lay in the darkness, my eyes wide and watchful. "You will not be a victim any longer."
"Who are you talking to?" a voice hissed from the shadows, making me jump. It was him, my father.
"You're not allowed in here anymore," I retorted, my pulse racing but my voice steady. In one swift movement, I pulled the knife from under my pillow and held it outstretched before me, the silver blade gleaming in the dim light.
"Put that down, Lillian" he growled, lunging forward to grab my wrist. But my instincts were sharper now, honed by fear and determination, and I sidestepped his grasping fingers with ease.
"Stop calling me that!" I cried, my heart pounding in my chest. "My name is Tuesday May!"
"God, you're just like her," he sneered, his eyes narrowing with malice. "Stubborn, defiant, and so eager to play the martyr."
"Leave me alone!" I shouted, backing toward the door, the knife still held defensively between us. "I won't let you hurt me anymore!"
"Get back here!" he roared, reaching for me again. But this time, I was ready. I ducked beneath his arm and bolted from the room, my bare feet pounding against the cold wood of the hallway floor.

"Lillian!" he bellowed after me, his footsteps echoing through the house as he gave chase. I raced towards the grand staircase, my breath coming in ragged gasps, my mind a chaotic whirlwind of thoughts and emotions.

"Please leave me alone," I prayed silently as I reached the top of the stairs, my body trembling with fear and adrenaline.

As if in answer to my desperate plea, My father lunged for me one final time, his fingers outstretched like the talons of a predator. But fate was on my side that night, and his grasp fell short, sending him stumbling forward onto the stairs. His body twisted unnaturally, limbs flailing as he tumbled down the steps with a sickening crunch. I stood at the top of the staircase, my chest heaving, my eyes wide with a mix of horror and relief. The knife slipped from my trembling fingers, clattering onto the floor as I stared down at the broken body of the man who had haunted my life for 3 long months.

As I whispered the words, "Freedom," tears rolled down my cheeks. Finally, I was free from the pain and suffering he had caused me. A sense of peace washed over me for the first time in what felt like forever. I felt empowered and in control, with a rush of adrenaline coursing through my veins. Already, I wanted to wake him up and push him down again, just to feel that sense of power all over again.

Chapter 8

Tuesday May

I stood there for a while, my heart pounding in my chest as I stared at the lifeless body of my father. Who now lay at the bottom of the stairs - broken and defeated. The eerie silence of the house enveloped me, making the scene before me feel surreal. His cold, calculating eyes that once held so much power were now glazed over, unseeing. I couldn't help but feel a sick satisfaction as I watched the blood surrounding him slowly cool, the dark crimson merging with the polished wooden floor.

My fingers twitched involuntarily, leaning down to grip the handle of the knife I'd been carrying. A voice inside me whispered, urging me to ensure he was truly gone. But no, I couldn't risk it. I had to be cautious and smart. Taking a deep breath, I forced myself to move, my steps slow and deliberate as I returned each sharp object to its rightful place. The knives slid back into their slots, the scissors nestled among the sewing supplies, and the letter opener found its home on his desk. Each action felt like a ritual, a cleansing of sorts, erasing all traces of my involvement.

With every item returned, the weight of what had happened began to sink in. My hands trembled as I picked up the phone, dialling the number for the police. "Hello? I need to report an accident," I said, my voice barely above a whisper.

"Can you please provide your location and details of the accident?" the operator asked, her voice calm and professional.

"25 Maple Drive," I replied, swallowing hard. "My father... I think he fell down the stairs. He's not breathing."

"An ambulance is on its way," she assured me. "Please stay on the line."

As I remained on the phone, listening to the operator's instructions, I fought to keep my emotions in check. Guilt and fear threatened to consume me, but I pushed them down, burying them beneath a steely resolve. This was what had to be done; there was no going back now.

"Thank you," I said quietly as the sirens approached in the distance. Hanging up, I closed my eyes, taking a moment to compose myself. The life I'd known was over, changed irreversibly by my own hand. And yet, despite the darkness that lay ahead, I couldn't help but feel a glimmer of hope, a flicker of freedom that had long been out of reach.

As the first responders entered the house, I watched from the shadows. Walking outside I sat on the cold stone steps of the mansion, my body trembling as the gravity of what I had done began to sink in. A faint breeze whispered through the night air, sending a shiver down my spine. The sound of more sirens entered my ears as to the crunch of gravel that announced Mr. Thompson's arrival. He appeared from the darkness, his face etched with concern as he sat down beside me. His eyes scanned me up and down, pausing at the bruises on my arms.

"Are you alright, Miss May?" he asked softly.

"Y-yes," I stammered, trying to mask my unease. "Thank you."

"Of course." His gaze lingered on the marks marring my skin. "You should cover your arms before the police arrive. We don't want them asking questions."

I nodded, pulling my sleeves down over the evidence of my father's wrath. A sudden suspicion bubbled up within me. "You seem to know a lot about... this sort of thing. Is there something you're not telling me?"

Mr. Thompson hesitated before responding. "Your mother, Lillian... I knew her well. I miss her every day," he said, his voice tinged with sadness.

"Did she..." I struggled to find the words, my heart heavy with grief and confusion. "Did she know what he was like?"

“Yes, that's why she ran. She wanted to protect you. I suspect that's why she left you at the church – to give you a chance at a better life."

My eyes filled with tears as I considered the possibility that my mother might have been looking out for me all along. The pain of losing her stung anew, sharp and unyielding.

"Once this is all wrapped up with the police," Mr. Thompson continued, "I suggest you search the house thoroughly. You might find answers to some of your questions."

"Thank you," I whispered, wiping away the tears that threatened to spill over.

"Of course, Miss May," he replied, his voice gentle but unwavering. "Just remember – no matter how dark things seem, there is always a way forward."

As I sat there on the steps with Mr. Thompson, his words echoing in my mind, I couldn't help but feel a strange sense of comfort. For the first time in a long while, I felt as if I wasn't completely alone in this world. And despite the horrors that awaited me, I clung to that feeling like a lifeline, determined to uncover the truth.

The distant wail of sirens grew louder, signalling the arrival of the police. I quickly made sure I was fully covered, so no bruises on my arms were visible. My heart raced, not from fear but anticipation – this was my chance to escape my father's twisted world.

The police cars came to a halt in front of the mansion, their flashing lights casting eerie shadows across our faces. Officers hurried out, their concerned expressions evident even in the darkness. I took a deep breath and steeled myself for what was to come.

"Miss May," one of the officers said, approaching me with caution in his eyes. "Can you tell us what happened?"

"I heard a loud noise," I explained, forcing my voice to tremble with feigned distress. "I ran out to find him at the bottom of the stairs, not moving."

The officer nodded, his gaze sympathetic but probing. As they moved past us to investigate the crime scene and join the first responders inside, I couldn't help but feel a strange sense of satisfaction – my father wouldn't be able to hurt me ever again.

As I watched the police work, their careful movements and hushed conversations a stark contrast to the chaos that had unfolded earlier, I felt my resolve harden. No longer would I be a prisoner in my own home; no longer would I live in fear. Whatever secrets lay hidden within these walls, I was determined to uncover them.

After what felt like an eternity, the officers began to pack up their equipment. The first responders carefully placed my father's lifeless body into a black body bag, zipping it shut without a word. As they loaded him into the ambulance, I struggled to suppress a smile – a small, twisted victory in the face of all that I had endured.

"Miss May," the officer who had spoken to me earlier said, his voice gentle. "A detective will be around in the morning to take your statement. In the meantime, try to get some sleep."

"Thank you," I murmured, my eyes never leaving the ambulance as it drove away. Sleep seemed a distant impossibility, but I knew that I needed to rest if I was going to face what lay ahead.

"Would you like a cup of hot chocolate?" Mr. Thompson asked quietly, standing beside me once more. His eyes held a mixture of concern and understanding – he knew that this was just the beginning.

"Yes," I whispered, the word almost catching in my throat. "That would be nice."

Chapter 9

Dimitri Costa

The rising sun cast a warm glow on the city as I walked into work that morning, coffee in hand. My thoughts were still heavy with the memories of last night's case, but I shook them off and focused on the day ahead. Just another day of putting the pieces together and seeking justice for those who couldn't find it themselves.

"Morning, Dimitri," greeted Officer Jenkins, flashing me a tired smile as he passed by my desk.

"Morning, Jenkins," I replied, taking a sip of my coffee. Its bitter taste grounded me in reality, awakening my senses and fuelling my readiness to tackle whatever lay ahead.

I noticed a new file sitting on my desk, left there by the night staff. Curiosity piqued, I set my coffee down and opened the file, immediately drawn into the details of the case. A man had fallen down the stairs at his home and died; his daughter was the only one present at the time. It was up to me to determine if this was a tragic accident or if something more sinister was at play.

As I read further, I could feel my heartbeat quickening. The victim's name struck a chord within me – Mr. Wellington, one of the wealthiest men in the country. Old money. I'd heard whispers about him throughout my career, but never imagined I would be investigating his death.

"Jesus," I muttered, running my fingers through my short-cropped dark hair. This case was going to be anything but ordinary.

"Everything okay, Costa?" asked Detective Martinez, looking over at me with concern.

"Yeah, just got assigned a high-profile case," I replied, my mind already racing with possible scenarios. "A man fell down the stairs and died. His daughter was the only one home."

"Damn," Martinez said, eyebrows raised. "That's rough. You think it might not have been an accident?"

"Can't say for sure yet," I said, closing the file. "But you know how these things go. Sometimes there's more than meets the eye. And with someone like Mr. Wellington... who knows?"

"Shit Mr Wellington?. Well, good luck, man. Let me know if you need any help."

"Thanks, Martinez," I said, offering him a small smile before turning my attention back to the file.

Grabbing my jacket and the files, I left the precinct, determination settling in my chest as I started the drive to the address. The landscape shifted slowly, from the bustling cityscape to the quiet tranquillity of the countryside. Rolling hills and thickets of trees stretched out before me, their beauty marred only by the grim purpose of my visit.

The further I drove, the more isolated I felt – a stark contrast to the crowded city streets I was used to. It gave me a sense of unease, as though the world was holding its breath in anticipation of what I might uncover.

"Damn," I muttered under my breath, the grip on the steering wheel tightening. "Why does this feel like I'm walking into a storm?"

As I approached the estate, the house loomed large and imposing, betraying its age through weathered stone and ivy creeping up the walls. My shock at seeing the grandiosity of the place was rivalled only by the name written in the file: Mr. Wellington, one of the wealthiest men in the country.

"Old money," I whispered, the weight of the situation pressing down on me. This man's death would have ripple effects far beyond his family, and I couldn't afford to make any mistakes.

I parked the car and took a deep breath, steeling myself for the task ahead. Before stepping out, I read the file once more, absorbing every detail about the tragic accident that had claimed Mr. Wellington's life.

"His daughter... Tuesday. She was the only one home," I murmured, trying to imagine what she must be going through.
As I opened the car door, the cold wind whipped around me, chilling me to the bone. I shivered, glancing back at the dark silhouette of the house.
"Time to find out what really happened here," I whispered, my breath misting in the air before me. With each step I took towards the imposing mansion, I felt a growing sense of foreboding – like a storm brewing on the horizon, waiting for the perfect moment to strike.
"Hello, I'm Mr. Thompson," said a man in his late 60s, waiting for me at the entrance. His eyes were kind but held a glimmer of sorrow that seemed to mirror my own thoughts. "I'm assuming you're the detective we've been expecting?"
"Detective Dimitri Costa," I replied, accepting his offered hand. His grip was firm, yet the lines etched into his face betrayed the weight of years spent serving the Wellington family.
"Please, come in," he said, leading me through the grand foyer and into a formal sitting room adorned with lavish furniture and gilded mirrors. Despite the opulence, a sombre atmosphere filled the air, as if the house itself mourned the loss of its master.
"Welcome, I'm Mrs. Collins," an older lady introduced herself, placing a tray of tea before me. Her eyes held a soft warmth, contrasting the chill within the room. I nodded my

thanks and took a sip of the steaming liquid, letting it soothe my frayed nerves.
"Thank you, Mrs Collins," I murmured, my mind racing through possible scenarios of what could have happened to Mr Wellington. Was it truly an accident, or was there something more sinister at play?
A few minutes later, Mr. Thompson returned to the sitting room, accompanied by a woman who seemed almost ethereal in her beauty. She was small and slender, with long dark hair that cascaded down her back like a waterfall of midnight silk. Her eyes were piercing and intense, as if they held the power to glimpse my very soul.
"Detective," Mr Thompson began, motioning toward the woman beside him, "this is Tuesday May, Mr Wellington's daughter."
"Miss May," I said, extending my hand with a polite smile. As our fingers touched, an electric jolt coursed through me, leaving me momentarily breathless. I couldn't help but be captivated by her beauty, and a part of me yearned to trace the curves of her body with my hands. I quickly dismissed these thoughts, focusing on the task at hand.
"Please, call me Tuesday," she replied softly, her voice like velvet. She took a seat nearby, her posture poised and graceful. "What can I do for you, Detective?"
"I need your statement about what happened the night your father died," I explained, trying to maintain a calm and

professional demeanour. My heart ached for her; the pain she must be feeling at the loss of her father was unimaginable. "I understand this may be difficult, but the more information you can provide, the better."

"Of course." Tuesday took a deep breath, steadying herself. "It was late, around midnight when I heard a loud thud and then a rumble of them to proceed that. I went to investigate and found my father at the bottom of the stairs. His body... it was twisted and broken."

Her eyes shone, not a normal response to seeing a dead body, but maybe shock was still running through her.

"Tuesday," I said gently, "did you notice anything unusual that night? Anything out of place or strange?"

"Nothing," she whispered, shaking her head. "It seemed like an ordinary night until I found him."

"Thank you for sharing your story with me," I reassured her, offering a warm smile. "I know it must have been difficult to recount those events." Reaching into my jacket pocket, I pulled out a business card and handed it to her. "If you think of anything else, please don't hesitate to call me."

"Thank you, Detective Costa," Tuesday murmured, accepting the card with a small nod. Her eyes met mine for a fleeting moment, and in that brief exchange, I felt the need to pull her close, wrap her in my arms, and kiss those full lips...

As I stood to leave, I couldn't help but wonder if this case would ultimately become more than just an investigation. I knew I wanted to taste her, but could I allow myself to get mixed up with someone from a case?

Chapter 10

Tuesday May

2 weeks later, the room was cold and sterile, filled with an eerie silence as the investigators whispered among themselves. I looked around, my heart pounding in my chest, waiting for their final verdict. Detective Martinez cleared his throat, breaking the tension. "After a thorough investigation, we have concluded that the incident was an accident."

I could feel the relief washing over me like a wave, but it was tainted by a strange longing—an attraction to the man who had been so dedicated to uncovering the truth about my father's death. Detective Dimitri Costa had been there from the beginning, offering me reassurance and a comforting presence.

"Thank you," I managed to whisper, my voice barely audible.

"Of course, Tuesday. If you need anything else, don't hesitate to call," Dimitri said, his warm brown eyes meeting mine.

As he left the room, I couldn't help but feel a pull towards him. The way he cared for others, his compassion and empathy; stirred something deep inside me. But I had never dated anyone before. How did people even go about asking someone out? Was calling him and asking for coffee too forward?

I paced back and forth in my bedroom, clutching my phone tightly as I wrestled with indecision. My thoughts raced, my mind a whirlwind of questions and doubts. What if he laughed at me? What if he thought I was ridiculous for even considering it?

"Ugh!" I groaned, collapsing onto the bed. It felt as if my heart would burst from my chest, so powerful were the emotions that consumed me. I wanted to take a chance, to reach out and connect with Dimitri, but how?

"Maybe... maybe I should just ask him," I whispered to myself, my pulse quickening at the mere thought of it.

Taking a deep breath, I dialled Dimitri's number, holding my breath as I pressed the call button. The phone rang, each tone echoing through my head like a ticking clock.

"Hello, Detective Costa speaking," Dimitri's voice echoed through the receiver, and just hearing him sent a shiver down my spine.

"Hi, it's Tuesday," I stammered, my voice trembling ever so slightly. "I was wondering if... if you'd like to grab a coffee sometime?"

There was a brief pause, a silence that felt like an eternity before Dimitri finally answered. "I'd love to."

My heart soared.

The sun dipped below the horizon as Mr. Thompson pulled up to the small, cozy coffee shop where I was meeting Dimitri for our date. As he opened the door for me, I couldn't help but feel a twinge of nervousness bubble up inside my chest. This was all so new to me.

"Thank you, Mr. Thompson," I said, stepping onto the sidewalk. He gave me a nod and a warm smile, acknowledging my gratitude before driving to the park and waiting for me.

As I pushed open the door to the coffee shop, the rich aroma of fresh brews enveloped me, soothing my nerves ever so slightly. I spotted Dimitri sitting in a corner booth, his eyes focused on a newspaper. Even from this distance, I could see the gentle curve of his lips as he read. My heart fluttered at the sight of him.

"Hey, Dimitri," I greeted softly as I approached the table.

"Tuesday!" His eyes lit up as he looked up from his paper, quickly folding it and setting it aside. "You look lovely."

"Thank you." I felt heat rise to my cheeks as I slid into the seat across from him. The intimacy of the brightly lit coffee shop surrounded us as we sipped our warm drinks, allowing our conversation to flow easily.

"Tuesday, tell me more about yourself," Dimitri asked, curiosity gleaming in his eyes. I hesitated for a moment, unsure of how much to reveal. But there was something about Dimitri that made me feel safe like I could trust him with my darkest secrets.

"I... I grew up in the foster system," I began, swallowing hard. "And when I was thirteen, I tried to stab a man who was abusing me. That's why I spent ten years in a mental institution."

Dimitri's eyes widened in shock, his grip on his coffee cup tightening. "I'm so sorry, Tuesday," he murmured, his voice thick with empathy. "You didn't deserve any of that."

"Thank you, Dimitri." I smiled weakly before continuing. "On my 23rd Birthday, my father came to the place I was in, and asked for a DNA test, I agreed and it came back positive, my mother had run away from him pregnant and left me on the church steps, I lived with my father for just three months before he died. And now... I've inherited billions from him. It's overwhelming, really. I don't know what to do with it all, or how to live like a normal person."

"Follow your passions," Dimitri suggested gently, reaching across the table and grasping my hand. "What brings you joy?"
“Art, Drawing," I admitted, feeling tears prick at the corners of my eyes. "It's been so long since I've done either."
"Turn a room in your house into an art studio," he encouraged. "Find your soul again through your creativity."
The weight of his words washed over me, filling my heart with gratitude. As the evening wound down, we stepped outside into the crisp night air. Dimitri looked into my eyes, hesitating only for a moment before leaning in and pressing his lips against mine. For the first time in my life, I was experiencing a real, wanted kiss, and it melted my heart toward him.
"Can I see you again?" Dimitri asked softly as our lips parted.
"Of course," I agreed. "But I understand if your job gets in the way sometimes."
"Call me whenever you want," he said, his brown eyes warm and sincere. "I'll come to see you when I'm off work."
"Deal," I whispered.

Chapter 11

Tuesday May

I had recently taken up running around the grounds of the mansion every day, something I never had the opportunity to do before. Surprisingly, I found that I loved it. Not only did it help with my recurring nightmares and flashbacks, but it also gave me a sense of control over my body. My morning routine now consisted of a gentle jog to the pond, a leisurely walk through the garden, and a final sprint back to the mansion.

As I stood there at the pond that morning, my heart racing with adrenaline, I realised how much I enjoyed it – seeing the life leave my father's eyes. It was intoxicating, this newfound sense of control over my demons. The power to decide who lived and who died. And for the first time since my innocence was stolen, I felt alive.

It dawned on me that I couldn't ignore my demons any longer; I needed to confront them head-on. As a sense of anger and fury rose within me, driven by my thirst for revenge, the memory of the Hamilton family flooded my mind. They were the first ones to hurt me, and they deserved to experience the same fear they had inflicted upon me. My hands clenched into tight fists as I made up my mind to take action.

I started to strategise, methodically gathering details about their whereabouts and daily schedules. Each bit of information brought me one step closer to facing the past I had been desperately trying to forget. My ultimate goal was to find them and figure out a way to eliminate them without getting caught. It would be a difficult task to plan, but luckily there were multiple rooms in this mansion that I could use as my war room. I would need to have Mr. Thompson clear out a space on the upper floor for me and install a lock on the door for added security.

The enormity of the mansion hit me like a ton of bricks as I stood at the foot of the grand staircase. I'd only managed to poke around three rooms so far, but each one seemed to hold more secrets than the last. With a deep breath, I began my ascent, eager to uncover what lay behind those closed doors.

"Alright, Tuesday," I muttered to myself, "let's see what you've gotten yourself into." My footsteps echoed in the vast emptiness, sending shivers down my spine. The air was thick with dust and mystery.

Reaching the top of the stairs, I glanced down the long hallway, lined with door after door. There had to be at least twenty of them spanning the hallways up and down stairs, though I hadn't bothered to count. Feeling like a kid in a candy store, I approached the first door, my heart pounding with excitement. The worn brass handle creaked beneath my touch, and the door swung open with a groan.
"Hello?" I called out jokingly, rolling my eyes at my own theatrics. The room was empty, save for an old wooden chair and a dusty chandelier hanging from the ceiling. I couldn't help but wonder what stories these walls would tell if they could talk. Shaking my head, I moved on to the next room.
"Jesus, how many rooms does one family need?" I huffed, feeling both exhilarated and slightly overwhelmed as I continued to explore. Each space held its own unique charm, some with ornate fireplaces or floor-to-ceiling windows that allowed moonlight to spill across the hardwood floors.
As I ventured further, I found myself getting lost in my thoughts. While I knew this place had been in the Wellington family for generations, it felt almost too big for someone like me. I couldn't deny the allure of starting fresh somewhere else, but at the same time, I wanted to uncover any hidden treasures that might be waiting for me in this labyrinth of a home. The thrill of discovery was just too enticing to resist.
"Tuesday May," I whispered under my breath, "professional treasure hunter and mystery solver extraordinaire." With a

grin, I continued to delve deeper into the mansion, eager to see what secrets awaited me behind each door.

"Mr. Thompson!" I called out, my voice echoing through the seemingly endless halls of the mansion. "Could you join me up here for a second?"

"Of course, Miss Tuesday," he replied, his footsteps growing louder as he ascended the stairs. His expression was stoic but slightly bemused as he approached.

"Alright, so here's the deal," I began, my tone casual yet determined. "I want to empty all these rooms one by one, clean them out, get rid of the furniture, the whole shebang. I know this place has been in my family for generations and all that jazz, but it's just too fucking big for little ol' me. Plus, you mentioned something about hidden treasure, and I'm not gonna lie – my curiosity is piqued."

"Very well, Miss," Mr. Thompson agreed with a nod, taking on an air of eagerness himself. "When shall we begin?"

"I was thinking we could order some moving boxes, ones for stuff I would like to keep and some for things I would like to donate, the furniture can we auctioned off" I explained

Mr Thompson laughed at me and said "We can manage that."

Chapter 12

Tuesday May

The next day, the front lawn was transformed into what looked like a storage facility. Three large container boxes sat there, waiting to be filled, while empty cardboard boxes were stacked up high like makeshift skyscrapers. Mr Thompson, the ever-reliable butler, stood next to me as we prepared to tackle the room at the end of the hall.

"Miss May," he began with his usual formality, "this room was originally a children's playroom a few generations back. As you can see, it's now mainly used for storage." He gestured towards the haphazard mix of toys and random furniture pieces scattered about the room.

"Damn, this place is a mess," I remarked, eyeing the clutter with both apprehension and excitement. Something was thrilling about uncovering secrets from my family's past, even if it meant sifting through piles of dusty junk.

"Indeed," Mr. Thompson agreed, clearing his throat. "Shall we get started?"

"Let's do it," I replied with a grin.

As we worked together, sorting through the room's contents, I found myself oddly enjoying the process. Sure, most of the stuff held no emotional value to me, but the act of unearthing buried treasures felt like an adventure. Plus, Mr. Thompson's presence, which I had initially thought might be a hindrance, turned out to be quite comforting. The man knew how to keep things light and fun.

"Hey, Mr. T," I called out, holding up a worn-out teddy bear, "do you think this little guy has seen better days?"

He chuckled softly. "I believe so, Miss May."

"Into the 'throw' pile he goes, then," I said, tossing the bear onto the overflowing boxes of discarded items.

"Another one bites the dust," Mr. Thompson mused, shaking his head with a smile.

As we continued our mission, I couldn't help but think about the room's original purpose. What sort of games had past generations played in here? Had they laughed and cried within these very walls?

"Mr. Thompson," I asked suddenly, "do you think this place holds any other secrets?"

"Miss May," he replied with a knowing look, "I believe every corner of this house has a story to tell."

"Guess we'll just have to keep digging, then," I grinned, determination flaring within me. "Who knows what we might find?"
My phone rang, interrupting our quest. Glancing at the screen, I saw Dimitri's name and couldn't help but smile.
"Hey there, handsome," I answered, trying to keep my voice playful despite my racing heart.
"Tuesday," he said warmly, "just checking in. I'm wrapping up a case soon and was hoping to see you. How about Sunday? It's my only day off."
"Sounds perfect," I replied, excitement bubbling within me. "I could use some help with this never-ending excavation anyway."
"Consider me your trusty assistant," he joked. "See you then, and good luck with your treasure hunt."
"Thanks, detective," I teased before hanging up.
With Dimitri's visit on the horizon, I felt an extra surge of motivation to uncover the mysteries of my family home. As Mr. Thompson and I continued our search through the room, I couldn't help but feel that we were just beginning to scratch the surface.
"Alright, Thompson, let's get this show on the road," I said with determination, rolling up my sleeves. "I've got a date with a detective on Sunday, and I want this place to be at least halfway decent by then."

"Of course, Miss May." Mr. Thompson nodded, equally determined. "Shall we begin assessing the furniture?"

"Lead the way, kind sir," I replied with mock formality, gesturing for him to proceed.

As we picked our way through the room, we examined the pieces one by one. Three rickety bookcases, covered in dust and cobwebs, stood in silent testament to the passage of time. Four broken chairs lay scattered like defeated soldiers on a battlefield. A worn rocking chair creaked ominously as if haunted by memories of long-forgotten lullabies. And several wooden storage boxes, now empty, stood as mute witnesses to the secrets they once held.

"Damn. This place is like a graveyard for furniture," I muttered, surveying the wreckage.

"Indeed, Miss May," Mr. Thompson agreed solemnly. "But perhaps it's time to put these old relics to rest."

"Couldn't have said it better myself," I grinned, feeling a strange sense of liberation. "Call the movers; let's get this stuff out of here."

With efficiency born from years of service, Mr Thompson arranged for the movers to haul the discarded items down to the containers outside. Watching them work, I felt an odd mixture of sadness and exhilaration. These things were part of my family's history, but they were also a burden, weighing me down with their oppressive silence.

"Alright, team," I called out as the movers finished up, wiping the sweat from their brows. "Great job today. We'll reconvene tomorrow for round two. Same bat time, same bat channel."
"Miss May," Mr. Thompson interjected, his lips twitching with the ghost of a smile, "I must admit, your enthusiasm is quite contagious."
"Damn right, it is," I replied, feeling lighter than I had in years.
As I strolled back into the now-empty room, my bare feet slapped against the hardwood floor, echoing through the space. The walls seemed to breathe a sigh of relief, free from the weight of years' worth of hoarded memories.
"Damn, it feels good to be a cleaner," I joked to myself, running my toes along the smooth surface of the floor where the antique rug once lay. That's when I noticed it - a slight gap between two of the floorboards. Curiosity piqued, I knelt down and wiggled the loose board, my heart pounding with excitement.
"Yo, Mr. T! Get in here!" I called out, trying to keep the thrill out of my voice. In a matter of seconds, the trusty old butler was at my side, eyeing the floorboard with interest.
"Good heavens, Miss May, what have you found?" he asked, his own curiosity evident.
"Only one way to find out," I winked, as we both gripped the edges of the board and pulled. With a satisfying creak, it came free, revealing a small hollow beneath.

"Jackpot," I whispered, reaching in to retrieve a few folded, yellowed pieces of paper. Unfolding them, I discovered a love letter written from my father to my mother, accompanied by a faded photograph of the two of them looking young and carefree. My heart clenched at the sight, of their happiness long gone.

The next note appeared to be some kind of diary entry, cryptic in nature: "Charming as you may be, I see through the facade. You can't fool me. I may be yours to take, but I'm not yours to own."

"Damn, that's deep," I mused aloud, feeling a chill run up my spine. Mr. Thompson looked sad, his eyes clouded with regret.

"I wish I was able to help her more than I did," he said softly, pushing himself up from the floor. He left the room, his footsteps echoing down the hallway, leaving me alone with my thoughts and the remnants of my parents' love.

"Shit," I sighed, rereading the mysterious note. "What kind of twisted game were you playing, Mom? And who were you playing it with?”

Chapter 13

Dimitri Costa

The shrill sound of my alarm cut into my dreams like a knife, yanking me from the comfortable depths of sleep. I groaned, fumbling for the snooze button. "Fuck," I muttered, rubbing my eyes and glancing at the glowing numbers on the clock. 8:15 AM. Shit, I'd only gotten five hours of sleep since getting home from work at 3 AM.

"Time to get up, Dimitri," I told myself, swinging my legs over the side of the bed. No time to waste, it was Sunday morning, and I had promised Tuesday, that intriguing woman with those piercing blue eyes, I'd help her with some cleaning. I quickly threw on clothes as my thoughts drifted back to our coffee date - it seemed ages ago, even though we'd been talking daily since then.

"Alright, let's do this" I mumbled, grabbing my keys and stepping out into the crisp morning air. My car roared to life beneath me, and I sped through the city streets, watching

buildings blur into the distance behind me. Forty-five minutes later, I pulled up to Tuesday's mansion, its imposing stature looming before me. Three large shipping containers sat on the pristine lawn alongside a couple of waiting removal men who looked bored as hell. She wasn't kidding when she said she was taking the clean-out seriously.
"Hey, guys" I greeted the removalists with a quick nod as I passed, making my way towards the open front door. As I stepped inside, the familiar figure of Mr. Thompson materialised before me like magic. He was always there when you needed him, wasn't he?
"Morning, Mr Costa," he said, his voice smooth and measured. "Miss May is in room three. I'll walk you up."
"Thanks" I replied, following him up the grand staircase, my footsteps echoing off the walls. As we reached the room, it looked like a tornado had ripped through it - packing boxes and furniture strewn about haphazardly. I spotted Tuesday sitting on the floor amid the chaos, carefully placing porcelain dolls into a box. My skin crawled at the sight of them.
“Hey," I called out, grinning as she turned to see me. Her face lit up and she practically leapt from the floor, throwing her arms around my neck. God, I could get used to this kind of greeting. Our lips met in a soft, lingering kiss before I set her back down on her feet.
"Hello, sweetness" I murmured, planting another quick peck on her inviting lips. "Seems like you've got your work cut out

for you today" I glanced around the room, taking in the disorder. She laughed a musical sound that sent warmth spreading through my chest.

"Tell me about it," she said, rolling her eyes. "But with you here, I'm sure we'll knock this out in no time" She flashed me one of those heart-stopping smiles that made everything seem possible.

My heart was beating wildly in my chest as we finished clearing out Room 3, or as Tuesday liked to call it. I couldn't help but marvel at her efficiency and determination, even with a task as mundane as this. It took us only two hours to empty the room, and the removal guys were quick to haul everything down into the awaiting shipping containers.

"Damn, we're good," I said, grinning at Tuesday as I wiped the sweat from my brow. "I didn't think we'd get through that so quickly."

"Neither did I," she admitted, a playful smirk on her lips. "But I guess when you've got two badass people working together, anything's possible."

Her piercing blue eyes met mine, and for a moment, I felt like she could see right through me. Despite her tumultuous past, there was an undeniable strength in her gaze that made me feel both humbled and drawn to her. She was cautious, yet brave - a survivor through and through.

"Hey, Detective," she teased, nudging me with her elbow. "You're not too bad yourself. Who knew you had such mad furniture-moving skills?"
"Years of practice," I joked, flexing my arm just to see her roll her eyes.
"Ha ha Dimitri." She shot me a genuine smile, and I felt a warmth spread through my chest at the sound of my name leaving her lips.
"Tuesday, why don't you give Dimitri a tour of the grounds while we take care of the room?" Mr. Thompson's voice pulled me from my thoughts as he poked his head in the doorway.
"Sure thing, Mr. T," she replied with a grin. "We could use a break, right?"
"Absolutely," I agreed
"Great!" She exclaimed, grabbing my hand like a child and practically sprinting down the hall. "Come on, there's so much to show you!"
"Slow down, Tuesday!" I laughed, struggling to keep up with her sudden burst of energy.
"Never!" She hollered back, her laughter echoing through the empty halls as we made our way outside.
The moment we stepped out into the open air, I felt a sense of freedom wash over me. The sun was shining, the birds were singing, and for a fleeting moment, it was easy to forget all the bad in the world.

"Isn't it beautiful out here?" Tuesday asked, finally releasing my hand as we strolled along the meticulously manicured gardens.

"Stunning," I agreed, unable to look away from the vibrant display of colours spread out before us. "I never would have guessed all of this was hidden behind those cold, stone walls."

"Appearances can be deceiving," she mused, her eyes scanning the horizon as if searching for something more. "But sometimes, you find beauty in unexpected places."

"True," I said, turning my gaze back to her. "Like in the middle of a dusty old room filled with forgotten belongings."

"Hey now," she teased, punching me playfully in the arm. "That room wasn't *that* bad."

"Sure, after we cleared it out," I chuckled, rubbing my sore bicep. "But seriously, Tuesday, I'm glad I got to share that experience with you. It felt like we were uncovering a piece of your history together."

"Thanks, Dimitri," she said softly, her voice tinged with a mix of gratitude and vulnerability. "I'm glad you're here too. I don't think I could have done it without you."

"Anytime, Tuesday. I enjoy seeing you." The sincerity in my words hung heavy between us, but it was the truth. And as we continued our leisurely stroll around the grounds.

Chapter 14

Tuesday May

The sun sat high, casting a golden glow across the serene pond. It was my favourite place outside, a little haven where I could escape and find peace. The soft rustling of leaves in the gentle breeze served as a soothing lullaby for my frazzled nerves.

"Damn, this is nice," I murmured, taking a seat on the chair facing the pond. I patted the empty space beside me, inviting Dimitri to join me. "Come sit."

"Beautiful spot, Tuesday," Dimitri said, his warm brown eyes reflecting the sunlight as he settled next to me. I could see the compassion etched on his handsome features, the empathy that made him such a great detective.

"Thanks," I replied, feeling a little nervous but excited at the same time. "So, um, there's something I've been wanting to tell you." My heart raced in my chest, threatening to burst free like a caged bird.

"Go ahead," Dimitri encouraged, his voice gentle and reassuring. "I'm all ears."
Taking a deep breath, I reached out and took his hand, marvelling at the warmth and strength it radiated. "I really like you, Dimitri," I confessed, my cheeks burning hot with embarrassment. "And I was wondering if... if you'd like to stay the night."
"Tuesday," he said softly, his thumb stroking the back of my hand. "I would be honoured."
"Really?" Relief flooded through me, and I couldn't help but smile at his sincere response. "That's awesome!"
"Of course," Dimitri replied, leaning in closer. His scent, a mix of cologne and something uniquely him enveloped me, making me feel secure and wanted. "There's nowhere else I'd rather be right now."
"Good," I said, my heart swelling with happiness. "Because I don't want you to go anywhere either."
I looked down at our intertwined hands, the contrast of his tanned skin against my paler complexion creating a beautiful juxtaposition. The thought of what I was about to say made my stomach flutter with nerves, but he needed to know. "Dimitri," I began, my voice barely audible. "There's something else I need to tell you."
"Of course, Tuesday," he replied, concern lacing his tone. "You can tell me anything."

Taking a deep breath, I gathered my courage. "I've never really had sex with anyone before." I paused, swallowing hard. "I mean, I'm not a virgin, but the only people who touched me were... foster parents who abused me." I felt vulnerable admitting this, but I needed him to understand. "I want to explore that side of myself with you."

His warm brown eyes filled with compassion as a single tear escaped and traced a path down his cheek. "I'm so sorry for what you've gone through, Tuesday," he said softly. "And I feel honoured that you want to explore that part of yourself with me."

He wiped away the tear, determination replacing the sadness in his gaze. "We'll take it slow, and only do what makes you comfortable. Alright?"

"Alright," I agreed, feeling a sense of trust and safety wash over me.

"Tuesday, you're a beautiful, strong woman," he whispered, his eyes searching mine. "Can I kiss you?"

I couldn't help the grin that spread across my face. "You never need permission to kiss me, Dimitri."

With that, he leaned in and pressed his lips to mine. They were soft and warm, and the sensation sent shivers down my spine. As he deepened the kiss, his hands found their way to my back, pulling me into his lap. I could feel his erection growing beneath his jeans, and surprisingly, it didn't scare me. Instead, I felt a spark of curiosity and desire.

As I ran my hands down his chest, feeling the grooves of his muscular torso beneath his t-shirt, I realised how much it turned me on. My body responded in kind, growing slick with want. For once, I wasn't afraid to take things further.
The warmth of Dimitri's body radiated through his shirt, and I couldn't help but let my hands wander beneath the fabric. As we kissed passionately, I marvelled at the contrast between his strong physique and the tenderness of his touch. He laughed softly, leaning back from our kiss to look me in the eyes, his warm brown gaze full of desire.
"Do you want to touch me, Sweetness?" Dimitri asked with a wicked grin. I bit my lip and nodded eagerly.
"Can I take off your shirt?" I asked, my voice barely more than a whisper.
Dimitri released his grip on my ass and leaned back further, expertly removing his shirt with one hand. The sight of him sitting there - clad only in jeans that bulged deliciously at the crotch - made my pulse race.
"Damn," I thought to myself as my fingers traced along his chest, playing with the small patch of hair just above his pecs. I followed the grooves of his well-defined abs down to the top of his jeans, feeling a mixture of excitement and nervousness.
"Tuesday," Dimitri said warmly, snapping me out of my thoughts. "You've got this wicked little smile. What are you thinking?"

"Nothing much," I lied, cheeks flushing. "I'm just... enjoying the view."

"Can I touch you too?" he inquired, his brown eyes filled with a mix of desire and genuine concern for my comfort.

"Okay," I agreed, biting my lip as anticipation built up within me.

I watched intently as Dimitri's hands moved slowly down my neck, then toward the sides of my breasts still clad in a t-shirt. The warmth of his touch sent shivers through my body. He traced a line down to my waist before gliding his fingertips back up, hooking his thumbs under the curve of my breasts and gently brushing against my nipples. My breath hitched, and I couldn't help but lean into his touch.

"Like that?" he asked huskily, gauging my reaction.

"Y-Yeah," I stammered, feeling a heady mix of excitement and vulnerability.

"Good," Dimitri murmured, leaning in to capture my lips in a passionate kiss once more. This time it was rougher and hungrier, and the intensity of it made my knees weak. As he touched my breasts more firmly, a deep, delicious ache began to build inside me. "God, Dimitri," I thought, "you're driving me absolutely insane."

Just when I felt like I couldn't take any more, Dimitri pulled away from the kiss. "That's enough for now, Sweetness," he said gently, concern etched on his handsome features. "I don't want to push it."

"Wait, no!" I protested, a rush of disappointment washing over me. "I'm okay with it, really."

"Tuesday," he replied, chuckling softly, "the first time I take you, it'll be in a bed. I promise."

"Fine," I pouted, feeling my cheeks heat up.

With my legs still wrapped around his waist, Dimitri stood and carefully lowered me back down to the ground. As he did so, our gazes locked, and I could see that the fire of passion still burned within him. "Let's go back inside the mansion, Sweetness," he suggested, his voice low and seductive. "You can show me your bedroom."

"Alright," I agreed breathlessly, knowing that despite the playful tone of our encounter, there was a deeper connection between us that couldn't be denied.

Chapter 15

Tuesday May

My heart races as I snatch Dimitri's hand, my fingers intertwining with his. It's like we're two teenagers sneaking around, but the thrill only amplifies the emotions swirling inside me. I can't hold it in any longer—I need to let it out, and I need him.

"Come on!" I grin, pulling him along as we sprint away from the pond, through the fragrant garden, and towards the back of the mansion. We're practically flying, our laughter mingling with the rustle of leaves and the distant hum of the world beyond.

"Tuesday," he gasps between breaths, awe in his voice, "you're a force of nature."

We continue racing up the stairs, my legs burning, but I don't care. The adrenaline pumps through me, making me feel alive.

We reach my bedroom door, and I fling it open. A sudden wave of nervousness washes over me, causing my steps to falter. This is really happening, isn't it?

I can practically feel the electricity between us as Dimitri walks in behind me, kicking the door closed with his foot. He stalks towards me like a predator, and I can't help but shiver in anticipation. His warm hands find my face, cupping it gently as if I'm some fragile piece of art. And then his lips crash into mine, obliterating all thought and reason.

"God, Tuesday," he murmurs against my mouth, "you have no idea what you do to me."

The way he says my name sends shivers down my spine. I twine my arms around his neck, desperate for more contact, for the heat of his body pressed against mine. Dimitri seems to sense my need, wrapping his arms around my back and grabbing my ass without hesitation. I let out a surprised squeak, but he just smirked against my lips.

"Trust me?" he asks, his voice rough with desire.

"Yes," I whisper, and that's when he lifts me off the ground, forcing me to wrap my legs around his waist. The feeling of powerlessness is thrilling and intoxicating, and I can't help but moan softly into his mouth.

"Jesus, Tuesday, you're driving me crazy," Dimitri pants, carrying me toward the bed with a determined stride. As he lays me down, I can see the hunger in his eyes, the barely contained lust that mirrors my own.

"Then let me drive you even crazier," I challenge my voice breathy and teasing.
"Fuck, don't tempt me," he growls, leaning down to claim my lips once more. The heat of our tangled bodies makes the room spin, and I know at this moment that we've crossed a line - one that neither of us can ever go back from. And yet, as Dimitri kisses me with such intensity that I feel like I might shatter apart, I can't bring myself to care.
"Please, Dimitri," I beg, my voice raw with need. "I need you."
"Sweetheart, you have me," he promises, his breath hot against my ear. "You have all of me."
Dimitri's weight settles on top of me, enveloping me in a cocoon of warmth and desire. The sensation is incredible like every cell in my body was waiting for this moment. I revel in it, feeling more alive than ever before.
"Is this okay?" Dimitri murmurs against my lips, his voice equal parts tender and hungry.
"More than okay," I breathe out, lost in the intoxicating mix of sensations coursing through me.
"Good," he says simply, our mouths never breaking contact as we continue to explore each other's taste and texture.
As if reading my mind, Dimitri begins to shift down my body, his hands gliding over my clothes with a possessive touch that sends shivers down my spine. He cups my breast gently, the heat of his palm searing through the fabric.

"Can I?" he whispers, already knowing my answer but still seeking consent.
"Get me naked, Dimitri," I demand, my voice husky and charged with need. "Now."
"Fuck, Tuesday," he smirks, his eyes darkening with lust. "You really know how to make a man feel wanted."
"Good," I confess, locking my gaze with his as he slowly peels my clothes away, piece by piece. As the cool air hits my heated skin, I tremble with anticipation, watching as his admiring gaze trails over my exposed body.
"God, you're beautiful," he murmurs, his fingers teasing the wetness between my legs. "And so ready for me."
"Your turn, Dimitri," I beg, my voice a sultry whisper. "I want to see all of you."
With a slow, deliberate motion, he removes his clothes, revealing the sculpted muscles. My breath catches in my throat as I drink in the sight of him, raw and exposed before me.
"Like what you see?" he teases, a wicked grin tugging at the corner of his mouth.
"God, yes," I breathe out, reaching for him with an almost magnetic pull. As his fingers slide through my slick folds, he groans in appreciation.
"Fuck, Tuesday, Can I taste you?"
I nod, entranced by the intensity burning in his eyes. He lowers his head between my legs, and the first touch of his

tongue sends shivers down my spine. He devours me, licking and sucking with ravenous hunger, until I feel my toes curl and my belly tighten. Waves of pleasure crash over me, and I cry out his name, coating his face in my wetness.

"Come here," I say, my voice quivering with desire. He leans up to kiss me, and I taste myself on his lips, an intoxicating blend of sweet and sinful.

"Please, Dimitri," I beg. "I need you inside me."

He retrieves a condom from his wallet, and I watch as he opens the packet, slowly rolling it down his impressive length. I reach out to touch him, feeling the weight of his dick in my hands. This time, sex isn't something forced upon me; it's a choice, a connection I'm willingly seeking with the man who has captured my attention.

"Are you ready?" he asks, his voice filled with tenderness and concern.

"Yes," I reply, my eyes locked onto his. The intimacy we share in this moment is something I've never experienced before.

"Tuesday," Dimitri groans, gripping the base of his dick as he climbs over me. The anticipation in his eyes reflects my own need, heightening the electric connection we share. He spreads my legs wide to accommodate his body between them, and as he runs the tip of his length through my wetness, I can practically feel the desire radiating off of him.

"Fuck, Tuesday, I can't wait to stretch you around me."

His warm brown eyes meet mine, filled with determination and care. "I'll be gentle," he promises, his voice steady despite the passion threatening to consume us both.

"Please, Dimitri," I say, my heart racing.

He lines himself up at my entrance and slowly pushes into me. His girth is considerable, forcing him to pull back and push in again, gradually sinking deeper inside me. My breath catches in my throat as I adjust to his size, feeling fuller than ever before.

"Are you okay?" he asks, genuine concern lacing his words. The tenderness in his touch sends shivers down my spine.

“Yes," I assure him, my fingers clutching at the sheets. "Please, move. I need you to move."

As Dimitri's eyes locked onto mine, I could see the intensity of his gaze. He began to move slowly inside me, each stroke deliberate and measured. It was like he wanted to savour every single moment, and he whispered, "Watch with me, Tuesday."

I propped myself up on my elbows, following his lead. We watched together as he continued, his dick disappearing within me and then reemerging, slick with our combined arousal. The sight was intoxicating and profoundly intimate.

"See that, right there?" he murmured, voice husky with lust. "That's pure heaven, Tuesday. Your body is gripping me perfectly."

His words sent a shiver down my spine, and I couldn't help but respond, teasing him with a smile. "Only the best for you, Detective."

With that, he took my admission as an invitation to increase his pace. His hands grasped at my hips, pulling me closer, burying himself deeper within me. The sensation was overwhelming – I had no idea sex could be this good. I could hear how wet I was, the slick sounds echoing around my room, betraying just how much he affected me.

My toes began to tingle again, and Dimitri must have noticed the telltale signs of my impending climax. "Oh, you're going to come again?" he asked

In response, I bit my lip and nodded, unable to form any coherent words. Dimitri reached down to rub my clit with his fingers, expertly coaxing me toward the edge. That was all it took. I exploded around him, a cry escaping my lips as pleasure coursed through me.

Dimitri's rhythm faltered as my inner walls tightened around him like a vice. "Oh, sweetness," he gasped, "I'm going to come." I could feel his legs shaking, the tension in his body reaching its peak.

He came, collapsing onto me as he continued to kiss me deeply and passionately. I felt his hips still slowly pumping, trying to draw out the last remnants of his orgasm. When he finally stopped, he looked into my eyes, a tender smile on his face.

"Sweetness, I'm already addicted to you," he confessed, tracing his fingers along my cheek.

Chapter 16

Tuesday May

As I sat in my dimly lit bedroom, the smell of lavender filled my nostrils. Time had a way of sliding past like a shadow in the night, and it had been three months since I started my relationship with Dimitri. I didn't regret a thing. He was sweet and kind, something I wasn't used to growing up, but had learned to trust my own instincts while I was in the clinic.

"Fuck, this place is like a time capsule," I muttered to myself as I surveyed the room. My thirst for revenge hadn't gone away though, and neither had my need to clean out the house. So far, I'd gotten six rooms completely empty, cleaned, and searched for hidden things from my mum.

The first room held a love letter and note, both yellowed with age and filled with secrets. The second room revealed much of the same. The third room was where I found the key – hidden in an unused fireplace with a pink ribbon on it. And the fourth room? Well, that's where I discovered a photo from her wedding day. Mum and Dad, standing in a room filled with other people, all smiles as they looked at the camera. It made me wonder what the hell happened to them after that moment. The others held nothing at all, and I continued to pick away at them sure they were concealing something I just hadn’t found yet.

"Tuesday, are you ready to tackle the next room?" Mr Thompson asked, poking his head into my bedroom. His eyebrows raised slightly at the sight of my laptop screen, but he didn't comment on it.

"Absolutely," I replied, snapping the laptop shut and hopping off the bed. "Let's get this show on the road."

The spare bedroom which would become my murder planning room was just down the hall.

As we entered, I took in the dusty, neglected space with a critical eye.

"Alright, let's start with the chest of drawers," I said, rubbing my hands together enthusiastically. Mr. Thompson nodded, understanding my need to search every nook and cranny for clues about my mother.

We pulled the drawers out, one by one, revealing old, moth-eaten clothes that smelled like damp and neglected. "Gross," I muttered, wrinkling my nose. "What do you think, Mr. T? Any hidden treasures in this mess?"

"Let's check, shall we?" he replied, maintaining his ever-present professionalism. Together, we sifted through the tattered garments, looking for anything unusual.

"Nothing here," I sighed, tossing the last decrepit item into the box for trash. "I guess we'll have to keep searching."

"Indeed, Miss Wellington," Mr Thompson agreed, adding the final drawer to the growing pile. "But don't lose hope. There's still plenty of room left to explore."

"True," I nodded, trying not to let my disappointment show.

As we continued our search, I couldn't help but think about the secrets still lurking within these walls – and how they might just be the key to unlocking my past and fuelling my future. With each new discovery, I could feel the exhilaration building inside of me, ready to burst forth like a firework.

We pulled out the drawers of the remaining furniture and examined them thoroughly – beneath, behind, and even within the hollow carcasses. Still, nothing caught our attention. It seemed like we were fighting a losing battle against my mother's secrecy.

"Damn it," I muttered, frustration bubbling up inside me. "She must've hidden something else here."

"Patience, Miss Wellington," Mr Thompson advised, his steady demeanour a stark contrast to my restless energy. "let me get the removalist up to take this furniture down now that we have searched it, they might be something we can’t see"

The men grunted and strained as they carried the heavy pieces of furniture down to the storage containers waiting outside. The once-beautiful 4-poster bed was now dismantled, its intricate carvings and fine woodwork hidden under a layer of dust. The queen Anne bedside tables were next, their elegant curves and polished surfaces weathered by time. Even though I had always loved old furniture, it now seemed tainted, just another burden to be passed on to someone else.

As the room was emptied, Mr Thompson and I carefully rolled up the old antique rug that had been partially covered by the bed. Its faded colours and worn fabric held memories of days gone by. But as we lifted it, the floorboards beneath groaned and creaked, revealing a loose panel. And there, hidden away for who knows how long, was our prize - a secret compartment

"Mr. Thompson!" I exclaimed, grinning from ear to ear.

"Shall we see what treasures await us?" he said, chuckling at my enthusiasm.

Inside the secret compartment, we found papers: deeds to a house just a few streets away. But the real kicker was the letter accompanying them – if my mother died, everything would pass to her child, or to charity if she remained childless. Her husband, however, would never be allowed to own it.

"Wow, Mom," I whispered, shaking my head in disbelief. "You really knew how to cover your tracks."

The lengths she went to hide all this only fuelled a hunger I didn't know I possessed. Suddenly, I realised I thrived in the chaos, in the hunt for answers and buried truths.

"Mr. Thompson," I said, turning to him with a coy smile. "Care to go for a drive? I'm dying to check this place out."

It had been exactly three months since I began my driving lessons. Every day, either Mr. Thompson or Dimitri would take me out for a driving session, weather permitting. In three more months, if I was able to pass my test, I would finally be able to drive on my own without supervision.

"Of course, Miss Wellington," he replied, his eyes twinkling with unspoken excitement. "After all, what's life without a little mystery?"

"Damn right," I agreed, clutching the papers to my chest like a lifeline. As we left the room, I couldn't help but feel a rush of adrenaline coursing through my veins. This was just the beginning, and I couldn't wait to see what other secrets lay hidden, waiting to be unearthed.

Chapter 17

Tuesday May

The fresh leather of the Audi's seats creased audibly as I dropped into the driver's side, a slight smirk playing on my lips. The car still had that new car smell - intoxicating, like success and freedom all rolled into one.

"I need an extra seat belt" Mr Thompson grumbled as he settled into the passenger seat, his tone dry but not without a trace of humour.

"Watch it, Thompson," I shot back with a wink, I flashed the mysterious key at him before slipping it into the pocket of my jeans.

I revved the engine, the purr sending a thrill up my spine. I wasn't usually one for possessions, but damn, this car made me feel powerful. "Buckle up, we're going for a little trip."

"Three streets down, was it?" Thompson asked, unfolding the crinkled paper that was the deeds to another property I now owned. He squinted at the address, old eyes betraying him.

"Yep, and let's hope it’s worth the intrigue." I manoeuvred the Audi out of the driveway, the smooth motion a stark contrast to the chaos that had surrounded me lately. My fingers tapped on the steering wheel, keeping time with the beat of some tune I had stuck in my head.
"Tuesday," Mr Thompson began, his voice laced with something akin to concern, "Are you certain we want to delve into this? Your father—"
"George Wellington may be many things, Mr. Thompson," I cut him off, the name leaving a sour taste, "but he's not here anymore, is he, how can a ghost still haunt the living"
"Very well," he conceded, and I could hear the cogs turning in his head, trying to piece together the mystery as much as I was. "Just three streets down, you said?"
"Exactly," I replied, taking the turn with a bit more zest than necessary. The Audi hugged the corner like a dream, and I couldn't help but laugh.
Mr Thompson held on to the "oh shit bar"
"Relax, Thompson. It's just an old house. What's the worst that could happen?" I teased, even though a part of me buzzed with the electric thrill of the unknown.
"Infamous last words," he muttered under his breath, but I caught it and laughed.
"Come on, lighten up. We're about to unlock a secret. That's not exciting to you?"

"Excitement isn't the word I'd choose," he replied, though the corner of his mouth twitched in what might have been the beginning of a smile.
"Suit yourself," I shrugged, the Audi slowing as we approached the destination. But inside, my heart was dancing a jig. Mystery keys, hidden paperwork, and now, an address that seemed to promise answers. Whatever lay ahead, it had my blood singing with anticipation.
Mr Thompson drew in a deep breath and muttered something under his breath before stepping out of the car to push on the old gates.
They groaned like a ghoul being stirred from slumber as it swung inwards, the Audi rolling to a stop just beyond its reach. An imposing silhouette of what once must have been grandeur loomed before us – a Victorian house that had succumbed to the relentless embrace of nature. Ivy clung to its walls with the tenacity of long-lost secrets, and the overgrown path seemed almost reluctant to lead us to its door.
"Jesus, this is straight out of every gothic novel I've ever read," I quipped, taking in the spectacle as we exited the car.
"I know whose house this is," Thompson murmured, his gaze sweeping over the forsaken edifice. "Remarkably preserved from intrusion, though."
"Or everyone's just scared shitless of what might be inside," I said, half-joking. My fingers traced the delicate pattern of the

wrought iron fence, finding beauty in decay. “And whose house is it?”
"This was where your mother grew up" he replied, a wry smile playing on his lips.
"Really," I said in astonishment, heading towards the front door, where nature had spun a green tapestry across the entrance. Pulling at the vines, they gave way with a satisfying rip, unveiling the keyhole that awaited our mysterious key. My heart skipped at the thought of unlocking more than just a door. What if answers lay beyond, waiting to be unearthed? What if this was the moment everything changed?
"Here goes nothing mum." I slid the key into the lock, feeling the tumblers shift with an ancient sigh. The click echoed through the silence, a tiny but mighty herald of new beginnings—or endings.
"Careful, Tuesday," Thompson warned, but there was a note of curiosity in his voice that matched my own pounding pulse.
Pushing the door open with a flourish, a cloud of dust motes swirled in the beam of light that sliced into the darkness. It was as if time itself had coughed up a memory. The air was dense with the scent of old wood and secrets, the kind that whispered of lives once lived with fervour, now just echoes in the hush.
"Looks like no one's been here since... well, forever," I mused, stepping inside. Each footfall kicked up a history of

dust, and I couldn't help but wonder about the stories it could tell. The furniture stood like silent sentinels, draped in grey cloaks that nobody had disturbed in years. Everything was frozen in a tableau of abandonment, each piece a testament to the past's reluctance to fade into obscurity.

"Remarkable," Thompson breathed, his eyes scanning the surroundings with an investigator's sharpness. But I could see it—the thin veil of excitement behind his professional facade.

"Totally gives off the 'haunted mansion' vibe, doesn't it?" I said, grinning despite the eeriness. It was thrilling, like dancing on the edge of a knife - danger on one side, adventure on the other.

"Indeed," he agreed, his tone lighter than before. "But let's not forget why we're here."

"Right, the mystery of the hidden paperwork and the key," I said, my voice bubbling with the thrill of the chase. "I wonder which room was my mother's?"

"Hopefully something less macabre than the exterior suggests," he replied.

"Macabre is my favourite I'm coming to realise," I retorted with a wink, leading the way deeper into the house's heart. Each creaking step felt like a conversation with the unknown, and I was bursting with questions. What would the house reveal? What shadows lingered within these walls, eager to leap out and claim their next victim?

"Let's just keep our wits about us," Thompson said, but the grin on his face told me he was as caught up in the moment as I was.
"Thompson, if these walls could talk, I'm sure they'd have quite the tales," I murmured, my fingertips grazing the ornate banister as we ascended the grand staircase. Each room we peeked into was like a still-life painting—unmoved, untouched, almost sacred in its preservation.
"Indeed, Miss May," he replied, his voice echoing softly against the high ceilings. "Though I daresay some stories are better left untold."
"Where's the fun in that?" I shot back with a chuckle, though my heart raced with anticipation. The mansion was a time capsule, each door we opened a portal to another era. A heavy layer of dust blanketed everything, and I couldn't help but imagine the hands that last touched these forsaken relics.
"Careful now," Thompson cautioned as I playfully hopped over a threadbare rug curled at the edges like a dried leaf. "Wouldn't want you to end up as part of the décor."
"Too late for that; I'm already enmeshed in the mystery," I said, winking at him over my shoulder.
We reached the final room upstairs, and there it was—an oddity among the mundane: a skeleton, stretched out on the four-poster bed like a macabre centrepiece. My breath hitched, a mix of horror and intrigue singing through my veins.

"Fuck me sideways," I breathed out, unable to tear my gaze from the grim display.

"Tuesday," Thompson's voice was sharp, a stark contrast to my awestruck whisper. "Don't go any closer. We need to call Dimitri right now."

"Right, right," I mumbled, fumbling in my pocket for my phone with hands that trembled—not from fear, but from the electric thrill of discovery. I dialled Dimitri, who picked up after the first ring.

"Sweetness?"

"Dimitri," I purred, my heartbeat a drumroll of excitement. "I have a new case for you.”

Chapter 18

Dimitri Costa

The last signature on the Henderson case file felt like a full stop to a long, drawn-out sentence. I leaned back in my chair, running a hand through my hair, and let out a breath that tasted of stale coffee and relief. That's when the shrill ring of my phone pierced the silence of my office. The caller ID flashed "Tuesday" in bold letters, and a small smile found its way onto my lips.

"Sweetness," I greeted, my voice carrying an easy warmth as I propped my feet on the cluttered desk.

"Hey, Dimitri, I have a new case for you," Tuesday's voice came through the line, light and teasing, but there was something in her tone that made the hairs on the back of my neck stand up.

"Spill it. What kind of trouble has fallen into your lap this time?" I asked, the playfulness in my voice tinged with concern.

She chuckled, a sound that usually sent a shiver down my spine, but now it just felt off. "Oh, you know, just a skeleton found in the house my mother grew up in."

I sat bolt upright, my feet thudding against the floor. "A skeleton? Tuesday, are you okay?"

"Relax, Dimitri, it's a skeleton; it can't hurt me," she laughed.

"Give me the address." My voice was sharp, the detective in me snapping to attention as I snatched up a pen to scribble down the details.

"Always the protector, huh?" Her words were light, but I heard the smile in them. And just like that, the mood shifted again, back to our usual dance of banter and unspoken things.

"Someone has to keep an eye on you," I shot back, already grabbing my jacket and heading for the door. "Stay put, I'm on my way."

"Wouldn't dream of moving," she said, the line goes dead, leaving me with the echo of her laughter and a gnawing feeling in my gut.

As I strode through the precinct, my mind churned with images of Tuesday—her piercing blue eyes that seemed to cut through facades, her dark hair that fell like a shadow across her face. She was enigmatic, a puzzle I'd spent too many nights trying to solve.

"Shit," I muttered under my breath, pushing through the doors and out into the brisk air. The city hummed around me, indifferent to the whirlwind that was Tuesday May, but I

couldn't shake the sense of foreboding that clung to me like a second skin.
I loved the chase, the thrill of unravelling mysteries—it was the lifeblood of my work. But as I slid behind the wheel and fired up the engine, barreling toward an address that promised yet another dive into the abyss of Tuesday's world, I realised something terrifying.
It wasn't just the chase that had me hooked—it was her. And goddamn if that realisation didn't scare me more than any skeleton ever could.
The Victorian loomed like a relic of forgotten times, its walls choked by ivy and the garden overrun with wild flora. Pulling up just three streets shy of Tuesday's mansion, I parked behind her sleek car that seemed almost as out of place as she did in this world.
"About time, Detective Costa," Mr. Thompson quipped, his stoic face betraying no sign of the macabre scene awaiting within.
"Traffic was a nightmare," I shot back, though my mind had been on anything but the road.
Tuesday stood beside him, the stark contrast of her dark hair against the pale façade of the house painting a picture I couldn't shake. She was like a spectre of beauty in a place forgotten by time, and it made my heart thrum in a way that was all too distracting.

"Come on, I'll show you upstairs," she said, leading the way with a grace that could make even these dust-ridden steps seem like a grand staircase.

"Lead the way, Sweetness."

In the room, the air felt thick, heavy with the weight of secrets long buried. There it was, nestled in the middle of the bed—a skeleton lying as if whispering its last testament to the peeling paint on the ceiling.

"Jesus," I muttered, crouching beside the remains. "Looks like you've got quite the family heirloom here."

"Charming, isn't it?" Her voice held a macabre humour that sent shivers down my spine.

"Always a laugh a minute with you." Sighing, I dialled the team. "We need forensics at 2 Little Gate Street, Yeah, it's one of those days."

As I ended the call, Tuesday extended something toward me —a single key, old and ornate. "Is this the key you found the other day? Hidden in the fireplace?"

"Yep, mom's little secret stash. Never thought it'd lead to this." She shrugged, her nonchalance not quite reaching her eyes.

"Well your treasure hunt was successful," I said, taking the key. Its metal was cold, yet it burned with the promise of untold stories.

"Sure was," she replied.

Mr. Thompson handed me a bundle of papers. "You'll be needing these, Detective."

I flipped through the dusty pages of paper, my fingers tracing over the words "deeds" and "Lillian Wellington." Tuesday, with a casual shrug, explained that she had found the book in a room they had just emptied. It had belonged to her mother, who had left it to her child, or to charity if she had no child. A note left with the pages also stated that Tuesday's father was not allowed to possess it. I let out an exasperated sigh, remarking on how intriguing her family history always seemed to be. The musty scent of old paper and ink filled my nostrils as I continued to scan the neatly penned words on each page

"Are you going to be okay with all this?" I asked Tuesday, the detective in me wanting to dig deeper, the man in me wanting to protect her from whatever ghosts this house held.

"Of course," she said with a smirk. "It's not every day you find a skeleton in your closet—literally."

"Ha, you're telling me." I pocketed the key and folded the deeds under my arm, my gaze lingering on her for a moment too long. "I'll take care of this, Tuesday. You just... go home and I'll come see you afterwards"

She beams at me, nodding her head in agreement before leaning in for a soft kiss. Her lips are warm and velvety, and I can't resist pulling her closer by wrapping my arm around her

lower back. The familiar smell of lavender fills my senses, calming my soul as she presses against me.
She pulls away from my embrace and gives me another small kiss on the lips before turning towards her car. She slips into the driver's seat and starts the engine, and I listen as the rumble of Tuesday's engine fades into the background. Her car becomes a speck in the distance as she drives away. I watched until it disappeared, the mystery she left behind far denser than the overgrown hedges flanking the driveway. I sank onto the crumbling steps, the cold stone beneath me, and exhaled a breath I hadn't realised I was holding.
"Damn, Tuesday," I murmured, raking a hand through my hair. The air was thick with the scent of must and earth, the kind that whispered secrets of bygone eras. How much could one woman take before she shattered? Then again, Tuesday wasn't just any woman; she was an enigma, a storm dressed in beauty – the kind that will be my damnation.
You'd think I'd know better by now. But no, there I was, Dimitri Costa, seasoned detective, utterly bewitched by a pair of piercing blue eyes that saw right through the bullshit. It was like she was crafted for a sap like me to fall for—hook, line, and sinker.
"Christ, she's got you bad," I grumbled to myself. Tuesday May had crept under my skin, settled in my thoughts, and staked her claim on whatever piece of me still believed in something beyond the grit and grime of this job. And as I sat

there, feeling the weight of her absence, the truth hit me like a sucker punch – I loved the woman. I loved her, and I didn't want to let go. Not now, not ever.

"Detective Costa?" A voice cut through my musings, and I glanced up to see the forensics team pulling up, their van coming to a halt with a crunch of gravel.

"Over here," I called out, standing and dusting off my pants. "Follow me."

I led them back to the house, the skeleton waiting for us like some grotesque centrepiece in a room untouched by time. As they unpacked their gear, the lead tech, a guy with more piercings than a punk band's frontman, whistled low.

"Wow, so perfectly preserved," he remarked, adjusting his gloves.

"Place looks like Miss Havisham decided to play hide-and-seek," I quipped, trying to keep the mood light despite the chill creeping up my spine.

"Untouched," another tech mused, her eyes scanning the room. "Means she could be years old. We're gonna need a forensic anthropologist on this."

"Great, more company," I said, half-joking. "Just what we need, another brainiac telling us how screwed we are."

"Hey, we love our brainiacs," Piercings shot back, grinning. "They make us look good."

"Speak for yourself," I retorted, watching as they began their ballet around the remains. But my mind was elsewhere, tracing the phantom warmth of a key that once lay hidden in a fireplace, and the woman who'd unearthed it along with my heart.

Chapter 19

Tuesday May

The evening air was still warm as I killed the engine of my car, a satisfying purr fading into silence. I stepped out onto the driveway, the gravel crunching softly under my boots, and the familiar grandeur of home towered before me. The place was starting to feel like home, as much as I hated that feeling.

"Quite the adventure," Mr Thompson remarked with his signature dry humour, his voice cutting through the twilight hush as he approached to take the keys from my hand.

I chuckled, the sound light and carefree. "You can say that again."

He smiled, a rare occurrence that made his usual stern features seem almost kind. Our laughter mingled, floating up towards the ivy that clung to the house's facade like nature's graffiti.

"Come on, let's see what culinary masterpiece Mrs. Collins has whipped up tonight." I breezed past him, my steps lite against the cool marble floor as we entered the foyer.
"Indeed, Miss May," he said, following behind me with the obedient click-clack of his polished shoes.
The scent of garlic and basil wafted through the halls, guiding me toward the kitchen where Mrs. Collins stood, apron-clad and the very picture of domestic efficiency. "Pasta for dinner, your favourite," she announced without turning, her focus on a pot that bubbled with promise.
"Smells divine, Mrs. C," I said, grinning as I caught a glimpse of the steamy strands being tossed in a rich, homemade tomato sauce. My stomach growled, betraying my attempt at nonchalance.
"Go freshen up, dear. It'll be ready by the time you're done," she instructed, and there was no arguing with that tone.
"Be back in a flash," I promised, taking the stairs two at a time.
Shedding the day's filth felt like a baptism, each droplet of water a tiny absolution as it chased away the dust and grime. The shower's embrace was brief but invigorating, and soon I was slipping into the comfort of sweats and a crop top—no designer tags, just pure, unadulterated coziness. As I looked in the mirror, my fingers combed through damp locks, teasing them into some semblance of order.

"Who knew being filthy rich had such perks?" I mused aloud, admiring the simplicity of my reflection. No more threadbare jeans or second-hand shirts. Just soft fabric hugging my skin, and the freedom to relax into myself.

Descending the staircase, I could already taste the tangy, savoury pasta on my tongue. Mrs Collins plated the dish with a flourish, her movements practised and sure.

"Looks amazing," I sighed, my mouth watering as I took a seat at the ornate dining table, feeling every bit the princess in her not-so-ivory tower.

"Enjoy, dear," she replied, a smile in her voice, and I dug in with gusto, twirling the fork with expertise born from years of pasta appreciation. Each bite was a symphony, each chews a step closer to culinary nirvana.

"Mrs. C, you've outdone yourself," I declared between mouthfuls, my eyes closing in reverence to her craft.

"Nothing but the best for you, Tuesday," she said, her tone affectionate yet tinged with something else—a knowing, perhaps, of the shadows that clung to the edges of our gilded cage.

"Wouldn't have it any other way," I quipped, my heart light despite the darkness that lurked just beyond the reach of the chandelier's glow. For now, this moment was mine, and I'd savour every damn second of it.

The doorbell's chime cut through the tranquillity of my post-dinner haze, a sharp note in the calm evening. I placed my book down, pages still warm from my touch, and padded barefoot to the door. There he stood—Dimitri, in all his rugged glory, dust clinging to him like a second skin.

"Sweetness," he greeted with an exhaustion that seemed to weigh down his smile, but his eyes... they were like coals, always burning for me.

"God, you look like hell," I said, the corners of my mouth turning up in amusement as I stepped aside, letting him into the house. "Shower. Now."

I nudged him towards the stairs, and with no more than a sheepish grin, he obeyed, trudging up like a soldier after a battle.

"Save some hot water for the fish," I called after him, shaking my head at the trail of dirt left in his wake. It was a good thing Mrs. Collins had retired for the night—she'd have had a fit at the sight.

The kitchen felt suddenly quiet without the hum of conversation, the clink of silverware a lonely sound as I reheated the pasta. Mrs. Collins had left it covered on the stove, her foresight almost psychic. Dimitri's portion was generous, steam curling up like little spirits as I stirred.

"Hope you're hungry," I murmured to myself, balancing the bowl carefully as I ascended the stairs.

He was there, perched on the edge of my bed, the image of vulnerability in just his boxers, his dark hair damp against his forehead. I couldn't help but notice the way the fabric clung to him, outlining muscles that whispered tales of strength and endurance.

"Your chariot awaits," I teased, presenting the food with a flourish. He chuckled, the sound rumbling from deep within his chest, and accepted the offering.

"Thanks, Sweetness," he said, his voice soft but laced with gratitude, those warm brown eyes meeting mine.

I watched him for a moment, devouring the pasta as if it was his first meal in days. The tension in his shoulders began to ease, his posture relaxing with every bite. My knees found the plush carpet as I lowered myself in front of him, drawn by an invisible string that left no room for resistance.

"Tuesday?" His question was half-concern, half-curiosity, the fork pausing midway to his mouth.

"Shh," I breathed out, a finger raised to silence him. "Just eat."

There was something electric about being at eye level with him, something intimate in the act of kneeling before this man.

"Always taking care of me, huh?" he mused with a crooked smile, his eyes never leaving my face.

"Someone has to," I shot back playfully, my heart swelling with a warmth that had nothing to do with the summer night outside. "And besides, I like it."

A coy smile played on my lips as I let my fingers trail down the hardening outline beneath the thin fabric of his boxers. The excitement zipped through me, a live wire sparking at the thought of what I was about to unveil. "I'm making sure you're well taken care of, in every way."

His breath hitched slightly as my touch grew more insistent, my hand moving with a boldness that mirrored the predatory glint in my blue eyes. I revelled in the power of my touch, watching the steady rise of his arousal under the gentle caress of my fingertips. It was intoxicating, this dance of flesh and desire.

"Tuesday, shit..." Dimitri's voice was a low growl, rough around the edges like sandpaper against silk. He was losing his composure, and I loved it.

"Language, Detective," I teased, though my heart was pounding in sync with his growing need. My hand slipped into the waistband of his boxers, grasping him firmly. It felt like holding onto a secret, something raw and pulsing with life.

The weight of him in my hand sent an electric thrill up my arm. I leaned forward, my breath ghosting over the sensitive skin before my tongue darted out to taste him. The tang of salt and soap met my lips, eliciting a groan from deep within his chest.

"Fuck, Tuesday," he gasped, and the sound of my name on his lips was like a victory chant. His empty plate clattered to the floor as if conceding defeat to the hunger we were about to indulge.

My response was a wicked grin as I enveloped him with the warmth of my mouth, licking the head like it was the most delicious lollipop. My tongue swirled beneath, tracing the pronounced veins with an artist's precision. Each lap, each suction was deliberate, designed to unravel him thread by thread.

"Sweetness," he murmured—a term of endearment that felt like a secret promise—and I could sense his legs beginning to tremble with the effort of holding back my signal that I was hitting all the right notes.

"Sweetness," he rasped again, his hands finding my head, fingers tangling in my hair. There was a firmness in his grip as he pulled me away. "I wanna cum in that pussy, not your mouth. Can I take you bare?"

His words, so raw and unguarded, shot through me like lightning. I paused, my heart hammering against my ribs.

“I'm not on birth control" I confess.

But he just shrugged, the corners of his lips tilting into a half-smile that made my core clench with desire. "It's okay, I'm fairly certain I'm under your spell and never leaving you."

Damn him for saying exactly what I needed to hear. My body responded before my mind could catch up, moisture building between my thighs, my inner walls pulsing with anticipation.
"Yes," I breathed out, surrendering to the moment.
In one fluid motion, I stood, my skin tingling from the heat of his gaze. Climbing onto his lap, his strong hands guided me, holding his dick perfectly still—a pillar of control amidst the chaos of our lust as I slide myself down his length.
The stretch was divine, filling me in ways that had my head spinning. I let out a throaty moan, lost in the sensation as I began to move atop him. Slowly at first, savouring every inch, every pulse that throbbed within me.
"Fuck, Tuesday," he groaned, his voice laced with both pleasure and awe. His grip shifted then, hands moving from guiding to owning as he laid back on the bed, pulling me along for the ride.
My hips found their rhythm against him, each roll forward sending sparks of pleasure straight to my clit. The room filled with the sound of flesh meeting flesh, our breaths mingling in the heated space between us.
"God, yes... just like that," I gasped, losing myself to the sensations, to the way he knew how to play my body like his favourite instrument. He was rough and gentle all at once, a contradiction that sent me spiralling towards ecstasy.
"Sweetness," he whispered, his voice strained with effort. "You're fucking incredible."

The praise was fuel to my fire, and I felt myself getting wetter, slipping easier over him, drowning in the sensation of being completely filled, completely claimed by Dimitri Costa.

Dimitri's hands, strong and unyielding, gripped my hips with a possessive urgency that sent ripples of excitement coursing through my veins. The pace he set was relentless, pulling me down onto him faster and faster, each thrust an echo of the desire that crackled between us like live wires.

"Jesus, Dimitri," I panted, feeling the coil of pleasure in my belly tighten to the brink of snapping. My toes curled as I braced myself against his chest, the tingling sensation spreading like wildfire. "Oh God... I'm—"

"Come for me, Sweetness," he commanded, his voice rough around the edges. The sound of it, so full of dark promises and want, was enough to tip me over.

I exploded around him, my climax shattering through me in waves that milked him of his cum, each pulse of his release a hot brand deep inside me. "Fuck, Dimitri!" The words were half-lost in my throat, muffled against the rapid thump of his heartbeat as I collapsed forward onto his chest.

Breathless, I lay draped over him, my body still humming from the intensity of our fucking. It took a moment for my breathing to find its rhythm again, for the room to stop spinning on its axis. But as I lifted my head, locking eyes with those warm brown irises that always seemed to see right through me, I knew the night was far from over.

"Ready for round two?" I teased, a playful smirk tugging at the corner of my lips. His chuckle was low and husky, a sound that promised more delicious sin to come.

"Sweetness, with you? Always." His fingers traced lazy circles on the small of my back, stirring the embers that had barely begun to cool. There was no mistaking the glint of anticipation in his gaze, the silent vow that he'd chase the dawn with me if that's what I wanted.

"Good," I whispered, nuzzling into the crook of his neck, already craving the next taste of him. "Because I plan on keeping you under my spell all night long."

Chapter 20

Dimitri Costa

I saunter into the precinct, a smug grin plastered on my face that would've earned me a slap on the back and a "go get 'em" from the guys—if they knew the source of my satisfaction. The night with Tuesday was still fresh in my mind; her skin, was soft and inviting, the way she arched beneath me—demanding, insatiable. I chuckle to myself, thinking how that little minx truly put me through my paces. I'm not exactly over the hill, but hell, moments like these remind me there's a full dozen years between us.

"Morning, Costa," calls out Jenkins, snapping me back to reality.

"Top of the morning, Jenks," I reply, sliding into my chair with a grace that belies the slight stiffness in my muscles.

Reaching for the coffee I desperately need, I notice the new file sitting on my desk. It's from yesterday's drop by forensics —the skeleton case. I exhale sharply, preparing mentally for the long haul ahead. Results on this kind of thing take an age to come back. I'm expecting nothing more than a mundane list: items catalogued, samples taken, yada yada. But as I flip open the folder, a Post-it note catches my eye, the handwriting all too familiar.

"Need Tuesday's DNA."

"Fuck me sideways," I mutter under my breath. That request is like a sucker punch, unexpected and leaving a sick twist in my gut. My mind races with questions. Why the hell do they need Tuesday's DNA?

"Something wrong?" Jenkins peers over, ever the nosy bastard.

"Nothing a gallon of coffee won't fix," I deflect with a half-smile, tucking away my personal turmoil. I can't afford to let my feelings for Tuesday cloud my judgment at work. Not when there's a mystery to unravel—and damn it, unravel it I will.

"Make it a strong one," he nods, his curiosity unsated but momentarily shelved.

"Like my women," I shoot back, the flirtatious banter a comfortable shield. But inside, my thoughts are tumbling. If they're asking for her DNA... Meaning they think she is related to the bones.

Pushing aside the creeping dread, I take another swig of coffee, letting the bitterness ground me. I'll have to play this close to the chest. Focus, Costa. Keep it professional. But

shit, it's hard when every instinct screams that Tuesday is wrapped up in this more than either of us could've imagined.
The sun filtered through the blinds, casting striped shadows across my desk as I tried to shake off the remnants of last night's indulgence. The case file sat in front of me like an unwelcome Monday morning hangover. My fingers drummed a restless beat on the mahogany surface, echoing the thrumming pulse in my temples.
"Could it really be her?" I murmured under my breath, the question clawing its way out. Lillian Wellington, the ghost haunting Tuesday's past, is now possibly more tangible than ever before. The house was hers, the skeleton's resting place for who knows how long. It wasn't just another mystery; this was personal, intimate—a Pandora's box I wasn't sure I wanted to open.
"Time to make some calls," I muttered, reaching for the battered phone that had heard too many secrets and not enough good news. Dialling the forensic lab's number, I tapped my foot impatiently. Old habits die hard, and patience was never a virtue I claimed.
"Forensic lab, Winters speaking.
"Hey, Winters, it's Costa. Who's playing with bones today?" I asked, trying to keep the mood light despite the weight pressing on my chest.

"Ah, Detective, we've got Dr. Tegan Smith on board for this one," Winters replied, the sound of rustling papers filtering through the line.
"Smith, huh? She any good?"
"Top of her class, sharp as they come. You'll like her, she's—"
"Thorough, I hope," I interjected, cutting him off before he could wax poetic about Tegan's credentials. I didn't need to be sold on her; I needed answers.
"Absolutely, Detective. Anything else?"
"Thanks, Winters, you're a peach." I hung up without waiting for a response. Sometimes pleasantries were just a waste of breath.
I dialled Dr. Smith's number next. "Dr. Smith, Dimitri Costa. We've got a set of old bones causing a stir over here."
"Detective Costa," her voice came through, crisp and professional. "I've been briefed. What can I help you with?"
"Look, Doc, I'm gonna cut to the chase. That skeleton... Any chance you can tell if it's our missing Mrs. Wellington?"
There was a slight pause, and I could picture her weighing her words. "The possibility is there, Costa," she said carefully. "But I'll need more to go on. The DNA request for Tuesday is crucial."
"Understood," I replied, clenching my jaw. This was playing out like a bad movie—one where I knew the ending was going to hurt.

"Anything else?" Her tone softened as if sensing my internal struggle.

"I have some preliminary findings on the bones." she sighed

"Hit me with it," I said, drumming my fingers on the desk, trying to keep the mood light despite the gravity pulling at my gut.

"So far I can say this, Female, early twenties, and she'd given birth," Dr. Smith stated.

"Christ," I muttered under my breath, the playful facade cracking. A vivid image of Tuesday flitted across my mind—her long, dark hair and those piercing blue eyes that seemed to echo generations of secrets. "Any idea how she died?"

"Her hyoid bone was crushed," Tegan replied curtly. "Strangulation is the likely cause of death."

"Shit." My heart sank like a stone in a still pond, sending ripples of dread through me. I leaned back, the chair creaking in protest, my fingers now stilled. "And the other injuries?"

"Numerous healed fractures to the phalanges and ribs." There was a pause as if she were choosing her next words carefully. "Consistent with regular, prolonged trauma."

"Damn..." I whispered, feeling the air thicken around me. "Regular beatings, huh? Can you pinpoint when they started?"

"Based on bone sizes and growth, after the age of sixteen."

"Tuesday's old man... Wellington. He had the reputation of a saint, but the ones with a good rep are always the ones with a different home life." I tapped the file on the desk, each tap a silent accusation against the man.

"Anything else, Detective?"

"Thanks, Doc. That's all for now." I hung up, the click of the receiver echoing in the room like a period at the end of a tragic sentence.

"Fuck me," I sighed, letting the implications wash over me. It was all coming together now—the pieces of Tuesday's past aligning like stars in a constellation spelling out 'trouble.'

I leaned back in the old, squeaky office chair, its creaks echoing the chaos inside my mind. The fluorescent lights above flickered as if they were mocking me and my tangled web of secrets. In my hand, I twirled a pen to distract myself, wishing it were a cigarette instead. Before I could delve into this case and talk to Mr. Thompson and Mrs. Collins for their perspectives, I needed to have a conversation with my boss first. This case was far from straightforward, especially since I was involved with someone connected to it.

"Damn," I muttered, running a hand through my hair in frustration. I was well aware of the rules; fraternising with key witnesses or...well, hooking up with them was definitely not allowed. It was as frowned upon as pairing ketchup with sushi.

"Boss man ain't gonna like this," I mumbled, hoisting myself from the chair with the enthusiasm of a kid facing the principal's office.

With a last glance at the case file, I strode out of my cubicle. It felt like walking the plank, each step heavy with the knowledge that this might be my last hurrah on the case. But if getting booted meant protecting Tuesday, then damn it, I'd hand over my badge with a bow on top.

"Here goes nothing," I whispered to myself, a half-grin spreading across my face despite the gravity of the situation. Time to face the music, detective style.

Chapter 21

Tuesday May

The last of the movers grunted as they hoisted the final chair from the room, its legs scuffing the threshold before they cleared it. I watched them go, my hands in a cloud of dust that settled back down like a disappointed sigh. Another room emptied, another chapter closed—except this one was as dull as a stack of blank pages. No hidden compartments, no lost letters, not even a forgotten penny. "So much for buried treasure," I muttered, wiping my hands on my jeans and leaving streaks of grey.

I glanced at my phone, the screen still lit with Dimitri's last message: 'Leaving the precinct now. See you soon, Sweetness.' A smile tugged at my lips; he had a way with words, even in text. I didn't see him as often as I'd like, thanks to his detective badge and the demanding mistress that was his job. But it was okay. I had grown too fond of the silence

that filled these expansive rooms, the kind of quiet where secrets whispered if you listened hard enough.
"Sweetness" was his name for me, and it always felt like a secret handshake, a word meant just for us. I flopped onto the floor where the furniture once stood, stretched out like a cat in a sunbeam. My phone buzzed again, and I snatched it up, hoping for another note, another hint of his presence.
"Stuck in traffic. Might be a bit longer," read the new message, and I let out a soft groan.
"Of course, you are," I said to no one, typing back a quick, "Drive safe, Detective." I chucked the phone beside me and sprawled out further, considering the ceiling as if it might offer some entertainment.
"Guess it's just you and me, old house," I sighed, the sound echoing off the bare walls. "But hey, we're pretty good company, right?" The house didn't answer, but the creaks and groans were familiar enough to feel like agreement.
I thought about rearranging my hair or maybe changing it into something less covered in dust but shrugged off the idea. Dimitri had seen me in worse states—and besides, something was thrilling about being seen as I am, unpolished and raw. It was a novelty after so long spent under the scrutiny of others.
My eyes drifted to the doorway, imagining his figure filling the frame, the warm brown of his eyes finding mine in the dimming light. Yeah, seeing him was always worth the wait.

"New beginnings, old ghosts," I muttered under my breath as Mr. Thompson handed me the gleaming key with a solemn nod. The lock clicked open, a satisfying sound that sent a shiver down my spine. The room—my room—was a blank canvas now, washed clean of its past, ready for the macabre artistry I had in mind.
"Thank you, Mr. Thompson," I said, turning the key over in my hand. It felt cold against my skin, heavy with promise.
"Of course, Miss Tuesday," he replied, his voice formal as ever, but I caught a glint of something like curiosity—or was it caution?—in his eyes as they swept over the desk and chair setup. "Your mother's Chesterfield looks quite at home in here."
I grinned, sauntering over to the stately chair that seemed to hold the shadows of a thousand secrets in its aged leather. It creaked invitingly as I sank into it, my fingers trailing over the desktop.
My laptop and notebooks were my next victims, snatched up from their temporary resting place on the side table in my room. They landed on the desk with a clatter that echoed in the empty space. I could feel the hum of excitement buzzing in my veins as I imagined the plots and schemes that would soon spill across these surfaces.
"Shall I leave you to it then?" Mr. Thompson asked, lingering by the doorway.

"Yep, fly free, Jeeves," I quipped, waving him off. He hesitated, a frown creasing his forehead, before finally shutting the door behind him.

Taking a moment to look around, I was thrilled to finally begin this much-needed cleansing. After walking out, I securely locked the door behind me and headed to my adjacent room to retrieve my phone before heading downstairs. Dimitri should be arriving any minute now. The last rays of sunlight played with the horizon, painting the sky a mischievous shade of red as Dimitri arrived right on schedule. "Good evening, Sweetness," he greeted, his detective's gaze sweeping over me like a soft touch against silk. I caught a whiff of his cologne, an alluring invitation to come closer.

"Hey, Detective," I shot back, my voice a melodic tease, watching him roll up his sleeves as we settled around the dinner table. The clink of cutlery against plates filled the air, interspersed with the soft hum of idle chatter. Every bite was an orchestrated dance of flavours, but anticipation curled within me, a serpent waiting to strike.

Dinner wrapped up with the kind of satisfaction only Mrs Collins' cooking could provide. Dimitri leaned back, his chair groaning in protest, and cleared his throat. "I need to talk to you all," he said. His warm brown eyes held each of us in turn, but it was me they lingered on—a silent promise that whatever came next, we'd face it together.

"Shoot," I said, folding my hands neatly on the table, the image of calm. Underneath, my pulse thrummed with curiosity.
"It's about the bones—" Dimitri's words were careful, measured. "We have reason to believe they might be related to you, Tuesday. Possibly your mother."
A hush fell over the room, the weight of his revelation pressing down like a heavy blanket. But inside, I felt light, almost hollow. I had always carried a ghostly sense of her absence, a void where maternal memories should have been.
"Can't say I'm shocked," I confessed, not missing the twin pallors of Mr Thompson and Mrs Collins. "Always figured she was gone. Dead, I mean." My voice didn't waver; truth be told, I wasn't sure if the news warranted a tear or a shrug.
"Mr. Thompson, Mrs. Collins," Dimitri turned to them, his voice gentle yet insistent. "I need to understand the relationship between Lillian and her husband—Tuesday's parents."
They exchanged a glance that screamed volumes, lips pressed into thin lines. Silence stretched, taut as a wire.
"Spit it out," I encouraged, my tone breezy despite the gravity of the moment. "No point in sugarcoating the past. It's already bitter enough."
"Your mother..." Mr Thompson began, struggling for words as if they were fish slipping through his fingers. "She... wasn't treated well by your father. After Mr. Wellington Sr passed..."

"Enough dancing around it," I interjected, a smirk playing at the corners of my mouth though my heart wasn't really in it. "You're saying he was a bastard to her, right?"
"Tuesday!" Mrs. Collins gasped, scandalised.
"Come on, we're all adults here." I shrugged. "Besides, if I'm going to dig up family skeletons—literal ones, at that—I'd rather know the whole sordid tale."
"Your father... he kept her isolated," Mrs Collins finally admitted, her voice barely above a whisper. "It was... not a happy home for her."
"Isolation can be a blessing or a curse, depending on who holds the key, huh?" I mused, tapping a finger idly on the table. Inside, I filed away every scrap of information, pieces of a puzzle I was only now beginning to assemble.
Mr. Thompson cleared his throat, a signal that he was delving into memories better left untouched. "Your father was... different then," he began, the weight of years pressing down on each word. "He cared for your mother, truly did. It was like watching spring bloom in the depths of winter."
"Love's got its seasons, huh?" I quipped, trying to keep the mood from sinking into gloom.
"Indeed, Miss Tuesday." He took a deep breath, his eyes darkening with the coming storm of recollections. "But after Mr Wellington Sr died in that boat accident, everything changed. It was as if a switch had been flipped inside him.

Your father became reclusive, buried in his work and his study."
"Mrs. Wellington, your mother..." Mrs Collins picked up where Mr Thompson trailed off, her fingers nervously twisting the edge of her apron. "She seemed to shrink back from the world. She'd always been such a vibrant thing, so full of life."
"Like a flower kept from the sun," I mused, imagining a woman withering in the shadows.
"Exactly," Mr. Thompson nodded grimly. "And there were times when she was locked away, in her room. Days would pass without a glimpse of her."
"Locked away?" My brows lifted in mock surprise. "Sounds like Dad was doubling as a jailer. Did he lose the keys, or was he just fond of solitary confinement?"
"Tuesday!" Mrs. Collins admonished again, but I could tell her heart wasn't in the scolding.
"Only he was allowed in," Mr. Thompson continued, ignoring our little exchange. "We never knew what transpired behind that door. We heard nothing, saw nothing. The silence was deafening."
"Isn't it just," I said softly, my mind weaving the threads of their words into a tapestry of hidden horrors. My father's image, already stained in my mind, took on a darker hue with each revelation. "So, the queen was in her tower, and only the king had the key. What a twisted fairytale they lived."

"Miss Tuesday," Mr. Thompson's voice was gentle, cautious. "There are some things—"

"Better left unsaid?" I finished for him, my eyes narrowing slightly. "I'm not a child, Mr. Thompson. I can handle the ugly truth. Besides, it's my story too, isn't it?"

"Of course, Miss Tuesday," he conceded, the lines on his face deepening. "Just know that your mother was... a remarkable woman. No matter what else happened here."

"Remarkable and caged," I whispered, the playfulness seeping out of my voice as I considered the gravity of what they shared. What monsters must have lurked in the silence of those rooms?

"George," Mr. Thompson's voice cracked like a whip, snapping me back from the abyss of my thoughts. "He was losing his grip on everything he held dear. His facade of control... it was crumbling."

"Mrs Wellington, one afternoon," he began, his gaze distant as if he were peering into the past, "she cornered me in the garden. *'Mr Thompson,' she said, 'I need to get away.'*"

I leaned forward, the anticipation prickling under my skin.

He swallowed hard before continuing, "Her eyes, Miss Tuesday, they were pleading. Desperate. I couldn't deny her that sliver of hope. So, I agreed."

"Jesus," I exhaled, and the room seemed to tilt on its axis.

"Your mother," he continued, his voice barely above a whisper, "she slipped out of the mansion like a shadow at

dusk. We met by the old oak tree, just beyond the gates. It was my day off—the only one I took each year to mourn my own loss."
"Your wife?" I asked gently, already knowing the sorrow that laced his words.
"Elizabeth," he confirmed, a melancholy smile touching his lips. "She passed giving birth to our son, who joined her in death shortly after." Taking a deep breath he continued.
"Anyway," he cleared his throat, pushing back the tide of memories, "I drove your mother far from here, towns over. She was six months along then, a tiny thing fighting a giant's battle."
"Six months..." I echoed, the pieces falling into place with a chilling click. "And you just left her there?"
"Her insistence," he affirmed, his hands trembling slightly. "She made me promise to return and act as though nothing happened."
"Sweetness," Dimitri chimed in, drawing my attention. His face was sombre, his brown eyes dark with the weight of his next words. "The skeleton we found—it had healed trauma indicative of regular abuse."
"Shit," I breathed out, an icy fist clenching around my heart.
"If those bones are Lillian's," he continued, each word deliberate, "then it's likely —your father—"

"Abused her daily," I finished for him, the horror of the revelation coiling in my stomach. "Not exactly the fairytale ending, huh?"

"Tuesday," he reached across the table, covering my hand with his own. The warmth of his touch was a stark contrast to the cold dread that filled me. There could have only been one person who would kill her, kill her for leaving him.

Chapter 22

Dimitri Costa

The flicker of my desk lamp seemed to mock the steady tick of the clock, counting down the moments I had left with this case. Three weeks had passed since the boss allowed me to stay on the case.

"Costa," I muttered to myself, "focus." My eyes skimmed the report once more, the words on the page blurring into a dance of fate and science. Dr. Tegan Smith's findings lay bare in black and white. The DNA was a match; Tuesday's mother had been found, and not in the way anyone would wish for.

"Jesus," I breathed out, leaning back in my chair, the leather creaking under the weight of the revelation. It was like trying to piece together a puzzle, only to find the final piece jammed right in the centre—it fit, but damn, did it change the whole picture.

I drummed my fingers, thinking about George Wellington's web of lies. No missing person report—just a story of abandonment that everyone bought. Lillian's entire family tree was uprooted and long dead; no one to cry foul. But her bones cried out from beyond the grave, telling a tale of a mother's love so fierce she'd leave her own flesh and blood on church steps to save her from the devil himself.

The relentless ticking of the station clock was like a metronome to my restless thoughts as I sat at my desk. It was piled high with paperwork I was avoiding.

"Costa," my boss's voice cut through the silence as he called me into his office. I stood up, letting out a sigh that seemed too heavy for such an empty room.

"Close it?" he asked, peering at me over the rim of his glasses, his fingers drumming on the mahogany desk. The question hung in the air like smoke from a snuffed-out cigarette.

"Yeah, closed." I leaned against the doorframe, feeling the cool wood press into my back. "Wellington's dead. The case is colder than the bones we dug up."

"Any loose ends?" His eyes, sharp and assessing, searched mine for any hint of doubt.

"None. We've circled this drain long enough." I shrugged the image of the decrepit Victorian flashing across my mind—silent save for the echoes of past horrors.

"Alright. Jenkins won't be pleased, but if you're sure..." He trailed off, giving me a look that told me he trusted my judgment.

"Sure as I can be when the only suspect is six feet under," I said, my voice tinged with a weariness I couldn't quite hide.

"Then that's that. Close it." He nodded once, decisively, and turned his attention back to the paperwork littering his desk.

"Thanks, Boss." I pushed off from the doorframe and walked out, the finality of the moment leaving a bitter taste in my mouth.

As the sun dipped below the horizon, painting the sky in shades of bruised purple, I found myself driving towards Tuesday's place, the city lights blurring past like distant stars. She never cared about the time, just that I made it to her side by the end of the night.

Tuesday's mansion rose before me, its silhouette hauntingly beautiful against the twilight sky. A chill ran down my spine —not from fear, but anticipation.

I let myself in, the familiar scent of her lilac perfume greeting me like an intimate whisper. Up the grand staircase, I moved silently, my thoughts a jumbled mess. The case might have been cold, but the memories were still alive, flickering in the dark corners of my mind.

I slipped into her bedroom, the soft glow of the bedside lamp casting shadows over the opulent space.

"Finally," Tuesday murmured without opening her eyes, her lips curving into a content smile.

"Miss me, Sweetness?" I teased, kicking off my shoes and shedding my jacket before sliding under the sheets beside her.

"Always do," she replied, her voice sleepy but warm.

I wrapped an arm around her, pulling her close, the feeling of her skin against mine chasing away the last of the day's ghosts. "Case is closed," I whispered into her hair, inhaling the scent that was now more home than any place I'd ever known.

"Good," she breathed out, turning to face me, her gaze soft yet resilient. "Now close your eyes. You're done being the detective for today."

"Am I now?" I grinned, relishing the lightness between us. "What am I supposed to be then?"

"Mine," she said simply, her hand finding mine under the covers. "Just...mine."

"Yours, huh?" I echoed, my heart skipping a beat, the gravity of those words pulling me deeper into her orbit. "That's a fact I can live with."

"Good," she repeated, closing the distance between us with a kiss that promised more than just tonight—it tasted like forever.

Chapter 23

Tuesday May

The sun had barely kissed the horizon when I stumbled out of bed, shuffling into another day that felt as repetitious as the last. Life had become a mirage of monotony. Every morning, with Mr. Thompson's efficient stride leading the way, we'd tackle a room in this labyrinthine mansion, dusting off relics and stripping away the heavy curtains of the past.

"Good morning, Miss Wellington," Mr. Thompson greeted me, his voice echoing through the hollow halls. "Shall we finish off the library this morning?"

"Let's just get it over with," I muttered, my voice tinged with the remnants of sleep. We moved methodically, our routine polished to perfection. Each sweep of the duster, each book evaluated and sorted, brought a sense of cleansing, as if with every cleared shelf, I was one step closer to shedding the skin of this house's history.

"Would you like some music while we work?" Mr. Thompson offered, ever attentive to the nuances of my moods.

"Sure, why not? Let's drown out the ghosts with something loud," I replied, a smirk playing on my lips. The air filled with the vibrant notes of an old rock tune, a stark contrast to the silent stories the books whispered.

As the hours ticked by, the familiar sense of anticipation curled in my stomach. Dimitri would be home soon. Home. The word felt foreign on my tongue, yet so right. This place was home because he was in it.

"Mr. Thompson, what do you think about Dimitri moving in?" I asked, pausing in my examination of a dusty tome.

"Detective Costa is a fine man," he said, his eyes crinkling at the corners. "If it brings you happiness, Miss Wellington, I believe it's a splendid idea."

"Thanks, Mr. T," I said, warmth blooming in my chest. "I'll pop the question tonight over dinner. Casual-like, y'know?"

"Very casual, indeed," he replied with a chuckle.

Later, as dusk painted the sky in shades of bruised purple, I heard the familiar sound of Dimitri's footsteps approaching. My heart skipped a beat. Dinner was laid out, candles flickered softly, and I waited for the perfect moment to broach the subject.

"Hey, Detective Handsome, how about making your visits more permanent?" I teased, swirling my wine glass playfully.

Dimitri raised an eyebrow, a smile tugging at the corner of his mouth. "Are you asking me to move in, Sweetness?"

"Maybe I am. Whatcha think?" I leaned in, my eyes locked on his.

"I think... I'd love nothing more," he said, his warm brown eyes reflecting the candlelight.

But amid the glow of new beginnings, there loomed the shadow of decisions yet to be made. My mother's house had been relinquished from the cold grip of forensics, its future uncertain. Would it hold treasures like this mansion? Or only the echoes of her laughter, trapped within walls?

"Tomorrow, I've got to figure out what to do with Mom's place," I told Dimitri, the flirtatious tone fading into seriousness. "Sell this mausoleum and make her happy house our new hideout?"

"Whatever decision you make, I'm with you," Dimitri assured me, reaching across the table to squeeze my hand. "We'll make it our sanctuary, wherever it is."

"Sanctuary," I echoed, rolling the word around in my mind. Yeah, I liked the sound of that. Sanctuary with Dimitri. Just maybe, the Groundhog Days were finally coming to an end.

"Inspections are such a drag, aren't they?" I mused aloud, watching Mr. Thompson's meticulous hands arrange the files on the dining table.

"Indeed, Miss Tuesday," he replied without looking up, "but necessary to ensure the structural integrity of your mother's house."

I let out a sigh, lounging back against the plush divan in the parlour. My gaze drifted to the ornate ceiling, where cherubs danced in a fresco of eternal spring. "Just set it all up for me, will ya? I want to wash my hands of the whole dusty affair."

"Already done," he responded, with that butler-like omniscience that always impressed me. "We'll meet with the assessors after lunch."

"Brilliant." I hopped off the divan and sauntered towards the murder room, humming a tuneless melody. The walls echoed with the promise of freedom; freedom that was a mere three weeks away.

"Planning another... escapade, Miss Tuesday?" Mr. Thompson called after me, one eyebrow arched in mild disapproval.

"Let's call it 'finalising arrangements'," I shot back over my shoulder, grinning wickedly. The door to the murder room creaked open, revealing my meticulously organised plans. Plans A through C lay sprawled across the table, each detailing the fate awaiting dear Mr. Hamilton.

"God, I'm good," I whispered to myself, admiring the web of contingency woven into every scenario. Each was a masterpiece of precision, a symphony of retribution.

"Miss Tuesday," Mr. Thompson's voice broke through my reverie as he appeared in the doorway. "Remember, curiosity and cats—"
"Have much better lives before they're dead," I finished for him with a smirk. "And speaking of, we've got a date with Daddy Dearest's study today."
"Ah, yes, the final frontier," he nodded, following me as I made my way to the looming study door.
"Or maybe we sell the damn thing as is," I said, half to him, half to myself. "Like a macabre mystery box, you know?"
"An intriguing idea," Mr. Thompson conceded, "but one mustn't leave stones unturned, especially those which might conceal treasure."
"Treasure or trauma," I corrected him, my hand hovering over the doorknob. "Time to nip this one in the bud, right? For Mom."
"For your mother," he agreed solemnly.
I stood hesitantly on the threshold of my father's office, the air heavy with the scent of his cologne. It was a smell that clung to the mahogany and leather like a sinister perfume, an aroma that could summon demons from the darkest corners of my mind. I knew him only briefly, but in those fleeting moments, he'd carved a canyon of dread into my existence. Yet, no nightmares ever featured his sneering face—probably because I'd been the one to send him off to hell. But even

with him gone, simple triggers like this godforsaken scent dragged me back through time.
"Miss Tuesday," Mr. Thompson said, his voice steady as he brushed past me. "Shall we?"
His nudge was gentle but firm, like a reminder that there were still pages to turn and secrets to uncover. The world didn't crumble when I stepped forward; reality held firm underfoot. I exhaled slowly, the mustiness of the room filling my lungs, and with a resolve I wasn't sure I possessed, I set to work alongside him.
"Alright, let's see what literary treasures Daddy dearest has hidden," I quipped, trying to mask the tremor in my voice with a dose of humour.
"Indeed," Mr. Thompson replied, his tone dry as the dust we disturbed. We reached for the books, our motions synchronised in a dance of discovery and disposal. One by one, I flipped through the pages, half-expecting secret messages or hidden compartments to reveal themselves. Old spy novels had nothing on us.
"Ha! Look at this... 'The Art of War'?" I couldn't help but laugh. "Subtle, Dad. Real subtle."
"Perhaps he fancied himself a strategist," Mr. Thompson mused, placing the book in the donation box. His eyes met mine, a glint of shared understanding passing between us.
By lunchtime, two entire cases stood bare, their contents sorted into boxes labelled 'Donate' and 'Dump.' The task felt

less like cleaning and more like exorcising ghosts, each title a spectre of the man who once cast a shadow over this mansion.
"Mrs. Collins outdid herself today," Mr. Thompson commented, nodding toward the sandwiches waiting on the heavy desk. They were a small comfort, a normalcy amidst the chaos of my inherited life.
"God bless that woman," I said, sinking my teeth into the homemade goodness. "She knows how to soothe the soul with mayonnaise and pickle."
"Indeed," he agreed, taking a polite bite.
"Right, then," I said after a few minutes of comfortable silence, brushing crumbs off my shirt. "Time to play house inspector and see what skeletons mom's closet is hiding."
"Quite literally, perhaps," Mr. Thompson added as we rose. He always had a knack for keeping pace with my dark humour.

The Victorian beast loomed before us, its tangled garden like the unruly hair of a once beautiful dowager. It was as if the house itself had been holding its breath, waiting for me to return.
"Quite the welcome committee," I quipped as Mr. Thompson and I approached the trio of men who seemed to have sprouted from the weedy front path like dubious mushrooms. Hard hats perched atop their heads, they clutched clipboards like shields against the encroaching wildness of the estate.

"Ms. May?" The one in the middle extended his hand; his grip was firm, callouses telling tales of labour. "We've completed our assessment."

"Hit me with it," I said, rocking back on my heels, hands stuffed into the pockets of my jeans.

"Structurally sound," he began, ticking points off on his fingers. "But you've got rot in some of the timber, the roof's a sieve, and the flooring's seen better days."

"Sounds like my life story," I joked, but my gaze was caught by the way sunlight struggled through the stained-glass window, throwing fractured rainbows onto the peeling wallpaper.

"Uh, right." He cleared his throat. "You'll also need to clear out the interiors so we can work without obstructions."

"Gotcha. Ghosts and all," I said, offering a thin smile that didn't quite reach my eyes.

"Here's the quote for the repairs," he handed me a slip of paper that felt like signing away a piece of my past.

"Thanks, boys. I'll give you a buzz when this old girl's ready for her facelift." Waving the quote like a white flag, I spun on my heel, the crunch of gravel underfoot satisfying punctuation to the meeting.

Back at the mansion, the study awaited, a mausoleum of memories housed in leather-bound tombs. "Round two, Mr. Thompson?"

"Indeed, Ms. May," he replied, already rolling up his sleeves.

"Let's see what secrets Daddy dearest has stashed between the pages," I said as we resumed our positions before the shelves. Book by book, we peeled back layers of dust and pretence, exposing each volume to the scrutiny of daylight.
"Ever think about just torching the lot?" Mr Thompson asked a glint of mischief in his eyes.
"Every damn day," I admitted with a chuckle. "But then where would the fun be in that?"
"True. Arson doesn't allow for the same... finesse."
"Exactly." I flipped through another book, a frown creasing my brow. "Thought I'd find something more... juicy by now."
"Patience is a virtue," he reminded me.
"Never been virtuous, Mr. Thompson, why start now?" I shot him a wink, and together we lost ourselves in the rhythmic dance of sort and sift, the afternoon waning as we waged war on the ghosts of the past, one page at a time.

Chapter 24

Tuesday May

"Ah, the last of them," I muse aloud, my fingers brushing over the spine of a weathered copy of 'Wuthering Heights' before dropping it into the cardboard box labelled 'Donate'. My gaze lingers on the now-empty seventh bookshelf. "Doesn't this one seem off to you?" I ask Mr. Thompson, nodding towards the towering mahogany structure.

The old butler squints, silver hair catching the dim light as he shuffles closer. His hands, aged yet steady, trace along the carved trim with a reverence that only years of service can instil. "Indeed, Miss May," he murmurs, his voice carrying the faintest hint of curiosity beneath its usual formality. "This back panel here... it's not quite like the others."

"Really?" The word is barely out before he leans in and presses against the wood. A soft click sends a thrill through me—it's almost like a scene straight out of a gothic novel.

With a creak of protest, the panel swings open, revealing darkness and dust. Cobwebs cling to forgotten secrets.
"Jackpot," I whisper, half-amazed, half-vindicated. This mansion has always been full of surprises, most of them darker than I care for. But this... this is what I live for—the hunt, the unravelling of Wellington mysteries.
"Treasure hunting at its finest," I say with a grin that feels a touch too giddy. It's not every day a hidden compartment decides to grace you with its presence.
Mr. Thompson chuckles—a rare sound—and nods sagely. "Perhaps your father was unaware of this particular nook. Given the age, it might predate even his time." He brushes a finger along the edge, where the varnish has worn thin. "These bookcases are part of the house itself; it wouldn't surprise me if he never knew."
"Can you imagine?" I jump up and down, excitement bubbling inside me. To think, something right under George Wellington's nose and he missed it? "Old man must be rolling in his grave"
"Miss May," Mr. Thompson starts, but there's no real admonishment there. Just the long-suffering sigh of a man who's seen more than his fair share of Wellington drama.
"Sorry, not sorry," I quip, biting back a laugh. Dad'd have a fit if he knew I was poking around his precious secrets—with his own butler, no less. But hell, if finding hidden compartments

isn't a perk of this twisted inheritance gig, I don't know what is.
"Let's see what the old house has been hiding, shall we?" I gesture grandly toward the opened panel, feeling every bit the heiress of mystery that I am—whether I like it or not.
The musty scent of age and secrets wafts through the air as I tug the wooden panel wider, revealing a hidden cavity that looks like it hasn't seen the light of day in forever. My fingers graze over the treasures nestled within—a trove of paperwork, stacks of cash bundled with faded paper bands, and several leather-bound notebooks aged to perfection.
"Jackpot," I breathe out, my voice a mix of awe and triumph.
"Indeed." Mr. Thompson's eyes widen slightly as he watches me extract the contents from their dusty tomb.
I fan myself with a thick wad of bills, feigning nonchalance. "Looks like you're getting a hefty bonus this year, Mr. T."
His gaze fixes on the cash as I pass the bundles to him. "Good heavens, there must be thousands here," he murmurs, thumbing through them with an appreciator's touch.
"Keep it," I insist, tossing another stack his way with a cheeky grin. "Consider it hazard pay for dealing with the Wellington brand of crazy."
"Miss May, I couldn't possibly—" he protests, but I cut him off with a laugh.

"Mr. Thompson, please. I'm swimming in more money than I can spend in a lifetime. Buy yourself something pretty, will ya?"
He chuckles, the sound dry as old leaves. "As you wish, Miss May. But only because you insist, and I shall halve it with Mrs Collins."
"Damn straight." The paper crackles under my fingertips as I flip open the first notebook, eager for more revelations. But instead of answers, I'm met with a scrawl of ink so elaborate it might as well be hieroglyphics. "What the hell is this? Some sort of code?"
"Let me see." Mr. Thompson leans over, and I catch the faint smell of his cologne, something warm and woodsy that's become reassuringly familiar over the past months.
"Old cursive," he says, amusement lacing his voice. "It's perfectly readable, Miss May."
"Show-off." I nudge him playfully with my elbow. "So what does it say?"
"Ah, it appears to be a journal," Mr. Thompson muses, tracing the looping letters with a finger. "And if I'm not mistaken, this belonged to Mr. Wellington Senior. He's discussing his wife, your grandmother, and a business transaction—tobacco shipments, it seems."
"Always about the bottom line with the Wellingtons, huh?" I lean back against the bookcase, letting the history seep into my bones.

"Did the Wellingtons actually deal in tobacco, Mr. Thompson?" I inquire, thumbing through the aged pages of the other journal, my curiosity piqued by the past's murky dealings.

"Your family has shipped everything from spices to silk, Miss May," Mr. Thompson replies, his voice carrying a note of pride mixed with a hint of something more solemn. "If there was profit, it was as good as done. Your lineage is a complex tapestry, woven with threads of ambition and secrecy."

"Sounds like I could be the bloody star of my own Wikipedia page." I chuckle, tossing a lock of hair over my shoulder, the dust motes catching in the sunlight streaming through the window.

"Indeed, you might find yourself quite infamous on the internet if you were to look," he adds with a knowing tilt of his head.

"Infamy has a certain ring to it, doesn't it?" My lips curl into a smirk as I picture my name etched across digital history—a legacy of both fortune and infamy.

"Quite so, Miss May." Mr. Thompson's eyes twinkle with amusement.

I settle onto the floor, the cool wood pressing against my legs, and motion for him to join me. "Well then, Mr. Thompson, how about you read this old man's secrets to me? I'm dying to know what skeletons the Wellington closet holds."

"Very well." He clears his throat, sitting down opposite me, the journal open on his lap. His voice takes on the cadence of the past as he reads, breathing life into the faded ink.
"Mr. Wellington Senior writes here of his wife, Grace. It seems he adored her—spoke of her with such tenderness it almost feels intrusive to read." He pauses, looking up at me, his expression softening.
"Keep going," I urge, leaning forward, eager to hear more about the woman whose blood runs through my veins.
"Tragedy struck them hard. They lost their first three children... never took a breath outside the sanctuary of the womb." Mr. Thompson's voice lowers, heavy with the weight of unfulfilled dreams.
"Shit," I mutter, a lump forming in my throat. Even I can't help but feel the sting of that ancient sorrow.
"Then came George..." He continues, his brow furrowing. "They gave him the world, but Mr. Wellington Senior worried. The boy was quiet, withdrawn, alarmingly... calculating."
"Why doesn't that shock me," I muse aloud, though the thought sends a shiver down my spine.
"Indeed," Mr. Thompson says, turning the page. "As George grew, he became fixated on a young girl from down the lane. When her family fell into debt, Mr. Wellington saw an opportunity—a chance to make his son happy."

"By buying him a bride? That's messed up," I snort, rolling my eyes.
"Unfortunately, happiness is often a fleeting guest in the Wellington house," Mr. Thompson observes. "George changed after the marriage. Became possessive, overprotective... Mr. Wellington Senior feared for his life, believed his son capable of... dark deeds."
"Well, now we are getting somewhere," I say, half-joking, but the truth of it gnaws at me. "So, Grandfather Dearest was scared of his own offspring. Now that's a plot twist."
"Life often outstrips fiction in its capacity for darkness, Miss May," Mr. Thompson remarks, closing the notebook with a sense of finality.
"Looks like I've inherited more than just a trust fund," I murmur, leaning back against the shelves, feeling the chill of history's shadow upon me.
"Mr. Wellington Senior met his end on a boat, you know," Mr. Thompson says, the words falling heavily in the now still air of the library. "Out at sea, the vessel exploded. Nothing left but debris and whispers of foul play."
"Damn," I reply, flipping a lock of hair behind my shoulder. "So old grandpa became fish food?"
"Indeed, Miss May," he continues with a solemn nod. "There were no witnesses; half the yacht sank to the ocean's depths. Curiously, George had taken it out just two weeks before with Lillian, claiming it was in perfect condition."

"Perfect, huh?" My voice drips with sarcasm as I skim my fingers across the coarse carpet, imagining the saltwater lapping at that sunken tomb. "Sounds like Grandpa might've known too much about darling Georgie's hobbies."

"Perhaps," Mr. Thompson agrees.

I can almost see it, the boat splintered into a thousand fragments, swallowed by waves. "He did it. Deep down, I know he did," I say, the conviction in my voice surprising even me. "Father clearly wasn't one for loose ends—especially not ones that could write in cursive."

"Allegations require proof, and in this case, the sea keeps its secrets," Mr. Thompson reminds me, though the corners of his mouth twitch, as if he knows the truth is as murky as those waters.

"Proof or not, I feel it in my bones." I lean back against the musty bookshelf, feeling its solidarity against my spine. "And speaking of twisted family traits..."

"Miss May?"

"Reading Grandpa's diary here," I tap the leather-bound journal, "it's like staring into a damn mirror. He was a loner, a thinker... a little unhinged. Shit, maybe I'm not just nursing a case of PTSD after all." A laugh bubbles up, but it's hollow, edged with a darker realisation. "Maybe I actually belonged in the loony bin from the start."

"Your resilience speaks otherwise," he counters softly, offering a conspiratorial smile. "You're stronger than you give yourself credit for."

"Thanks, Jeeves." I flash him a grin, trying to shake off the cobwebs of lineage. "But strength aside, knowing where I come from... it's like finding the missing piece of a jigsaw puzzle. The piece that's covered in blood."

"An unsettling revelation," he concedes, adjusting his cufflinks with a practised motion.

Unsettling, sure. But it makes sense. Explains why I've got this itch for revenge that won't quit. I push myself to my feet, dusting off my jeans. I guess it's true what they say—the apple doesn't fall far.

"Revenge is a dish best-served cold, they say," Mr Thompson quips, a wry smile playing on his lips.

"Then consider me the fucking ice queen," I retort, my pulse quickening with the thrill of the hunt. "Now, let's dig deeper into these dirty little secrets, shall we?"

"By all means, Miss May. After you." Mr. Thompson gestures grandly towards the rest of the hidden compartment, ready to unearth more of the Wellington darkness.

"Let the treasure hunt continue," I declare, my heart thudding with anticipation and something else—a fierce, unyielding desire for retribution.

Chapter 25

Tuesday May

The musty scent of old leather and ink-filled my nostrils as I stepped back into the sanctum of secrets that was my father's study. The air felt thick with the past, each breath like inhaling whispers of a life lived in shadows. "You know," I began, running a finger along the edge of the desk, "this room is like a damn time capsule."

"Indeed, Miss Tuesday," Mr. Thompson replied, his voice as steady as the ticking grandfather clock in the corner. "In all my years of service, not a single thing has been altered or removed."

"Sort of creepy when you think about it." I chuckled, trying to shake off the chill that seemed to cling to every surface. We moved on to the cupboards behind the desk the next day, their dark wood looming like silent guardians of the Wellington empire.

"Let's see what Daddy has hoarded away here." My hands danced over files and business papers, each one a reminder of the Wellington Enterprises behemoth that now, by default, belonged to me. I flicked through them with disinterest, the numbers and contracts blurring into an indistinguishable mess.

"Mr. Thompson, I think I'd rather stick my hand in a blender than try to run this circus," I confessed, tossing another file onto the growing pile.

"Perhaps it would be wise to consider selling the company, Miss Tuesday," Mr. Thompson suggested, his voice cutting through the playful banter. "I could arrange for it to be liquidated on your behalf."

"Best idea you've had all day," I quipped, but my heart wasn't really in it. The thought of letting go, of severing the last tangible ties to George Wellington, sent an unexpected pang through me.

"Alright, let's box these up for whoever's brave enough to take over." My fingers worked deftly, sealing away the legacy of a man who was both a stranger and blood. But first, I had to make sure there were no hidden messages among the mundane. "Wouldn't want to miss out on any juicy secrets, now would we?"

"Very thorough, Miss Tuesday," Mr. Thompson said, approval lacing his tone as we sifted through each document with painstaking care. It was tedious work, but something in the

back of my mind buzzed with the possibility of uncovering... anything that might give me a glimpse into the enigma that was my family.
"God, imagine if this was all just some elaborate riddle leading to the world's most disappointing prize," I joked, breaking the monotony. But the truth was, I ached for a connection, for a clue that would bring me closer to understanding more about why my mother left, why my father became the man he did, and ultimately, who I was meant to become in the wake of their legacies.
"Life has a way of revealing its answers in due time," Mr. Thompson mused. I shot him a wry smile, wondering if he knew just how right he was.
The cupboards surrendered their final secret with a sigh, barren and echoing as we stared into the void of empty space.
"Well, that's that," I mumbled, my fingertips brushing along the smooth inner walls for any sign of deception—a hidden latch, a false back—anything. But there was nothing. Just the stark reality that sometimes, a cupboard is just a cupboard.
"Onto the desk then," Mr. Thompson prompted, his voice steady like the ticking of the grandfather clock in the corner.
"Right. The heart of the beast." I moved to the massive oak desk, a relic from an era of austere businessmen and ruthless dealings. Drawers gave way under my insistent tugs, revealing nothing but dust motes dancing in the sliver of sunlight sneaking through the curtains. Until the last one.

"Jesus," I breathed out, the word slipping past my lips like a prayer as I thumbed through the pile of photographs that spilled out, covering the desk like a glossy carpet. "She was... she was beautiful."

"Very much so," Mr. Thompson agreed solemnly, standing at my shoulder, peering down at the images of Lillian Wellington—my ghost of a mother—frozen in time.

"Look at her," I said, a mix of awe and sorrow tightening my chest as I held one up. It was a candid shot, Mom laughing, her dark hair wild around her shoulders, those familiar blue eyes sparkling with life. "I mean, look at us. It's like staring into a mirror."

"Indeed, Miss Tuesday. The resemblance is quite remarkable."

Nostalgia clung to the edges of each photograph, whispers of love etched into the paper. And there, nestled among them all, were letters scrawled in elegant handwriting—love notes that spanned the years, tangible proof that once upon a time, George Wellington's heart wasn't made entirely of stone.

"Damn, Daddy had game." My chuckle felt hollow as I flipped through the declarations of undying affection, the promises of forever. "Who knew?"

"Love often brings out the poet in even the most stoic of men," Mr. Thompson observed, his gaze lingering on a photo of my parents, arms wrapped around each other, lost in their own world.

Sifting through more snapshots of the past, my fingers brushed against something solid beneath a stack of legal documents detailing joint ownerships and shared assets—a marriage certificate, faded with age, bearing their signatures entwined at the bottom.

"Wow." The word escaped me in a whisper, heavy with the weight of discovery as I unearthed three treasures buried within the drawer: my mother's wedding ring, glinting softly; a letter addressed to my father, dated the day she vanished; and lastly, a set of three keys, mysterious in their ordinary appearance.

"Bet these open another three houses," I quipped, trying to infuse some levity into the gravity of the moment.

Mr. Thompson plucked one key from the bunch, examining it carefully. "I assume this one," he gestured to the ornate key, "would fit the lock to his bedroom. It's always been locked. Never been inside, never seen what lies beyond those doors."

"Secrets upon secrets," I murmured, rolling the cool metal between my fingers. "Guess there's only one way to find out."

"Indeed, Miss Tuesday," Mr. Thompson replied.

"Let's go see what Daddy Dearest has been hiding all these years," I say, the words tumbling out of my mouth with a blend of dread and excitement. I can't help but sprint up the stairs, two at a time, my heart pounding against my ribcage like it's trying to break free. The last room on the right has been an enigma, a space in this sprawling house I've skirted around since the clean-out began.

Slipping the key into the lock, there's a satisfying click, and something inside me feels unlocked too. With a deep breath to brace myself, I turn the handle and push the door open. A flick of the wall switch and the room floods with light, chasing away shadows that have lurked here far too long.

"Jesus..." The word is a half-whisper, half-gasp as we freeze. Four mannequins, decked out like guests at some macabre tea party, stare back at us with their blank, lifeless eyes. One perches primly in a chair, her dress a vintage swirl of lace and secrets. Another stands sentinel by the en suite, her pose rigid, eternal. The third lies sprawled across the bed, a tableau of twisted slumber, while the fourth kneels in the corner—penitent or predator, I can't tell.

A shiver races down my spine, a visceral reaction that has nothing to do with the temperature of the room. "Holy shit," slips from my lips before I can stop it.

"Miss Tuesday?" Mr. Thompson's voice cuts through the eerie silence, tinged with concern.

"Look at them," I whisper, my voice sounding foreign even to my ears. "Dressed to the nines for a party that never happened."

I back away, the weight of unseen eyes pressing against me, heavy and unyielding. My hand shakes as I reach for the door, eager to put a barrier between us and this... shrine. Closet?

Mausoleum? "Nope. We are not touching this one. I can't—I just can't go in there." The door slams shut with a finality that echoes in the pit of my stomach.
"Understandable," Mr Thompson murmurs, and I can hear the wheels turning in his head, trying to rationalise, categorise, explain away the inexplicable.
I twist the key again, locking the door and, hopefully, whatever ghosts linger behind it. "Let's pretend we saw another boring old bedroom, huh?"
"Of course, Miss Tuesday," he agrees, and I can't tell if the tremor in his voice is from fear or the effort to maintain our fragile normalcy.
"Let's get the hell out of here," I mutter, my voice devoid of its usual buoyancy as we descend the staircase. The memory of those lifeless figures in that room clings to the edges of my mind like cobwebs.
"Quite the collection he had up there." Mr. Thompson's attempt at nonchalance falls flat, the words hollow against the grandeur of the stairwell.
"Yeah, a freaking waxwork horror show." My laugh is an abrupt bark, too loud in the silence enveloping us. I can't help but glance over my shoulder, half-expecting one of those mannequins to be gliding down the stairs after us.
"Shall we have some tea, Miss Tuesday?" His suggestion is a lifeline back to normality.

"Tea," I echo, the word foreign yet comforting. "Tea sounds bloody brilliant."
We reach the bottom, and I shove my hands into the pockets of my jeans, fingers brushing against lint and loose change, grounding me. "You think that's what he did for kicks? Played dress-up with dummies?"
"Perhaps it was his way of coping, I've seen your mother wearing every single one of those outfits" Mr. Thompson muses, his eyes not quite meeting mine. He's always been good at spinning things just so, making the intolerable seem almost palatable.
"Or maybe he was just batshit crazy." I snort, trying to push away the chill that has nothing to do with the drafty halls of Wellington Manor.
"Miss Tuesday, your father..." He trails off, then clears his throat. "He was a complex man."
"Complex," I repeat, the word tasting like ash on my tongue. "That's one way to put it."
"Indeed." He nods, and we move through the foyer, our footsteps a soft drumbeat against the marble floor. "Shall I prepare the Earl Grey or the chamomile?"
"Earl Grey," I decide, craving the bite of bergamot over the soothing lull of chamomile. "And maybe something stronger to spike it with."
"Of course, Miss Tuesday." His lips twitch in what might be a smile, or perhaps a grimace.

"Thanks, Mr. T." I manage a wink, throwing bravado over my unease like a shawl. "You're a real gem."
"Merely doing my job." He inclines his head, ever the professional.
"Right." I breathe out, forcing myself to look around at the familiar walls, the portraits, the vases of fresh flowers. "Just another day in paradise, huh?"
"Something like that," Mr Thompson agrees, and there's a sombre note in his voice that tells me he's seen far more than he'll ever let on.
"Fuck me sideways," I mutter under my breath, scratching at the back of my neck. "This place is going to be the death of me."
"Miss Tuesday!" He tsk, though I catch the flicker of amusement in his eyes.
"Sorry, sorry." I grin, sheepish. "But seriously, if this house doesn't kill me, the paperwork will."
"Then we best get to the tea posthaste." He gestures toward the kitchen, his shoulders relaxing ever so slightly.
"Lead the way, Jeeves." I fall into step behind him, the playful jab at his formality slipping out easily.
"Very droll, Miss Tuesday." But the corners of his mouth are turned up now, and I know we'll be okay. We'll sip our tea, spike it with something less genteel, and pretend that upstairs is just an ordinary bedroom, full of dust motes and forgotten dreams, not secrets dressed in silk and satin.

Chapter 26

Dimitri Costa

The cardboard boxes stacked in the corner seemed to mock me with their modesty. "I really don't own a lot," I muttered, watching as the removalist crew efficiently wrapped my few possessions. Every action they took was a reminder that Tuesday had orchestrated this move. It felt like a strange dance where I was always a step behind.

"Careful with that one, it's got my vinyls," I called out, but my voice lacked its usual authority. Being the recipient of Tuesday's generosity chafed at me. I'm not some kept man, I wanted to scream. But each time I tried to settle a bill or buy her a gift, she'd wave me off with a laugh that sent shivers down my spine.

"Dimitri, I've got more money than I know what to do with. Live a little on me, won't you?" she had said the night before, blue eyes alight with mischief.

I shook my head, trying to dispel the memory and the feelings it stirred. The crew moved with a silent efficiency that would have impressed me under different circumstances. "Is that everything, sir?" one of them asked, gesturing to the last box – the one holding the mismatched dishes I'd collected over the years.

"Yeah, that's it," I replied, feeling the weight of my life condensed into a handful of containers. As the movers carried my past out the door, a mix of emotions tangled inside me.

"Who am I to argue with a woman who wants to give me the world?" I told my empty apartment. The echo of my words bounced back, hollow and questioning. Tuesday didn't just inherit millions; she inherited a golden heart too. And here I was, caught in the web of her kindness.

I trailed behind the movers, locking up the place that had been my sanctuary. My pride fought a losing battle against the truth that bubbled up within me: I was head over heels for Tuesday. If she lived in a damn hut or if she turned out to be a yeti in disguise, it wouldn't have made a difference to me.

"Mr Costa, we're ready to go when you are," one of the movers called, snapping me back to reality. I sighed, running a hand through my hair. The sun was setting, casting a warm glow over the moving van, and I couldn't help but smile.

"Alright, let's get a move on then," I said, clapping the nearest guy on the shoulder. They didn't need to know that inside, I was a mess of nerves and excitement – all because of a

woman who called me 'hers' and treated me like I was the most important thing she'd ever had.
The jangle of keys echoed in the empty hallway, a clinking requiem for my bachelor life. I dropped them into Mr. Patel's outstretched hand, his wrinkled fingers closing over them like he was trapping a ghost.
"Take care of her, will ya?" I said, nodding toward the apartment door.
"Always do, Detective Dimitri," he replied, the corners of his eyes crinkling with a smile. "She'll be waiting if you ever come back."
"Thanks, but I'm not planning on doing any haunting around here." I patted the doorframe one last time and turned to go, the finality of the moment settling in my chest like the last piece of a puzzle.
With a lump in my throat, I followed the removalist truck, its engine growling like some caged beast hauling my past toward Tuesday's mansion. The city's skyline shrank in the rearview mirror, each building a silent witness to a chapter now closed.
"Big house, big problems, huh?" I muttered to myself, thinking about the looming mansion that would soon swallow me whole. A fortress of secrets, each room whispering tales of old money and older sins.
"Hey, detective, how's it feel to be moving up in the world?" Tuesday's voice crackled through the speakerphone.

"Like I'm Jack climbing the beanstalk, except this giant's got better taste in curtains," I shot back, grinning despite the nerves dancing in my stomach.

"Watch out for the golden goose, then. Wouldn't want you getting pecked to death before you've even unpacked." Her voice was light, but I could picture the concern knitted between her brows.

"Speaking of flying solo, heard you aced your driving test. Should I be worried about you tearing up the streets without Mr. Thompson riding shotgun?"

"Please, he's more likely to grab the wheel and drive us both into a hedge. I think he's secretly thrilled to be spared my 'exhilarating' driving style," she quipped, but there was an edge of pride in her tone.

"Can't blame him. But hey, freedom suits you, Tuesday, May. Just promise me you'll keep it under ninety, alright?"

"Scout's honour," she laughed, though I doubted either of us knew the first thing about scouts or their honour.

"Good, 'cause I kinda like having you in one piece."

"Kinda?" There was mock indignation there, but also something softer, something that made my heart beat just a bit faster.

"Alright, more than kinda. Now, let's get me moved into your haunted mansion before I start getting cold feet."

"Too late for that, detective. You're stuck with me. And believe me, the only spirits in my house are the ones we'll be drinking."

"Then lead the way to the bar, lady. I'll follow you anywhere."

I couldn't see her, but I knew she was smiling. And as the road stretched out before me, leading me away from the life I knew toward one filled with unknowns, I realised I meant every word.

The dust from the moving truck's tires hadn't even settled when I swung my car door open. There she was, Tuesday, May, a silhouette against her mansion's imposing front entrance—the kind of place you'd expect to find in a gothic novel, not your future digs. She spotted me and with the grace of a dark-haired, blue-eyed tempest, she bolted down the steps.

"About time, detective," she called out, launching into my arms with an eager embrace that almost knocked the wind out of me. Her laughter was infectious, a melody that could make a haunted house feel like home.

"Traffic was a nightmare," I said, but the truth was, I'd lingered outside my old apartment, hesitant to leave the last shred of my independence behind.

"Let's get you moved in," she said, pulling back just enough to give the removalists a nod. They shuffled past us, carting boxes and furniture towards the first room on the left—a temporary holding cell for my worldly goods.

"Right here?" I asked, thumbing over my shoulder as I set her down.
"Yep, until I finish exorcising the ghosts from the other rooms," she quipped, her eyes twinkling with mischief. "Then we're off to Mom's place."
She explained how she'd packed up Mother Lillian Wellington's possessions, storing them in containers around the estate like some kind of modern-day pirate burying treasure. "Thought about tearing through it, but..." She shrugged, and I caught a glimpse of vulnerability. "If there were secrets, Mom would've stashed 'em here."
"Guess we'll be playing Nancy Drew and Hardy Boy for a while then," I remarked, scratching the back of my neck.
"Something like that, Sweetness," she replied, her use of my private nickname sending a shiver down my spine.
Before I could tease her about our upcoming adventures, Mrs. Collins, the keeper of this colossal crypt, emerged from the shadows. "Tea and sandwiches while you wait?" Her voice was warm, a stark contrast to the cool air that seemed to perpetually hang in the halls.
"Starving," I admitted, grateful for the reprieve. My stomach had been in knots all day, twisted by more than just the move.
"Come on, let's eat," Tuesday said, tugging at my hand. "Tell me about your case."
"Ah, it's nothing. Just a woman who forgot she was a mother first, teacher second," I said, trying to keep the darkness at

bay. But the image of the boy, the same age as her own son, haunted me. "I want to lock her up and throw away the key."

"Process, Dimitri," Tuesday reminded me gently, her gaze softening. "It'll be okay."

"Easy for you to say," I muttered. "You weren't looking into his eyes, seeing... Well, doesn't matter now. Kid's with his dad."

"Good," she said firmly. "Now eat. You'll need your strength for unpacking... and for whatever else you might need strength for later."

"Is that a promise or a threat, Miss May?" I teased, letting the casual banter distract me from the gnawing unease that came with the case—and the move.

"Guess you'll have to stick around to find out," she shot back, with a sly grin that promised trouble—or maybe something infinitely better.

Chapter 27

Tuesday May

The dawn had barely broken the night's hold as I slipped out of bed, the twisted sheets a testament to the restless sleep that had been my only companion. My fingers curled around the edge of the comforter, pulling it back into place with a habitual neatness that felt almost sacrilegious on a day ordained for destruction.

"Today's the day," I whispered to my reflection in the mirror, a grim smile tugging at the corners of my mouth. Dimitri was already out, chasing his own demons in the guise of justice. He'd left in that quiet way of his, all soft footsteps and tender, lingering glances cast back toward the bedroom where he thought I still lay asleep. His obsession with the case—a sleazy teacher with roving hands—meant his mind wouldn't be on me. Perfect.

I dressed with care, my movements deliberate. Each article of clothing was chosen for ease of movement, dark fabrics that would keep me hidden in the shadows. Today wasn't about seduction; it was about retribution. Once ready, I padded down the stairs, the soft thud of my boots a steady drumbeat against the hardwood.

Mr. Thompson was in the kitchen, his back a rigid line as he attended to his morning duties. The man had an air of unspoken secrets, and hell, today, he was going to become part of one more.

"Morning, Mr. Thompson," I chirped, sliding onto a barstool as if it were any other day. "I'm planning on taking a little drive today. You know, put that new license of mine to good use."

"Very good, Miss May," he said, handing me a plate stacked with pancakes. "Will you be needing anything from me?"

"No thank you." I bit into the fluffy stack, syrup sweet on my tongue. "Why don't you take a day off" I winked at him, my tone light.

"Of course." His eyes didn't quite meet mine, but there was an understanding there that sent a shiver down my spine.

I finished breakfast quickly, eager to get on with the day. As I stood, I slung my bag over my shoulder, its contents—a coil of rope and a ball gag purchased under the cloak of internet anonymity—were innocuous separately but together spelled out my intentions clear as day.

"See you later, Mr. Thompson," I called out, the flirtatious lilt in my voice belying the cold anticipation coiling in my gut. "Wish me luck!"

"Good luck, Miss May," he replied, and I could almost hear the silent prayer for my damned soul.

With each step towards the door, the playful mask I wore for the world began to slip. Today, I'd confront the monster of my past. And by the time the sunset, there'd be one less hiding in plain sight.

The leather of the driver's seat hugged my body like a promise as I slid behind the wheel, the soft creak welcoming me into its embrace. My fingers danced over the ignition, a ballet of anticipation. The plan that had consumed my thoughts, that had nestled in the crevices of my mind for countless nights, was finally breathing life. My heart, a wild drumbeat in my chest, thrummed with the kind of excitement that edged on mania. I was keen—no, desperate—to finish what I'd so meticulously orchestrated.

"Fuck yes," I whispered to myself, tasting the vengeance like sweet venom on my tongue. Today would be the day Hamilton took his last sip of freedom.

As the engine purred to life beneath my touch, a testament to my resolve, the passenger door opened with a soft click that shattered my focus. Mr. Thompson slipped into the car, his movements as silent as the secrets we kept. He wore an

impassive mask, but his eyes gleamed with something akin to mischief—or was it pride?
"Miss May," he said, his voice smooth as aged whiskey, "you'll be needing an alibi, and I plan to be just that."
My pulse skipped. Shock rippled through me, cold and quick as a flash flood. How? My gaze snapped to him, wide-eyed and searching. Did the shadows of my past reflect so clearly in my eyes?
He must have seen the question written all over my face because he let out a low chuckle, the sound wrapping around me like a conspiratorial hug. "You don't get to be a butler without learning a few things, miss."
"Shit," I muttered under my breath, a smirk playing at the corner of my mouth despite the surprise still echoing through my veins. "You're full of surprises, aren't you, Mr. Thompson?"
"Only when it counts," he replied, steepling his fingers in front of him as if we were plotting over tea and scones rather than revenge and retribution.
"Alright, then." I flicked on the turn signal, the rhythmic tick-tock a metronome to our impending deed. "Let's not keep destiny waiting."
With a sharp intake of breath, I swung the car out onto the open road. The landscape blurred past us, a watercolour of greenery and asphalt. My mind raced faster than the car, thoughts tumbling and colliding.

"Mr. Thompson," I said, glancing at him, "after today... things can never go back to how they were."
"Miss May," he responded, his gaze locked ahead, steely and unyielding, "some things were never meant to stay the same."
The morning sun was playing hide and seek with the clouds as I took the wheel, the taste of anticipation sweet on my tongue. Mr. Thompson beside me was quiet, his presence a solid reassurance that I wasn't alone in this twisted game. The engine purred beneath us, a promise of the vengeance we were speeding toward.
"Nearly there," I whispered to myself, a smile tugging at my lips. The drive to Hamilton felt like a lifetime and a blink all at once. Every mile that rolled under us was another step away from the haunted past and toward a future where ghosts might be laid to rest.
"Remember to breathe, Miss May," Mr. Thompson murmured, glancing at me with a faint smirk as if he could hear the drumbeat of my heart against the silence.
"Breathing's overrated," I quipped, but I took his advice anyway, inhaling the scent of leather and the crisp air slipping through the cracked window.
When we arrived, the world seemed oblivious to our intentions, birds chirping merrily as I parked down the street from Hamilton's place. Mr. Thompson gave me a nod, his eyes sharp behind the aviators he'd donned.

"Showtime," I said, more to brace myself than anything. My fingers worked swiftly, pulling my hair back and securing it with military precision before hiding it under a net and beanie. The gloves slipped on, a second skin of black latex—my warpaint.

"Let's not dawdle, shall we?" I chuckled, feeling the thrill lick up my spine like a flame. We stalked down the back path, the world reduced to the sound of our footfalls and the thudding of my pulse.

The rear entrance greeted us, its door ajar like an invitation or a dare. "Well, that's convenient," I muttered, half disappointed I wouldn't get to play with my new lock-picking toys. But today wasn't about fun and games; it was about justice—a word that tasted like metal and resolved on my lips.

Creeping inside, I found him there. Hamilton, in all his smug ignorance, sat sipping coffee and rustling his newspaper. I sauntered in, casual as you please, and planted myself across from him. His head snapped up, and for a moment, he just gaped, like a fish suddenly yanked from its cozy pond.

"Who the fuck are you?" He scrambled to his feet, the paper fluttering forgotten to the floor.

"Me?" I flashed him a cheeky grin, brandishing the knife with a flourish fit for a magician. "I'm just a girl looking to have a little chat."

"Get out!" He pointed towards the door, his voice cracking with the strain of authority and fear.

"Uh-uh," I tutted, shaking my head slowly. "We've got some catching up to do, you and I."

I perched on the chair, twirling the knife like a baton in a parade. "The name's Tuesday May," I said, my voice a feather drifting across the tension-thick room. "And you, Hamilton, are about to learn why hell hath no fury like a woman scorned."

His face drained of colour as if someone had pulled the plug on his very soul. He knew—the bastard actually knew who I was and why I'd come.

"Tuesday... what are you here for?" His attempt at nonchalance was as flimsy as wet tissue paper.

"Justice," I replied, sweet as poison. "For the innocence, you snatched away from me. See, you were the first, so it's only fitting you're the first to go, too."

Hamilton bolted, all pretence of bravado gone. He made it two steps before bumping into an immovable object—Mr. Thompson, standing in the doorway like the grim reaper's more dapper brother, a gun aimed with practised ease.

"Nope," Mr. Thompson drawled, the corner of his mouth ticking up ever so slightly. "The lady asked you to sit, so please sit."

"Ha!" I couldn't help but chuckle, adrenaline dancing like sparks along my veins. "You really are earning that bonus now, aren't you?"

"Miss Tuesday," Mr. Thompson said, his smirk widening just a fraction, "if someone had done to my child what was done to you... well, they wouldn't be breathing." There was a chilling finality in his tone, a promise of swift retribution. "So consider this me helping you right some wrongs."
"Such a gentleman," I mused, the words laced with sarcasm while inside, something warm flickered to life—a feeling I thought had been extinguished long ago.
"Shall we?" I gestured to Hamilton with the knife, a morbid invitation to the last waltz he'd ever stumble through.
Mr. Thompson's grip was firm as he ushered a trembling Hamilton back into his chair, the kind of hold that spoke of years serving under my father's roof, where strength and silence were virtues. Even now, with his tailored suit and grey-streaked hair, Mr. Thompson had the air of someone you didn't mess with.
"Behave," I cooed, circling around to face our captive audience, my movements deliberate and unhurried. "It's not every day you get front-row seats to your own downfall."
Hamilton's eyes were wide, darting between me and the butler-turned-accomplice. A bead of sweat slid down his temple as Mr Thompson secured his wrists behind his back with the rope I had bought with me, tying him with perfect knots akin to a boy scout.
"Comfortable?" I asked, my tone dripping with mock concern as he tightened the last knot. His muffled grunt was all the

answer I got; the ball gag was already doing its job. "Good. We're about to begin."
My fingers played along the hem of his slacks, undoing them with an ease that belied the pounding of my heart. This was it —the culmination of countless nights spent plotting in the dark, fuelled by memories I wished I could scrub away. The fabric gave way, and there it was, the physical manifestation of my nightmares.
"Aw, look at you," I teased, though my stomach churned. "All exposed and vulnerable. Kinda like how you left me, huh?"
The knife felt cold and heavy in my hand—a stark contrast to the warmth spreading through my chest at the sight of his terror. It wasn't joy, no, but something far more primal. With precision I didn't know I possessed, I severed the piece of him that had taken so much from me and others.
"Let’s call this an unkind cut, shall we?" My words were flippant, but the gravity in my chest was like lead. "I'm sure I'm not the first or last child you touched, so think of this as karma."
Hamilton's muffled screams filled the room as I pinned his dick to the table with the blade, a grotesque trophy for the world. The blood pooled, crimson against the polished wood, and for a moment, I felt victorious, powerful.
Leaning down I picked up the tire iron I had bought with me, the iron felt righteous in my grip, a cold extension of my own seething rage. I approached Hamilton's trembling form, his

eyes wide with the sort of fear that only comes when you know you're about to get exactly what you deserve.

"Time for the grand finale," I murmured, almost sweetly, as if I were discussing the weather rather than the prelude to his end.

The first blow was a symphony of crunching bone and splattering gore. I swung again, relentless, the tire iron rising and falling like a conductor's baton orchestrating a silent requiem. Each impact was a release, a liberation of years of bottled fury. The room - a canvas of white walls - was now splashed with a new, visceral kind of paint: brain matter and blood.

"Tuesday..." Mr. Thompson's voice broke through the red haze of my vengeance, tinged not with reproach, but with an eerie calm. "It's time to go."

His hand on my shoulder was grounding, a lifeline pulling me back from the abyss I'd gleefully danced along. I dropped the tire iron; it clattered against the hardwood floor, its work done.

"Right behind you, Mr. T," I answered, a manic grin tugging at the corner of my lips as I caught my breath. He wrapped me in one of Hamilton's towels, hiding the evidence of my catharsis beneath terrycloth folds.

We slipped out the back door, shadows blending into the twilight gloom of the alley. My heart raced, not just from the

exertion, but from a sense of accomplishment. The car welcomed us back, a silent accomplice to our dark deed.
"Feeling any better?" Mr. Thompson asked once we were on the road, his tone light but eyes searching mine.
I leaned back in the seat, letting out a sigh that felt like it carried the weight of the world. "Why yes, I do," I confessed with a chuckle that bubbled up from a place I didn't often visit. "One monster down, four to go.”

Chapter 28

Dimitri Costa

The fluorescent lights of the precinct buzzed overhead, a discordant symphony to the chaos that swirled in my mind. Three damn months. That's all the justice system had deemed fit for a crime that'd scar a kid for life. The papers on my desk were blurred, the words 'sexual misconduct' and 'minor' echoing in my head like some sick mantra. I raked a hand through my hair, frustration knotting my brow.

"Fuck," I muttered, slapping the file shut. It was a mockery, this sentence. A teacher, someone entrusted with the care of children, walks away with barely a blemish on her record while that boy... Christ. My fist clenched involuntarily.

The sudden shrill ring of my phone jerked me out of my brooding. I snatched it up, more out of irritation than any real desire to talk. "Costa."

"Hey, Dimitri." Tuesday's voice was a soothing balm, instantly disarming me. "Are you coming home for dinner? Or should I put something in the fridge for you?"
"Sweetness," I sighed, the edge in my tone softening at her concern. "I'm on my way now. Just leaving the precinct."
"Okay. Drive safe." Her voice was warm honey, the kind that made you want to drown in it.
"Will do." I ended the call, already feeling the pull of home—the pull of her. Snatching my jacket from the back of my chair, I stuffed the case files into my bag; they felt like lead, heavy with injustice.
As I strode through the bullpen, I could feel the eyes of my colleagues on me. They knew about the case, knew how it gnawed at me. But right then, none of that mattered. All I could think about was getting home to Tuesday.
"Costa, heading out?" called out Sanchez, his eyebrow raised knowingly.
"Got a hot date with a certain lady," I shot back, flashing him a grin that didn't quite reach my eyes.
"Give her my best," he chuckled, shaking his head.
"Sure thing," I said over my shoulder, pushing through the glass doors and stepping out into the cool evening air.
My footsteps echoed on the pavement as I made my way to the car, the weight of the case momentarily forgotten. Three months, huh? I'd find a way to keep that woman off the streets longer, one way or another.

The moment I slid behind the wheel of my car, the tension in my shoulders began to ease. The engine purred to life, a familiar sound that promised escape. As I navigated through the streets, painted orange and pink by the setting sun, my thoughts turned to Tuesday. She'd been so damn excited about her driving plans—her first taste of real freedom since she got her license.

"Bet you're flying high, baby girl," I murmured to myself, imagining her behind the wheel, that wild mane of dark hair whipping around her face, those piercing blue eyes alight with exhilaration. Knowing her, she was probably grinning ear to ear, just like I did when I was seventeen and the road opened up before me for the first time.

My grip on the steering wheel relaxed as I pulled into the familiar spot outside our place, the concrete rectangle that might as well have my name etched into it. Before I could even kill the engine, the front door burst open, and there she was—Tuesday May in all her tempestuous glory.

"Hey, Dimitri!" she called out, and goddamn if her voice didn't sound like music after the day I'd had.

"Hey yourself," I said with a grin, stepping out of the car.

In two heartbeats, she crashed into me—a whirlwind of limbs and energy. Her arms wound around my neck, her body pressed against mine, and the scent of lavender filled my senses. It was like coming home to a living, breathing spring garden, and I soaked it all in, letting it wash over me and cleanse away the grime of the day.

"Missed you," she whispered, her breath warm against my ear.

"Missed you more," I teased back, my hands finding their way to her waist, holding her close.

"Impossible," she retorted, pulling back just enough to look up at me with those eyes—bright, mischievous, and brimming with secrets I was still unravelling.

"Tell me about your day," I said, eager to hear about her adventures. "Did you give Mr. Thompson a heart attack with your driving?"

She laughed, the sound tinkling through the air, and I couldn't help but join in. There was something infectious about her joy, something undeniably pure despite the shadows that sometimes crossed her gaze.

"Let's just say he was unable to let me go alone and ended up riding shotgun again," she confessed, and the image had me chuckling.

"Good. He is protective of you."

We stayed locked in our embrace, unwilling to let go, the world around us fading to nothing. It was moments like these—simple, unguarded, filled with the promise of us—that made everything else bearable.

"Come inside," she said, finally stepping back but keeping hold of my hand. "I've got stories to tell, and you look like you need to relax."
"Lead the way, darling," I replied, allowing her to tug me toward the door.
"Hope you're starving," Tuesday said with a grin, her blue eyes sparkling like shards of the clearest ocean. "Mrs. Collins outdid herself today—made a roast that's to die for. I swear, I must've had three helpings."
Her laughter was music to my ears as she waltzed over to the microwave, setting the timer for my portion. The scent of rosemary and garlic filled the kitchen as the microwave hummed softly. I settled into a chair, observing Tuesday move about with an ease that made the space seem like it belonged to her. She reached for the cocoa powder, her long, dark hair swaying with every movement.
"Is that your fourth hot chocolate today?" I teased, taking in the sight of her. The way she bit her lip when concentrating, or how her cheeks flushed a soft pink when she laughed—it was a sight that never got old.
"Maybe," she replied with a coy smile, her back still turned to me. "A girl needs her fix."
I watched her every move, captivated by the dance of her hips, and the delicate arch of her neck. The microwave beeped, signalling my dinner was ready, but my appetite was suddenly more for her than food.

"Damn, Mrs. Collins wasn't playing around," I mumbled, digging into the tender meat and perfectly roasted vegetables. With each bite, I felt some of the day's tension slip away, replaced by the comforting warmth of a home-cooked meal. I glanced up occasionally to catch Tuesday's gaze, that little smirk on her lips telling me she knew exactly what kind of effect she had on me.
"Good, huh?" she asked, sipping on her hot chocolate, the steam framing her face like a misty halo.
"Unbelievable," I agreed, though I wasn't just talking about the food.
Finishing up, I carried my plate to the sink, feeling a bit more human with my stomach full. As the clink of porcelain echoed through the kitchen, I sidled up behind Tuesday, wrapping my arms around her waist. Her body leaned back into mine, the roundness of her ass pressing against me, igniting a familiar heat beneath my skin.
"Someone's happy to see me," she murmured, a playful note in her voice as she glanced over her shoulder, her piercing blue eyes meeting mine.
"Can't help it," I confessed, my voice a low rumble. "You do things to me, Sweetness."
Her laughter rang out again, and she wiggled ever so slightly, teasing me further. I tightened my grip, both of us caught in that electric space where flirtation sparked into something more—a fire we were all too willing to stoke.

"Careful, Sweetness," I warned with a husky chuckle, the heat of her body searing through my clothes. "I'll take you right here on this kitchen bench if you don't stop pushing back."

But Tuesday was all about defiance wrapped in temptation, her body pressing back once more, firm and inviting against mine. The air between us crackled with an unspoken dare.

"Is that a promise, Detective?" she teased, turning her head to throw me a look that could start fires.

"Fuck, Sweetness," I groaned, my restraint snapping like a dry twig underfoot. My hand glided up to her throat, fingertips barely grazing her skin, while the other slipped into the waistband of her shorts. The slick warmth I found there drew a deep growl from within me. "I'm not waiting to get you upstairs."

Her breath hitched as I tugged her shorts down, exposing her to my hungry gaze. With a silent plea written in her eyes, she surrendered to the passion we both craved. I unbuckled my belt swiftly, the sound loud in the quiet kitchen, and freed my dick from the confines of slacks, my arousal undeniable.

"Dimi..." Her whisper was a feather across my senses.

"Shhh," I hushed her gently, nudging her forward onto the cool surface of the bench. The contrast of her heated skin against the stone sent a shiver through her that I felt in my own flesh. I lined myself up, sliding through the slickness, coating myself with her juices.

"Tuesday," I murmured, taking in her form splayed beneath me, "you're perfection."

Lining my head up to her pussy, I push all the way in till my hips met her flesh, a slow invasion that gathered intensity with each breath we shared. The world outside our little cocoon didn't exist—it was just her and me, moving together in a rhythm as old as time, racing towards a finish line that promised nothing but pure ecstasy.

The softness of her moans pierced the silence of the kitchen, a sound so laden with desire it sent a shockwave straight through me, hardening my resolve along with every inch of my body. I watched her beneath me, a vision of pure temptation, as I began to fuck her faster. "Sweetness," I groaned, feeling her clench around me, gripping me like she never wanted to let go.

"Dimi... more," she panted, and God, how could I deny her anything?

I seized her hips in my hands, skin on skin, my fingers digging in just enough to surely leave a memory on her flesh come morning. With urgency born of a hunger that had long since stopped being solely physical, I thrust into her, each movement punctuated by the music of her moans bouncing off the walls. The thought that Mrs. Collins or Mr. Thompson might overhear was like a distant whisper against the roaring need in my veins. "You feel incredible, Tuesday."

"Ah... don't stop," she begged, writhing beneath me, her movements stoking the fire that blazed between us.
"Never," I promised, picking up the pace. I sensed her teeter on the edge, her body a live wire. Leaning over her, I reached for her swollen clit, pinching gently, and she shattered spectacularly around me, pulling me into the vortex of her release. Her inner walls clenched, milking me in waves, and I followed her over the precipice, pouring myself into her as I emptied every ounce of frustration and passion I had.
"Fuck, I love you," I gasped, collapsing onto her back, trying to catch my breath, my heart racing a marathon in my chest.
She turned her head, her eyes sparkling with mischief and satisfaction. "I love you too, detective, but now you owe me a new hot chocolate." She nodded toward the bench where the remnants of her previous cup lay spilled.
I couldn't help but chuckle, the sight of my cum trailing down her thighs enough to make any man feel victorious. "Only the best for my girl," I muttered, slipping out of her with a sense of loss, already missing the heat of her embrace.
Tucking away the evidence of our fuck, I set out to craft the perfect apology in the form of a steaming cup of hot cocoa. As I worked, I found myself whistling—an unfamiliar tune of contentment—as I watched Tuesday collect herself with that grace she wore like a second skin. This woman, this incredible force of nature, had taken the raw edges of my world and smoothed them into something resembling peace.

And I'd be damned if I didn't spend the rest of my days making sure she knew just how much she meant to me.

Chapter 29

Tuesday May

I blinked my eyes open, my body heavy with warmth. Dimitri's arm was slung over my waist, his breath steady against the back of my neck. Damn, he's like a human furnace.

"Hey," I whispered, hoping to stir him without actually having to push him off. No reaction. With a soft groan, I wriggled beneath his grip, trying to shimmy my way out of our tangle of limbs. "Dimitri, babe, you gotta let go."

No luck. He murmured something incoherent and pulled me closer. A laugh bubbled up in my chest. That man could sleep through an apocalypse. But I was too hot, too restless to stay put. Carefully, I peeled his arm away and slid out from under the sheets.

"Sorry, love," I said softly, even though I knew he couldn't hear me. Standing up, I stretched, feeling the delicious pull in my muscles. The air was cooler here, and it kissed my bare

skin, making me shiver just a little. I walked to the bathroom, doing my best to avoid tripping over the clothes thrown on the floor.
Once inside, I took care of business, flushing away the remnants of last night's romp. I caught my reflection in the mirror. Dark hair tousled, blue eyes blinking back sleep.
I smirked at myself, splashed some water on my face, and quickly got dressed. Jeans and a tee, nothing fancy.
Slipping quietly out of the room, I left Dimitri to his slumber. The house was quiet, but the smell of coffee was already wafting up the stairs, beckoning me. Breakfast awaited, and I wasn't one to ignore the call of caffeine and carbs. Time to see what kind of day it would be.
The scent of cinnamon and cooked oats led me down the grand staircase, each step bringing the warmth of Mrs. Collins' kitchen closer. The old house, with its secrets and shadows, felt less oppressive in the morning light, especially when there was porridge involved.
"Morning, Mrs. Collins," I greeted, slipping into a chair at the massive dining table that could probably seat an army but mostly just accumulated mail.
"Good morning, dear," she replied, not missing a beat as she stirred the pot on the stove. "I thought some hearty porridge might do you good today."
"Sounds perfect," I said, leaning back and breathing in the comforting aroma. I couldn't help but think about the day

ahead. "Hey, Mrs. Collins, did Mom ever use her own bedroom much?" I asked, twirling a strand of hair around my finger.
She turned a soft smile on her face. "Oh, yes. Even though she slept with your father, tradition meant she kept her own room. She'd spend hours in there, lost in her books."
"Think I'm gonna tackle it today," I declared. "Might be time to let some light into that mausoleum."
"Very well, Tuesday," Mr. Thompson's voice chimed in from the doorway, stern as ever but with a hint of something softer just beneath the surface. "I'll call the removalists to assist. That armoire won't budge without a fight."
"Thanks, Mr. T," I smirked, knowing full well he hated the nickname but loving that he'd let it slide for me. "Don't suppose they can handle ghosts too, huh?"
"Only the living kind, Miss Wellington," he retorted, pulling his phone from his pocket and stepping away to make the call.
As I scooped up a spoonful of the golden porridge, now topped with a dollop of honey and a sprinkle of almonds courtesy of Mrs Collins, I pondered the task ahead. My mother's room was like a time capsule, one I wasn't sure I was ready to open, but my curiosity was killing me. What secrets did those walls hold? What whispers hid in the creases of her bedsheets?

"Your mother had a way with spaces," Mrs Collins remarked, breaking into my thoughts as she set down a steaming mug of tea next to me. "Her room... it's got her spirit, it does."
I nodded, swallowing a mouthful of porridge that warmed me from the inside out.
"Miss Wellington," Mr. Thompson returned, phone in hand. "The removalists will be here within the hour. We'll start with the heavy lifting and then see where the day takes us."
"Perfect." I pushed the bowl away, suddenly full of nervous energy. The prospect of rifling through my mother's most personal space felt invasive yet necessary, like ripping off a Band-Aid to let an old wound breathe.
"Tuesday," Mrs. Collins said gently, placing a comforting hand on my shoulder. "Whatever you find in there, remember your mother loved you fiercely."
"Thanks, Mrs. C." I forced a smile, feeling the weight of the day pressing down on me like a thick summer heat. "Let's hope I can handle whatever skeletons she kept in her closet."
"Or under her bed," Mr Thompson quipped, his rare attempt at humour surprising a giggle out of me.
"Under her bed, huh?" I teased back. "Wasn't aware we were hiding bodies in this place, Mr. T."
"Only the metaphorical kind, Miss Wellington," he replied, his eyes glinting with mischief that belied his usual stoic demeanour.

The clinking of porcelain and the rich aroma of freshly brewed coffee heralded Dimitri's arrival into the kitchen. Mrs Collins, ever the attentive housekeeper, had his cup ready before his backside even hit the chair.

"Morning, Sweetness," he greeted, leaning across to press a kiss to my forehead—a mix of affection and stubble.

"Hey, handsome." I teased, moving my head just enough so his lips brushed my hair instead. "Slept like a chilli pepper."

"Chilli pepper?" His warm brown eyes sparkled with amusement.

"Yep," I said, pushing my tangled dark hair out of my face. "I woke up with a bear wrapped around me making me sweat."

Laughter bubbled up from the depths of Mrs. Collins' throat while Dimitri's own chuckle mingled with the sounds of the morning kitchen.

"Should I be offended or flattered?" His grin was all charm and mischief as he sipped on his coffee.

"Deliciously flattered, Detec—" The ring of his mobile phone cut me off.

Dimitri's warm gaze turned cold as he glanced at the caller ID, then flicked back to me with an apologetic tilt to his mouth.

"Costa here," he answered all business now. I watched the playfulness drain from his demeanour as the chief rattled off details I wasn't privy to but could piece together from the tension lining Dimitri's jaw.

"Are you fucking kidding me?" he muttered under his breath, scrubbing a hand down his face. "Yeah, I'll be there in twenty."
"Bad news?" I ventured once he'd ended the call. How did he switch gears so fast? From lover to detective in a heartbeat.
"Murder case," he grumbled, setting the phone down with more force than necessary. "So much for our day off."
"Guess the dead don't have much respect for personal time, huh?" I couldn't help the snark that laced my words.
"Sorry, sweetheart." He stood, pressing a brief, firm kiss to my lips that had me swooning. "Duty calls."
"Go save the world, Detective Costa." I waved him off, trying to ignore the sudden tightness in my chest. Mr. Thompson caught my eye from the doorway, a silent understanding passing between us.
"Save the world," Dimitri echoed with a half-smile, already heading upstairs to change into whatever armour detectives wore to shield themselves from the horrors they faced daily.
The silence in the kitchen was a stark contrast to the laughter that had filled it just moments before. Dimitri's departure left a palpable emptiness, and I found myself fidgeting with the hem of my shirt, trying to find solace in the mundane action.
"Tuesday, love, would you fancy a hot chocolate?" Mrs. Collins' voice cut through the quiet like a beacon, her maternal tone wrapping around me like a warm blanket.

I glanced up, my lips curving into a genuine smile. "You're reading my mind, Mrs. C." The thought of something sweet and comforting was enough to lure a sigh from my lips.

"Coming right up." She bustled around the kitchen, the clink of cups and the soft whoosh of the milk steamer filling the space between us.

Chapter 30

Dimitri Costa

I leaned over her, taking in the scent of lavender and something wild that was just... her. I pressed a kiss to her forehead, a promise for later. "See you tonight, yeah?"

"Be careful," she murmured, the blue of her eyes piercing even through the dim light. It was like she could see straight through all the bullshit. Maybe that's why I couldn't help but lean in for another kiss, this one brushing her lips softly.

"Always am." But her frown told me she wasn't buying it. She never did.

I grabbed my keys from the bowl by the door, my badge a cold, solid weight in my pocket—a reminder of what I signed up for. The job was a cruel mistress, always calling at the worst damn times.

Stepping out into the chill of the early morning, I squinted against the low-hanging sun as I made my way to the car. My mood was a mix of irritation and resigned acceptance—wasn't the first time I'd been called in on a day meant for nothing but relaxing.

"Fuck it," I muttered, tossing myself into the driver's seat with less care than usual. The leather creaked under me, familiar and strangely comforting. I punched in the address into the nav system, the screen glowing blue as it calculated my route. Forty-five minutes to the other side of town; forty-five minutes of wondering what kind of hell awaited me.

As the engine hummed to life, I couldn't help but let out a low chuckle. Here I was, Dimitri Costa, supposedly enjoying a rare day off, now driving towards god knows what. But hey, I chose the badge, the late nights, the crime scenes that stuck to your soul like tar...

"Let's see what fresh hell you've got for me today," I said to no one in particular, hitting the gas a little harder than necessary. The town blurred past, each block melding into the next—a monotonous symphony of waking life that had no clue about the darkness I was heading into.

The gravel crunched beneath my shoes like a morbid countdown, my heart ticking in sync with each step. The cool morning air did little to clear the dread coiling in my stomach. I flashed my badge at the uniformed officer who manned the gate—a silent exchange as he nodded me through.

"Morning, Detective Costa," he said, his voice a low rumble that didn't quite match the sympathetic glance he threw my way.
I slipped on the forensic booties with practised ease, followed by a hair net that threatened to tame my unruly dark locks—ha, good luck with that—and finally pulled on the latex gloves until they hugged my hands like a second skin. At the door, I found Martinez, his face a mask of professionalism that barely concealed the grimness in his eyes.
"Martinez," I greeted, tilting my head in acknowledgment. "So, what do we have?"
He exhaled sharply, passing over the pleasantries. "White male, late 60s, name's Henry Hamilton works at the local hardware shop," Martinez began, his words clipped. "Looks like someone used his head for batting practice. And well... let's just say there's a knife involved in a very personal way."
"Christ." I ran a hand down my face, feeling the stubble scratch against my palm. "His dick?"
"Speared to the table," Martinez confirmed, and I could hear the subtle strain in his voice despite his stoic front.
"Damn... that's one hell of a 'Fuck You' to go out on," I mused aloud, trying to keep the mood from sinking into the abyss. But even my flirtation with dark humour felt hollow.
"Neighbour says they carpool together. Found him this morning." Martinez's gaze flickered away, then back to mine.
"All right, let's take a look at what we're dealing with."

"Follow me. Watch your step," Martinez warned, leading the way.

"Always do," I shot back, though my bravado was starting to wear thin. These scenes, they always took a piece of you—nibbled away at your soul like a starved rat. And yet, here I was, walking into another nightmare because someone had to make sense of the senseless.

Following the path laid out in tape, my mind already racing with the questions I'd need answers to. Who hated Henry Hamilton enough to turn his death into a spectacle? How deep did the darkness go in this quiet slice of suburbia?

"Long day ahead, partner," Martinez said, echoing my thoughts as we approached the threshold.

"Long day, indeed," I agreed, bracing myself for the grisly tableau that awaited us inside.

Stepping over the threshold, I was slammed by the coppery stench of blood—a surefire way to kill any appetite. It clung to the air like an unwelcome guest, and there it was—the body. The sight was something out of a butcher shop nightmare. Henry Hamilton's head had been reduced to a crushed melon, his brain matter splattered across the walls and floor in a grotesque Rorschach test.

"Shit, what the fuck..." My voice barely carried over the ringing silence that followed my curse. I'd seen my fair share of bodies, but this? This was a new brand of horror. "I mean, whoever did this was angry, a deep type of anger."

"Anger?" Martinez snorted softly, "That's putting it mildly."

I approached the corpse, careful not to disturb the evidence. The old man's penis was pinned to the table with a kitchen knife, displayed like a perverse trophy. My stomach churned, but I kept my face stoic.

"Anyone else lives here?" I managed, my tone steadier than I felt.

"Nope, his wife died, so it's just him," Martinez replied, thumbing through his notes.

The image before me seared into my memory; it'd be a mainstay in my nocturnal reruns for weeks. I swallowed hard, trying to keep my breakfast where it belonged. Whoever orchestrated this little display of rage wasn't going to be an easy nut to crack. And something told me this was only the overture to a symphony of madness.

"Shit," I exhale, a plume of breath fogging in the crisp morning air. The scene inside had been enough to suck the warmth right out of my bones.

"Long case?" Martinez asks, his brows knitting together above tired eyes as he watches me step back from the threshold, peeling off gloves that were starting to stick to my skin like a second, sweat-slicked layer.

"Feels like it." My voice is low, a reluctant admission. "This isn't just some random act of violence. It's personal, theatrical even." I gesture vaguely with a nod towards the house, not wanting to paint that picture again in front of my eyes.

"Could be a message," Martinez muses, flipping his notepad shut with a snap that seems too loud in the hush that follows horror.

"Or someone's twisted idea of art." I can't help the shiver that runs down my spine at the thought, and I turn away, giving myself a moment under the guise of inspecting the perimeter. The grass is dew-kissed, the sun casting long shadows that feel like they're reaching for us with cold fingers.

"Hey, Dimitri," Martinez calls after a beat, "you okay?"

"Never better," I lie, flashing him a grin that doesn't quite reach my eyes. "Just thinking about what kind of sick fuck we're dealing with."

"Let's hope it's not a series," he says, and I can hear the edge of concern in his voice.

"Here's to hoping." But even as I say it, there's a sinking feeling in my gut that tells me we're not going to be that lucky. Whoever did this didn't seem like the type to stop at a one-hit wonder.

"Alright, let's canvas the area, and talk to the neighbours," I suggest, slipping into work mode like a comfortable pair of jeans. "Maybe someone saw or heard something useful."

"Already on it," Martinez replies, thumbing through his notes once more before heading off to do just that.

Left alone, I glance back at the house, its windows like unblinking eyes holding secrets I'm not sure I want to know. The foreboding sense of this being only the beginning sits heavy in my chest.

A crow caws overhead, and I watch it circle before it disappears beyond the tree-line, taking with it the last shred of normalcy this day might have held. I shake my head; there's no room for superstition when you've got a killer to catch.

Chapter 31

Tuesday May

The door creaked open, like the first note of a forgotten symphony, as I stepped into the mausoleum that was Mom's bedroom. Mr Thompson, ever the silent shadow, followed suit, his eyes scanning the room with practised indifference.

"Wow," I muttered, "It's like stepping into a dollhouse." Dark timber furniture clawed at the pastel walls—a twisted contrast to my own taste for minimalist darkness. The Queen Anne bedside tables were like sentinels flanking the four-poster bed, its pink and white linens too pristine, too untouched.

"Indeed, Miss May," said Mr. Thompson, his voice a soft echo in the floral-scented air. "A room frozen in time."

I couldn't help but roll my eyes. "More like frozen in a nightmare of frills and ruffles."

We moved through the space, our shadows dancing across the shelves that lined the walls. Books spilled over the edges, a cascade of knowledge and escapism that had been left to gather dust. An armoire stood nearby, its doors slightly ajar as if it yearned to spill its secrets.

"Looks like Mom was preparing for an episode of 'Hoarders: Victorian Edition,'" I quipped, trying not to sneeze from the perfume of age that wafted from every crevice.

"Your mother had eclectic tastes," Mr. Thompson observed, his fingertips grazing a spine-bound classic. "She found comfort in these pages."

"Eclectic?" I cocked an eyebrow. "That's one way to put it. I call it 'old lady chic'." I brushed my fingers along the bookshelf, leaving a line in the dust—my mark on this untouchable shrine.

"Shall we commence with the sorting, Miss Tuesday?" His voice barely broke the heavy silence that blanketed the room.

"Let's do it," I said, more to myself than to him. "Out with the old, in with...well, anything that doesn't look like it belongs to Marie Antoinette's ghost."

As we waded through the sea of femininity, the stark absence of anything that felt remotely like the woman I've become—or am trying to be—was jarring. No sleek lines or bold contrasts here; just the soft curvature of a life that wasn't mine.

"Your father," Mr. Thompson started, then stopped, as if catching himself. He never did speak much about Dad,

always kept his thoughts tucked away, ironed flat like the linens before us.
These relics, they weren't just remnants of her existence; they were proof of her disappearance—a disappearance that left me questioning the fabric of our family tapestry. But beneath it all, I couldn't shake the feeling there was something more, something hidden beneath the layers of silk and page.
"Alright, let's see what sort of skeletons the armoire's hiding," I said with a smirk, rolling up the sleeves of my shirt. Mr. Thompson, ever the silent partner in crime, simply nodded and opened the doors with a flourish fit for a stage magician.
I pulled out dresses and coats, each more delicate and dainty than the last. "God, did she wear anything that didn't scream 'damsel in distress'?" I muttered under my breath. There was the scent of lavender sachets and a hint of her perfume, a ghostly reminder that lingered like cobwebs.
"Your mother had quite the collection," Mr. Thompson observed, his voice betraying no emotion as he helped me pile the garments into boxes for donation.
"Collection?" I scoffed, yanking out a particularly frilly blouse. "This is less 'collection' and more...costume wardrobe for a Victorian melodrama." Not a single item sparked joy, nor a whisper of intrigue. Just fabric and memories, all destined for someone else's story.
"Next up, the literary fortress!" I announced with a forced cheer, marching towards the bookshelves. I imagined myself

an intrepid explorer, braving the dense jungle of romance novels and poetry anthologies.
"Any first editions, you reckon?" I called over to Mr. Thompson as I tugged at a volume of Shakespeare's sonnets so tightly wedged it seemed to protest its own removal.
"Unlikely," he replied, dust motes dancing in the beam of sunlight as he flipped through a leather-bound book.
"Damn," I sighed, hoping for some long-lost manuscript worth millions—or at least a scandalous love letter. Instead, it was just page after page of unblemished text, the margins void of secrets or scribbles.
"Empty-handed again, huh?" I dropped the last book on the growing pile bound for the second-hand store. "I thought for sure we'd uncover at least one racy historical romance tucked away. You know, Lady Chatterley's Lover hidden behind the Bible or something equally cliché."
"Perhaps your mother was less secretive than we thought, Miss May," Mr. Thompson suggested, closing the cover on another fruitless find.
"Or maybe she was better at hiding things than we thought," I countered with a wink, though the hollow feeling in my chest begged to differ.
"Alright, a fortress of solitude, your secrets are mine," I muttered, eyeing the four-poster bed like it was the final boss in a game of domestic espionage. I gripped the pink and white linen, the fabric a stark contrast to my preferred shades of

midnight and onyx. Yanking back the bedding with more force than necessary, I exposed the mattress beneath—a barren landscape devoid of intrigue.
"Expecting a treasure map?" Mr. Thompson quipped, his arms crossed, an amused smirk tugging at the corner of his mouth.
"Treasure, skeletons, hell, even a diary filled with teenage angst. Anything to make this snooze-fest worthwhile." I flopped onto the edge of the now naked mattress, watching a small puff of dust rise up like a ghost disturbed from slumber. "Instead, nada. Zip. Zilch," I continued, drumming my fingers against the bare springs of the bed frame. "It's so... clean. Like, annoyingly clean."
Mr. Thompson approached, running a hand along the polished wood of the bedpost. "Sometimes the best place to hide something is in plain sight, Miss May."
"Or maybe she knew Dad would look here," I mused aloud. "Knew he'd rip this room apart looking for... I don't know what. A sign? An explanation? Anything that hints at why Mom bolted and left him wondering his whole life."
"Tuesday—" Mr. Thompson started, but the sound of heavy footsteps interrupted him.
"Removalists," I announced, standing up as two burly men entered, ready to whisk away the remnants of Lady Lillian Wellington's existence. They grunted acknowledgments,

moving to the bookcases first, sliding them away from the walls with practised ease.

"Careful with those, will ya?" I called out half-heartedly. "They're antiques or some shit."

"Got it, lady," one of them said with a nod before he froze, his gaze fixed on something behind where the bookcase stood moments ago.

"Hey, what's this?" the other removalist said, reaching down and pulling out a stack of weathered leather journals. My heart skipped a beat, something akin to excitement—or was it dread?—fluttering in my stomach.

"Shit, jackpot," I exclaimed, snatching the journals from his rough hands. "These must be..."

"Your mother's," Mr. Thompson finished, peering over my shoulder with a reverence that bordered on sacred.

The journals felt heavy in my grip, saturated with the essence of a woman I didn't know. The embossed covers were worn at the edges, the pages tinged with the sepia tone of secrets long kept. I fanned through them quickly, my eyes catching snippets of the elegant script that danced across the paper like some kind of cryptic ballet.

"Look at that penmanship," Mr. Thompson murmured from over my shoulder—close enough that I could feel his breath stir my hair. "That's definitely your mother's handwriting."

"Lillian had class," I said, more to myself than to him, as I traced the loops and flourishes of ink with my finger. "Let's hope she had some juicy secrets to match."
"Indeed," he replied, his voice tinged with a respect that bordered on reverence. "I'm sure you will find everything written in these."
"Secrets, lies, or an old grocery list—I'll take anything at this point." The corners of my lips curled up into a half-smile. I clutched the journals tighter, the thrill of the chase igniting something wild within me.
"Be careful, Miss May," Mr. Thompson warned, a hint of caution lacing his words as he straightened up. "Sometimes the past has claws."
"Good thing I like a little scratch." I winked at him before turning on my heel, my boots clicking against the hardwood floor as I made my way to the murder room—a place that felt more mine than anywhere else in this mausoleum of a house.
Once inside, I ran my hand along the familiar cold metal of the new filing cabinets, the dim light from the single bulb overhead casting long shadows across the room. It was my sanctuary of sleuthing, where every curiosity could be dissected, every mystery unravelled. And now, it would hold my mother's enigmatic words.
"Sorry, lovelies," I cooed to the journals as I found them a temporary home in the top drawer of the cabinet. "You'll have

to wait your turn." I lock the drawer with a satisfying click, sealing away the potential bombshells for just a bit longer.
I sauntered back into what was once the forbidden garden of my mother's existence, her room now stripped bare, a tabula rasa save for the vintage rug lying like a slumbering beast on the polished floor. Mr. Thompson, in his butler's stoicism, joins me at one end of the rug, and together we roll it up, the old fabric crackling in protest.
"Expecting a trap door, Miss May?" Mr. Thompson's voice is dry as he catches my hopeful gaze darting across the exposed floorboards.
"Wouldn't that be something," I quip back, not quite ready to let go of the fantasy. "But no, just the last act of a daughter playing detective."
We scour the room with methodical thoroughness, lifting, tapping, searching for hollows, for seams, for anything that might hint at hidden treasures. But all we unearth is the lingering scent of lavender and dust motes dancing in the shafts of light — the ghosts of a past life.
A sigh escapes me, the dusty air filling my lungs with resignation. All we had were those journals, leather-bound enigmas waiting to be unravelled.
"Shall we head down for dinner?" Mr. Thompson gestures towards the door, ever the faithful timekeeper.
"Lead the way, Jeeves," I say, with a half-smile that doesn't reach my eyes.

Dinner is a blur of cutlery and chewing. Each bite is mechanical, my mind already upstairs in the locked drawer, picking at the edges of my mother's words. I'm shovelling in the last forkful of salad when my phone vibrates against the tablecloth.

"Go ahead, Miss May. It might be important," Mr Thompson nods towards the insistent device.

"Hey, Sweetness," Dimitri's voice is a warm balm, even if tinged with the weariness of his work.

"Hey yourself," I answer, trying to keep the flirtatious lilt alive despite the butterflies doing kamikaze dives in my stomach. "Everything okay?"

"Ah, you know, just another murder case keeping me late. The usual romantic evening plans," he says, and I can picture the grimace that accompanies his attempt at levity.

"Stay safe, Detective Handsome. And bring me back a story," I reply, keeping it light though part of me cringes at the casualness. I miss him, sure, but tonight, solitude feels like a guilty pleasure I want to indulge in.

"Will do, Tuesday. Lock up tight, okay?" There's that protective edge, always.

"Always do. Love you, Dimitri."

"Love you, Sweetness."

The call ends, and I'm left with the echo of his voice and a plate scraped clean. I toss a smile Mr. Thompson's way, eager

to get back to those journals, to that locked room where secrets wait patiently for my prying eyes.
"Thank you for dinner, Mrs Collins. It was... nourishing." I push back from the table, feeling the pull of the unread pages.
"Of course, Miss May. Do take care this evening," she says, with a knowing glance.
"Like a cat, always landing on her feet," I assure her, already halfway to reclaiming the key from its hiding place. My mother's words are a siren song, and I am all too willing to crash upon their shores.
Climbing into bed, the journals clutched like a lifeline in my hands, I flip to page one. It's dated 25 years ago—the ink faded but still legible. The handwriting is elegant, loops and swirls of a bygone era, speaking of love penned down with youthful exuberance.
"George," the name written with a flourish that makes my heart clench, "you have turned my world into a canvas painted with the colours of passion and tenderness." My mother's words leap off the page, vibrant and full of life, painting a picture of a love so fierce it could burn the stars.
"Sweet George, how you dance around me, a gentle orbit, always pulling me closer. Your touch ignites fires that I never knew lay dormant." I can almost hear her laughter between the lines, the warmth of her voice as she recounts days drenched in sunlight and nights alight with desire.

Halfway through the journal, though, the narrative shifts, like a play where the backdrop suddenly darkens. "Lately, George seems... altered. He flinches at the thought of me wandering the grounds alone, insists on being my shadow, yet the door to his second office remains ever shut—a barrier he claims is work, but feels far more sinister."

I bite my lip, turning the pages with fingers that now tremble slightly. "Trapped" is the word she uses next; like a bird in a gilded cage, her wings clipped by the man who once swore to be her sky. "Why does he change our rules? Why does the very air feel heavier, laced with something unsaid?"

The room is too quiet, each creak a whisper of secrets long buried. As I reach the final entries, the sudden crunch of tyres against gravel cuts through the silence—Dimitri. With a start, I stash the journal's back in its hiding place next door, feeling like a thief in my own home.

"Hey, you still up?" Dimitri's voice carries through the darkness as he enters, his presence a balm to the chaos of my thoughts.

"Uh-huh, just couldn't sleep," I murmur, shifting to make room for him.

"Rough day?" I ask as he sheds his clothes, the weariness in his movements evident even in the dim light.

"Understatement of the year," he sighs, sliding into bed beside me. His arms envelop me, strong and reassuring. "But right now, this is exactly where I need to be."

"Me too," I confess, snuggling closer, the scent of his cologne mingling with the faint mustiness of old paper still clinging to my skin.
"Tell me about your day," I prompt, eager to lose myself in his stories rather than dwell on my mother's.
"Let's not," he whispers, pressing a kiss to my forehead. "Some things are better left outside the bedroom. Tonight, let's just be us."
"Deal," I agree, a sense of peace settling over me as we drift into sleep, wrapped up in each other's arms, away from nightmares and ghostly words of the past.

Chapter 32

Dimitri Costa

The scent of the dark roast invaded my senses before the bitter warmth even touched my lips. I leaned back in my squeaky office chair, savouring the first sip like a lifeline as I braced myself for the day.

"Early bird gets the worm, huh, Costa?" Martinez sauntered over, his voice gravel mixed with amusement. The overhead fluorescents glinted off his badge, reminding me that the job never really sleeps—you just doze off and hope the phone doesn't ring.

"Or the last cup of good coffee," I replied, tilting my mug in a mock salute. There's something about the precinct at this hour, a quiet hum that's almost peaceful—if you can ignore the undercurrent of last night's misdemeanours hanging in the air.

"Leave any for me, or am I stuck with the sludge again?"

"First come, first served," I shot back with a grin. I watched him pour himself a cup of the tar-like remnants, his nose crinkling in disgust. Detective Martinez—man could sniff out a clue better than a bloodhound, yet he couldn't tell a decent brew from mud.
"Christ, Dimitri, you're merciless." He knocked back the coffee like a shot of cheap whiskey, grimacing. "So, are we cracking this bastard wide open today or what?"
"Plan on it." I leaned forward, elbows on my desk, meeting his determined gaze. Martinez was a force of nature; hurricane might be a more fitting description. But hell if he wasn't one of the best. I thumbed through the case notes, feeling the familiar itch of anticipation.
"Any bright ideas on how to start charming the truth out of this mess?" His question hung between us, though we both knew the dance too well—the push and pull of interrogation, the silent language of crime scenes.
"Charm's your department, Martinez," I quipped, even though the guy had the subtlety of a sledgehammer. "I'll stick with the tried-and-true method of actually looking at the evidence."
"Touché," he said with a chuckle, leaning against my desk, his eyes scanning the room as he could already see the pieces falling into place. It was part of his magic, seeing the invisible threads that connected everything, that led us down the rabbit hole to the cold, hard truth.

"Listen, when you've got the instincts I have" —he tapped his temple— "you don't need charm."
"Instincts, right..." I muttered, smirking. The man was cocky, but he had every damn right to be. In another life, he'd have made a hell of a poker player.
"Let's cut the crap and dive in, yeah? I want this sicko behind bars before they get a taste for it." His playful tone belted out the seriousness of his words. For all his bravado, Martinez had a heart that bled blue through and through.
"Agreed. Let's not keep our date with the coroner waiting." I pushed up from my seat, tossing back the last of my coffee and hoping it carried enough kick to keep up with Martinez's relentless pace.
"Traffic gods willing?" I quipped, grabbing my jacket from the back of the chair. The city had a way of turning minutes into hours.
"Let's roll the dice and hope they're feeling generous today." He slapped the desk with an open palm, already halfway to the door.
The patrol car felt like an old friend as we eased into its familiar embrace, the leather seats conforming to our well-worn grooves. We hit the road, Martinez behind the wheel, his fingers drumming an impatient rhythm on the steering column.

The city loomed ahead, buildings clawing at the sky. It was a steel beast, alive and indifferent to the dramas unfolding within its belly.
"Twenty-five minutes if we're lucky," I calculated aloud, watching the snarl of traffic ebb and flow like a hesitant tide.
"Optimist," Martinez grunted, but he expertly wove through the lanes, cutting precious seconds off our journey.
Stepping out of the patrol car, the city's pulse thrummed beneath our feet. The coroner's office stood like a silent monolith—a place where secrets were stripped bare and laid out for cold examination.
"Time to dance with the dead," Martinez said, a morbid invitation hanging between us as I followed him through the glass sliding doors.
The sterile chill of the room greeted us like a slap—antiseptic and final. The coroner, a compact old man with salt-and-pepper hair, turned to us with a grin that belied his grim profession.
"Detectives, you're right on time!" He extended a hand that had known more death than most could handle.
"Morning, Doc. You always know how to give a warm welcome," I said, shaking his hand.
"Only the best for my boys in blue," he chuckled, swearing colourfully as he stubbed his toe against the foot of a stainless-steel table. "Fucking hell. Let's get down to business, shall we?"

"Lead the way," Martinez said, his voice brimming with a respect reserved for those who spoke the language of the dead.
We stood shoulder to shoulder, Martinez, the coroner, and I, forming a triad around the body that held the answers we sought.
"Blunt force trauma to the cranium," he said, pointing to the grotesquely deformed head. "Consistent with a tire iron, similar to the one found at the scene." He enunciated each word as if it were a sacrament. "Skull fragments indicate multiple impacts—enough to liquefy brain matter."
"Jesus," I muttered under my breath, swallowing down the bile that threatened to rise. The sight was a special kind of hell, but I prided myself on having a stomach as sturdy as my resolve. Still, there are some things you can't unsee.
"Genital mutilation perimortem," the coroner went on, not missing a beat. "Clean cut, straight edge blade, akin to the kitchen knife wedged into... Well, you see where." His hand fluttered briefly towards the bloodied mess between the victim's thighs before he moved on.
"Any idea on the knots?" Martinez asked, squatting to inspect the bindings that held the victim’s wrists and ankles.
"Ah, now that's an interesting tidbit," the coroner said with a spark of grisly enthusiasm. "These are bowline knots—common among sailors. Pretty secure stuff."

"Someone with sea legs, then," I chimed in, trying to keep the mood from sinking too deep into the abyss.

"Or someone who's good with rope," Martinez added, eyes narrowing thoughtfully.

"Could be your killer's calling card," the coroner suggested, scrubbing a hand across his stubble.

"Alright, let's head upstairs to the lab," I said, clapping Martinez on the shoulder as we backed away from the table. "Maybe they've got something to make our day."

"Hope springs eternal, Dimitri," Martinez replied, his voice tinged with the weariness that came from too many bodies and not enough answers.

"Hey, maybe our perp left us a love note in invisible ink," I joked, because what else could you do but laugh in the face of death's ghoulish dance?

"Or a treasure map," Martinez quipped back, but the set of his jaw told me he was already piecing together the puzzle, knot by bloody knot.

"X marks the spot, partner," I said, as we exited the chill of the morgue for the relative warmth of the hallway, heading for the forensic lab.

The fluorescent lights hummed a monotonous tune as we entered the forensic lab. The place always had that clinical, antiseptic smell that seemed to scrub away any trace of the outside world. I watched the techs move about with an efficiency that was both impressive and slightly robotic.

"Costa, Martinez," greeted our lead forensic analyst, her eyes tired behind her glasses. "We're still sifting through everything, but we've got some tidbits for you."

"Hit us with it," I said, leaning against a stainless-steel counter, my gaze tracing the room's organised chaos.

She handed us a printout, pointing at two distinct footprints. "Here. The killer's likely over six feet, based on stride and impression depth. And this," she tapped on the smaller footprint, "suggests a female—or someone with very dainty feet for a dude."

"Any chance these smaller ones are from the neighbour?" Martinez inquired, his brow furrowing as he studied the measurements.

"Unlikely. His prints were found out back; bigger, work boots type. We'll need to confirm his shoe size though, to see if they match up."

"Nothing on prints or DNA yet?" I pushed off the counter, my mind already racing through scenarios. It was like hunting ghosts sometimes, chasing after shadowy figures that slipped just out of grasp.

"Still looking. The scene is clean. Either our perp is good, or they got lucky." She shrugged. "But luck eventually runs out."

"Doesn't it just," I muttered, the frustration nipping at my patience. "Alright, let's go have a chat with the neighbour. See if Cinderella left us a glass slipper."

"Or a steel-toed boot," Martinez added, folding the paper and tucking it into his jacket.

"Glass slippers don't suit the neighbourhood anyway," I quipped, pushing through the door to head back downstairs. "More like worn sneakers with holes."

"Those would be your sneakers, Costa," Martinez shot back with a smirk.

"Hey, they're vintage," I defended, my lips twitching. "Adds character."

"Sure," he chuckled. "Let's hope our neighbour's footwear is in better condition."

"Size matters, after all," I said, hitting the button for the elevator, and when the doors opened, we stepped inside. "Especially in a murder investigation."

"Very profound, Detective Costa," Martinez deadpanned, and I couldn't help but grin.

"Years of wisdom, partner," I said, as the doors closed on us, sealing us together in our own little world of crime and conjecture.

The elevator dinged at the basement floor, and we stepped out into the parking lot.

"Costa," Martinez said as we wove through the parked cars, his voice cutting through the din. "You think this is personal? Our Vic, Henry Hamilton—he wasn't exactly Mister Congeniality."

"Personal?" I quipped, stepping over a random puddle, "With a guy like Hamilton? Could be his mailman for all we know."

"True," he conceded, tugging at his tie, which always seemed to strangle him more than adorn him. "But considering the, uh, 'surgical removal' job... if a female did this, we might be looking at someone scorned."

"Like an ex-girlfriend firestorm. Hell hath no fury," I mused aloud.

"Exactly. We should dig into his past. Since his wife kicked the bucket, who knows what kind of skeletons are rattling in his closet." Martinez nudged me with his elbow, a silent signal that he was onto something.

"Maybe Hamilton played fast and loose, pissed off the wrong woman," I said, "I say we grab his files, see who he's been cozying up to since Mrs H took the eternal nap."

"Could give us our why," Martinez agreed, his eyes sharp beneath furrowed brows. "And maybe even our who."

"Can't hurt to look." My brain started to tick, piecing together potential scenarios. A jealous lover, a spurned fling, a revenge plot—the possibilities were as tantalising as they were twisted.

"Alright, so background check on Hamilton it is. Let's see what kind of dirty laundry we can air out." Martinez's grin was all business, the thrill of the hunt evident in his stance.

"Nothing like airing some dirty boxers to brighten up your day." Laughter bubbled up in my chest, a needed release from the darkness we'd been steeped in since dawn.
"Let's just hope they lead us to our Cinderella before she disappears at midnight," he said, opening the door to the car and sliding in.

Chapter 33

Tuesday May

The air in the murder room was always cooler, a permanent chill that seemed to seep from the walls themselves, as if they were steeped in secrets and silent screams. I sat there, legs tucked beneath me on the plush chair that contrasted sharply with the room's purpose, flipping through one of my mother's journals. Her neat script danced across the pages, a waltz of words that I was desperately trying to follow.

"Your lunch, Miss May," Mr. Thompson announced, his voice as crisp as the white shirt he wore beneath his impeccably tailored suit. He entered with the grace of a man who knew how to move silently, setting down a tray with a porcelain plate of sandwiches and a crystal glass filled with iced tea beside the scattered journals.

"Find anything exciting yet?" His question was casual, but the undercurrent of curiosity was unmistakable.

"Nothing but the usual parental love story turned twisted thriller," I said, tapping the edge of the leather-bound book. "It's like one day he just snapped—Dad went full-on psycho, started seeing shadows in Mom's every move."

"Paranoia is a peculiar beast," Mr. Thompson mused, leaning against the dark mahogany desk. "It creeps up, unannounced, and sinks its claws in deep."

"Tell me about it." I sighed, brushing a lock of hair behind my ear. "One minute he's Prince Charming, the next he's the Big Bad Wolf." I glanced up at him with a smirk. "But you know all about playing multiple roles, don't you, Mr. T?"

"Indeed, Miss May," he replied, the corner of his mouth twitching in amusement. "I wear many hats, as it seems I have adorned a new one recently to"

"Add 'detective' to that list as well," I quipped, taking a dainty bite of my sandwich. The crunch of fresh lettuce and the tang of mustard hit my tongue.

"Indeed," he echoed, eyes glinting with a shared understanding of the darkness we were wading through. "And perhaps one day, we'll unravel the mystery of George Wellington's descent into madness."

"Here's hoping," I murmured, my gaze returning to the journal. "Because right now, it's like looking for a black cat in a coal cellar."

"Patience and perseverance, Miss May," Mr. Thompson advised, straightening up. "They often illuminate the darkest corners."
"Let's hope they do it before I lose my damn mind too," I said with a laugh that didn't quite reach my eyes.
"Sanity is overrated" — Mr. Thompson's laughed.
I traced the faded lines of my mother's handwriting, each word a breadcrumb leading me through the labyrinth of my father's psyche. "He was always a bit off-centre," I mused aloud, the journal resting on my lap. "But he adored her—worshipped the ground she walked on. Then, like a switch flipped, he just... snapped."
Mr. Thompson leaned against the doorframe, his presence a comforting shadow in the dimly lit room. "It's quite the conundrum," he said, the words hanging between us like an unsolved riddle.
"Conundrum is putting it lightly," I scoffed, flipping another page. "It's like trying to piece together a jigsaw puzzle with half the pieces missing."
"Perhaps the missing pieces lie elsewhere." He straightened, brows furrowing in thought. "Your father's room, perhaps?"
"God, that place..." I shivered at the thought of the mannequins posed like silent sentinels around his personal museum of madness. "That room gives me the creeps."
"I'll ensure they're removed before you set foot in there," Mr. Thompson assured, already plotting the logistics in his head.

"Thanks, Mr. T. You're a real knight in shining armour." My voice dripped with sarcasm, but there was genuine gratitude beneath it.
"Speaking of quests," he ventured with a hint of caution, "are you planning another outing soon?"
"Ah, yes," I said, my lips curling into a smile that didn't quite reach my eyes. "The Kents are due for a visit—an hour's drive from here. A little family reunion, you might say, complicated by their living arrangements"
"Complicated how?" Mr. Thompson's tone was light, but there was steel behind it.
"They bunk with their night owl son now," I replied,
"Nighttime is the right time," I mused aloud, tapping a finger against my chin. "Their son works the graveyard shift, which means the Kents are ripe for the picking."
"Under cover of darkness, then." Mr. Thompson's voice sliced through the silence, a smooth blade sharpened with intent. He stood there, the loyal butler, his eyes betraying nothing of the storm brewing behind them.
"Exactly. But that leaves me with one hell of a question—how do I slip away without Dimitri sniffing out my little escapade?" I leaned back in my chair, the leather creaking a soft protest.
"Perhaps something a touch more... medicinal might aid in ensuring Detective Costa's slumber," Mr. Thompson offered, his brows arching just so.

"Drugging Dimitri? Now that's low, even for me" I frowned at the thought. "No, I need to play this smarter."

"Then perhaps a business trip is in order. A little getaway from dear Dimitri under the guise of liquidating the family assets?" There it was—that sly twinkle in Mr. Thompson's eye.

"Ooh, now you're talking my language!" Excitement bubbled up inside me like champagne fizz. "A legitimate trip out of town, sign some papers, shake some hands, and while everyone's sleeping soundly, I'll be off playing the vengeful foster child."

"Should I set it up?" Mr. Thompson asked, already halfway to making it happen.

"Make it happen, Jeeves," I said with a wink, using the nickname I knew irked him.

"Or better yet," Mr Thompson's voice cut through the room, his smile devilish as his eyes met mine, "Let's give the Kent's son a holiday. A return trip to Bali for a week?" He leaned against the door frame, casual as sin. "There should be cash stashed in the main safe we could use. Set it up as a fake competition at his work."

I paused, my fingers hovering over the yellowed pages of my mother's journal. The idea was genius—sinister and sweet like a forbidden fruit. It might take longer, but it would mean we could do everything in broad daylight, with Dimitri none the wiser.

"Fuck me sideways, that's brilliant." I couldn't help but admire the devious spark in Mr. Thompson's eye. "You're not just a pretty face and a crisp suit, are you?"
"Only on Sundays," he quipped, the ghost of a smirk playing on his lips. "Shall I arrange it?"
"Make it so," I said, leaning back in my chair, the leather creaking under my weight. My heart thrummed with excitement—a deadly dance I was all too eager to lead. "And while you're at it, please liberate my father's room from those creepy-ass mannequins. We'll tackle that horror show tomorrow."
"Consider it done, Miss May." Mr. Thompson dipped his head, already plotting the logistics in his meticulous mind.
"Tuesday," I corrected him, the informality rolling off my tongue as easily as the lies we spun.
"Tuesday," he echoed, a hint of warmth seeping into his otherwise frosty demeanour.
With a nod, he vanished, leaving me alone with the ghosts of ink and paper. I turned back to my mother's words, her elegant script weaving tales of a gilded cage. So far, she had only chronicled the house arrest my father imposed upon her—the true horror, the abuse, was an unwritten storm looming on the horizon.
My eyes traced the loops and lines of her handwriting, each word a breadcrumb leading me deeper into the labyrinth of my family's past. Yet even as I delved into the darkness of my

mother's journals, part of me lingered on the plan brewing, on the thrill of the hunt.

Chapter 34

Tuesday May

The moon hung low and heavy, a silver eye peering through the gauzy curtains of my bedroom. I lay sprawled on the bed, legs tangled in sheets that still held the scent of Dimitri's cologne. He'd kissed me with those warm brown eyes before he left, whispering "Stay out of trouble, Sweetness" like he always did. But as the grandfather clock chimed down the hall, each toll echoed my mounting curiosity.

"Come on, Dimitri..." I muttered to myself, tracing the outline of the cool metallic lamp base beside me. The case he was working on consumed him, and it gnawed at me too. Not because of the late hours or the missed dinners, but because of a nagging itch in my gut—one that whispered the name Henry Hamilton in hushed, venomous tones.

I fluffed the pillow behind my head, trying to shake off the unease. *Maybe he'll slip up, give me something to go on.* I

knew better than to hope; Dimitri guarded his cases like family secrets. Still, I couldn't help but wonder if the man I'd snuffed out—Hamilton, that vile creature—was sprawled across my boyfriend's case files without either of them knowing it.
"Shit," I sighed, rising from the bed to pace the room. My bare feet padded across the plush carpet.
It must've been past midnight when I heard the front door creak open and close, the sound muffled but unmistakable. My heart gave a traitorous leap.
"Sweetness?" Dimitri's voice floated up the staircase, husky and tired. I slipped on a dressing gown, not bothering with the tie, and darted downstairs.
"Hey, Detective Late Night," I greeted him with a cocked hip and a smirk, watching as he shrugged off his coat. "Catch any bad guys?"
"Something like that." He offered a weary smile, but his eyes were sharp, scanning me as if I were a puzzle he couldn't quite solve. "Why are you still up? You should be sleeping."
"Could say the same to you, couldn't I?" I sidled up to him, looping my arms around his neck. The familiar smell of his skin chased away the chill of the night. "Besides, I wanted to ask about your day... or night, rather."
"Tuesday," he said, a note of caution threading his tone. He searched my face, looking for what, I wasn't sure.

"Relax, I'm just being nosy." I tapped his nose with my finger, feigning innocence. "Can't a girlfriend take an interest in her boyfriend's work?"
"An interest, huh?" His hands found my waist, thumbs stroking softly. "You know I can't talk much about it."
"Much leaves room for a little." I pouted playfully, though my heart hammered.
"Sweetness, you have a way with words," he chuckled, pulling me closer.
"Come on, let's get some sleep," he said, kissing the top of my head.
"Race you to the bed?" I suggested, already knowing I'd win.
"Only if I get to catch you," he replied with a grin that promised more than sleep, and together we stumbled toward the stairs, and up to our room.
The glow of the bedside lamp cast a soft golden hue over Dimitri's features, accentuating the weariness etched into his rugged face. I propped myself up on one elbow, watching him as he loosened his tie with a sigh.
"Rough night?" I murmured, tracing patterns on the duvet to distract myself from the gnawing curiosity.
"You could say that," he replied, tossing his tie onto the dresser. He slumped down beside me, the bed dipping under his weight.
"Tell me about it?" I asked, trying to keep my voice light despite the storm of thoughts raging in my mind.

"Tuesday, you know I can't—" he started, but I cut him off with a soft peck on his lips.
"Please? Just a snippet?" I pleaded, batting my lashes at him. "I promise I'll be your favourite distraction afterwards."
He chuckled, the sound rumbling deep in his chest, and I felt a thrill knowing I could coax that out of him. "Alright, Sweetness, just a bit then." He ran a hand through his hair, looking into my eyes. "It was brutal—a man beaten to death with a tire iron."
My breath hitched slightly, but I masked it with a practised smile. "Sounds like something out of a horror flick."
"Kind of is," he said, his gaze darkening. "The footprints around the body... they're from a woman. Small size. It's got us thinking we might be dealing with a serial killer."
"Jesus, that's intense," I managed, my heart pounding against my ribcage. *A woman's footprints...* A shiver ran down my spine despite the warmth of the room.
"Intense doesn't quite cover it," he agreed, his warm brown eyes searching mine. "The lack of empathy needed to do something like that... It points to some serious mental issues. Whoever did this could very well be on the path to becoming a serial killer."
"Serial killer," I echoed, my voice airy as I tucked a stray strand of hair behind my ear. The term felt alien and yet not entirely unsuitable, like a dress I'd never wear in public but kept hidden in my closet just because it fit so well.

"Terrifying thought," Dimitri continued, oblivious to the storm brewing inside me. "To think someone could be so... unfeeling."
I hummed in agreement, tracing a pattern on the back of his hand with my fingertip. The cool metal of the tire iron still seemed to linger there, a ghostly weight in my palm. "Yeah, you'd have to be pretty messed up in the head, huh?"
"Absolutely," he said, pulling me closer, his arm warm around my shoulders. His touch was meant to comfort me, but all it did was remind me of the power that surged through me when I swung that iron.
"Speaking of messed up..." I started, tilting my head to study his face, "How's your day been otherwise? Catch any bad guys, or just chasing after potential psychos?"
Dimitri laughed, a rich sound that always made my heart flutter. "Oh, you know, the usual. Paperwork, leads, more paperwork. The glamorous life of a detective."
"Sounds enthralling," I teased, pressing a quick kiss to his cheek. My mind, however, was racing. As much as I wanted to lose myself in him, in us, I couldn't shake the knowledge that bubbled under my skin – the knowledge of what I had done, of what I was capable of.
"Hey, what's on your mind?" he asked, peering down at me with concern etched into his brow.
"Nothing," I lied smoothly, offering him my best innocent smile. "Just wondering if you've managed to eat today."

"Does coffee count?"
"Only in your world, Detective." I poked his chest playfully. "You should take better care of yourself."
"We don't all have a Mrs Collins," he chuckled, leaning in to steal another kiss.
"You do have a Mrs Collins," I quietly said back allowing the silence to follow.
Staring into the abyss of his brown eyes, I could tell he was worried. The furrow in Dimitri's brow deepened as he watched my silence grow like a chasm between us. "Sweetness," he said softly, a note of concern in his voice that felt like a gentle hand on a bruise. "You've gone quiet on me. Everything okay?"
"Uh-huh," I lied with a half-hearted nod, feeling the weight of tomorrow's task pressing down on me. "It's just... I'm tackling Dad's room. Kinda feels like I'm walking into the lion's den without a chair or a whip."
"Need me to clear out the mannequins?" His offer came so effortlessly like he'd take on a legion of demons for me.
"Mr. Thompson handled it." My words were clipped, but a small, grateful smile emerged at the thought of the butler's efficiency. I didn't need to see those hollow, plastic stares.
"Okay, then." He pulled me close, wrapping his arms around me. The warmth of his body was a welcome contrast to the chill creeping up my spine at the thought of facing the remnants of my father's twisted world.

His lips found mine, light as a whisper, and something inside me sparked. Enough with the fears—my lips hungered for more. I wanted to feel alive, bright, burning with something other than this cold dread. So I deepened the kiss, tasting the mix of concern and coffee lingering there.
In one swift motion, I flipped him onto his back, a playful laugh escaping me as I straddled him. My hands fumbled at the hem of my nightdress—the flimsy fabric no match for my sudden impatience—and off it went, fluttering to the floor like a discarded shadow.
"Jesus, Tuesday," Dimitri breathed out, his gaze devouring every inch of me. "I swear, I could spend forever just looking at you like this. You're stunning."
The compliment washed over me, filling some of the emptiness with a warm glow. "Don't look too long, Detective," I teased, leaning down to claim his lips once more.
His hands roamed across my skin, tracing fire wherever they touched. A shiver ran through me, but not from cold—from pure, unadulterated desire. This is what I needed—to drown in the sensation, to forget the darkness waiting to spill from my fingertips.
The heat between us was a living thing, wrapping its tendrils around my senses, making the world outside this room, this bed, fade into insignificance. I could feel every ridge and

pulse of him beneath me as I ground down, the firmness of his dick pressing insistently against my core.

"Fuck, Sweetness," he groaned his voice a rough whisper that sent a shiver of anticipation down my spine.

Leaning forward, I let my fingers trace the bulge in his boxers, teasing him through the fabric before freeing him from the confines. His dick sprang free, and I couldn't help but smirk at the effect I had on him. Clasping him firmly in my hand, I felt the silken hardness, the subtle twitching that beckoned for attention.

"Look at you, all eager for me," I murmured, letting my lips hover over the tip, tasting the salty hint of his precum. With deliberate slowness, I wrapped my mouth around him, sliding down until I felt him at the back of my throat. The groan that escaped Dimitri was music to my ears, raw and unguarded.

"Jesus, Tuesday... if you keep that up—" He didn't finish his sentence, lost in the sensation, but his hands found their way to my hair, gently guiding me.

I gave his balls a gentle squeeze, eliciting another moan from him. "What's that, Detective? Can't handle a little foreplay?"

"Get up here. Now," he demanded, his eyes dark with need.

With a final lingering suck, I released him from my mouth and clambered up his body. Positioning myself above him, I met his gaze, fierce and full of that silent communication we'd always shared. Then, without further warning, I impaled myself onto him, taking him deep inside me. The stretch, the slight burn – it was delicious.

"Ah, fuck..." I gasped, relishing the fullness, the exquisite pain that was so much better than the shadows clawing at my soul.

"Ride me, Sweetness," Dimitri encouraged, his hands firm on my hips.

I obeyed, lifting and dropping myself onto him, each movement building the pressure, the pleasure spiralling tighter within me. His hand left my hip, trailing upward to pinch a nipple sharply, and that was all it took. My orgasm hit me like a tidal wave, walls clenching around him as he thrust upward to meet me, prolonging the sweet torture.

"Tuesday," he growled, and I could feel him thicken, pulsing inside me as he came, spilling his cum within me.

"God, Tuesday," he panted as I collapsed onto his chest, spent and satisfied. "You make me feel like I'm a teenager again. All I wanna do is sink myself into your pussy and stay there for hours."

"Only hours?" I teased, breathless, tracing lazy circles on his chest. "I was hoping for days."

"Days, then," he agreed, laughter in his voice, even as his arms tightened around me. "As long as you want, Sweetness."

Chapter 35

Tuesday May

The cool morning air nipped at my cheeks as I watched Dimitri's form shrink into the distance, his car a fleeting speck on the horizon. With a sigh that carried more weight than the breeze, I turned and faced the monolithic structure of my home. The house stood silent, as if holding its breath, awaiting my next move. I squared my shoulders, sucking in a deep breath laced with the scent of dew and the faintest hint of jasmine from the garden.

"Alright, old man," I muttered to myself, referring to the ghost of my father that seemed to hover in every shadowed corner, "let's see what secrets you've left behind."

With each step up the grand staircase, the light-hearted air from my morning kiss dissipated, replaced by a sense of foreboding. My hand gripped the banister, the wood cool and unyielding beneath my touch. The door to my father's room loomed before me, a barrier to both the past and truth.

Pushing it open, the sunlight poured in through the windows, casting away some of the darkness that used to cling to the drapes like cobwebs. Mr. Thompson, ever the stoic butler, awaited me inside, his posture impeccable despite the grim task at hand.

"Tuesday the floor is yours," he intoned, his voice steady as always.

"Looks less like a horror show now that those damn mannequins are gone," I remarked, trying to keep the mood light as I stepped over the threshold.

Mr. Thompson gave a short nod, his lips twitching in what might pass for a smile on a less composed day. "Ah, yes, the mannequins. Well, their attire found a new home in a donation box. I made sure they were... unencumbered by anything hidden." His eyes darted around the room, not quite meeting mine.

"Jesus, Thompson, did you frisk them too?" I chuckled, imagining him patting down the lifeless figures with a clinical detachment.

"Quite thoroughly, Miss May. And then off to the tip they went. Couldn't very well have them scaring someone else, could we?" He paused, adding, "I wore triple-layered gloves if you must know."

"Triple? Damn, afraid they'd come to life and strangle you?" I teased, my laughter bouncing off the walls.

"Precautions are necessary when dealing with your father's... eclectic tastes," he replied dryly.
"Fair enough," I conceded, glancing around the room that seemed to breathe easier without its eerie occupants. The light filtering through the window caught dust motes dancing like spirits in the air.
"Shall we?" Mr. Thompson gestured towards the remaining pieces of furniture, his sleeves rolled up in readiness.
"Let's do this," I said with a determined nod. "I'm ready to lay some ghosts to rest."
The armoire loomed like a relic of a bygone era, its dark wood carved with intricate patterns that seemed to swirl and dance as Mr. Thompson and I approached it.
"Alright, Tuesday, let's tackle the beast," he said, his voice steady but not unkind.
"Beast is right," I muttered, pulling open the heavy doors with more force than necessary. The scent of mothballs and aged cedar wafted out.
"Your mother had good taste," Mr Thompson remarked, holding up a silk scarf, the colours still vibrant against the gloom. "Beautiful."
"Too bad she didn't have better taste in husbands," I quipped, though my heart wasn't in it. I grabbed a handful of my father's stiff-collared shirts, tossing them into the box labelled 'Donations.' They fell with a whisper, a soft hush of fabric bidding farewell to its former life.

"Next, the drawers." Mr. Thompson's voice pulled me back to the task at hand.

"Let's see what secrets you're hiding," I murmured to the chest of drawers as we slid them out one by one. My fingers trailed along the bottom of each drawer, searching for hidden compartments or forgotten treasures. Nothing but the smooth, empty wood greeted me.

"Seems like Dad was only mysterious on the surface," I said with a half-laugh, trying to ignore the twist of disappointment in my gut.

"Appearances can be deceiving," Mr. Thompson replied, his eyes scanning the room as if he expected the walls to whisper confessions.

"Or maybe they're just appearances," I countered, watching the removalist crew as they began to haul out the furniture piece by piece. Each thud and scrape against the floorboards was another echo of a past being carted away.

"Make sure to check every inch," I called out to the men. "Who knows what could be wedged in there?"

"Will do, Miss May!" came the reply, muffled by the effort of shifting the heavy wood.

I leaned against the wall, arms crossed, observing the procession. The sunlight cut through the dust-laden air, casting long shadows that reached out like fingers, trying to hold on to the remnants of history now being paraded out the door.

"Empty carcasses, all of them," I said, more to myself than to Mr. Thompson. "Not a single secret."
"Sometimes, it's the lack of secrets that's the real surprise," Mr. Thompson noted, giving me a knowing look.
"Ha! If only that were enough to satisfy my gnawing curiosity" I shot back, a smirk playing at the corner of my mouth.
"Curiosity killed the cat, but satisfaction brought it back," he said, his voice tinged with humour.
"Good thing I have nine lives then," I retorted. "I'm going to need them all to get through this house."
The four-poster bed loomed in the middle of the room, its once grandeur now just a stark reminder of what used to be.
"Alright, let's strip this beast," I announced with an exaggerated sigh, pulling at the aged linen like it was hiding the last secret of Atlantis.
"Beast indeed," Mr. Thompson echoed, joining me in yanking off the sheets. We worked in tandem, the crisp sound of fabric snapping in the air as we bared the mattress.
"Seems clear," Mr. Thompson confirmed, his voice carrying a trace of disappointment. Together, we dismantled the skeleton of the bed, leaving the room feeling emptier with each piece carried out.
"Down to the bare bones," I muttered, scanning the room once the bed was gone. My gaze landed on the twin bedside

tables, little sentinels keeping watch over nothing but memories.
"Let's check these puppies," I said, opening the drawers with a flourish. Empty. Nothing but the scent of old wood and the echo of a time past. "And...nothing here either. But why are they empty?."
"Miss May, not every search yields treasure," Mr. Thompson reminded me, his voice steady and calm.
"Tuesday. Please, it's Tuesday," I corrected him for the umpteenth time, flopping onto the carpet where the bed had been. "All this work, and for what? A whole lot of empty?"
"Patience is a virtue," he said, patting my shoulder in a fatherly way.
"Patience can kiss my ass," I shot back, rolling my eyes but unable to suppress a grin. "We're running out of rooms, Mr. T."
"Indeed," he acknowledged, casting a look around the near-barren space. "The attic, your bedroom, one lounge, and our modest quarters are all that's left."
"Guess it's time to face the cobwebs in the attic next," I sighed, pushing myself up from the floor. I couldn't help but feel a pang of defeat. Every corner of this house held a memory, a shadow of the past, but none revealed the secrets I yearned to uncover.
"Come on, let's get this rug rolled up," Mr. Thompson urged with a brisk clap of his hands. "Can't very well leave it here to

gather more dust. And those curtains—down they go. Mrs. Collins will have the room spotless in no time."
"Spotless and empty," I quipped, bending down to grab one end of the heavy Persian rug. We worked in tandem, rolling the ornate fabric into a tight cylinder. The room echoed strangely without its trappings, like an abandoned theatre after the final act.
"Like a goddamn tomb," I murmured under my breath, tugging at the curtains which once shielded my father's twisted torture chamber from prying eyes. With each tug, puffs of dust motes took flight, dancing in the slanting light like malevolent little spirits. I gave them a glare, half expecting them to coalesce into some tangible clue. But, as always, they dispersed into nothingness.
"Miss May, if you'd be so kind as to steady the ladder for me?" Mr. T's voice pulled me from my daze. I moved to where he stood, positioning a rickety old ladder beneath the last curtain rod. My hands gripped the sides, steadying it as he ascended.
"Careful up there, Mr. T. I'm not cut out for nursing duties," I warned, offering him a wry smile.
"Never you fear, I've survived worse than a tumble from a few feet," he assured me, his tone teasing.
"Like managing my father's affairs?" I shot back, arching an eyebrow.

"Ah, that would certainly be one for the books," he agreed, pulling down the heavy drapes with efficient movements. They fell in a heap at our feet, their opulence reduced to mere fabric.
"Damn," I muttered, glancing around the barren room. "I was so sure this place held the answers. That behind every corner, under every creaky floorboard, there'd be something... anything."
"Sometimes the answers we seek aren't always the ones we find," Mr. Thompson said sagely, climbing down from the ladder.
"Or maybe there never were any to begin with," I mumbled, feeling the sting of disappointment sharp in my chest. The last vestiges of hope I'd clung to seemed to unravel with the threads of the discarded curtains.
"Tuesday, your father was a complex man. His greatest secrets might not have been hidden in rooms or drawers," Mr. Thompson offered, giving me a knowing look.
"Maybe," I conceded, my voice barely above a whisper. "But right now, all I see is a whole lot of nothing where something should be."
"Let's just finish this up," I said louder, straightening my back and squaring my shoulders. "Who knows what the attic holds, right? Or maybe it's just more cobwebs and disappointment."

"Indeed," Mr. T replied, the corners of his mouth turning up just slightly. "But let's hold onto the notion that sometimes, it's the journey that counts, not the destination."

"Journey, destination... I'll take either at this point," I said, flashing him a grin despite the frustration curling in my gut. "Let's just hope the journey doesn't end with me becoming the crazy lady in the haunted house, talking to walls and scaring the neighbourhood kids."

"Perish the thought," he chuckled, beginning to gather the fallen curtains. "You're far too charming for such a fate."

"Flattery will get you everywhere, Mr. T," I teased, bending to help him. "Especially if it gets me out of this haunted echo chamber faster."

"Then by all means, let's hasten our departure," he quipped, and together we carried the weight of fabric and folded dreams out of the room.

Chapter 36

Dimitri Costa

The manila folder had a weight to it like sin itself was pressed between those flaps, and it was staring at me from my otherwise immaculate desk. I tapped a rhythm on the polished wood with my fingers, trying to coax out some courage or maybe just procrastinate a little longer. My gut was doing flips, and not the good kind I get from a glance of Tuesday's electric gaze.

"Would you just open the damn thing?" Jenkins grunted from his desk adjacent to mine, his eyes flickering up from his own stack of paperwork. "You're giving me anxiety."

I swivelled in my chair and finally reached for the report. The cover felt cold under my touch. I flipped it open slowly, knowing that most of what lay inside were things I'd already pieced together from the crime scene photos and preliminary briefings; the bruising patterns, the blood spatter, Henry Hamilton's last stand against his own mortality.

"Anything new, Costa?" Martinez called out, not even looking up from his screen.
"Give a man a chance to read, will ya?" I shot back, but my ribbing tone was losing its edge as I scanned the lines, looking for whatever piece I hadn't been privy to before. My eyes snagged on a couple of phrases, ones that didn't fit the puzzle yet. No DNA evidence? Not a damn strand of hair or a whisper of a fingerprint?
"Looks like our killer's cleaner than Mr Thompson's silverware," I muttered, letting out a low whistle. "Whoever did this is meticulous. Scary meticulous."
"Or lucky," Martinez chimed in. "Sometimes it's just dumb, blind luck."
"Maybe," I conceded, leaning back in my chair and raking a hand through my cropped hair. "But I don't believe much in luck when it comes to serial killers. They're like cockroaches, always more of them hiding in the shadows."
"Cheery thought, Dimitri," Jenkins commented dryly.
"Always here to brighten your day." I flashed a grin. But inside, my mind was racing. There was a hunger to this case, an itch that told me we were dealing with someone who didn't make mistakes—or if they did, they were minuscule, lost in the larger chaos they orchestrated.
"Anything else?" Martinez asked, now giving me her full attention.

"Nothing yet." I closed the folder with a snap. Our perp was out there, breathing the same air as us, maybe even watching. And until she decided to grace us with another performance, all we could do was wait and watch right back.

"Let's hope our lady killer's patience is shorter than yours, Costa," Jenkins said, half-serious.

"Let's hope," I echoed, but I couldn't shake the feeling that our killer—this shadow-wraith of a woman—was playing a game whose rules only she knew. And I'd be damned if I wasn't going to learn them, beat her at her own twisted game.

The office was silent except for the scratching of my pen as I scribbled a few notes in the margin of the coroner's report. Mr Hamilton's unfortunate end had been a messy affair, but the forensic details were like breadcrumbs leading us through a dark forest. I caught sight of Jenkins hovering by the door, his expression unreadable as always.

"Hey, Jenkins, ever seen an arm-wrestling match?" I asked without lifting my gaze from the papers.

"Indeed, though I find them rather boring," he replied, his voice smooth like aged whiskey.

"Boring is right," I murmured. "Looks like our killer didn't have the muscle to make it quick. Had to really go at it with Mr. Hamilton's head." I shook my own in mock sympathy. "That's gotta be a bitch on the ol' biceps, huh?"

"Quite distressing, I'm sure," Jenkins said, the corner of his mouth twitching slightly.

I flipped another page, and there it was—the photo that would turn stomachs less accustomed to the grotesque theatre of crime. "Ah, here we come to the pièce de résistance. Our perp's got finesse, I'll give her that. Snipped off his manhood like she was pruning roses."
"Precision indeed suggests a certain... resolve," Jenkins commented back, rubbing his chin.
"Resolve? Hell, it's downright artistic," I quipped, leaning back in my chair. The image was stark—an act of violence so deliberate it bordered on ritualistic. And yet, my gut twisted not from the gore but from the cold intention behind it.
"Costa—does this not perturb you? This level of brutality?" Jenkin's question hovered in the air, laced with a rare note of curiosity.
"Sure, it's fucked up," I admitted, tapping the photo. "But it tells us something, doesn't it? Tells us we're looking for someone who's not just angry. They're sending a message, loud and clear."
"Indeed. A message most grim."
"Grim my middle name, buddy." I grinned, but inside, my mind was already churning. This wasn't some random act of savagery; it was calculated, a statement made in blood and flesh.
My mind wandered to Tuesday. As I read the shoe size of the killer, a twisted waltz played in my head as I imagined her

delicate steps in size 7 shoes—dancing around a crime scene with the grace of a sick ballerina.
"Costa, you've been staring at that page for an eternity," Jenkins' voice cut through my reverie, his tone laced with concern and mild annoyance. "Find something juicy?"
"Juicier than a peach in summer," I replied, flipping over another glossy photo, the edges crinkled from my tight grip. "Our lady killer has dainty feet, but she's not dancing solo. She's got a partner with boats for shoes."
"Size 11?" Martinez chimed in, peering over my shoulder with a raised eyebrow. "That's a big fella."
"Big enough to stomp out trouble—or create it," I said, tapping the photograph where the imprints were marked next to a ruler. "But get this, no DNA, no fibres, no damn prints. It's like our perps are ghosts, floating through the crime scene without leaving a trace."
"Or they're just careful," Jenkins mused, polishing his glasses on his shirt. "Real careful."
"Careful or not, they can't be perfect forever," I shot back, leaning back in my chair with a creak. The fluorescents above flickered like they were winking at me.
"Damn, this reads like one of those puzzles you get in the cereal box, except all the pieces taste like shit," I continued, thumbing through the report once more. "Not even a single strand of hair? That's some next-level meticulousness."

"Or they're bald," Martinez joked, but his smile didn't quite reach his eyes.
"Ha! Maybe," I laughed, though the humour felt hollow against the backdrop of brutality. "But nah, this was planned. Our girl and her oversized shadow knew what they were doing."
"Sounds like you admire them," Jenkins noted, his gaze sharp.
"Admire's a strong word, buddy. Let's say I'm... intrigued. They've got style—I'll give 'em that. But they've also got a date with a pair of handcuffs, courtesy of yours truly."
The clock on the wall ticked away, each second a reminder that somewhere out there, a killer was probably planning their next move.
"God, this is twisted," I muttered, flipping through the pages with a grim fascination. "You think you've seen it all, and then—"
My eyes wandered back to the report, to the details that screamed experience. A woman's touch, delicate yet deadly; her male partner, an enigma.
"Martinez, tell me something," I started, my voice low. "When was the last time we had a case this clean? No evidence, no nothing?"
"Can't remember," he answered, furrowing his brow. "Why? What's cooking in that detective brain of yours?"

"Patterns, my friend," I said, tapping the paper. "Serial killers have them, like a signature. And I'd bet my badge she's danced this dance before."
"Fuck," he sighed. "That's not good news."
"Understatement of the year," I replied.
I leaned back in my chair, considering the cold detachment necessary to carry out such brutality. Women serial killers, they were unicorns in our line of work—rare, enigmatic, and damn hard to track down. They didn't kill on impulse; they planned, they plotted, they perfected.
"We're not going to solve this one," I said, settling back in my seat.
"Then what's the plan, boss?" Martinez asked.
"Patience," I told him, a bitter taste on my tongue. "We wait for her next move. Because there will be a next move. People like her can't stop at just one twirl around the floor."
"Shit," he cursed softly. "So, we just sit tight and wait for another body to drop?"
"Seems so," I confirmed. "But we'll be ready. We'll learn her steps, and anticipate the music. And when she least expects it, we'll step in and steal her partner away."

Chapter 37

Tuesday May

The flutter of the envelope through the mail slot at Kent's son's workplace was almost as delicious as the anticipation curling in my stomach. Mr. Thompson, with his usual meticulousness, had set up the sham with an artistry that would've made a con artist swoon. A holiday competition —how quaint, how utterly normal.

"Tuesday, it's done," Mr. Thompson informed me, an edge of smugness in his tone. "The bait has been sent."

"Perfect," I replied, twirling a lock of my dark hair around my finger. "Now we wait for the fish to bite."

I lounged on the chaise, draped like a cat in the sun, feigning disinterest as Mr. Thompson busied himself with other tasks. But inside, oh, inside I was a tumult of wicked glee. The plan was simple, elegant, and wickedly deceptive—qualities I found most appealing in all aspects of life.

Two days later, as expected, Mr Thompson received the completed paperwork—the Kent spawn eagerly to claim his prize. It was almost too easy; sometimes, I felt a pang of disappointment at the lack of challenge.

"Congratulations," Mr. Thompson's voice carried from the dining table where he'd made the call, his tone convincingly cheerful. "You've won a return trip to Bali for one week. Your departure is in three days."

"Really? Oh man, that's amazing!" The muffled exuberance from the other end of the line caused my lips to curve into a sly smile. Fools paraded their ignorance like peacocks, didn't they?

"Make sure you pack plenty of sunscreen," Mr Thompson continued, the perfect picture of a helpful servant. "Bali can be quite unforgiving this time of year."

"Will do, will do! Thank you so much!"

"Think nothing of it. Enjoy your trip." Mr. Thompson hung up the phone, and I could hear the soft click as he placed the receiver back in its cradle.

"Hook, line, and sinker," I murmured, rising from my lazy repose. I strolled into the dining room, finding Mr. Thompson straightening the papers on the table, already moving on to the next task at hand.

"Indeed, Tuesday. Our young traveller is none the wiser," he said without looking up.

"Mr. Thompson, you devious old fox," I teased, leaning against the doorway. "You have outdone yourself."
"Merely following your lead, Miss May," he replied, finally meeting my gaze with a flicker of something akin to pride.
"Flatterer," I chided playfully, but the warmth in my chest betrayed my affection for the man who had been both accomplice and mentor. "Now, let's prepare for our own little excursion, shall we?"
"Indeed," he agreed, the corner of his mouth lifting ever so slightly before he returned to his ever-present list of tasks.

The room is cold, the kind of chill that seeps into your bones and makes a home there. It's fitting, I suppose, for a place we've christened the 'murder room.' Mr Thompson stands at the centre of the desk, poring over maps and schedules like some twisted party planner.
"Okay, so our little prince is off to his fairy-tale vacation," I start, sauntering into the room. The morbid setting does nothing to dampen my spirits; if anything, it's an exhilarating backdrop for what's to come. "Three days, Mr. Thompson. We have three days to turn the Kent residence into a scene from Dante's Inferno."
"Quite the poet today, aren't we?" Mr. Thompson responds without missing a beat, his eyes never leaving the papers spread before him.

"Poetry in motion, that's me," I quip, pulling up a chair next to him. My fingers dance across the tabletop, tracing invisible lines between the various documents. "So, Dimitri will be at work, nose deep in murder files, oblivious to our own little contribution to his caseload."
"Indeed. Dimitri will be out of our hair until 6 PM at the earliest," Mr Thompson confirms, tapping a pencil thoughtfully against his chin. "The Kents stay home during the day"
"Perfect," I breathe out, leaning forward with renewed interest. "We'll have to be swift — in and out like a whisper on the wind." I catch Mr. Thompson's eye and wink. "A deadly whisper."
"Precision is key," he agrees, marking a time on the schedule. "We'll need to account for traffic, potential delays, and any... unexpected occurrences."
"Speaking of which," I interject, "we can't be too predictable, can we? Our dear detective is getting antsy for a serial killer case."
"Variety is, as they say, the spice of life," Mr. Thompson nods sagely. "Or, in our case, the spice of death.
Mr. Thompson leans down and grabs 2 boxes off the floor, and opens them up. A mischievous glint danced in his eyes as he watched me saunter over, my gaze fixed on the oversized footwear we'd procured.

"Size twelve and eight, Miss May," he said. "A necessary misdirection."

"Like Cinderella's ugly stepsisters trying to fit into the glass slipper," I quipped, picking up a size twelve shoe. It was comically large in my hand, like some sort of clown prop. "Except we're not trying to snag a prince; just staging a little exit scene."

"Indeed," Mr. Thompson replied with a smirk. "Though remember to tread lightly. We don't want these to look too out of place."

"Never fear, Jeeves," I chuckled, slipping my feet into the oversized shoes. They felt alien, like boats floating around my ankles. "I'm a natural at playing dress-up."

As I tied the laces, making them snug despite the size difference, Mr Thompson opened another box, revealing a sleek backpack. "And for your added weight? Bricks, Miss May. They'll add heft to your step, quite literally."

"Brick by brick, we build our alibi," I mused, hoisting the pack onto my shoulders. The heaviness settled against my back, grounding me. It was an odd comfort, a reminder of the gravity of what we were about to do.

"Quite poetic," he observed, watching as I adjusted the straps.

"Isn't it just?" I said with a grin. "A regular Shakespeare, I am."

"More like Macbeth," Mr. Thompson retorted dryly.

"Ooh, I do love a good tragedy," I responded, twirling once in my new, clunky attire. "But let's not foreshadow our own downfall, hm?"
"Of course not," he agreed, but there was a hint of laughter in his tone. "Just stick to the plan, and all will be well."
"Plan, schman," I scoffed playfully. "You worry too much. We're a dynamic duo, remember?"
"Infamous is more like it," he countered, but he couldn't hide the pride that swelled in his chest.
"Infamous, notorious, call it what you will," I said, feeling the bricks shift as I moved. "It adds a certain...je ne sais quoi to our escapades."
"Let's hope that 'je ne sais quoi' doesn't include prison bars," Mr. Thompson muttered under his breath, though I caught the twinkle in his eye.
The oversized shoes felt like boats on my feet, each step a clumsy dance with the floor. I glanced up at Mr. Thompson, the thrill of our sinister plan buzzing through me like a live wire.
"Consistency is the hobgoblin of little minds," I mused, twirling a lock of my dark hair around my finger as I pondered our next move. "And we're anything but consistent, aren't we?"
"Variety is key," Mr. Thompson agreed, his tone serious despite the whimsical subject. "Change the game before they even know they're playing."

"Exactly!" I exclaimed, the backpack's weight settling comfortably against my back. "Dimitri thinks he's on the trail of a serial killer." The words rolled off my tongue with a sardonic twist, and I savoured the irony like a fine wine.

"Speaking of which," Mr Thompson interjected, his brow furrowing in concern, "I must advise against...repeating certain...signature moves."

"Ah, you mean our dear Mr. Kent's penis?" I said, feigning innocence while batting my lashes. "But it's such a compelling statement, don't you think?"

"Compelling or not," he chided, "it's a dead giveaway. We need to be smarter."

"Fine, fine," I conceded with a playful pout. "But what about Mrs. Kent's shrill little instrument? It's been begging for a trim."

"Tuesday," he warned, but there was no real bite to it. "We have to be careful."

"Careful is my middle name," I lied cheerfully, shifting to balance the load on my back.

"Let's focus on making this look random," he insisted, his eyes scanning the room – our designated murder room – with meticulous care. "Leave nothing that can lead back to us."

"Random, schmandom," I quipped, a smirk tugging at the corner of my lips. "I'll make it artful. An ode to chaos."

"An ode to staying out of handcuffs, more like," he retorted, but the corners of his mouth betrayed him, curling upwards ever so slightly.
"Handcuffs could be fun," I winked, "but not in the way Dimitri would use them. I would miss him too much."
"Focus, Tuesday," Mr. Thompson sighed, though the affectionate exasperation was clear in his voice.
"Alright, alright," I relented, my mind already racing with possibilities. "No souvenirs from Mr. Kent, and a different kind of silence for Mrs. Kent. Something poetic but discreet."

Chapter 38

Tuesday May

The dawn barely broke as I watched Dimitri's silhouette blend with the greying light, his badge glistening briefly before he vanished into the nascent day. "Got called in early, Sweetness," he'd murmured against my hair, his breath warm with the scent of coffee and mint. "A body in the harbour, Detective Matthew Rocklan needs me for the tide charts."

"Go be the hero," I teased, feigning a pout that flirted with the edges of genuine disappointment. "Just promise to make it up to me later."

"Cross my heart," he said, pressing a firm kiss on my forehead before slipping out into the world where death waited with its cold hands.

I turned from the window, the playful mood hanging by a thread as the weight of the day settled on my shoulders. Mr.

Thompson stood by the door, his face an unreadable mask. "Ready, Miss May?"
"Ready as I'll ever be," I replied, a smirk playing about my lips. It was time to dive headfirst into the twisted game only I knew how to play. I grabbed the keys to my father's car, the sleek monster of metal I once swore would become a compact square under my wrath. Funny how fate enjoys its little jokes—today, Daddy's precious ride was our chariot for mischief.
"Let's not keep adventure waiting," I chirped, tossing the keys from hand to hand as Mr. Thompson followed me out. The car hummed to life beneath my touch, and I couldn't help but feel a twinge of power steering this beast. "You know, Georgie Porgie would have a fit seeing us take his baby for a spin."
"Indeed, Miss May," Mr. Thompson intoned, the ghost of a smile almost reaching his eyes. "Your father valued this car more than most things."
“Let's crush after today," I quipped, winking at him through the rearview mirror. Adventure beckoned, and for all its dark promises, today felt like it would unfold exactly as I intended.
"Seatbelt, Mr. T," I reminded him, as the engine purred eagerly.
"Of course, safety first," he said, the click of the seatbelt punctuating his words like the final note of a prelude.
The car slid down the driveway like a whisper of danger dressed in black. I allowed myself a moment to relish the

anticipation coiling tight in my stomach. Today was about settling scores, old debts paid with the currency of pain and fear. And yet, despite the gravity of our intentions, I drove with a lightness that defied the heaviness of revenge.
The tyre iron from my car was left at the first murder, and now I wish I had kept it. "You got a new tyre iron coming, right Mr. T?" I asked as we cruised down the highway, an hour's drive stretching out like a promise.
"Indeed, Miss May," he replied, glancing at the rearview mirror. "It should arrive by Friday if all goes well."
"Sweet," I said, tapping my fingers on the steering wheel to the rhythm of some tune playing only in my head. "Wouldn't want to get caught with our pants down because it was missing from my car."
The landscape blurred past us, a palette of greens and browns smeared across nature's canvas. We turned off into the quieter streets, the ones that whispered secrets of suburban lives behind closed doors. Two streets over from the Kents' place, I pulled up and killed the engine, the silence suddenly loud in its absence.
"Here we go," I murmured more to myself than to Mr. Thompson, as we slipped out of the car. My boots hit the pavement with a thud that felt like a drumroll. I shrugged on the hair net, smoothing back strands of rebellious dark hair that always seemed to have their own agenda, followed by gloves that hugged my fingers like a second skin.

"Backpack," I commanded, and Mr. T handed it over without a word. Bricks. Check. Tools of choice nestled in my pocket. Double check. We were armed for destruction in the most domestic way possible.
"Let's take a stroll, shall we?" I suggested, leading the way around to the back where freedom and revenge waited with open arms. The fence loomed ahead, a picket obstacle course so quaint you could almost hear it apologising for being there.
"Cute," I snorted, placing a boot on the top and swinging my leg over with ease.
"Quite," Mr. Thompson agreed, following suit with a grace that betrayed his age.
"Ready for some fun?" I asked, my voice low and playful as we approached the back door.
"Always, Miss May," he replied, his tone matching mine.
"Good," I said, a wicked grin spreading across my face. "Because it's showtime."
A crisp click resonated through the stillness, and I flashed a triumphant smile at Mr T. "And that, my dear fence-hopper, is the sound of victory." The doorknob turned with ease under my gloved hand, and together, we slipped into the dimly lit kitchen-like shadows craving solace from the noonday sun.
"Shh," I whispered, more out of habit than necessity—The Kent's squabbling voices were a cacophony that could drown out a marching band. We crept closer to the archway leading

to the living room, where the discordant symphony grew louder.
"Ungrateful little shit," sneered Mrs. Kent, her voice scraping against my eardrums like nails on a chalkboard. "Goes off on a bloody holiday, and leaves us here like we're yesterday's newspaper."
"Only a single ticket," grumbled Mr. Kent, his tone soaked in self-pity and scotch. "What sort of son does that?"
I bit back a laugh, the absurdity of their complaints tickling at the edges of my mind.
"Let's just say he's not winning any 'Son of the Year' awards," I murmured, sharing a conspiratorial glance with Mr. T, who only nodded, his face an impassive mask. Our steps were silent, our breaths measured—predators closing in on the unsuspecting prey wallowing in their own bile of entitlement.
The scent of lemon cleaner and the muffled tirade of Mrs Kent's voice were my welcome as I eased into the living room, the cold kiss of steel pressed against my palm. Mr. T's shadow loomed behind me, a silent giant in this twisted pantomime we were about to perform. I slinked behind Mrs. Kent, the knife gliding from my pocket like a secret being whispered.
"Shh," I breathed against her earlobe, the blade resting against the delicate skin of her neck. "Not a peep now, darling."
Her eyes widened in the mirror, reflecting terror laced with recognition. With the tenderness of a lover, I steered her like a

prized mare towards the closest chair. She stumbled slightly, her breath hitching in little jerky sobs that tickled my insides. Mr. T worked with the efficiency of a seasoned sailor, ropes securing her wrists and ankles before she could even think to struggle.

"Stay put, sweetheart," I cooed, patting her cheek, an almost affectionate gesture if it weren't for the malice dancing in my gaze.

As if on cue, Mr T returned from his brief sojourn, marching a dishevelled Mr. Kent at gunpoint into the room. His face was a comic display of boozed bewilderment and dawning horror. He was bound and parked right beside wifey—two peas in a very pathetic pod.

"Hello, hello," I chimed, crouching down to their level, all smiles and bad intentions. "Miss me? It's been what, 13 years since you spewed venom at me?" My eyes locked onto Mrs. Kent's; she flinched under my stare. Turning to Mr. Kent, I continued, "And you, swinging your dick around in my direction like you owned the place."

Their wide-eyed silence begged for mercy, but all they received was my flirtatious tilt of the head and a mocking pout. "I think it's time for some payback, don't you reckon?"

Inside, I was dancing—a jive, a tango, a macabre ballet. Thirteen years of pent-up rage and hurt pirouetting behind my ribs. Every insult, every sneer, every time they made me feel

less than dirt—it all came bubbling up to the surface, ready to spill over in the most delightful of ways.
The sweet scent of terror mingled with the musty air as I circled around Mrs Kent like a vulture, my footsteps soundless against the plush carpet. "Shh," I cooed, almost lovingly, as I reached into my pocket and pulled out the ball gag. "We wouldn't want the neighbours to hear our little reunion, now would we?"
"Tuesday, you don't have to do this," she tried to plead, her voice quivering.
"Correction, sweetie—I don't HAVE to do anything." I pressed the gag to her lips, watching her eyes widen in helpless fury. "I GET to do this."
As I secured the gag behind her head, Mr. Thompson mirrored my actions with Mr. Kent, who was spitting curses that were cut short by his own mouthpiece. Their muffled grunts became the twisted harmony to the melody of revenge playing in my head.
"Much better," I said, clapping my hands together with glee. "Now, where were we? Oh, right—payback."
My fingers danced over the tools in my pocket before settling on the cold, sleek piano wire. I showed it to Mrs. Kent, letting her see the instrument of her finale. The way her eyes fixed on it, I could tell she knew its purpose. Hell, I'd watched enough crime shows with her as a kid; she was practically an expert.

"Ever hear how they describe strangulation?" I asked, drawing out the wire. "They say it's intimate. Up close and personal." With a flourish, I looped the wire around her neck, my hands steady as a surgeon's.
"Let's get acquainted, shall we?"
I crossed the ends at the back of her neck and pulled. The wire bit into her flesh, a thin line of blood blossoming like a cruel necklace. The gurgling noise that bubbled up from her throat was music to my ears—a symphony of suffocation. Her body thrashed beneath the ropes, but the chair held her fast.
"Isn't it just delicious?" I whispered, leaning in close to catch every nuance of her struggle. The coppery smell of blood mixed with her Chanel No. 5, a cocktail of bitterness and death.
"Tuesday, stop this madness!" came Mr. Kent's garbled plea through the gag, but it was all white noise to me.
"Shh, darling, let me enjoy the moment," I scolded him without taking my eyes off Mrs. Kent. My grip on the wire never wavered, even as her movements grew sluggish, her eyes bulging with the horror of impending oblivion.
"Deep breaths, Mrs. Kent," I mocked, though we both knew she couldn't take any. "Oh wait, my bad."
Her struggles ceased, the silence thickening around us. Her head lolled forward; it was done. I released the wire, stepping back to admire my handiwork.

I sauntered behind Mr Kent with a playful bounce in my step, the weight in my bag promising another round of twisted fun. "Time for your surprise," I cooed, rummaging through my satchel of horrors until my fingers closed around the life-sized dildo—the pièce de résistance.

"Open wide, you son of a bitch," I murmured as I yanked out the ball gag from his quivering mouth. Mr Thompson, ever the dutiful accomplice, clamped Mr Kent's jaw open, his grip unyielding. With a devilish grin, I introduced the rubber monster to Mr Kent's gaping maw, pushing it deeper and deeper, watching his eyes widen in terror.

"Isn't this just a choke?" I chuckled, keeping one hand firmly on the base of the toy, anchoring it like a ship's mast in a stormy sea. His breath hitched and sputtered, the clear struggle for air music to my ears.

"Look at me, Mr. Kent," I demanded softly. His bloodshot gaze met mine, and I watched, fascinated, as a single blood vessel in his eye popped like a balloon, painting the entire orb a splendid shade of crimson. "Oh, darling, red really is your colour," I whispered, more to myself than him.

His body's fight was epic, almost admirable, but futile against my relentless hold. As his thrashing subsided into weak twitches, a serene smile stretched across my lips. A sense of liberation washed over me—a cleansing flood after years of toxic sludge. My past was drowning before my eyes, and I couldn't help but feel reborn.

"Tuesday," Mr. Thompson's voice broke through my reverie, his hand on my shoulder grounding me back to the now still room. "We gotta go."

"Right, right," I replied, a little dazed by the rush. We exited just as we had entered, blending with the shadows. The car ride home was cloaked in silence, thick enough to slice with a knife. But inside, I was doing cartwheels; the world seemed a bit brighter, a touch lighter.

We pulled into the driveway at 1 pm sharp—my timing was always impeccable. Detective Costa wouldn't be off work for hours, the perfect alibi. I stepped into the shower, letting the hot water cleanse away any lingering traces of the day's exploits.

Meanwhile, Mr. T played his part, packing up our stained garments along with the bricks in the backpack, and tossing it all into the pond. To anyone else, just another sack sinking out of sight—but to us, a secret nestled in plain sight.

Chapter 39

Tuesday May

The dust motes played in the slanting light as I idly swirled the last dregs of cold coffee in my mug. It had been a few days since we'd darkened the doorstep of the Kents' place, and the silence from their end was thick enough to choke on. I tapped my fingers against the ceramic, casting a glance at Dimitri who was sprawled across the kitchen chair, his brow furrowed in concentration over the morning paper.

"Sweetness," he said without looking up, "you're tapping Morse code with that cup. Something on your mind?"

"Nope," I sighed, letting the mug rest. Maybe they don't have friends to call around? Who'd want to visit a family more twisted than a pretzel?

Dimitri stood up and stretched his arms above his head, the hem of his shirt lifting to reveal a sliver of tan skin. "It's too nice a day brooding."

"Brooding?" I echoed, mock offended, pushing away from the table. "I was going for pensive with a touch of mysterious allure."

"Keep telling yourself that." Dimitri's laugh was a low rumble as he crossed the room to me. "Now, how about we take advantage of this rare day off? The sun's calling your name."

"Is that so?" I teased, tilting my head to look up at him. "And what does it say?"

"It says," he leaned down, his breath tickling my ear, "Get your ass upstairs to the attic and stop thinking"

"Charming," I laughed, grabbing his hand and allowing him to tug me towards the stairs. "You should write greeting cards."

"Only if you're my muse," he quipped, squeezing my hand.

The musk of old timber and a hint of mothballs welcomed us as Mr Thompson led the way, his posture rigid with the sort of discipline only years in service could carve into a man's spine. Today was a day unlike any other; we were venturing into the attic of the Wellington estate, an unmapped territory in a house that held more secrets than warmth.

"Looks like it's us against the forgotten relics of the Wellington dynasty," I quipped, watching Dimitri roll up his sleeves. He was a rare sight on his day off – all casual energy and eagerness, contrasting sharply with his usual cool, detective facade.

"Bring it on," he declared with a grin that could've rivalled the Cheshire Cat. "This place could hide a million stories."

"Or skeletons," I added, unable to resist poking fun at the grim history threading through the air.

"Only one way to find out." His eyes sparked with that adventurous glint I adored.

We trudged up the creaking staircase, my hand trailing along the banister polished by time. The second floor was just as grandiose as the rest of the house, each step echoing with the whispers of the past. And then, there it stood – the door to the attic, straight out of a gothic novel and begging to be opened.

"Bet this door has seen some things," Dimitri mused, his fingers ghosting over the ornate handle.

"Like what? Scandalous affairs? Secret rendezvous?" My imagination was running wild, buoyed by the thrill of exploration.

"Or just a lifetime of dust bunnies plotting their takeover," he said, chuckling as he pushed the door open, revealing the narrow staircase leading up to the attic.

"Guess we're about to join the rebellion," I said, taking the first step into the unknown.

The attic was cavernous, a vast expanse shrouded in shadows and swathed in cobwebs. It was as if the room itself breathed, the stale air whispering across our skin, inviting us into its confidence.

"Shit, this is... impressive," I whispered, awestruck by the sheer size of it.

"Could've been a ballroom," Dimitri agreed, his voice hushed in reverence.

"Or my ultimate childhood hideaway," I mused, imagining myself as a kid claiming this space as my kingdom. The attic had an eerie charm, the kind that tickled the spine but beckoned you closer.

"Could still be," Dimitri teased, bumping his shoulder against mine. "Queen of the Attic, her royal highness of dust and antiques."

I laughed, the sound bouncing off the walls, filling the space with a semblance of life. "Long may she reign."

"Over broken furniture and boxes of... who even knows what," he gestured at the clutter that awaited our inspection.

"Every queen needs her treasure trove." I stepped further into the room, the floorboards groaning underfoot, ready to unearth the mysteries camouflaged amidst the chaos.

"Then let's get to it," Dimitri said, his tone light but determined, as we ventured deeper into the heart of the attic.

Dimitri let out a low whistle, the sound slicing through the hush of the attic. "This is no joke, Sweetness," he said, his brown eyes wide as they took in the space crammed with memories and forgotten belongings.

"Right?" My voice echoed back at us. The removalist guys had done their part, leaving behind a sea of cardboard boxes, each labelled and lined like soldiers ready for battle. "They've set us up for success, at least."

"Or an epic voyage." His chuckle was infectious, and my heart did that annoying little flutter every time I heard it.

"Every box could be Pandora's, for all we know," I warned him, running a hand along the nearest stack. "We have to empty each one before hauling it out. And check every nook and cranny."

"Ah, so we're on a quest!" Dimitri's hands mimicked the shape of a telescope over his eyes. "Arrr, matey! Perhaps we'll find the buried treasure of the infamous Attic Pirates!"

"Shut up!" I swatted at him playfully, but the corners of my mouth betrayed me by turning upward. "Just help me open this first chest."

A cloud of dust puffed into the air as I flipped the lid, sending both of us into a fit of coughs. "Christ, it's like opening a tomb," I muttered, waving away the particles.

"X marks the spot," Dimitri continued with his pirate act, pointing to an imaginary mark on the chest. He broke into a grin, his teeth bright against the dim light filtering in from the small attic window.

"More like 'Ex marks the regret,'" I said, pulling out a moth-eaten scarf and a pile of yellowed newspapers. "There's more junk in here than treasures."

"Ah, but that's where you're wrong, Sweetness." He bent down next to me, his shoulder brushing mine as he reached

into the chest. "It's all about the hunt. And who knows what secret fortunes we might uncover?"
"Or secret horrors," I countered, winking at him. "With our luck, we'll find a cursed amulet or something."
"Then we'd better be careful not to unleash any ancient evils." He winked back, the playful glint in his eye making the dust and the work ahead seem less daunting.
"Or incur the wrath of the Attic Queen," I added, my title from earlier returning with a smirk.
"Her Majesty's wish is my command." He gave an exaggerated bow, knocking his head against the chest with a thud.
"Careful!" I couldn't help the laughter bubbling up. "You'll dethrone yourself before we even start."
"Can't have that." Dimitri rubbed his head with a mock grimace. "All right, Captain Sweetness, lead the way to our next grand adventure."
"Captain, huh?" I played along, standing tall. "Well then, loyal subject, let's dive into this sea of antiquity and see what fortunes—or failures—await us."
"Anchors aweigh," I announced, stepping over the threshold into the sea of forgotten relics. The attic loomed before us, a graveyard for memories and discarded dreams.
"Shiver me timbers," Dimitri chuckled, peeking into an old chest by the door, the creak of its hinges echoing through the vast space. "Looks like we hit our first treasure trove."

"Treasure" was a generous term for the assortment of oddities we uncovered; a one-legged doll with vacant eyes, a stack of vinyl records warped beyond recognition, and a collection of porcelain figurines, each missing some vital piece. They felt like echoes of someone's history, whispers of the past that had somehow washed up in this dusty attic.

"Who even keeps this stuff?" I mused, sifting through a box of tarnished silverware that hadn't seen the light of day in decades.

"Sentimental souls, or those too busy to deal with the past," Dimitri replied, holding up a rusted toy car between his fingers. "Each of these objects has a story to tell if only they could speak."

"Or scream," I joked, tossing a frayed hat back into the box. "Imagine the secrets they're hiding."

"Sweetness, if these walls could talk..." He trailed off, his gaze scanning the room. "They'd probably beg for a good dusting."

"Ha! You're not wrong," I agreed, wrapping my fingers around the handle of a heavy suitcase. The effort it took to drag it out from under a table sent a plume of dust into the air, causing us both to cough. "Sorry about that!"

"Occupational hazard," he said, waving away the dust with a grin. "I'm just glad I'm here to help you navigate these treacherous waters."

"Much appreciated, Captain Costa," I replied, using my foot to prop open the lid of the suitcase. Inside, a tangled mess of fabric, faded photographs, and random knick-knacks greeted us.
"Look at this." I held up a sepia-toned photo of a couple, their faces worn by time but their smiles still bright. "Think they ever imagined their life would end up boxed away like this?"
"Maybe not," Dimitri said softly, taking the photo and studying it. "But at least they had moments worth capturing."
"True." I smiled, though a pang of longing prickled at the back of my mind—a yearning for moments of my own worth preserving.
"Hey," Dimitri nudged my shoulder gently, pulling me from my thoughts. "We've got plenty of our own moments ahead of us. No box required."
"Promises, promises," I teased, brushing off the sentimentality. We moved on to a cupboard, its doors swinging open to reveal a jumbled mess of china and glassware. Some pieces were whole, others chipped or cracked, all of them coated in a film of neglect.
"From riches to rags," I quipped, handling a teacup with a faded floral pattern.
"More like from rags to riches," Dimitri corrected, a smirk playing on his lips as he wrapped an armful of dusty linens in a newspaper.

"Ever the optimist," I said, rolling my eyes but unable to suppress a smile. His presence made the work feel lighter, the day less grey.

"Only when I'm with you, Sweetness," he shot back, winking as he sealed another box.

"Flatterer," I accused, though my heart skipped at the endearment.

"Guilty as charged." He shrugged, unabashed. "Now, let's see what other 'treasures' we can unearth before this day is out."

"Lead the way, Detective," I said, following him deeper into the attic, eager to discover whatever lay hidden beneath layers of dust and time.

The sun had climbed high enough in the sky to begin its slow descent by the time we paused, hands on hips, surveying the attic. A graveyard of possessions still loomed around us, mocking our morning's effort with its sheer volume of clutter.

"Shit," I muttered under my breath, "it's like trying to bail out the ocean with a teacup."

Dimitri chuckled, wiping sweat from his brow with the back of his hand. "Well, if it's any consolation, I think you're the prettiest little teacup I've ever seen try to take on the sea."

"Ha-ha," I replied, sarcasm lacing my voice though my lips couldn't help but curve upwards. "I'm all about that Sisyphean aesthetic."

"Can't fault you for ambition." He stretched, arms reaching toward the rafters. "But sweetness, we're gonna need more than ambition to tackle this beast."
"Or maybe just a sandwich and a cold drink," came the welcome interruption, as Mrs. Collins appeared at the top of the attic stairs, her arms laden with refreshments.
"Mrs. C, you're an absolute lifesaver," I said, genuinely grateful as I plopped down onto the floor, welcoming the break.
"Sandwiches, iced tea, and a little pick-me-up," she announced, setting down a tray with a motherly kind of pride. "You two have been at it like the world's ending. You need your strength."
"Thanks, Mrs. Collins." Dimitri grinned, accepting a sandwich wrapped in wax paper and taking a hearty bite. "This is better than treasure."
I reached for a sandwich, the bread soft and fresh, and took a sip of the sweet, cool tea. It was heaven against my parched throat. "Mmm, this is perfect," I sighed contentedly.
"Balance," he said, mouth full, gesturing with his half-eaten sandwich. "A bit of chaos, a bit of calm."
"Pretty deep for a guy who was making pirate noises earlier," I teased, nudging his knee with mine.
"Even pirates appreciate the finer things in life," he quipped back, winking over the rim of his drink.

"Like plundering attics and stealing hearts?" I asked playfully, feeling the fatigue slip away just a little in the lightness of the moment.
"Especially hearts," Dimitri agreed, mock-serious. "Though, not necessarily in that order."
We lapsed into a comfortable silence, munching on our sandwiches and sipping our drinks. The dust motes danced in the shafts of sunlight filtering through the attic windows, and I felt a weird sense of peace amidst the chaos.
"Round two after lunch?" I asked finally, steeling myself for the afternoon ahead.
"Wouldn't miss it for the world," Dimitri said, standing and offering me a hand up.
"Good," I replied, "because there's no way I'm letting you off the hook that easily."
"Never doubted it for a second, Sweetness," he said.

Chapter 40

Tuesday May

The dust danced like mocking spectres in the shafts of light that sliced through the attic's gloom. I wiped a bead of sweat from my brow, my arms aching from the relentless hefting and sorting of forgotten relics. "Christ on a cracker, how much stuff did one family need to hoard?" I muttered under my breath.

"Miss Tuesday," Mr. Thompson's voice was steady as always, but even he sounded weary, "we're nearly there. Just a few more boxes."

"Nearly there" had become our mantra over the last three days, but this time, as I glanced around the now sparse attic, it felt true. I grabbed another box, its cardboard damp with age, and heaved its contents out. A cloud of dust puffed up, making me cough and wave my hand frantically in front of my face. "You know, the Wellingtons sure knew how to stockpile junk."

"Indeed," Mr. Thompson agreed, a rare hint of dryness in his tone. He lifted a tattered teddy bear by one arm and inspected it with a furrowed brow. "Yet, not all is without value. Memories, for instance."

I snorted at that, tossing aside a stack of moth-eaten clothes. "Memories can't pay bills, Mr. T. And they sure as hell can't buy happiness."

"Perhaps not," he conceded, placing the bear atop a pile destined for donation. "But they do provide context for who we are."

"Who we are or who we were?" I lifted an eyebrow, a smirk playing on my lips despite the exhaustion tugging at them.

The last box lay between us, and together we pried it open. Inside, nothing but old newspapers and faded photographs.

"Great, more anticlimactic crap." I sighed heavily, flipping through the photos with disinterest.

"Seems so," Mr. Thompson murmured, though his eyes scanned every inch meticulously. "Yet, one never knows where a secret might hide."

"Secrets..." My voice trailed off, and I stared at the empty expanse where cobwebs clung to the rafters. The thrill of uncovering some long-lost heirloom or scandalous diary had evaporated like morning mist. "Empty. Just like everything else in this attic."

"Perhaps it's best this way," he suggested, folding the flaps of the box back down. "A clean slate, as it were."

"Clean slate..." I echoed, my thoughts drifting to the plans I had, the future I wanted to carve out—free from the shadows of this mansion and the family who'd built it. "Yeah, a clean fucking slate. That's what I need."

"Then let us take solace in the fact that the attic is empty, and we've found nothing further to burden you," Mr. Thompson said, offering a small smile as he surveyed the bare room. "Come on let’s carry the last boxes down"

The sun dipped low, painting the horizon in hues of tangerine and lavender as I stood outside, surveying the row of hulking shipping containers lining the driveway. "Seven," I said out loud, just to feel the weight of the number on my tongue. "We've packed seven of these metal beasts, Mr. T."

"Indeed, Miss Tuesday," Mr Thompson replied, his voice carrying from where he stood by the last container, clipboard in hand. "And four trucks' worth donated. Quite the achievement."

"Feels more like a yard sale at a giant's house," I chuckled, tossing a lock of hair over my shoulder. I couldn't help but feel a sense of weariness mixed with pride.

"Only your room, mine, Mrs. Collins', and the kitchen remain." Mr Thompson checked something off his list and looked up at me with an eyebrow raised. "Shall we tackle your quarters tomorrow?"

"Ugh, let's." I groaned theatrically. "I'm ready to torch it and call it a day."

"Let's not resort to arson just yet." His lips twitched in amusement. "It might raise a few eyebrows."

"Fine, spoil my fun." I mock pouted, leaning against one of the cold steel containers. My breath fogged up in the air, a ghostly echo of my thoughts. "You know, soon we'll be setting up camp in Mum's old place down the road. Just two months left."

"Are you looking forward to it?" He closed the distance between us, his hands finding refuge in his pockets.

"Looking forward? I'm practically leaping out of my skin," I confessed. The big mansion with its echoing halls and dark corners had become a cage. Once upon a time, it felt like a playground of mysteries, but now, it suffocated me.

"Change can be exhilarating," he mused, studying my face for a reaction.

"Exhilarating, terrifying, liberating..." I let out a half-hearted laugh. "All rolled into one. But seriously, I need out. This whole treasure-hunting gig in Daddy Dearest's haunted house is losing its charm."

"Understandable." Mr Thompson nodded sagely.

"By the time we move to Mum's, I want to be... free," I emphasised the last word, feeling its promise on my lips. The past was a shackle I was desperate to shed. "Done with all this," I waved a hand around, encompassing the mansion and all its unseen chains.

"Then consider the countdown begun." There was a glint in Mr. Thompson's eye that matched the resolve in my heart. "A fresh start awaits, Miss Tuesday."
“Damn, straight it does." I pushed off from the container, my boots crunching on the gravel. "And hey, if we find any more skeletons in the closet, we can always use them to scare the trick-or-treaters come Halloween, right?"
"Ever the optimist." He chuckled, locking the container with a satisfying clank.
"Optimist, realist, badass extraordinaire." I flashed him a grin, already plotting my next moves in the dance of life. "Pick your poison, Mr. T."
"Badass extraordinaire it is," he agreed, and together we walked back toward the house, leaving the orange glow of sunset to fade into twilight.
The merciless claws of twilight had yet to pry into the night's domain as I leaned against the cool marble of the kitchen counter, a mug of hot chocolate cradled in my hands. Mr. Thompson methodically sorted through the files scattered across the dining table, his meticulous nature a stark contrast to the chaos of our recent days.
"Got something new on Jennings?" I asked, taking a sip. The bitter warmth slid down my throat, a much-needed balm for the chill that seemed to cling to my bones these days.
"Indeed, Miss Tuesday," he replied without looking up, his fingers pausing over a particular sheet. "Our dear Mr

Jennings is now scrubbing toilets at the local bowling club. Seems like karma has quite the sense of humor."

"Scrubbing toilets? God, that's poetic." A smirk played on my lips. "And the hours?"

"Unearthly early. Before the first bird chirps."

"Perfect for a worm like him." My voice was light, but the undercurrent of disgust was palpable. I pushed off from the counter and strolled over to peer at the file. "What about the dynamic duo?"

"Ah, the foster children," Mr. Thompson said as he handed me a couple of photographs. "One found God, apparently. Preaches against the very sins he was subject to."

"Good for him." I examined the photo of a young man with haunted eyes. "He gets a pass. The other one?"

"Street-bound in the city. Reports suggest he's made a pact with heroin rather than redemption."

"Seems we're dealing with a lost cause then." I tossed the photo back onto the pile. "Easiest to start with, don't you think?"

"Logically speaking, yes." He gave a small nod, his expression unreadable.

"Then it's settled." I leaned back against the chair, feeling the weight of the past heavy on my shoulders. "Two ghosts left to exorcise before I can truly call this life mine."

"Exorcisms can be... messy affairs," Mr. Thompson observed quietly.

"Can't make an omelette without breaking some eggs, right?" I replied flippantly, though my heart wasn't in it.

"Indeed, Miss Tuesday." His gaze lingered on me, a silent question in his eyes.

"Let's just get it done," I said, more to myself than to him. "Before we move to Mum's. I can't drag all this shit with me."

"Understood." He closed a folder with a snap. "I suppose it's time to plan our next move."

"Time indeed." I stood up, stretching out the kinks in my muscles, feeling the restless energy coursing through me. There was a certain thrill in plotting, a perverse pleasure in orchestrating the downfall of those who'd wronged me. But beneath it all was a burning desire for closure, for freedom.

The musty scent of old leather and dust clung to the air, a fitting backdrop for our sordid little scheme. I leaned against the weathered wall of the garage, tapping my foot impatiently on the oil-stained concrete. With every passing second, the anticipation twisted like a knife in my gut.

"Got it," Mr. Thompson's voice cut through the thick silence as he sauntered back into sight, a set of grimy keys dangling from his finger. "She ain't pretty, but she'll do the job."

"Show me this beast," I said with a smirk, pushing off the wall.

We walked together to where the truck was parked—a hunk of rusted metal that looked like it had been chewed up and spit out by life itself. The tyres were bald, the paint was flaking, and one headlight was cloudier than the eyes of a dying fish. Perfect.

"Christ, she's hideous. I love it." My voice was laced with a wicked glee.

"Only the best for us," Mr Thompson quipped a rare flicker of humour in his steely demeanour.

“Ready to go?" I asked, sliding into the passenger seat and relishing the creak of the worn upholstery beneath me.

"Are you sure you don't want to drive, Miss Tuesday?" he asked, a twinkle in his eye as he started the engine, which coughed to life like an old man waking from a deep sleep.

"Sweetheart, I wouldn't dream of taking away your joy," I replied, fastening my seatbelt with a click. "Besides, I've got to look the part, remember?"

"Indeed." He nodded, pulling out onto the street, the truck groaning in protest. "And what is your disguise?"

"Think... disenchanted junkie with a taste for trouble," I mused, picturing the filthy streets where our prey lingered.

"Charming," he deadpanned, but the corner of his mouth twitched upward.

As we drove, I let my mind wander, picturing the face of the one we were after. A kid turned puppet, strings pulled by that sick fuck Jennings. The thought made my blood boil, but the rage was a fire I'd learned to cook on.

"Once we get him alone, we slip him the poison—easy peasy," I explained, rolling down the window to let in the city smog. It smelled like desperation and decay—a fitting bouquet.

"Rat poison," Mr. Thompson echoed. "Cruel to rats, lethal to humans."

"Karma's a bitch, and so am I," I retorted, leaning my head out the window to feel the bite of the wind. My hair whipped around my face, a wild tangle of rebellion.

"Indeed," he said again, eyes fixed on the road ahead. "But we must tread carefully."

"Y'know, they say revenge is a dish best served cold," I mused aloud, watching the dilapidated buildings pass by in a blur. "But I say fuck that—it's all about the presentation."

"Quite," Mr. Thompson murmured, the truck rumbling beneath us like a beast ready to pounce. And in that moment, I felt the thrill of the hunt surge through me, fierce and undeniable.

"Let's go sell some poison," I whispered, more to myself than to him, my smile sharp enough to cut glass.

Chapter 41

Tuesday May

The engine hummed a low, comforting purr as Mr. Thompson and I made our way into the city's belly, its skyscrapers looming like silent judges above us. We were incognito, decked out in moth-eaten rags that smelled of dust and time, relics we'd unearthed in the attic.

"Feels like we're undercover agents or something," I mused aloud, breaking the silence as I tugged at the frayed hem of my makeshift disguise. "Like in one of those old spy movies."

Mr. Thompson spared me a glance, his lips curving ever so slightly. "Indeed, Miss May. Though, I believe our mission is somewhat darker than your typical espionage."

"Dark but necessary," I replied, letting the words hang between us as the cityscape blurred past. My hand found the edge of the seat, gripping it tightly. There was a certain thrill in this, a wicked dance with fate.

"Quite so." His voice held the weight of unspoken truths. "You remember the plan?"
"Find the guy, give him his 'lucky' dose, and then leave," I confirmed, rolling my eyes for effect. The casual flippancy in my tone belied the gravity of what we were about to do. "Easy peasy."
"Here," Mr. Thompson said, producing a small, crinkled bag from his pocket. The contents were ominous, a sandy mixture that promised eternal sleep. "The heroin, cut with a... special ingredient."
"Rat poison, right?" I snatched the bag from his hand, examining it under the pale light. It was almost funny, how something so deadly could look so benign. "I'm guessing he won't be checking for purity."
"Unlikely," Mr. Thompson replied dryly. "Given his current state, he'll be more than eager to indulge."
"Shit, this is twisted," I said, chuckling despite the sick nature of our task. "But after everything, it’s kind of poetic, don’t you think?"
"Poetry comes in many forms, Miss May." He navigated a sharp turn, the car’s suspension groaning beneath us. "Sometimes in verses of vengeance."
"Speaking of verses..." I began, sifting through my thoughts like pages of an unwritten book. "You ever wonder if we're the bad guys in someone else's story?"

"Every story needs its villain, Miss May," he replied with a hint of wistfulness. "But remember, even villains believe they are the heroes of their own tales."

"Heroes and villains just depend on the day."

"Or the deed," Mr. Thompson added quietly, his gaze fixed on the unfolding road ahead.

"Right. The deed." I squeezed the bag once more, feeling the grains shift between my fingers. There was no turning back now. Not when I was so close to scratching off the second last name on my list.

The city's underbelly had a pulse of its own, one that throbbed with the kind of life that only desperation could breed. Mr Thompson and I navigated through its veins—the back alleys and dimly lit corners—where society's forgotten found their refuge.

"Here," I whispered as we approached an overpass, the stench of urine and decay hanging heavy in the air. "This is where they huddle up."

As if on cue, the truck sputtered to a stop, the engine cutting out like it was respecting the silence of the slumbering forms before us. We stepped out, our rags blending seamlessly with the backdrop of discarded dreams. I could feel the weight of the bag in my pocket, its contents a cruel twist of fate concealed within white powder.

"Stay close," Mr. Thompson murmured, his voice barely above the whisper of wind through trash-strewn streets.

"Wouldn't dream of wandering," I replied, matching his tone.
We walked, and the gravel crunched beneath our feet like a depressing applause for what was about to unfold. Each step felt like a betrayal to the beat of my heart, which had begun to pound with a ferocity that bordered on excitement—or was it dread?
"Ah, there he is." My voice broke the silence as we came upon a figure curled beneath the bridge, his body so thin it seemed a breath could blow him away.
"Matt? Matt Smith?" I bent down to his level, peering into the hollows that once held eyes full of life. Now, they were just glazed windows to a soul long departed from hope.
"Y-yes," he rasped, voice brittle as dried leaves.
"Your lucky day, Matt." I couldn't help the sardonic curl of my lips. "Someone paid me to give you some heroin. Want it?"
His reaction was primal, eyes igniting with a hunger that made my stomach turn. He reached out with a hand trembling from more than just withdrawal, not even questioning the origins of his unexpected boon.
"Sure you do," I said as I handed him the bag, fingers brushing against his clammy skin. The contact sent a shiver up my spine, a silent requiem for the man who'd lost himself to the abyss.

I straightened up, feeling the gravity of the moment pressing down on me. "Enjoy the high, Matt," I added, though the words tasted like ash in my mouth.
"Thanks," he mumbled, already fumbling with the bag.
"Anytime," I lied, turning on my heel to walk away.
Mr. Thompson fell into step beside me.
"Let's get out of here," I said, eager to leave the scene behind, to shed the rags and the role I had played. But as we climbed back into the truck, I knew some parts you never truly take off; they cling to you, seep into your pores, and become part of your very essence.
The rattle of the truck's engine was a dull hum compared to the cacophony in my head as we pulled away from that dingy underpass. My fingers twined and untwined in the hem of my makeshift attire, the fabric rough against my skin.
"Quite the performance back there," Mr. Thompson remarked, his voice steady but not without a tinge of something tender underneath.
"Performance?" I scoffed lightly, attempting to keep the mood aloft. "More like a one-act tragedy."
Thompson shot me a glance, his eyes searching mine in the rearview mirror. "You're awfully quiet. Everything okay?"
"Sure," I lied, knotting my brow. The usual rush, that sweet surge of righteous retribution—it wasn't coursing through my veins. Instead, guilt gnawed at my insides like a starved rat. "It's just... this one didn't feel quite so satisfying, you know?"

"Ah." Mr. Thompson's sigh was almost inaudible over the hum of the tires on asphalt. His lips curled into a soft, sad smile—a rare crack in his stoic butler facade. "I have a hunch that might be because Mr. Smith is already paying for his deeds in life, maybe even more deeply than you or I could fathom."

"Is that supposed to make me feel better?" I quipped, though my heart wasn't in it. I gazed out the window, watching the city blur by, each faceless building mirroring my own numbness.

"Perhaps," he said gently, "you've given him an escape, a twisted kind of mercy."

"Mercy" was a funny word, that felt foreign on my tongue. But there it was, hanging between us, stubborn and unmovable.

"Maybe Matt was more messed up than we thought," Thompson continued, his voice low and thoughtful. "In the end, people who do bad things—they were often taught those things. Perhaps he never knew any different, or maybe—just maybe—Mr. Jennings screwed him up so much that hurting you was his only outlet."

"An outlet," I mused aloud, rolling the concept around in my mind like a loose marble. "Everyone's got their demons, I guess. Some just wear them on the inside."

"Exactly." Mr. Thompson's nod was slow, deliberate. "At least now, you can be certain he'll do no more harm. And who knows? Maybe in the end, he'll find some peace, too."

"Fuck, I don't know," I confessed. "I thought it would feel like...victory. But it feels more like I kicked a dog while it was down."

"Revenge can be a fickle friend," Mr. Thompson mused, stopping at a red light. The eerie glow illuminated the weariness etched into his features.

As we left the city's embrace, the slight darkness outside mirrored the one within me, and I settled into its familiarity. Maybe Mr. Thompson was right; maybe some peace was found tonight. But for whom, I wasn't entirely sure.

Chapter 42

Dimitri Costa

The morning sun filtered through the blinds, casting lazy stripes of gold across the worn surface of my desk. The precinct was waking up, a low hum of activity steadily growing as the clock ticked towards nine. I leaned back in my chair, hands behind my head, and allowed myself a rare moment of reflection.

Tuesday, the thought of her brought a smile to my face. With her dark hair that cascaded in waves over her shoulders and those piercing blue eyes that could cut through a man's soul, she was more than just a sight to behold. She was a force that had unknowingly coiled herself around my heart, tightening with every laugh, every knowing glance, every time she ran to me, arms flung wide as if I were the answer to a question she hadn't known she'd asked.

Damn, the woman didn't just understand me; she got me. Never once did she judge the demands of my job or the gruesome details that sometimes followed me home. Instead, she'd throw her arms around me, her embrace a sanctuary from the harsh realities of my day-to-day grind. It was bliss—an unexpected, addictive kind of bliss. For a guy who spent his days wading through the city's underbelly, her love was like a damn lifeline.

"Costa!" The shrill ring of the phone shattered the tranquillity, yanking me from my reverie. "We got a call—two bodies found out of the city. You're up."

"Shit." I bolted upright, my previous warmth instantly replaced by the cool, sharp focus of Detective Dimitri Costa on the job. I snatched the receiver, "This is Costa. Give me the details."

"Nearly two hours out," the voice crackled on the other end. "Looks bad."

"Got it." I slammed the phone down, already on my feet, the familiar adrenaline surge kicking in. My hand flew to the phone again, punching in Martinez's extension. "Martinez, grab your coat, we've got a double homicide. Looks like we're taking a trip."

"Christ. On a Friday?" Martinez's voice came through, tinged with both annoyance and intrigue.

"Wouldn't be a good start to the weekend without a little blood and mystery, right?" I said though the jest felt hollow against the backdrop of what awaited us.

"Always with the charm, Costa," he shot back, but I could hear the scrape of his chair, the telltale sign he was ready to roll. "I'll meet you in the car."
"Make it quick. Something tells me this is gonna be one for the books." I grabbed my jacket, thoughts of Tuesday tucked away for now. The detective in me took over, cold and calculating, chasing down the next lead, ready to peer into whatever darkness we were about to uncover.
The morning sun had barely climbed its way into the sky, painting everything with a soft golden hue. It seemed almost sacrilegious that something so serene could serve as a prelude to what we were about to face.
"Ready for this?" Martinez asked as he shrugged on his coat, his voice betraying a hint of that Friday fatigue.
"Born ready," I quipped with a smirk, though my stomach twisted at the thought of what 'this' could entail. I tossed him the keys and we both clambered into the patrol car, the engine springing to life under the command of Detective Martinez's steady hand.
"Two hours, huh? You'd think trouble would have the decency to happen closer to town," I mused, my eyes fixed on the blur of the cityscape giving way to sprawling countryside.
"Trouble never liked convenience," Martinez grumbled, his knuckles white on the steering wheel. "Especially not our kind of trouble."

"Touché." My mind drifted, the drive stretched long, filled with the hum of the road beneath us and the occasional crackle of the radio, until finally, the GPS announced our arrival.

"Shit," I breathed out as we pulled up to the house, an old weatherboard house surrounded with flurries of officers and tape fluttering in the breeze.

"Welcome to paradise," Martinez said dryly as we stepped out of the car.

"Looks like hell got a makeover." I straightened my jacket, trying to shake off the last vestiges of tranquillity from the drive.

We approached the house, greeted by the lead officer who looked like he had seen better days. "Family reunion turned torture chamber," he said, gesturing towards the lounge. "Son came home from Bali to find mom and dad tied up like Christmas presents."

"Jesus Christ," I muttered, my gaze stealing across the threshold where the once-wellborn lounge room was now a grotesque stage. Two figures, bound and lifeless, sat as if mocking the very idea of human decency.

"Guess this is one-holiday slideshow no one's gonna want to see," Martinez added, his usual humour darkened by the grim spectacle.

"Can't even imagine..." My words trailed off as the son, a young man in his twenties, caught my eye. He sat on the

steps, hands buried in his hair, a portrait of anguish. Or guilt? Time would peel back the layers.
"Let's get to work," I said, squaring my shoulders. "And hope to God this isn't the start of a trend."
"From your lips to God's ears," Martinez replied. We donned our gloves and stepped into the scene.
"Coroner, what's the story here?" I asked, nodding toward the bodies as we stepped over the threshold into a chilling air thick with decay. My senses were assaulted by the sharp tang of blood mixed with other bodily fluids, and beneath it all, the cloying scent of death.
"Hard to say for sure until we get them back to the lab," Dr. Langley replied, brushing a lock of hair from her face with the back of her gloved hand. "But it looks like the female had her throat cut." She gestured to the woman, her head lolling at an unnatural angle, matted blood darkening her blouse. "Decomposition makes it tricky. We'll need more time."
I swallowed hard, feeling the remnants of this morning's coffee sour in my stomach. "And him?" I nodded toward the male victim, his posture one of grotesque repose.
"Ah, well, he was easier to read," the coroner said dryly. She pointed to the object protruding from his mouth. "Seems someone took a very... personal approach to silencing him."
"Christ," Martinez whispered beside me, his usual bravado momentarily quenched.

"Any chance his—" I started, not sure how to phrase the question delicately, but it was necessary. "Was he... castrated?"
Dr. Langley shook her head, a strand of chestnut hair falling across her brow. "No, no signs of that. This is more a message than anything else. Humiliation, maybe control. We'll know better after the autopsy."
"Message received loud and clear," I muttered under my breath.
"Alright, let's give the forensics team room to work." I clapped a hand on Martinez's shoulder. He nodded, and we both stepped away, our minds undoubtedly racing with the same questions. Who would do something like this? And why?
Martinez's gaze flickered back to the grotesque display in the lounge, something gnawing at his expression. "Shit, Dimitri, you remember the Hamilton case? The way old man Hamilton was left?" His voice was a low murmur only I could catch.
"Vividly," I replied, my stomach tightening at the memory of that bloodbath. "But this...it's different." I ran a hand through my hair, trying to shake off the eerie feeling clinging to me like cobwebs.
"Yeah, but it's got that same stink of hate, doesn't it?" Martinez said, his eyes narrowing as he scanned the room, hunting for invisible clues in its shadows. "We'll need to dig

into the son's alibi. Check if he really was sunning himself in Bali while his folks were being turned into gruesome art pieces."
"His tan does look authentically baked," I quipped, though humour felt out of place in the grimness of the scene. I caught Martinez's eye and shrugged.
"Sure dose." Martinez pulled out his own phone, thumbs flying over the screen. "And I hope to hell the kid did it because, honestly, if this is another masterpiece from the same twisted artist who did in Hamilton..."
"Then we're up the proverbial creek without a paddle," I finished for him, feeling my chest tighten. The thought sent a shiver down my spine that no amount of Tuesday's warm embrace could chase away.
"Fuck paddles, we won't even have a canoe." His tone was a half-hearted jest, but his eyes betrayed the gravity of his words. "We might as well be shark bait."
"Charming imagery, Martinez," I said, forcing a grin. "Let's just focus on what we can control. Right now, that's making sure Junior's passport stamps aren't from the local gift shop."
"Right." He clapped me on the back, a silent pact between us to weather whatever storm was brewing. "Let's reel in our fish and see if he bites."

Chapter 43

Tuesday May

The Kents' demise was a slow, silent sonata I never planned to hear. They sat, bound and unvisited, their lifeless bodies marinating in the stillness of their living room for an entire week. It was both fortunate and chilling that no one came looking for them, not even a nosy neighbour or a distant relative. The stench of decay would've been heavy, and cloying, the kind that clings to your clothes like a desperate lover.

"Sweetness, don't sound so glum," Dimitri murmured over the phone late one night, his voice a mix of concern and exhaustion.

"Can't help it, Detective. Just thinking about all the work you're doing," I replied, twirling a lock of dark hair around my finger. "Must be taking a toll on you."

"Ah, you know me," he said with a half-hearted chuckle. "I live for the thrill of the chase. Although, in this case... it's a tough nut to crack."

"Maybe you need a break. A little distraction could do wonders," I teased, picturing him hunched over his desk, piecing together the puzzle with that furrowed brow of his.

"Only if my distraction comes in the form of a certain young woman with eyes that pierce the soul," he shot back playfully, but I heard the underlying strain. Dimitri was close, too close, and that made me nervous.

"Be careful what you wish for," I warned, a smirk playing at the corners of my mouth.

"Always am, Sweetness." He yawned, the sound crackling through the line. "Got to go. Another long night ahead."

"Love you, Detective," I whispered before hanging up, a sly smile spreading across my face. It's time for Mr. Jennings to take his final bow while my dear detective is buried in work.

"Mr Jennings won't see it coming," I mused aloud, my thoughts drifted to the Kents, I hoped against hope that nature had done its job well, erasing any trace that might connect the dots back to me.

As I turned away from the ghost of that scene, my thoughts shifted to the task at hand. Eliminating Mr. Jennings while Dimitri was wrapped up in his investigation seemed almost serendipitous. It was as if the universe conspired to give me this window of opportunity – one that I couldn't let pass by.

The old grandfather clock in the corner tolled, its deep chimes marking the hour with an ominous echo that seemed to resonate with my mood. I leaned against the mahogany desk, fingers tracing the intricate carvings as I pondered our dilemma.
"Thompson," I began, not bothering to look up from the woodwork, "you know I adore a good challenge, but this Mr. Jennings predicament is like trying to thread a needle with boxing gloves on."
"Indeed, Miss Tuesday," came Thompson's ever-calm voice from across the room. He stood by the window, his silhouette outlined by the waning light. "The man's living situation does make a direct approach... problematic."
I sighed, pushing away from the desk and sauntered toward him. "And here I thought life post-stabbing trial would be all roses and retribution." I paused, catching a glint of something in Thompson's eye. "Tell me you have something juicy to report from your little excursions."
"Mr. Jennings' routine is painfully mundane," he reported, straightening his tie with a flick of his wrist. The action was so quintessentially Thompson – all poise and precision. "Work and groceries, work and groceries. But there may be a sliver of opportunity..."
"Spill it, Jeeves," I teased, nudging his arm playfully.
"His place of employment," Thompson continued, undeterred by my nickname for him, "It's quiet in the hours before he

clocks off. A small window where the streets are nearly empty."

"Nearly empty isn't empty, though," I pointed out, biting my lip in thought. "We can't risk a peeping Tom spoiling our little game."

"True, Miss Tuesday." He gazed out the window, thoughtful. "But it may be our best option. We just need to ensure we're not seen."

"Which means we'll need a plan that's tighter than a corset on a harlot." I flopped down onto the nearby chaise lounge, pulling a throw pillow into my lap. "Any bright ideas?"

"Several, but they require... finesse."

Mr Jennings's shift at the bowling club wrapped up at the ungodly hour of 6 AM – prime time for the early birds and the late-night stragglers mingling in the grey light of morning. Too many witnesses. Too risky.

"Every damn plan we've cooked up falls flatter than a pancake under a steamroller," I muttered, running a hand through my long dark hair. The frustration was a bitter pill, sticking in my throat.

Thompson, ever the stoic shadow in the corner, nodded solemnly. "It appears Mr. Jennings lives quite a monotonous life. Work and groceries, nothing more."

"Thrilling." I rolled my eyes. "He's like a mouse in a maze with only one piece of cheese at the end. Predictable."

"Perhaps too predictable," Thompson mused, his fingers tapping against his chin. "We'll need to catch him off guard somehow."

"Right-o, but how? We can't exactly waltz into the bowling alley and ask him for a slow dance to the exit." I chuckled at the thought before standing up and pacing across the room. My feet sank into the plush carpet that I would soon strip away, just like everything else in this godforsaken house.

With the rest of the house now empty, stripped of its memories and secrets, all that remained was my sanctuary. Boxes had been piled high on the front lawn, turning it into some kind of suburban graveyard. The gardener was outside, cursing under his breath as he tried to revive the grass crushed by the weight of my past.

"Damn storage containers left me with more bald patches than my uncle Harold's head," he grumbled, running his rake through the dirt with more aggression than necessary.

"Easy there, tiger. It's just grass," I called out from the doorway with a sardonic grin. "It’ll grow back, unlike Uncle Harold's toupee."

"Miss, I want it perfect for when the buyers come. Can't have 'em thinking the place is cursed or somethin'," he shot back, not looking up from his labour.

"Wouldn't that be a shame?" I replied, my tone dripping with mock concern.

As the first real estate agent stepped onto the lawn, I leaned against the doorway, twirling the house key around my finger like a dubious prize. "So, what's the damage?" I asked my voice light despite the heaviness in my chest.

"Ms. Tuesday," he began, clipboard in hand, "comparable estates are fetching quite the sum these days." He started pacing the perimeter, jotting down notes with an intensity that made me want to roll my eyes.

"Figures," I muttered under my breath, following him with a measured stride. The grass crunched beneath my boots, a testament to the gardener's battle with nature. He'd been cursing those damn storage boxes for weeks.

"May I say, this property has great potential," another agent chimed in, her heels sinking into the freshly resurrected lawn. "Families will be tripping over themselves to create memories here."

"Memories," I scoffed, flashing her a grin that didn't quite reach my eyes. "We've got plenty of those, don't we, Mrs. Collins?"

The housekeeper gave me a stern look that could curdle milk. "It's not the house's fault for what transpired within," she said, her tone softening as she patted my hand. "Let it bring joy to others."

"Joy," I echoed, watching as the next five agents paraded through the door. They talked amongst themselves, throwing around terms like "market value" and "investment opportunity" while I stifled a yawn.

"Look at them," I whispered to Mrs. Collins, "like vultures circling a carcass. Can't they smell the stench of death?"

"Your sense of humour always was... unique," she replied with a weary smile. "But think of the future, dear. A new beginning."

"New beginnings," I mused aloud, my gaze lingering on the parade of suit-and-ties.

Mrs. Collins shook her head. "One step at a time, Tuesday."

"Right, right," I said, winking at the last agent who had the audacity to suggest turning my personal hell into a bed and breakfast. "One foot in front of the other, away from the flames."

"Exactly," Mrs. Collins agreed, her eyes brimming with something akin to hope. "And no arson, please."

"Fine, fine," I conceded, throwing my hands up in mock surrender. "You win, Collins. We'll sell the damn place. Let some other poor soul deal with the demons. I'm off to find my own slice of paradise—minus the pitchforks and brimstone."

"Good girl," she said, patting my cheek. "Now let's show these people out so we can focus on the task at hand."

"Lead the way," I said, offering my arm in a dramatic gesture. "I've got a date with destiny—or at least a bottle of wine and a hot bath. Whichever comes first."

"Both sound divine," Mrs. Collins agreed, linking her arm with mine as we ushered the eager agents toward the exit. "But remember, Tuesday, life is about more than just escaping the past."

"Is it, though?" I teased, closing the door behind the last of them. "Because from where I stand, the future's looking pretty damn bright."

"Especially without all those storage boxes ruining your view," Mrs Collins quipped, and we shared a laugh that felt like the start of healing—or maybe just the calm before the next storm.

Chapter 44

Dimitri Costa

The coroner's report landed on my desk with a resounding thud, causing papers to scatter and my heart to sink. The rain pounded against the precinct windows, mimicking the turmoil churning in my gut. With a sense of dread, I flipped through the pages, noticing how quickly this report had been delivered compared to the last one. It wasn't due to improved bureaucracy, but rather the grotesque details that demanded urgent attention. The smell of formaldehyde wafted from the pages, reminding me of the lifeless bodies that lay on the examining table.

I reclined in my chair, the worn leather creaking under my weight like an old man's bones. With a flick of my wrist, I opened the folder and read its contents. Mrs. Kent, may she rest in peace, had been brutally strangled--not just any strangulation, but a method that sent shivers down my spine as I read the report. The murder weapon? A thin wire,

resembling the strings of a piano used for creating music, now transformed into a deadly tool of silence.
The name "Jesus" escaped my lips in a hushed gasp, as my mind raced with the gruesome image of cold, thin metal slicing through flesh. I could almost feel the wire digging into my own neck from behind, tightening with enough force to crush my windpipe and silence me forever. It was like a twisted symphony, the killer's hands steady and calculated like a maestro conducting an orchestra, using a wire no thicker than a B string to bring about death. The thought alone sent shivers down my spine and made the hairs on the back of my neck stand on end.
As the words tumbled from my lips, I could feel the weight of them, heavy and full of meaning. They hung in the air like a dense fog, swirling around me in the silence of the room. My eyes darted around as if expecting to see faces appear in the shadows, listening to my macabre monologue. "Pressure would've severed the carotid arteries too," I continued, my voice low and grave. "Blood flow to the brain cut off—a few seconds feeling like an eternity before darkness hits." My fingers subconsciously grazed my own throat, tracing the path of an invisible line. It was personal, a kill that required both patience and an unsettling intimacy.
A curse slipped out of my mouth, a faint whisper in the cold room. I shuddered, but it wasn't because of the draft. "Who does this shit?" The question lingered, unanswered and

ignored. I knew what was coming next - the autopsy photos. Glossy prints that would reveal the aftermath of a brutal steel embrace on pale skin. I braced myself for the onslaught of gruesome images, dreading what they would reveal about the victim's final moments.
"Alright, Dimitri, focus," I chided myself, tapping the file against my desk. "There's a sicko out there turning life's soundtrack into a mute button, and you need to find them."
With a sigh, I closed the folder, the image of Mrs. Kent's final moments etched behind my eyelids. It was going to be a long night, chasing ghosts and piano wires.
With a sense of dread, I flipped the page and braced myself for the next act of this macabre play. The photo that greeted me was grotesque in every way imaginable; Mr Kent's face was distorted and bloated, his eyes bulging like a pair of overripe cherries about to burst. Each line on his face seemed to tell a different story - one of fear, pain, and ultimate demise. I couldn't help but release a low curse under my breath, running a hand through my hair in frustration. This scene was like something out of a nightmare, yet I knew it was all too real.
"Got something nasty?" asked Jenkins from across the room, his voice tinged with curiosity.
"Kent was choked out, but not your garden variety strangulation," I replied, leaning back in my chair. The image

clung to my retinas—those distended lips, the horror etched into his features.

"Rubber dildo," I said flatly as if reading off a grocery list. "Shoved down his throat."

"Christ..." Jenkin's eyebrows shot up. "That's one hell of an exit."

I looked over at Jenkins and tapped on the coroner's notes, my heart heavy with sorrow and anger. "Tell me about it," I said, my voice low and shaky. According to the report, the object had completely blocked the airway and crushed the epiglottis. The thought of someone experiencing that kind of suffocation made me want to claw at my own throat in sympathy. But there was no chance for this victim; with that foreign object lodged in their throat, they never stood a chance. Horrified images flooded my mind as I tried to imagine their final moments, gasping for air but only finding pain and fear. It was a cruel and brutal way to die, and I couldn't help but feel a strong urge for justice to be served.

"Someone had to hold his mouth open for it." I could almost see the struggle, the perverse intimacy of the act, the killer prying jaws apart to insert the fatal faux phallus. It took strength, determination, and a sick sense of poetic justice—or humour.

"Forensics?" Jenkins inquired, shifting uncomfortably.

"Zilch. Nada." I tossed the report onto the desk. "No DNA, again. But we've got shoe prints—a size 12 and a size 8. Different from Hamilton's murder scene."
"Doesn't add up," he mused, scratching his chin.
"Except it does, in a twisted way." My gaze flicked to the shoes imprinted on the forensic sketch. "The smaller print's deeper. Means our size 8 is carrying more weight than Hamilton ever did."
"Two killers then?"
"Maybe, maybe not." My mind raced, chasing shadows and patterns where others saw only chaos. "But they're connected. Even if the evidence is playing hard to get, I can feel it in my bones."
"Instincts, huh?"
"When you've waltzed with death as much as I have, you learn the tune." I cracked a grin despite the grim topic. "Now all I have to do is find the bastards who changed the music."
Jenkins nodded, his expression solemn. I stood up, stretching my legs before sitting again. I was a detective, and hunter in a concrete jungle, and the prey had just left another breadcrumb.
The fluorescent buzz above my desk was the only sound in the room, save for the scrawl of my pen and Detective Martinez's impatient tapping. Papers littered everywhere, mugshots staring back like a deck of ghoulish playing cards. I leaned back, thumb and forefinger kneading the bridge of my

nose as I tried to make sense of it all—the silence, the chaos, the dead ends.

"Dammit, Dimitri," Martinez broke the quiet, "there has to be something that links them together." He came over, leaning against my cluttered desk, his eyes dark pools of frustration. "My gut tells me they're linked; I just don't know how."

"I know," I murmured, dropping my hand. "When has your gut ever steered us wrong?" The scent of stale coffee hung between us, a testament to the long hours we'd already put in. "Let's dive deeper. Background checks, from birth till now. Every single day. There's gotta be a thread—if not, we'll make one."

Martinez straightened up, his face etching into a determined scowl. "You got it. I'll take Hamilton; you take Mr. Kent." His voice had that gravelly edge like he was ready to tear the city apart brick by brick. "We'll work our way through it and see if anything matches."

"Sounds like a plan, partner." My grin was the silver lining on a very dark cloud. As he walked back to his desk, I felt the itch—a nagging hunch that was part tickle, part burn, scratching at the back of my mind.

I swivelled in my chair, reaching for Mr. Kent's file, the wheels creaking beneath me. The picture of the man stared back—rigid, high-collar, the kind of starched life that screamed more secrets than a confessional.

"Alright," I spoke to the photo as if he could hear me, "let's see what closets you've got because I'm betting you've got skeletons to match." My fingers danced over the keyboard, each tap a step closer to the abyss we were about to tumble into.

"Here goes nothing," I muttered under my breath, diving into the digital sea of Mr. Kent's existence. But even as I did, my thoughts couldn't help but waltz back to the crime scene, to the grotesque parody of death that awaited us there.

"Link up, boys," I whispered to the silence. "Show me the dance steps."

Chapter 45

Tuesday May

The heavy wooden doors creaked open, and the real estate agent strode in like she owned the place. I couldn't help but smirk as I watched her confident stride across the ornate tiles of the mansion's grand entrance.

"Miss May!" she called out, her voice echoing through the vast space. "I have some wonderful news!"

"Spill it," I said with a sly grin, leaning against one of the wooden pillars that framed the staircase.

"Someone's interested in buying the mansion," she beamed, her excitement contagious.

"Shut up!" I squealed, my heart racing in anticipation. "Seriously?"

"Dead serious," she replied, unable to hide her own enthusiasm. She held out a crisp white envelope, sealed with an elegant wax stamp. "They've made an offer."

"Fuck, yes!" I exclaimed, snatching the envelope from her hand and tearing it open. My eyes scanned over the details, my fingers twitching with excitement. "So, when can we finalise this shit? Like, how soon can they sign and take this massive hunk of stone off my hands?"

"Typically, it takes about a month or so for all the legal processes to go through," she explained, her eyes sparkling with a hint of mischief. "But I can try to expedite things if you'd like."

"Yes, I'd like," I replied, feeling the weight of my past starting to lift off my shoulders. Selling this monstrosity would be like shedding a suffocating layer of skin, and I couldn't wait to get on with the next chapter of my life.

"Consider it done," she winked, already pulling out her phone to start making calls. "We'll have you out of here in no time, Miss May."

The sun poured through the grand windows, casting an ethereal glow over the room as Mr. Thompson entered with a sense of urgency that was unusual for him. I glanced up from the pile of papers I'd been half-heartedly organising, feeling a spark of curiosity at his sudden appearance.

"Miss May," he began, his voice tinged with excitement. "I have some wonderful news."

"Better than selling this place?" I asked, raising my eyebrows in playful disbelief.

"Perhaps not better, but certainly complementary," he replied cryptically. "Your mother's house—it's ready for you to move in."
"Wait, seriously?" I gasped, my heart leaping in my chest. "But I thought it was still a disaster zone."
"Indeed, there is still work to be done," he admitted. "The interior needs decorating, and the grounds require attention, but the house itself is quite liveable."
I jumped up from my seat, unable to contain my excitement. "That's fucking amazing! I can't believe we're really going to be out of this place soon."
"Indeed, Miss May," Mr. Thompson nodded solemnly, though I could see the glimmer of happiness in his eyes. "It's time to let go of the past and embrace the future."
"Damn straight," I agreed, grinning widely. The thought of leaving behind the memories that haunted the mansion's halls filled me with a sense of euphoria.
As I wandered through the empty rooms, imagining them filled with life and laughter once more, I couldn't help but feel a sense of bittersweet nostalgia. It was where I'd met Mr. Thompson and Mrs Collins, who had become like family to me.
"Hey," I called out to him as he trailed behind me. "You know you're coming with me, right? You can't back out, I need you with me!"

"Miss May," he began, his voice choked with emotion. "I am honoured to be a part of your life, and I will gladly follow wherever it may lead."
"Good," I smiled, feeling a warmth in my chest, "Mr. Thompson, I've been thinking," I said, twirling a strand of my dark hair around my finger, a mischievous glint in my eyes. "I've got an idea for Mr. Jennings."
His eyebrows raised in curiosity, the corners of his mouth threatening to break into a grin. "Oh, do tell, Miss May."
"Picture this," I began, pacing back and forth as if I were presenting a master plan to a room full of scheming villains. "We casually stroll up to his front door like we're old friends dropping by for tea. I tell him I forgive him for whatever sins he's committed against me, and as a peace offering, we leave him a box of chocolates. Poisoned, of course."
"Miss May," Mr. Thompson chuckled, shaking his head. "You do have quite the imagination. But are you sure that'll work? It seems a bit… risky."
"Risky?" I scoffed, my hands on my hips. "Where's your sense of adventure, Mr. Thompson? Besides, it's the only idea that we have come up with that might work?"
"Very well," he conceded with a sigh, clearly amused by my enthusiasm. "If you believe this is the best course of action, then I will support you."
"Of course!" I grinned, clapping my hands together. "

"Mr. Thompson," I whispered, as we carefully arranged the chocolates in their elegant box. "Do you think this is truly the beginning of our new life? Will we finally be free once Mr. Jennings is gone?"
The glow of the midday sun cast a warm, golden light through the window, bathing us in its embrace as we stood side by side, our wicked plan laid out before us like some twisted masterpiece. I couldn't help but let out an excited giggle at the thought of Mr Jennings's face when he bit into one of our poisoned chocolates.
"God, I can't believe we're actually doing this," I said, unable to contain my devious delight. "It's like something straight out of a fucked-up fairy tale, but instead of an apple we use chocolates."
Mr. Thompson chuckled softly, his eyes gleaming with mischief. "Well, Miss May, every fairy tale needs a touch of darkness. And if this works, we'll finally be able to close this godforsaken chapter of your life and move on to something better."
"Damn right," I agreed, grinning wickedly, my excitement bubbling up inside me like champagne. The thought of finally being free from this mansion and all its terrible memories was intoxicating, a sweet promise I couldn't wait to fulfil. With each passing moment, vengeance and freedom seemed to be drawing nearer, tantalisingly within reach.

"May the darkness of the night only serve to make the dawn of our new life that much brighter," I murmured, my gaze fixed on the sun outside.

Chapter 46

Dimitri Costa

It was a Tuesday the day it happened like the universe was taking a fucking dig at me. As if Tuesdays already didn't have enough baggage in my life, what with my Sweetness, Tuesday May, being named after them. But today, the office air felt heavy with tension as I sat at my cluttered desk, pouring over case files.

"Detective Costa, you've been staring at those papers for hours," Detective Martinez said, poking her head into my office. "You found something?"

"Maybe," I muttered, pushing aside the frustration that was building up inside me. I combed through hundreds of files, social medias, online lives, and mountains of paperwork. And there it was – the goddamn link. The one thing that linked the Kents with Hamilton. My heart sank, and I couldn't shake off that nagging feeling that this was going to lead somewhere I didn't want it to go.

A light bulb flickered on in my mind, casting a shadow on the immaculate image of Tuesday May. I couldn't deny that something was connecting these cases – and that something was foster care.
"Shit," I muttered, rubbing my temples as if it would somehow alleviate the gnawing feeling in my gut. I picked up the phone and dialled the number for the foster unit, trying to keep my voice steady. "Hey, it's Detective Costa. I need the paperwork for the Kents and Hamiltons, like, yesterday."
The receptionist on the other end assured me they'd have the files sent over as soon as possible, but it felt like an eternity before they finally arrived. When they did, I tore into them like a man possessed, scouring each page for any hint of a connection. And then, there it was – a name that stood out like a sore thumb: Tuesday May.
"Fuck me," I whispered, staring at her name scrawled across the pages. She had been a foster child in both homes. The universe was laughing at my expense, wasn't it?
"Got something interesting there, Dimitri?" Detective Martinez sauntered into my office again.
"Maybe," I hedged, not wanting to reveal too much until I was certain.
"Alright, well, let me know," he smiled and walked out. ,
As I continued rifling through the paperwork, I could feel my heart rate steadily climbing. There was no way that sweet, beautiful Tuesday could be involved in something so

sinister... right? But the more I investigated, the harder it became to deny the possibility.
"Fuck this coincidence," I muttered as I sipped my coffee, trying to make sense of it all. "Tuesday had to be involved somehow, but what if she's just a pawn?" My mind raced, struggling to find an explanation that didn't betray my trust in her.
The sun dipped low in the sky, casting a golden glow on the stacks of paperwork that cluttered my desk. I couldn't shake the nagging feeling that gnawed at me, so I grabbed my jacket and hastily stuffed the files into my bag. Time was running out, and I needed to do something about it.
I made my way to the exit. I could feel the weight of the files pressing against my chest, a reminder of the uncomfortable truth I might be about to uncover.
As I slid behind the wheel of my car, I took a moment to collect myself. My thoughts raced, circling around Tuesday like a moth drawn to a flame. I wanted desperately to be wrong, to find an explanation that didn't make her the killer. But I couldn't ignore the evidence that seemed to be piling up against her.
"Shit," I whispered under my breath, my fingers drumming anxiously on the steering wheel. "Alright, Dimitri, you've got this. Just gotta investigate every angle first. Can't let my feelings cloud my judgment."

I pulled out of the precinct's parking lot and began the drive home, all the while mulling over the case in my head. The more I thought about it, the more ludicrous it seemed that my sweet Tuesday could be responsible for such heinous acts. And yet...

"Fuck it," I muttered, gripping the wheel tighter. "I'll get to the bottom of this, even if it kills me."

I took a deep breath and hit the call button, my fingers tapping nervously on the dashboard. The phone rang twice before she picked up.

"Hey, Tuesday," I said, trying to keep my voice steady. "What are you up to?"

"Hi Detective," she replied sweetly. "Just at home, filling out some paperwork for the sale of the mansion." She chuckled lightly, and I couldn't help but smile.

"Sounds like fun," I said with a hint of sarcasm. "I'm heading home now, see you soon baby?"

"See you soon Detective" she purred back.

My heart raced as I continued on my way home, the drive feeling longer than ever. I shook my head, trying to clear away any negative thoughts. There was no way Tuesday could be the killer. She was beautiful, sweet, and caring. No one that sweet could possibly commit such atrocities.

"Dammit, Dimitri," I muttered to myself. "You can't let your feelings get in the way of your job. You have to consider every possibility, even if it hurts like hell."

As the miles stretched on, my gut twisted uncomfortably, warning me that something wasn't right. But I refused to accept it without concrete evidence.

Chapter 47

Tuesday May

A stack of papers lay before me, the ink on the last signature barely dry. The sale of the house was finally official, and I couldn't help but feel a strange blend of relief and excitement. My fingertips grazed over the smooth surface of the documents as I imagined leaving this dark mansion behind, trading its shadows for the warmth of my mother's home.

The sound of the front door creaking open tore me from my reverie. Dimitri was back. In an instant, I leapt up from my seat at the kitchen table, my heart racing with anticipation. It felt like he'd been gone for an eternity, even though it had only been hours since we'd shared our morning coffee.

"Sweetness!" Dimitri called out, his voice echoing through the empty halls.

"Dimi!" I shouted in response, sprinting toward the entrance. As soon as I saw him, I launched myself into his arms, my

legs wrapping around his waist as I clung to him like a lifeline. "God, I've missed you today."
His strong arms encircled me, and I could feel the comforting rhythm of his heartbeat beneath my cheek. "I missed you too," he murmured, pressing a tender kiss to my forehead.
"Guess what?" I whispered, pulling back just enough to look into his warm brown eyes. "I have fantastic news!"
Dimitri's laughter was a warm embrace, filling the air as he hugged me closer. With my arms still looped around his neck, he effortlessly carried me back toward the kitchen like I weighed nothing at all. The familiar scent of his cologne mixed with the lingering aroma of stale coffee and ink from the paperwork I'd been working on. I couldn't help but smile, feeling a surge of love and gratitude for this man who had walked into my life and changed it so irrevocably.
"Alright, Sweetness," Dimitri said, gently lowering me back into my seat at the kitchen table. His hand lingered on my waist for just a moment longer before he pulled out the chair beside me and sat down. "I've waited long enough. Spill the beans."
"Okay, okay," I giggled, unable to contain my excitement any longer. My heart hammered in my chest, anticipation building as I watched the curiosity flicker in Dimitri's eyes. "I just finished signing the papers. The house is officially sold!"

"Seriously?" Dimitri's face broke into a grin, and he reached for my hand, giving it a reassuring squeeze. "That's fantastic news, Tuesday! I'm so happy for you."
"Me too," I sighed, leaning against the back of my chair and staring wistfully at the ceiling. "Finally, we can leave this godforsaken place behind and start anew."
"Yes we can," Dimitri agreed, his voice full of conviction. "We'll make new memories, fill our days with laughter and love, and never look back. And, uh, maybe find some less creepy decor?"
"Ha! You know, I think I might actually miss the cobwebs," I teased, sticking my tongue out at him.
"Ah, well, we can always bring some with us," Dimitri chuckled, playfully nudging my shoulder. "But seriously, Tuesday, this is a huge step, and I'm so proud of you."
"Thanks, Dimi," I replied, feeling a warmth in my chest that had nothing to do with the hot chocolate I'd been sipping earlier. We sat there for a moment, basking in the glow of our shared happiness.
The smell of victory lingered in the air. I couldn't believe it was finally happening – we were breaking free from this haunted mansion and its dreadful memories.
"Alright, Dimi, so here's the deal," I began, excitement bubbling up inside me. "The house is officially sold! We'll be out of here in a week, and the new owners will take over a few weeks after that."

Dimitri's eyes lit up, and he couldn't help but grin. "Seriously? That's amazing, Sweetness! This place has been nothing but trouble since day one."

"Tell me about it," I agreed, rolling my eyes. "But guess what? My mom's house is actually liveable, so we can move there as soon as possible and leave this horrible mansion in the dust."

"Wow, you really did it, did you?" Dimitri teased, raising an eyebrow. "I'm impressed, sweetness."

"Hey, I'm a woman of action," I retorted playfully, giving him a mock-serious look. "When I set my mind to something, there's no stopping me."

"That is true," Dimitri said with a chuckle, reaching across the table to squeeze my hand. "But seriously, Tuesday, thank you for making all this happen. You're incredible, you know that?"

"Aw, shucks," I replied, pretending to be bashful as I glanced down at my lap. "You're not so bad yourself, Detective Costa."

"Is that right?" he asked, smirking as he leaned closer. "Well, I'm certainly glad you think so, Miss May."

"Of course," I murmured, unable to resist the pull of his warm brown eyes. "And now that we have our fresh start, just think of all the fun we can have together, exploring new places and making our own memories."

"Absolutely," Dimitri agreed, his voice full of warmth and promise. "Here's to the future, Sweetness. May it be filled with nothing but love, laughter, and adventure."
"Cheers to that," I said with a smile, raising an imaginary glass in a toast. And as we sat there, fingers entwined and hearts beating in sync, I knew without a doubt that whatever lay ahead, we were more than ready to face it – together.
At that moment, Mrs. Collins entered the room with a steaming pot of pasta in her hands. "Dinner is served," she announced, her voice as warm and welcoming as ever. As she set the pot down on the table, the delicious aroma wafted through the air, making my stomach rumble in anticipation.
"Thank you, Mrs. Collins," I said gratefully, giving her a genuine smile. She nodded in response, her eyes crinkling at the corners, before excusing herself and leaving us for our meal.
Dimitri and I dug into the pasta, savouring each flavourful bite while we chatted about our plans for the future. It felt so good to finally see a light at the end of the tunnel, to know that we were moving forward together.
With our stomachs full and hearts' content, Dimitri and I cleared the table and said our goodnights to Mrs Collins before making our way upstairs. As we entered our bedroom, I couldn't help but feel a sense of anticipation for what the future held – not just for the next week, but for all the weeks, months, and years to come.

Dimitri headed toward the shower, stripping as he went, the view was sensational, drawing me towards him with every step he took away. I walked into the bathroom and watched as the steam from the hot shower filled the room, creating a warm, inviting cocoon that seemed to beckon me as Dimitri stepped in. I watched as he closed his eyes and tilted his head back, letting the water cascade over his body before I couldn't help but join him.
"Hey," I murmured, wrapping my arms around his waist from behind. The slick feel of our wet skin against each other sent a shiver down my spine despite the heat from the shower.
"Hey yourself," Dimitri replied with a soft chuckle, his voice slightly muffled by the spray of water. "You couldn't resist, huh?"
"Absolutely not," I admitted, pressing a light kiss on his back. "I'm just so happy, Dimitri. I feel like everything is coming together nicely. We can go live in Mum's house, and I have enough money for us to live more than one lifetime. If you want to quit your job, you can. You can stay at home with me, and we can travel, go places I've never had the chance to go, see things I could only dream of."
Dimitri turned to face me, his strong arms encircling my waist as the water continued to wash over us both. He gazed into my eyes, his own filled with warmth and affection. "I love you, Sweetness," he confessed, his voice barely audible

over the sound of the shower. "You're the best thing that ever happened to me."

I searched his eyes, looking for any hint of doubt or hesitation, but all I saw was love – and a tiny flicker of sadness that disappeared almost as quickly as it had appeared.

Before I could ask him about it, Dimitri leaned down and captured my lips in a passionate kiss. My heart raced and my breathing grew shallow as he lifted me up by my ass, my legs instinctively wrapping around his waist as he deepened the kiss.

"Promise me we'll always be like this," I whispered against his lips, my fingers entwined in his wet hair.

"Forever and always, Sweetness" Dimitri promised, sealing it with another soul-stirring kiss that left me breathless and completely, utterly in love.

Chapter 48

Dimitri Costa

The light danced across the bathroom walls, casting a warm glow on Tuesday's wet skin as she stood beneath the shower head. Water streamed down her long, dark hair, tracing rivulets down her back and over her round, firm ass. She looked up at me, her piercing blue eyes locking onto mine, and a devilish grin spread across her face.

Losing myself in Tuesday was easy. It was like second nature. I gripped her ass firmly, lifting her so she could wrap her legs around my waist. Her warmth against my own hardened desire made me quiver with anticipation.

I couldn't control myself around this woman; she was a magnet drawing me in, always leaving me wanting more. My fingers dug into her soft flesh, eliciting a gasp from her lips that only served to fuel my desire.

"Tell me what you want, Sweetness," I murmured, seeking her approval before taking her completely. I needed her to say it, to voice her own need for me.

"Fuck me, Dimitri," she breathed, her voice trembling with urgency. "Take me right here, right now."

The steam from the shower surrounded us like a warm embrace, our bodies entwined and slick with desire. As I looked into Tuesday's piercing blue eyes, I couldn't help but be captivated by her raw beauty and the way she made me feel.

My thoughts flickered to the accusations that had been haunting me – the idea that she might be responsible for a string of brutal murders in our city. It seemed ludicrous to entertain such doubts, especially when I was drowning in her intoxicating presence.

I pressed her against the shower wall. The heat from the water contrasting with the cool surface sent shivers down my spine. She eagerly wrapped her legs around my waist, giving me easy access to what I craved most – her body.

"God, you're amazing," I murmured as I pushed my already hard cock into her waiting pussy. She was tight but also wet enough already to take me.

"Fuck, Dimitri... don't stop," Tuesday moaned, her voice music to my ears.

As I continued to move inside her, thoughts raced through my head. How could I doubt this woman? How could I even

entertain the idea that she was capable of something so heinous? But logic had no place here, not now. All that mattered was losing myself in Tuesday, drowning out everything else but her taste, her touch, and her cries of pleasure.
Water droplets clung to Tuesday's long, dark hair as they made their way down her body, eventually merging with the steamy shower spray. The sight of her was intoxicating, and I couldn't help but let out a low growl.
"Fuck, Dimitri, you're driving me crazy," she gasped, her piercing blue eyes locked on mine.
"Good," I replied, smirking as I set a slow rhythm, savouring every inch of her warmth enveloping me. The water cascaded down us both, steam rising and fogging the glass shower door. It felt like we were in our own little world, separate from everything else.
"Harder," Tuesday urged, her voice breathy and full of need.
"Patience, Sweetness," I teased, maintaining the same tantalising pace.
"Asshole," she muttered with a playful glare, clearly enjoying our banter even in this intimate moment.
"Guilty as charged," I admitted with a grin, loving the way her eyes sparkled when she was feisty.
Tuesday brought her hands up to her breasts, pinching and flicking her own nipples with a mischievous smile. That sight alone nearly did me in. To keep myself from losing control, I

focused on supporting her weight with both hands on her hips, lifting her slightly with each thrust.
"God, you're beautiful," I groaned, feeling my desire for her building to an almost unbearable level. My thoughts raced, and my heart pounded, but all that mattered right now was Tuesday and the pleasure we were sharing.
"Touch yourself for me, Tuesday," I commanded, my voice low and husky. Her fingers immediately slid down to tease her clit. The sight of her touching herself so willingly lost in pleasure, made my heart race.
"Fuck, you're so sexy," I groaned, my thrusts becoming more forceful as I struggled to maintain control despite the overwhelming passion coursing through me. My legs began to cramp from holding her up, but I refused to let that slow me down. I needed this.
"More... please," she whimpered, her fingers moving faster over her swollen nub, her moans growing louder and more desperate with each passing moment. Her body was my sanctuary, a place where I could forget everything else and simply lose myself in her warmth and desire. And right now, there was nothing I craved more than to see her unravel in my arms.
"God, you feel incredible," I told her, my voice barely audible over the sound of the water pounding against the shower wall and floor. She looked up at me, her blue eyes wide and filled

with lust, silently begging for the release she so desperately needed.
"Come for me, baby," I urged, increasing my pace as the tension in my lower abdomen became almost unbearable. "I want to feel you fall apart around me."
Her hand moved even faster, her breathing coming in ragged gasps as she teetered on the edge of ecstasy. I watched, entranced, as her body tightened, her thighs quivering with anticipation.
"Fuck, Dimitri, I'm so close..." she cried out, her nails digging into my shoulder as she clung to me for dear life.
"Let go, Tuesday," I whispered into her ear, hoping my words would be enough to push her over the edge. "I've got you.
And then, with one final, desperate moan, she shattered in my arms, her inner walls clamping down on me as she milked every last drop of pleasure from my body. The sensation was so intense that I couldn't hold back any longer, pumping my cum deep inside her greedy pussy. As we came down from our joint high, I set her back down on the shower floor, making sure her legs were steady enough to hold her up.
With water droplets glistening on her naked body like tiny diamonds, Tuesday looked ethereal as she leaned against the shower wall, catching her breath. The steam in the room added an otherworldly haze to the scene, and I couldn't help but smile at the sight of this woman who had such a hold on me.

"Come here, Sweetness," I said softly, pulling her towards me so we could rinse off the remnants of our passion. As I gently washed her with a soapy cloth, she closed her eyes and sighed contentedly. "You okay?"
"Mmm, better than okay," she murmured, her blue eyes flicking open for a moment before closing again as she leaned into my touch.
I took my time cleaning every inch of her body, enjoying the feel of her silky skin beneath my hands. When I finished, she took the cloth from me and returned the favour, her fingers trailing over my chest and down my abdomen, causing my dick to twitch back to life.
"Looks like someone's ready for round two," she teased, a wicked grin playing on her lips.
"Can you blame me?" I replied, raising an eyebrow. "You're fucking addictive."
She laughed a melodic sound that always made my heart swell. "Well, I'm not going anywhere, Detective. You can have all the tastes and moans you want."
As she continued washing me, I couldn't help but marvel at how insatiable she made me feel. It was rare for me to desire someone with such intensity, and yet, with Tuesday, it felt like I could never get enough of her. Her scent, her touch, the way she whispered my name when we were lost in each other – it was intoxicating.

"Promise me something, Dimitri," she said, her voice suddenly serious.
"Anything, Sweetness," I responded, my brow furrowing with concern.
"Promise me that no matter what happens, we'll always find our way back to each other. In this shower, in our bed, anywhere. Just...promise me you'll never let go."
Her words were heavy with emotion, and I could see the vulnerability shining in her eyes.
“Tuesday, May, I promise," I whispered, pulling her close and pressing my lips to her forehead. "No matter what, I'll stay." And I meant it, I would stay, even if she was the killer. I had never loved anyone like her before, she was my soul mate.

Chapter 49

Tuesday May

The sun had barely risen when Dimitri kissed me goodbye, his warm brown eyes filled with concern. "Be careful, Sweetness," he whispered before heading off to work. As soon as the door closed behind him, I turned to Mr. Thompson.

"Today's the day," I said, trying to sound brave. But inside, I was a storm of emotions - anger, fear, and a thirst for vengeance.

"Indeed it is, Miss May," Mr Thompson replied, his stoic expression belying the gravity of our plan. He handed me a plastic shopping bag containing a box of chocolates. "I've taken care of everything," he assured me. "These chocolates are now filled with poison. The box is wrapped in plastic so there won't be any fingerprints left on it."

"Damn, Mr. T, you really thought of everything." I grinned at him, though I couldn't shake the feeling that we were dancing

on a razor's edge. My heart raced as I imagined the end game unfolding, finally getting justice for my childhood pain.
"Miss May," Mr. Thompson said, his voice serious. "This is a dangerous path we're taking, and there's no turning back once it's done. Are you absolutely certain about this?"
I looked into his eyes, seeing the genuine concern for my well-being there. I knew he'd support me no matter what, but the weight of my decision settled heavily on my shoulders.
"Fuck yeah, I'm sure," I said, my voice unwavering. "Mr. Jennings deserves everything that's coming to him. It's time karma paid a visit."
"Very well, then," Mr. Thompson nodded, determination shining in his eyes. "Let's bring down the curtain on this twisted performance."
The sun streamed through the kitchen window, catching the buttery glint of our croissants as Mr Thompson and I shared a light breakfast. We ate in silence, the tension between us palpable as we both knew what lay ahead. My heart raced in anticipation, a mixture of excitement and fear coiling within me like a snake ready to strike.
"Alright, Mr. T," I said with forced cheerfulness, brushing crumbs off my fingers and tossing my napkin onto the table. "Time's a-wasting, and we've got a date with destiny."
"Very true, Miss May." He stood up and cleared our plates, his movements efficient but betraying a hint of unease. He

knew this was dangerous, and so did I. But there was no turning back now.
We headed out to the garage, where my car waited like a predator eager for the hunt. The thought of finally confronting Mr. Jennings made my palms sweaty, but I gripped the wheel with determination. Mr Thompson settled into the passenger seat, his eyes locked on the road ahead as if he could will our success into existence.
"Ready?" I asked, more to myself than to him.
"Ready," he confirmed, and I could hear the steely resolve in his voice. It helped steady my own nerves as I started the engine and backed out of the driveway.
The drive to Mr. Jennings' place was one of silent contemplation. While I manoeuvred through the morning traffic, my thoughts swirled around the memories of my past – the pain, the shame, the anger. And intertwined with it all was the burning desire for revenge, for justice. Today, karma would come calling.
"Miss May," Mr. Thompson finally spoke up, breaking my reverie. "Remember to stay calm and focused."
"Got it, Mr. T," I replied, trying to keep my voice steady. "Just stick to the plan."
"Exactly." He gave me a small, reassuring smile that warmed my heart. For all his seriousness and precision, Mr. Thompson had a soft side that showed through every now and then.

I took a deep breath, steeling myself for what was to come. This was it – the moment of truth. And as much as I wanted to dance around it like a giddy schoolgirl, I knew I had to face it head-on. No more hiding, no more running. Today, I would make Mr. Jennings pay for what he had done.
The early morning sunlight glinted off the polished chrome of mailboxes all neatly lined up as we parked out front. My heart raced like a wild stallion, eager to be unleashed. "Showtime," I whispered, feeling a wicked grin stretch across my face.
"Remember, Miss May, stay collected and composed," Mr. Thompson reminded me, his tone steady and calm.
"Of course, Mr T." I winked at him before stepping out of the car, my heels clicking confidently on the pavement.
We strolled up the path towards the front door, the scent of freshly cut grass tickling my nose. I couldn't help but feel a perverse sense of excitement at the prospect of finally getting even with the man who had tormented my childhood. Knocking on the door with a few sharp raps, I squared my shoulders, ready for our little tête-à-tête.
The door swung open, and there stood Mr. Jennings in his work uniform. His eyes widened like saucers when they landed on me. "Tuesday? What the fuck are you doing here?"
"Surprise, surprise," I drawled, playfully twirling a lock of my hair around my finger. "Can't a girl drop by to see an old... friend?" The word tasted bitter in my mouth, but it was all part of the game.

"Uh, sure," he stuttered, clearly flustered by my unexpected arrival. "Come on in, I guess."
"Thanks, doll," I purred, stepping inside with Mr. Thompson following closely behind. The familiar sensation of being back around this man sent shivers down my spine, but I pushed it aside – I had a job to do, and nothing was going to stand in my way.
The warmth of Mr. Jennings' hallway wrapped around me as I stepped inside, a stark contrast to the chilly air that nipped at my cheeks just moments before. "So, Tuesday," he said, his voice dripping with false concern, "it's been a while. What can I do for you?"
"Actually, I just wanted to chat." I gestured towards Mr. Thompson. "Oh, and this is my butler, Mr. Thompson."
"Your... butler?" Mr Jennings raised an eyebrow, trying to hide his surprise poorly. "Well, isn't that fancy?”
"Isn't it?" I replied, letting a coy smile play on my lips. The bastard didn't know what was coming.
"Take a seat," Mr. Jennings offered, gesturing to the couch. I could practically feel the tension radiating off Mr. Thompson as he sat down next to me, but I kept my own emotions locked away tight. We were playing a dangerous game, and I wasn't about to let myself be vulnerable.
"Would you like some tea or coffee?" Mr. Jennings asked, trying to sound hospitable and failing miserably.

"Neither, thanks," I replied, my voice light and airy. "We won't be staying long."
"Here," I said with a sly grin, extending the plastic bag with the box of chocolates towards Mr. Jennings. "I brought you some chocolates as a token of goodwill. But can I have the bag back?"
"Uh, sure," he stuttered, pulling the wrapped box from the bag and handing it back to me. I felt a rush of adrenaline knowing that he held his own demise in his hands.
"Anyway," Mr. Jennings said, trying to regain his composure. "What can I do for you both today?"
"Isn't it obvious?" I giggled, feeling giddy at the prospect of finally getting my revenge. "I just wanted to drop by, say that I've forgiven you for...you know, what happened all those years ago. And maybe hear a sincere apology from you."
"Sorry? For what?" he blinked at me, playing coy. The audacity of this man.
"Really?" I scoffed, rolling my eyes. "For molesting a 13-year-old without consent. But hey, if that doesn't ring a bell, no worries."
"Tuesday, I think it's time to leave," Mr. Jennings growled, standing up abruptly.
"Fine by me," I shrugged nonchalantly, though my heart was pounding in my chest.
I sauntered out of the living room, taking in the sight of Mr. Jennings' face – a mixture of confusion, anger, and fear. Just

as he was about to slam the door behind us, I turned back with a wicked grin.
"Remember, karma always finds you, Mr. Jennings," I called out sweetly before the door shut with a loud bang, leaving me a little thrill in my chest.
"Damn, Tuesday," Mr. Thompson chuckled, holding out his hand for me to take.
Placing my hand in his as we walked back to the car. The sun shone brightly on our faces, but it couldn't compare to the warmth radiating from within me. Finally, I was one step closer to getting the justice I deserved.
As we reached the car, Mr. Thompson pulled me into a sideways hug, squeezing me gently. "You did good, kid. Now let's go home."
"Thanks, Mr. T," I said, returning the embrace. Mr Thompson had been there for me through thick and thin since I met him. His loyalty and protection meant more to me than anything else. "Couldn't have done it without you."
"Ah, don't mention it," he replied, releasing me from the hug. "It's about time that bastard faced the consequences of his actions."
With that, we climbed into my car, the leather seats welcoming us like old friends. As I started the engine, I couldn't help but think about how much had changed since that fateful day years ago when Mr. Jennings violated my trust.

"Ready to head back?" I asked, feeling a newfound sense of freedom and power.
"Absolutely," Mr. Thompson responded, his eyes meeting mine with unwavering support. "Let's go home."

Chapter 50

Dimitri Costa

I left early that morning, the sun barely peeking over the horizon. As I stepped out of the house and sauntered towards her car parked in the garage. "Forgive me, Sweetness," I whispered under my breath, snapping a tracker onto the underside of her car before slipping away like a ghost. I jumped in my car and parked a few streets away, my breath fogged up the windshield as I parked hidden behind an old oak tree.

I needed to be sure she wasn't the killer, but if she was... Damn it, I'd do whatever it took to keep her safe. I couldn't understand why I felt this way – I'm a detective, for fuck's sake! But Tuesday had wormed her way into my heart, and now I was in too deep.

I leaned against the steering wheel, watching the house from a distance. "Come on, Sweetness," I murmured, my fingers

tapping impatiently on the wheel. "Show me what you're up to."
When she finally emerged with Mr Thompson in tow. She looked like she was on a mission, and I couldn't help but admire her determination. They climbed into er car and took off down the driveway.
"Alright, Sweetness," I muttered under my breath, starting the engine. "Let's see where you're off to."
I trailed behind at a distance, following the tracker rather than her car, careful not to draw attention. The tension in my chest grew with every turn, each mile bringing me closer to the truth – or so I hoped. It wasn't like me to play it safe, but something about Tuesday had me wrapped around her finger, and I couldn't risk losing her.
"Shit, what am I doing?" I sighed, gripping the steering wheel tighter. "This isn't how I roll."
Yet, there I was, acting like some love-struck fool. Despite all logic and reason, I couldn't help but feel a connection to her – one that went beyond anything I could explain. And that scared the hell out of me.
"Damn it, Dimitri, get your shit together," I chastised myself, shaking my head. "You're a detective, not a damn teenager."
As I followed the tracker, Tuesday's car pulled up outside a set of townhouse units. My heart raced as I parked a distance up the road and watched, trying to discern what she was up to.

"Of course, it can't be that easy," I grumbled, squinting into the fading light.
I watched Tuesday and Thompson approach the door, my heart thudded in my chest like a goddamn jackhammer. What the hell was she doing here?
I quickly pulled out my phone and ran an address check on the house number. Bingo – the name Jennings popped up. I remembered him as the bastard who had molested Tuesday, the one she'd tried to stab in retaliation. What was she up to now?
"Okay, Dimitri, think," I whispered to myself, drumming my fingers on the steering wheel. "You're just here to keep an eye on her, right? Just another job."
But even as I said the words, I knew it wasn't true. This was more than just a job – this was personal. And that scared me more than any criminal I'd ever faced.
"Fuck it," I muttered, watching intently as Tuesday and Thompson disappeared into the house. "You've got this, Detective. It's just another case."
Except it wasn't. And I knew that no matter how hard I tried to deny it, there was something about Tuesday May that had changed me – and that terrified me more than anything else.
I leaned back in my car seat, the cold leather sending a shiver down my spine. Tuesday and Thompson were inside Jennings' house now, and there was nothing left for me to do but wait. I pulled out my notepad, thumbing through the

pages of notes I'd compiled on Tuesday. When we'd first done a background check on her after her father died, it hadn't been this in-depth. But now, with the stakes so much higher, I couldn't help but dig deeper.
"Let's see what we've got here," I muttered, scanning over the lines of information. "Tuesday May, twenty-three years old, charged with attempted murder but placed in a Mental Health Ward and diagnosed with psychosis, in the foster unit since birth, jumped from family to family..."
"Fuck, this is a mess," I sighed, rubbing my temples as I tried to make sense of my feelings. Normally, I could separate myself from a case – stay objective and focused on the task at hand. But when it came to Tuesday, everything was a tangled web of emotions and desires. And that wasn't something I was used to dealing with, especially when it came to murderers.
"Shit, get a grip," I scolded myself, trying to shake off the confusing thoughts swirling around in my head. "You're a goddamn detective, remember?"
"Alright, so maybe she's out for revenge," I reasoned, thinking back to the incident with Jennings. It would make sense, given her past. But was that really enough to turn an otherwise law-abiding citizen into a killer?
"Can't say I blame her, though," I admitted, feeling a pang of sympathy despite my better judgment. After what she'd been through, who wouldn't want to make the bastards pay? But

getting involved with her like this – letting my emotions cloud my judgment – was a dangerous game to play.
"Alright, Dimitri, focus," I told myself firmly, forcing my attention back to the task at hand. "You're here to keep an eye on her, not to play Romeo and fucking Juliet. Just watch and learn – figure out if she's the killer or not."
I was getting antsy in my car, drumming my fingers on the steering wheel while keeping a close eye on the door Tuesday and Mr. Thompson had disappeared behind. My heart raced like a fucking stallion every time I thought about what might be going down inside that house.
"Come on, come on," I muttered to myself, not quite sure if I wanted them to hurry up or take their sweet time. The longer they were in there, the more likely it was that something had gone wrong.
Just when I was starting to consider getting out of the car and doing some investigating of my own, the front door burst open, revealing a fuming Mr Jennings. His face was beet red as he practically shoved Tuesday and Mr. Thompson onto the sidewalk, saying something to them that I couldn't make out from where I was sitting.
"Shit," I whispered, watching Tuesday and Mr Thompson exchange a few words before making their way back to her car. She looked strangely happy, and unharmed – and more importantly, so did Mr. Jennings. If she'd been planning to hurt him, she clearly hadn't gone through with it.

"Damn it, Tuesday," I muttered under my breath as they drove away. "What the fuck are you up to?"
As I watched the tracker on my phone move in the direction of the mansion, I couldn't help but feel a strange mix of relief and disappointment. On one hand, it was good to know that she wasn't the cold-blooded killer I'd initially suspected – but on the other, it meant that I was no closer to figuring out what the hell was going on.
"Maybe I'm losing my touch," I mused, drumming my fingers on the steering wheel once more. "Or maybe…maybe she's just that good at hiding her true nature."
I revved the engine and sped towards the office, my heart pounding in my chest. The adrenaline was pumping through me like a drug – I couldn't help but feel alive, even as the stakes grew higher and higher.
"Sweetness," I whispered to myself with a small grin. "What kind of mess have you gotten yourself into?"
As soon as I stepped into the office, I caught a glimpse of Detective Martinez hunched over his desk, papers scattered everywhere. The creases on his forehead deepened as he squinted at something on his computer screen.
"Hey, Martinez," I called out, casually leaning against his desk. "Whatcha got there?"
Martinez hesitated for a moment, then sighed. "You're not going to like this," he muttered, sliding a folder across the desk.

"And why is that," I stated, snatching up the folder. As I flipped it open, my eyes were immediately drawn to Tuesday's name – right at the top of the suspect list.
"Shit," I muttered, feeling a surge of protectiveness well up inside me.
"Looks like your girl has some skeletons in her closet," Martinez quipped, clearly enjoying my discomfort. "Guess she's not so innocent after all."
"Fuck off," I snapped, slamming the folder shut. I knew what I had to do – I had to find a way to clear her name, even if it meant bending the rules a little. Or a lot.
"Hey, Costa," Martinez called out as I stormed towards the door. "Just remember – we're not in the business of playing favourites. We're here to catch a killer, and if she's guilty…"
"I know," I cut him off, gritting my teeth. "I'll do what needs to be done."
But as I left the office, the thought of turning Tuesday in – of losing her forever – felt like a dagger to the heart. And I knew, without a doubt, that I'd do anything to keep that from happening.

Chapter 51

Tuesday May

The rain splattered against the windowpane, distorting the view outside. I sighed and took a sip of my lukewarm hot chocolate, trying to shake off the heaviness that had settled in my chest. It had been a few days since Mr Jennings' death made headlines, and I couldn't help but feel some sort of twisted pride that I had been the reason he made the news at all.

“I'll always keep you safe," Dimitri said softly to me last night. His long hours at work left me feeling lonely, and the silence in the mansion only amplified my racing thoughts when he was gone.

The musty scent of old furniture and faded memories hung in the air, creating a heavy atmosphere in the nearly empty mansion. I wandered through the barren rooms, my footsteps echoing like a ghostly whisper. It felt surreal – this house was now just a shell, waiting to be left behind.

"Sweetness, you alright?" Dimitri's voice snapped me back into reality as he appeared in the doorway of what used to be my bedroom, concern etched on his face.
"Of course," I lied, forcing a smile. "Just taking one last look around, y'know?"
"Understandable," he replied, stepping closer and wrapping an arm around me. "We'll be out of here in two days, starting fresh."
"Can't come soon enough," I muttered, leaning into him for comfort.
"Hey, remember when I caught you and Mr. Thompson in that heated discussion yesterday?" I asked, eager to change the subject. "You never did tell me what it was about."
Dimitri sighed, his grip tightening ever so slightly. "It wasn't anything important, Sweetness. Just work stuff. You know how it is."
"Right," I responded, though I couldn't shake the feeling that there was more to it than that. But I let it go – I trusted Dimitri, even if he was keeping something from me.
"God, this place looks like a scene from a post-apocalyptic movie," I joked, trying to lighten the mood as we continued walking through the house. Mr. Thompson and Mrs. Collins were staying at their own homes until we moved to my mother's house.
"Ha, yeah," Dimitri chuckled, his brown eyes glancing around the room. "All we need are some zombies or mutants roaming

around." As he held his arms up and started to chase me around the barren rooms.

"laughing as I ran, I allowed him to catch me and scoop me up. breathing in his scent I asked how his case was going only to get the same generic response I got daily.

"Can't talk about it, Sweetness," he reminded me gently, though I could see the tired lines around his eyes deepening as he spoke. "You know that."

"Right," I sighed, frustrated but understanding.

The glow from the setting sun illuminated the empty mansion, casting long shadows across the barren rooms as I sat on the lone mattress in my once-luxurious bedroom. The phone rang, its sharp trill breaking the eerie silence.

"Hey Sweetness," Dimitri's voice sounded tired and distant on the other end of the call, making me frown with concern. "I'm going to be home late again."

"Again?" I sighed, trying to ignore the pang of loneliness that constricted my chest. "It's fine, I understand. You have a case to solve, after all."

"Thanks for understanding," he replied softly, his tone apologetic. "I'll see you later, alright?"

"Alright," I agreed, hanging up the phone and sinking back onto the mattress. As much as I missed him, I couldn't blame Dimitri for working late. After all, this mess was my doing.

Hours passed in solitude, the heavy air of the empty house pressing down on me like a suffocating blanket. It wasn't until around 7 pm that there was a sudden knock on the door, the sound echoing through the vacant halls.

"Who could that be at this hour?" I muttered to myself, curiosity piquing as I listened to Mr Thompson's footsteps approach the entrance as I headed for the stairs.

"Good evening, sir. How can I hel—" Mr Thompson's polite inquiry was cut off by angry shouts and the unmistakable sound of armed police and a SWAT team barreling into the mansion.

"Mr. Thompson!" I cried out, leaping from the stairs and sprinting towards the hallway. My heart raced as I skidded to a halt, my eyes widening in shock at the sight before me.

"Mr Thompson, you are under arrest for the murders of Mr Hamilton, Mr and Mrs Kent, and Mr Jennings!" one of the officers barked, roughly cuffing Mr Thompson's wrists as he struggled against their grip.

"Wait, what the fuck is going on?!" I screamed, feeling my world crumble around me. "Dimitri! Where are you? Help him!"

Just as my heart threatened to burst from my chest, Dimitri finally appeared in the doorway. His eyes were downcast, and he refused to meet my gaze. Fury surged through me like a wildfire.

"Sweetness, I'm so sorry..." Dimitri's voice was barely above a whisper.
"Sorry? What the fuck is happening, Dimitri?" I screamed at him, tears streaming down my face. "You need to help Mr. Thompson!"
But he remained silent, his jaw clenched tightly. I couldn't believe it – the man I trusted more than anyone else was just letting this happen.
"Miss Tuesday Wellington," another detective stepped forward, his cold, unfeeling eyes boring into mine. "You're under arrest for accessory to murder. You have the right to remain silent, anything you say can and will be used against you in a court of law..."
His words washed over me, but my focus remained on Dimitri, pleading with him to do something, anything. Yet he stood there, frozen, unable or unwilling to come to our aid.
"Fuck you, Dimitri," I spat out, feeling more betrayed than I ever had in my life. As the handcuffs clicked around my wrists, I wondered what he had found. My heart raced as I stared at Dimitri, desperately seeking a shred of the man I knew in his eyes. But he refused to meet my gaze, leaving me feeling abandoned and vulnerable.
"Dammit, Dimitri! Do something!" I screamed, my voice raw with emotion. But he remained silent, a bystander in this nightmare unfolding before us.

"Alright, let's move," one of the officers barked, shoving Mr. Thompson and me toward the door. I stumbled, but the detective holding me kept me upright.

The biting cold outside hit me like a slap in the face, but it was nothing compared to the emptiness settling in my chest. The flashing blue and red lights of the police cars cast eerie shadows across the mansion we were leaving behind.

"Get in!" another officer commanded, pushing us into the back of a cruiser.

"Hey, watch it!" I protested, my feisty nature refusing to be completely extinguished.

"Tuesday," Mr. Thompson whispered urgently as soon as the door slammed shut behind us. "Whatever you do, say nothing. Not a word. I'll handle this."

"Mr. Thompson," I began, fear creeping into my voice. "What the hell is going on? How did we end up here?"

"Shhh," he hushed me, his usually calm demeanour cracking under the pressure. "I'm not certain, but I promise you, you'll get through this."

"What do you mean by you'll what about you?" I couldn't help but challenge him, my faith in everyone around me was dangerously close to shattering. "Because right now, it feels like everyone I've trusted has turned their backs on me."

"Trust me, Tuesday," he implored, his eyes searching mine for understanding. "We're not going down without a fight. Just keep quiet, and let me handle things for now. Can you do that?"

I swallowed hard, nodding my agreement. As the police car pulled away, I couldn't shake the uneasy feeling gnawing at me, whispering that things were about to get a whole lot worse before they got better. But for now, all I could do was sit in silence, clinging to what little hope remained.

Chapter 52

Dimitri Costa

The rain tapped against the window like a lover's impatient fingers, reminding me of how I used to call Tuesday "Sweetness" as we lay tangled in each other's arms. But now, things had turned sour. I was removed from the case when Detective Martinez worked out the link. He was thorough, I'll give him that. As much as it pained me, I knew he only did his job.

"Costa," he said, leaning against the doorframe of my office, "it's time to pick them up. You're coming with us, but you know the drill – no interference."

My heart raced, and I nodded. "Sure thing, Martinez. Just along for the ride, right?"

His eyes narrowed, but he didn't question my intentions. We walked together to the unmarked police car, the rain still pouring down, drenching our clothes like the cold truth soaking into my very soul.

"Sweetness" – the nickname echoed through my mind, mocking me as I climbed into the car and we drove in silence to the mansion.

"Alright, Costa, remember your place," Martinez reminded me as we pulled up to the house. "Let us handle this."

"Fine," I agreed, gritting my teeth. "But if you hurt her..."

"Relax," he replied, stepping out of the car. "We'll be gentle."

As they went to the door, I stayed back, watching from a distance as they prepared to take away the woman I loved. My heart ached, and I felt helpless, but I knew I'd prove her innocence.

"Costa, come on!" Detective Martinez called out to me, his voice snapping me back to the present. I followed him and the other officers into the house.

The cold fluorescent light flickered above me as I paced back and forth in front of the chief's office like a lion whose territory had been invaded. The door swung open, and the Chief beckoned me inside with an air of concern.

"Costa, come in," he said, his voice weary. "Have a seat."

I lowered myself into the chair across from him, feeling the weight of my emotions pressing down on me. He studied me for a moment before he spoke.

"Look, Dimitri, I know you're going through hell right now. I'm worried about you. We all are," he said, his brown eyes filled with genuine concern.

"Thanks, Chief," I replied, rubbing my hands together nervously. "But I'd be doing a lot better if everyone would just get off Tuesday's case. She didn't do it, I know she didn't."
"Alright, let's talk about that" he sighed, leaning back in his chair. "You're sure about her innocence?"
"Damn straight," I shot back, my heart pounding in my chest. "There's no concrete evidence against her. No DNA, no fingerprints, nothing. You can't tell me a foster kid with a history of abuse doesn't deserve a fair shake."
Chief Davis rubbed his temples, considering my words. "You're right, Costa. The evidence is circumstantial at best. But the fact remains, she accused her foster parents of molesting her, and now they're all dead. It's not looking good for her."
"Its bullshit," I snapped.
"Costa, I understand your loyalty. But this is out of our hands now," He said, his voice heavy with resignation. "We have to let the system do its job. If Tuesday and Mr. Thompson are innocent, they'll be acquitted."
"Fuck the system," I muttered under my breath, clenching my fists tightly. "It wasn't there for her when she needed it most."
"Sometimes we have to believe in the justice system, Dimitri" he said softly, placing a hand on my shoulder. "I know it's hard, but you have to trust it."

"I thought i did, now im not sure" I replied bitterly, shaking off his hand.

"Costa, you need to take some time off" he insisted, concern etching deeper lines into his already worn face. "You're too close to this case, and you need to clear your head."

"Fine" I spat, standing up abruptly. "But I'm not giving up on her. Not now, not ever."

As I stormed out of the office, I couldn't help but feel like the walls were closing in on me. But one thing was certain - I'd fight for Tuesday until my last breath, no matter what it took.

Chapter 53

Father David

I sat at the kitchen table, nursing a steaming mug of black coffee as I crunched into my bowl of Weetabix. With a sigh, I unfolded the newspaper, eagerly anticipating the day's headlines.

"Oh," I muttered, nearly falling out of my chair when I saw the front page. There, in bold print, was the headline: *"23-year-old Tuesday May and Her Butler Mr Thompson on Trial for Murder."*

"Miss Kellie?" I asked Mrs. Kellie, one of the nuns, who just happened to be passing by with a tray of freshly baked scones. She glanced over at the paper, her eyes widening in shock.

"Good heavens! Tuesday May? That little baby you found all those years ago?"

"None other," I replied, shaking my head. "And she's accused of being a serial killer"

"Dear Lord," she gasped, setting down the tray before taking a seat beside me. "Who would've thought that sweet little girl could do such a thing?"

"Exactly," I said, my mind racing with memories of the little baby left on the church doorstep.

"Father David," Mrs. Kellie said gently, interrupting my thoughts. "You seem troubled. Is there anything I can do to help?"

"Thank you," I sighed, running a hand through my hair in frustration. "But I'm not sure there's much anyone can do right now."

"Indeed," she agreed, patting my hand reassuringly before rising to her feet. "Just remember, Father David, the Lord works in mysterious ways. Perhaps there's a reason for all this that we can't yet see."

"Maybe you're right," I conceded, my thoughts drifting back to that little baby with bright blue eyes.

My fingers trembled as I flipped to the middle of the paper, my heart pounding like a jackhammer. The full article sprawled across two pages, detailing every twisted aspect of Tuesday's life.

23 years ago, a baby was discovered on the steps of a church in Willows End. Her mother Lillian Wellington had abandoned her. Tuesday spent 13 years in foster care before being committed to a mental health facility for 10 years. This came after she attempted to stab her foster father, whom she accused of molesting her.

At the age of 23, Tuesday discovered that her presumed father was actually Mr George Wellington through a DNA test. Shortly after moving in with him, Mr. Wellington was found dead at the bottom of the grand staircase. Tuesday was investigated for any involvement in his death but was cleared of all suspicions. She then began a sexual relationship with Detective Dimitri Costa, who had been assigned to the case.

Mr. Costa was initially handling the case for Mr. Hamilton, Mr. and Mrs. Kent until he was taken off after Mr. Jennings' death. Despite being cleared of any involvement, he firmly believes in Tuesday and Mr Thompson's innocence. As the case remains unsolved, Detective Dimitri Costa has been put on administrative leave. Miss May and Mr Thompson's court appearance today will determine the outcome of their charges.

I practically sprinted out of the kitchen, my mind racing a mile a minute. How could I have let this happen? Wasn't it my responsibility to look after those who came into my life, especially the most vulnerable? I should have done more.

The church doors seemed heavier than usual as I pushed them open, my chest tightening with guilt. I fell to my knees in front of the altar, tears streaming down my cheeks.

"Lord," I whispered, "forgive me for not helping that beautiful little girl when she needed it the most. I should have done more, watched over her, guided her... something, anything."

Nurse Amanda

I leaned against the cold wall in the back of the courtroom, shivering despite the warmth of my sweater. Curiosity had driven me here - I needed to know what happened to that tiny baby I cradled in the emergency room 23 years ago. The fluorescent lights above cast an eerie glow on the scene before me.

"Your Honour, I would now like to call Tuesday to the stand," announced the prosecutor. She was a small woman with glasses perched precariously on her nose, but she exuded confidence.

Tuesday stood up slowly and walked toward the witness stand, her long dark hair trailing behind her. God, she looked so different from that helpless infant I held two decades ago. Her eyes now held a sadness that could crush the soul, but there was a fierce determination in her stride.

"Please state your full name for the record," the prosecutor instructed. For a moment, Tuesday hesitated. Then, looking

straight at the judge, she spoke in a voice barely above a whisper: "Tuesday May."
"Alright, Tuesday, please tell the court your story." The prosecutor's tone softened, and I couldn't help but sense an air of camaraderie between them.
"Your Honour, members of the jury..." Tuesday paused, taking a deep breath. "I'm not sure where to start, but I guess I'll begin with a fact that might shock some people here: I know nothing of my birth, as I was abandoned by my mother Lillian Wellington on the steps of a church in Willows End. My mother had run away from my father George Wellington in a bit to keep me safe."
A murmur rippled through the courtroom, and I could feel the tension in the air. I stared at Tuesday as she continued, her voice growing stronger.
"From that point on, my life became a twisted roller coaster ride. I was passed around from one foster family to another. It seemed like nobody wanted me. Nobody cared." She stopped, her gaze drifting to the ceiling as if searching for the right words.
"Your Honour," she continued, her voice steady despite the weight of her words. "I want you to understand that I'm not asking for pity or sympathy. I'm here to tell you how the system, which was supposed to protect me, failed me over and over again."

She didn't flinch in the slightest as she recounted the horrors she had gone through at the hands of her foster families. Her eyes locked onto the judge's, daring him to look away.

"From the age of five, I was molested by the very people who were meant to care for me." The courtroom seemed to hold its breath as she spoke, and even I felt the sting of tears threatening to spill over.

"By the time I was thirteen, I'd had enough. I knew what Mr. Jennings did to me was wrong, but no one ever listened. So I fought back. I tried to stab him when he came for me one night. And you know what? I was the one who was locked away."

Her admission sent a shiver down my spine, but I couldn't help admiring her courage. She was taking control of her own narrative, refusing to be a victim any longer.

"Your Honour, members of the jury," she continued, her gaze sweeping the room, "I stand before you today pleading not guilty to all charges. Because I refuse to be punished for the death of monsters, ones that the police had no evidence of me even committing."

A murmur went through the audience, and I could see a few heads nodding in agreement. My own heart hammered in my chest, silently cheering her on.

"Thank you, Ms. May," the judge said solemnly, her face giving nothing away. But I saw a flicker in her eyes, a hint of understanding.

"Your testimony will be taken into account. The court is adjourned for today."

As the crowd began to disperse, I stood there, marvelling at Tuesday May. She had become a symbol of resilience and strength, a beacon for others who'd suffered like her. As she left the courtroom with her chin high and her steps purposeful, I knew that women would keep fighting, no matter what life threw at her.

Nurse Kyile

"Ms. Kylie, you're up," the bailiff called out, his voice echoing off the sterile walls.

"Shit," I muttered under my breath, my stomach lurching. I nearly vomited when I was called up to talk, but I knew I had a duty to my ex-patient, Tuesday. We had grown close over the course of the ten years she was in my care. My heart raced, pounding like a jackhammer in my chest as I got up from the uncomfortable plastic chair.

"Deep breaths, girl. You got this," I whispered to myself, trying to steady my nerves. I smoothed down my hair, which had tangled itself into unruly curls around my face, and brushed a nervous hand over my bright green eyes.

As I walked towards the door, I could feel the weight of the situation settling on my shoulders. This wasn't just any

ordinary day at work; this was about justice for a young woman who had been through hell and back. I owed it to her to be strong, to be the reassuring presence she needed in this godforsaken place.
"Please state your name and occupation for the record," the attorney asked me as I took my place on the stand.
"Kylie - uh, Kylie Rolls," I stammered, cursing my sudden inability to remember my last name. "I work at Hillcrest Mental Health Facility."
"Thank you, Kylie," the attorney said with a warm smile that didn't quite reach her eyes. She continued, "Can you tell us about your relationship with Tuesday?"

My palms were sweaty as I sat outside the courtroom, fidgeting with my scrubs. The fluorescent lights above buzzed softly, casting a harsh glow on the linoleum floor. I couldn't help but feel like a rabbit caught in a snare, just waiting for the verdict of Mr. Thompson and Tuesday May's trial.
A wave of hushed anticipation swirled through the hallway like a hungry ghost as the court attendant swung the door open, his voice cutting through the air. "The jury has reached a verdict."
"Shit," I muttered under my breath, heart pounding in my chest. I glanced over at Tuesday, who looked as pale as a damn ghost herself. She tried to offer me a faint smile, but it crumbled before it ever really formed. Poor girl.

As we filed back into the courtroom, I noticed Detective Dimitri Costa waiting in the pew behind Tuesday. Our eyes met for a fleeting moment, and he gave me a subtle nod – almost like a silent 'thank you.'

We all took our seats, the room practically buzzing with tension. I could've cut it with a knife – hell, probably even a spoon. My hands clenched around the edges of my seat, knuckles turning white, as I fought the urge to chew my nails down to the quick.

The smell of stale coffee and old wood filled my nostrils, while the hard wooden bench dug into my ass. It wasn't much, but it was better than letting my thoughts run wild.

"Order in the court!" the bailiff barked, snapping me out of my thoughts.

"Here we go," I sighed, bracing myself for whatever was coming next.

The judge rose from his seat like a conductor about to lead an orchestra, and the jury members took their places as if perfectly choreographed. The woman in the middle, the spokesperson for the jury, stood up with her shoulders squared and chin held high. I couldn't help but admire her confidence – hell, I could barely keep my breakfast down.

"Your Honour," she began, her voice clear and steady, "we, the jury, have reached a verdict."

"Fuck," I muttered under my breath, my heart pounding like a jackhammer against my ribs. It felt like the whole courtroom

was holding its collective breath, waiting for those fateful words.
"We find Mr. Thompson guilty of the murders," the woman announced, and a wave of murmurs rippled through the room. I let out a shaky breath, feeling nauseated by the verdict. But what about Tuesday? What would happen to her?
"Regarding Tuesday May," the woman continued, pausing just long enough for me to hold my breath again, "we believe she was taken advantage of in this situation. Therefore, she is sentenced to spend a further five years in the mental health facility and be placed back on medication."
"Five fucking years?" I hissed, my shock turning to anger. Sure, she wasn't going to prison, but damn, that was still a hefty chunk of her life.
"Fucking Hell," I hissed, trying to process the decision. But even as I tried to rationalise it, the unfairness of it all gnawed at me like a restless itch. She'd already lost so much time, and now she had to give up even more.
"Mr. Thompson," Tuesday choked out, her voice barely a whisper as she slumped in her seat. Her once strong and defiant demeanour crumbled like a house of cards, leaving behind a fragile, broken girl.
"Sweetness, it's okay," Detective Dimitri Costa murmured from the first row. He stood behind her, his hand reaching out to offer comfort. As his warm fingers brushed against her trembling shoulder. It was clear that he cared for her deeply.

"Dimitri," she managed to say, wrapping her arms around his solid frame and burying her face in his chest. His strong arms enveloped her, providing a safe haven as her sobs wracked her body.

The system had failed Tuesday once again, sentencing her to five more years in a mental facility when she deserved to be free. By the time she got out, she'd be twenty-eight years old.

Chapter 54

Dimitri Costa

To say the past three months were hard would be a lie. No, the last three months have been pure-fucking-torture. I've been walking through a maze of shattered glass, and with every step, the shards dig deeper into my soul. The only thing keeping me going is the thought of Tuesday - my Sweetness.

"Five more years," I mutter to myself, gripping the steering wheel as if it could somehow change the outcome. "Five more goddamn years."

There's nothing left to do now but push forward. For her sake, I'll visit her every week, keep her mother's house intact, and hold onto the hope that one day she'll walk free. That's all we have left - hope.

"Sweetness, I won't let you down," I whisper, making a silent promise to the woman who cracked open my heart and made

me feel alive again. Even if I have to crawl through broken glass for the rest of my life, I'm not giving up on her.
After hours of painstaking investigation, I finally uncovered the truth - Tuesday was the murderer. My heart had raced that day, as I pulled Mr Thompson aside and confronted him on the matter. We hashed out a plan, one where he would take the fall and Tuesday would be safe from prosecution. The courtroom was tense as the verdict was read, but it didn't quite give us the ending we had hoped for. Though she was only sentenced to 5 years at Hillcrest, at least I would be allowed to visit her weekly.

Sunlight streamed through the large bay windows, casting a warm glow on the vintage wallpaper and the antique furnishings that now filled Tuesday's mother's house. Mrs Collins and I had been rummaging through storage containers for weeks, breathing new life into this once-abandoned home.
"Mrs. Collins, what do you think of this old armchair?" I asked, giving it a playful spin. "Doesn't it give off that 'haunted mansion' vibe?"
"Indeed, Mr. Dimitri," she replied with a chuckle. "It has character, just like this house."
"Character" was an understatement. This place was a treasure trove of memories – some beautiful, some heart-wrenching.

But as Tuesday demanded, we were making sure everything was in perfect order for when she could return.
"Can you believe she insisted on us moving in here?" I mused, dusting off an ornate mirror. "I mean, I get wanting to keep the place up, but living here? That girl is full of surprises."
"Miss Tuesday always did have a flair for the dramatic," Mrs. Collins said with a knowing smile. "But she trusts you, and she knows you'll take good care of her home."
"Damn right," I murmured, my thoughts drifting to our last visit. She had looked so vulnerable, yet so determined. I'd do anything to make her happy, even if it meant playing housekeeper for 5 years alone with Mrs Collins.
"Speaking of surprises," Mrs Collins called from across the room, "I found a book that looks a lot like a Diary."

“I'm out!" I exclaimed, tossing my detective’s badge onto the kitchen counter. The metallic clang echoed through the empty room, mirroring the finality of my decision. I had officially resigned from the police force this week, and honestly, it was a relief.
"Language, Dimitri," Mrs. Collins scolded, but I could see a smile playing on her lips. "Congratulations"
"Sorry, Mrs. C," I replied, rubbing the back of my neck sheepishly. "I'm glad I’m no longer working for a system that

doesn't care about people. They put a lot of truly bad people behind bars, but they screw up too many innocent ones as well."
Mrs Collins nodded sagely, understanding the turmoil I felt. As we continued to organise the house, I couldn't help but think about Tuesday's situation—how she had been dealt a shitty hand in life, yet still managed to fight for her freedom.
"Mr. Thompson has written another letter to Tuesday," Mrs. Collins mentioned casually, handing me the envelope. "Such devotion…"
"Damn right," I agreed, admiring the man's unwavering commitment. Although Tuesday wasn't allowed to receive the letters until she was released, I suspected Mr. Thompson would continue to write them weekly for the rest of his life. What he did for Tuesday was the most loving thing anyone could do for another person. He gave her the life she deserved, and for that, I'd be forever grateful.
"Promise me something, Dimitri," Mrs. Collins said suddenly, her eyes serious. "Promise me you'll look after her when I'm gone, too."
"Like she's my own," I vowed without hesitation. If there was one thing I knew for certain, it was that Tuesday May had my heart, and I wouldn't let anything harm her again.
"Good," she replied, satisfied with my answer. She patted my arm affectionately before returning to her task, leaving me to ponder the immense responsibility I had willingly taken on.

"That delivery is arriving today" Mrs Collins smiled at me
“I'll get my tools, and put it together the second it arrives, the room needs to be ready, we only have 3 more months till it is needed" I replied.

Chapter 55

2013
5 Years Later
Tuesday May

I had refused to allow Dimitri to pick me up today; I was finally being released. The sun was setting, casting a warm golden glow over the facility as I took my first steps toward freedom. My heart raced with both excitement and anxiety. After all this time, I would be in control of my own life once again.

"Sweetness, are you sure?" Dimitri's voice came through the phone, his concern evident. "I don't mind picking you up."

"I'm sure," I insisted, trying to sound more confident than I felt. "You already did enough by bringing my car here yesterday. I want to drive myself home, feel the wind in my hair, you know?"

"Alright," he sighed, relenting. "Just call me if you need anything, okay?"

"Of course, Dimitri. See you soon," I replied, hanging up the phone.

As I approached the sleek black car that Dimitri had delivered, the keys jingled in my trembling hands. It had been years since I'd driven, but the familiar hum of the engine and the smooth leather beneath my fingertips brought a sense of comfort.

"Okay, Tuesday," I murmured to myself, taking a deep breath. "You can do this."

With that, I shifted into gear and eased onto the open road, feeling the cool breeze whip through my long, dark hair. As the scenery changed from the sterile grounds of the institution to the lush, green countryside, my spirits began to lift.

"Freedom," I whispered, a smile tugging at the corners of my mouth. The thought of reuniting with Lillian, Dimitri, and Mrs. Collins filled me with an indescribable warmth.

"Home, here I come," I whispered, feeling the wind in my hair and the promise of a new beginning just around the bend.

For the past 5 years, Dimitri and Mrs. Collins had poured their love and care into preparing our home for my return and looking after our most precious gift - Lillian Costa, our daughter. It was a shock to discover my pregnancy upon returning to Hillcrest, but with the help of Dimitri's supportive presence, I was able to carry and give birth to our beautiful daughter. Though I wasn't permitted to raise her, Dimitri was granted permission to bring her to see me every week. And every time she arrived, my heart would burst with love and adoration. With her glossy black hair cascading down her back like mine, and deep brown eyes that mirrored those of her father's, she was a perfect blend of both of us. Each week, she would regale me with fantastical stories of dragons and ghosts that roamed the corridors of the castle where she lived. Her imagination knew no bounds, and I eagerly anticipated being able to be a part of it with her.

Mrs. Collins, with her kind and gentle demeanour, continued to work diligently as our trusted housekeeper. But in addition to her duties, she also took on the role of a nanny for Lillian. Though we didn't necessarily need one, Mrs. Collins' loving presence was welcomed and appreciated. Meanwhile, Dimitri had made the decision to leave his job and become a stay-at-home dad for our little girl. It was evident that fatherhood suited him effortlessly - he was always beaming with pride and joy whenever he held our daughter in his arms.

The sun glinted off the windshield as I turned onto the street that led to my new home, anticipation bubbling in my chest.

"Holy shit," I whispered, pressing a hand to my heart.

As I drove up to the gate, I marvelled at the transformation that had taken place. Vibrant flowers danced along either side of the driveway, their petals swaying gently in the breeze. The once-rusty gate had been lovingly restored, now gleaming in the sunlight and swinging open smoothly with just a tap of a button.

"Damn," I said, grinning from ear to ear.
The crunch of gravel beneath my tyres had been replaced by the soothing sound of cobblestones, guiding me toward the beautifully renovated Victorian standing tall and proud before me. Its fresh coat of white paint seemed to shimmer as if it were welcoming me home.
I drove down the long driveway and parked the car in front of the house. I quickly got out of the car and made my way up the steps. The sweet aroma of blooming roses surrounded me as I approached, and I could see Lillian, Dimitri, and Mrs. Collins standing there, their expressions lighting up like radiant suns. Their warmth filled my heart and eased my mind.
"Mommy!" Lillian squealed, racing down the stairs to throw her arms around my waist.
"Hey, Princess," I whispered into her hair, holding her close. "I've missed you so much."
"Welcome home, Sweetness," Dimitri said, his voice deep and velvety smooth, causing shivers to run down my spine. He descended the steps and wrapped his strong arms around us both, cocooning us in his love.
"Thank you, Dimitri," I murmured, feeling his heartbeat against my back. "For everything."
"Anything for you, Sweetness," he replied, pressing a tender kiss on my temple.

"Miss Tuesday, it's good to have you home," Mrs. Collins chimed in, her eyes glistening with unshed tears. God, had I missed that gentle, motherly voice.

"Thank you, Mrs. Collins," I responded, disentangling myself from Lillian and Dimitri to give our housekeeper a heartfelt hug. "You've all made this place truly magical."

"Damn right, we did," Dimitri teased, taking my hand and leading me up the front steps.

As I stood there, surrounded by the people who meant the world to me, I couldn't help but marvel at how far I'd come. Back when I was battling my demons, I never thought I'd get to experience such happiness. But here I was – free, loved, and ready to start anew.

Dimitri leaned over and kissed my cheek as he whispered into my ear, "Welcome Home".

Chapter 56

Epilogue
Tuesday May

As I sat up in bed, a dim glow from the moonlight illuminated the box of letters on the floor next to me. Each envelope had a date neatly written on it, a collection of memories that made my heart race with anticipation. These were not ordinary letters - each one was addressed to me from Mr Thompson, that beautiful man who had been writing to me once a week for four years straight while he sat in jail for the crimes I committed.

I smiled as I picked up an envelope, feeling its weight and texture between my fingers. Running my thumb over the seal, I couldn't help but think about how much effort Mr Thompson had put into these letters, considering his circumstances. It warmed my heart, knowing that even in prison, he thought of me so often.

"Damn you, Mr. Thompson," I whispered under my breath, both cursing and praising him at the same time. I tore open the envelope, pulling out the letter inside. Every single word he wrote was like a piece of his soul, given to me willingly, without hesitation. He spoke of his days in jail, his thoughts on life, and most importantly, his unwavering faith in me.
I traced my fingers over the inked words, savouring the connection we shared through these letters.
A cool breeze swept through my open window, carrying the scent of distant roses and stirring the curtains like ghosts in the moonlight. I shivered, pulling the blanket tighter around me, trying to shake off the chill that settled in my bones as I thought about Mr. Thompson.
"Did you know he was sick?" I asked Dimitri, who was leaning against the doorframe with his arms crossed.
"Of course, sweetness," he replied softly, pushing himself off the frame and crossing the room to sit beside me on the bed. "He told me that day you found us having that heated discussion."
"Six years ago... He knew he was dying the whole time?"
Dimitri nodded solemnly, his expressive brown eyes reflecting the weight of the secret he'd been keeping. "Mr. Thompson confided in me about his stage 4 prostate cancer. It was why he gave you your freedom."

I looked at Dimitri, my heart aching for the man who had given so much to me. "So, you two came up with the plan together?"

"Indeed." Dimitri's voice carried a hint of pride. "We secretly hashed out the details for him to take the fall for your crimes. It wasn't an easy decision, but Mr. Thompson insisted. He wanted to give you a chance at life, even if it meant sacrificing his own."

"Jesus, Dimitri. All this time and I never knew..." My voice cracked, tears stinging my eyes as I thought about the depth of Mr. Thompson's devotion. "How could he have kept something like that from me?"

"Because he loved you, Tuesday," Dimitri said gently, placing a comforting hand on my shoulder. "And he believed in the person you could become, free from the darkness of your past."

I wiped away a tear and forced a small smile, grateful for the support of these two incredible men. "Well, I'm not going to let his sacrifice be in vain. I'll make sure of it."

"Good." Dimitri squeezed my shoulder reassuringly, a warm smile lighting up his face. "Together, we'll honour Mr. Thompson's memory and build a better future for you."

"Thank you," I whispered, my heart swelling with gratitude and determination.

Since returning home from the mental health facility, I had taken to reading one of these precious missives every night, finding solace and strength in his words.

"Have you read them all?" Dimitri asked.

"Yes," I replied, running my fingers over the smooth paper of the last letter.

"How are you holding up?" Dimitri asked.

I shrugged, attempting nonchalance. "You know me, tough as nails." But even as I said it, I could feel the emotion welling up inside, threatening to spill over.

"Mr. Thompson really loved you" Dimitri mused, his voice soft with understanding. "He was a beautiful man."

"More than we'll ever know," I whispered, my throat tight with unshed tears.

"Tuesday, there's something else," Dimitri began hesitantly, pulling a worn leather-bound diary from his jacket pocket. "We found this among your mother's things. I thought you should read it, but only if you've finished with the letters"

"Ok," I said, curiosity piqued by the mysterious tome. "But why all the secrecy? What's so important about this diary?"

"Let's just say it might help to shed some light on certain... unresolved issues." Dimitri's eyes held a hint of sadness as he passed the diary to me.

"Okay," I replied, my fingers itching to crack open the cover. Steeling my resolve, my fingers traced the cracks along its spine.

"Here goes nothing," I muttered under my breath as I took a deep breath and opened the diary. My heart pounded in anticipation, an impatient rhythm demanding answers.

My eyes widened as I scanned the first page, recognising the familiar, angular handwriting. "Um... this is my Father's writing."

With a shaky hand, I began to read my father's words – words I never thought I'd find answers to. Each sentence brought with it a new wave of emotions: anger, sadness, confusion. It was like peeling back layers of an onion, each one revealing something darker, something deeper beneath the surface.

The pages of the diary seemed to tremble in my hands as I delved deeper into my father's mind, a place I never thought I'd venture. His fascination with my mother Lillian was evident from the very beginning. The way he described her – those long, flowing locks and kind eyes that held an underlying sadness – it was like seeing her through his eyes.

As I continued reading, it became apparent that my father had gone to great lengths to be near my mother. He stalked her, watching her every move, until fate finally presented him with the opportunity to marry her. And once he did, he showered her with love and affection.

But despite the seemingly perfect love story laid out before me, I couldn't shake the feeling that something was amiss. Each entry grew more erratic, like a storm brewing in my father's mind. His obsession with my mother morphed into something darker, more possessive. A chill ran down my spine as I imagined the extent of his madness.

"Shit, this is getting intense," I muttered under my breath, unable to contain my unease. My fingers traced the lines on the page where he recounted witnessing my mother walking the grounds with Mr Thompson, their laughter echoing through the air. Another entry detailed seeing her leave his sleeping quarters, clutching a book to her chest as if trying to shield herself from prying eyes.

"Dammit, Mom," I whispered, feeling a mixture of anger and sadness at the thought of her being trapped in this twisted web of deceit.

As I continued reading, it became clear that my father had considered firing Mr Thompson after she ran away but decided against it, hoping she would return for him. The entries stopped abruptly when he discovered my existence, leaving me wondering what other secrets were hidden in this diary.

Flipping through the remaining pages. That's when I found them: two folded sheets tucked in the back of the diary, alongside a lock of pure silver hair bound with a rubber band.

"Okay, what do we have here?" I mused, unfolding the first page. It was a DNA test result, a mouth swab, stating "No familiar match found." But the second one, done with the strand of hair, declared a parental match. My heart pounded in my chest, and my hands shook as the realisation hit me like a freight train.

"Fuck... This hair, it's not my father's." I stared at the silver strands, remembering how my father's hair was salt and pepper. "This can only belong to Mr. Thompson."

The End

ABOUT CASSANDRA DOON

Originally from around the Sydney area, Cassandra now resides on the Gold Coast Queensland in Australia. Originally starting out as a book cover illustrator she slowly worked her way into writing. Her Current jobs are Full-time Child Wrangler, Soccer Mum and servant to 1 fluffy cat.

Join her Facebook readers Group:
https://www.facebook.com/groups/1113426753355119/
Or follow on Instagram:
https://www.instagram.com/doon_co/

ALSO BY CASSANDRA DOON

The 4 Seats Series:

Matteo

Felix (Coming Soon)

Standalone:

The Boys Of Hastings House

The Kings of Willows Peak

Damaged Goods

Oakland Harbour Series:

Missing (Coming Soon)

Found (Coming Soon)

Home (Coming Soon)

Milton Keynes UK
Ingram Content Group UK Ltd.
UKHW020915050424
440683UK00004B/156